Praise for

The Talented Miss Farwell

"Stylish. . . . The fictional Becky is playing a more morally complex game." *—New York Times Book Review*

"Becky Farwell is one of the most wickedly compelling characters I've read in ages—a Machiavellian marvel, a modern Becky Sharp, a character to root for despite your better judgment—and her story, both topical and timeless, will knock you off your feet." —Rebecca Makkai, author of *The Great Believers*

"The gritty underbelly of the art market and the pathology of decades of financial chicanery meet their delirious match in Tedrowe's Miss Farwell, who stands glaring up at the reader from the intersection of Hitchcock's Marnie and Highsmith's Ripley. Watch out for paper cuts." —Jonathan Lethem

"There's just nothing as compelling as a juicy, sordid scam—which makes Emily Gray Tedrowe's latest a-must-read." *—Harper's Bazaar*

"Perfectly executed. . . . Tedrowe does a spectacular job of demonstrating the mindset of a character who justifies her criminal activity while believing she's ultimately good." *—Publishers Weekly* (starred review)

"If ever you are looking for a book to provide an escape from your own reality, I heartily recommend Emily Gray Tedrowe's *The Talented Miss Farwell*. Becky Farwell is the most sympathetic, art-collecting, money-laundering villain I have ever encountered. She literally bleeds her hometown dry—the empty swimming pools of Pierson are heartbreaking—and yet somehow, I loved her." —Marcy Dermansky, author of *Very Nice e Talented Miss Farwell* is utterly magnificent. Not since Tom Ripley have I fallen so hard for a con artist. . . . Becky Farwell is an unforgettable character. She is the beating heart of this spellbinding page-turner about art, greed, and self-invention."

—Cristina Alger, *New York Times* bestselling author of *Girls Like Us*

"A read-it-to-believe-it page-turner about a con artist whose luck can't last." —*Real Simple*

"Both lighthearted and deeply conflicted, Tedrowe's caper, with its Becky Sharp allusions, raises significant moral issues." —*Booklist*

"Sharp, darkly comedic, and full of fascinating facts about the art world." —CrimeReads

"Riveting. . . . With Becky Farwell, Tedrowe has created one of the year's most fascinating, complex, nuanced characters."

—Medium

"A page-turner about a con woman who steals from her town government to make it big in the art world. . . . A fantastic character—and compelling story." —Alma

"Tedrowe has a talent for incrementally (and believably) stacking a house of cards and keeping readers wondering just how crazy things will get. The answer: way crazier than you'd expect for a small-town art lover." —*Chicago* magazine

"Smart, psychologically insightful. . . . Tedrowe makes the pages fly through the secrets and self-delusions, skillfully inspiring empathy and identification with a criminal mastermind."

—The National Book Review

The Talented
Miss Farwell

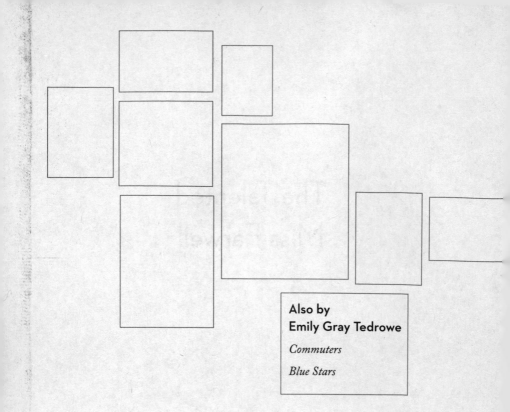

The Talented
Miss Farwell

A NOVEL

Emily Gray Tedrowe

CUSTOM
HOUSE

P.S.™ is a trademark of HarperCollins Publishers.

THE TALENTED MISS FARWELL. Copyright © 2020 by Emily Gray Tedrowe. All rights reserved. Printed in the United States of America. No part of this book may be used or reproduced in any manner whatsoever without written permission except in the case of brief quotations embodied in critical articles and reviews. For information, address HarperCollins Publishers, 195 Broadway, New York, NY 10007.

HarperCollins books may be purchased for educational, business, or sales promotional use. For information, please email the Special Markets Department at SPsales@harpercollins.com.

A hardcover edition of this book was published in 2020 by Custom House, an imprint of William Morrow.

FIRST CUSTOM HOUSE PAPERBACK EDITION PUBLISHED 2021.

Designed by Nancy Singer

Library of Congress Cataloging-in-Publication Data has been applied for.

ISBN 978-0-06-289771-8

21 22 23 24 25   BRR   10 9 8 7 6 5 4 3 2 1

To Courtney

Even now, however, she was not always happy. She had everything she wanted, but she still felt, at times, that there were other things she might want if she knew about them.

Edith Wharton, *The Custom of the Country*

The Talented
Miss Farwell

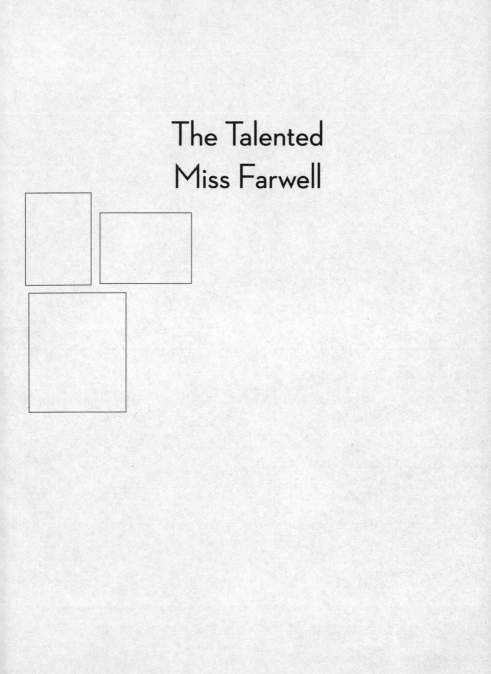

1

Pierson, Illinois
1979

FOURTEEN-YEAR-OLD BECKY FARWELL LAY ON the truck horn with her forearm.

"Daddy, let's go!"

Engine running, she tilted the rearview to study her eye makeup, a wash of greens running dark to light from her eyelashes to eyebrows. Greens, of course, because the magazines said all redheads had to, even indistinct blond-red mixes like her own. What she really wanted was the set that gave you three kinds of purple, pale violet to dusky eggplant. Becky ran a quick calculation on how much she was owed by the four girls she did homework for—geometry and algebra, although she could stretch up to pre-calc too, even as a ninth-grader. Though for pre-calc all she could guarantee was a B, not that any of the girls complained. Sometimes she took payment in shoes, like the almost-new Tretorns she had on now, without socks because no one did. Becky flipped the mirror back with a snap. They needed cash too bad to daydream about makeup.

Getting squeezed at all ends. One of her father's sayings that didn't make sense but sure as hell got across how bad it was that spring.

After another minute she jumped down from the truck and went inside. Even though it was one of the first nice days in March, the front rooms of their farmhouse were dark and stuffy, closed in. Becky pushed up a window and propped it open with a can of beans. This morning's cereal bowls were tumbled milky-white in the sink and a thin sticky layer of grease and dust filmed everything, but Becky had no time to wipe it up. In the family room, one patch of carpet stood out darker and new. Last week her father had pawned the TV set, all her mother's jewelry (he thought all: Becky had hidden a few bits), and the blender. He wouldn't tell her how much he'd gotten—*it's only temporary*—but the crumpled receipt she'd found proved it was less than a hundred.

"Daddy?" she called, from the bottom of the stairs. Then ran up lightly, bracelets jingling. "We have to— Have you not even showered?"

For there he was, her bear-like father, curled on his side in bed. His silver hair mashed down low over his forehead, perspiration speckling his nose. Stomach flu, but there was no time for it. A buyer was driving in from Rockford, and her father was supposed to meet him at noon.

"You said just turn on the engine! Daddy, it's already—"

He groaned and threw a hand over his eyes. "Show him the drills. The Lite-Trac air seeder, make sure he sees that one. And the spreaders, even if he says he don't—"

"I can't . . ." Becky looked wildly around the room. "How am I supposed to—"

"Tell him not the Masseys, or any John Deere. You can walk

2

him back by the two Vicons, he'll want those. But say no. Just drills, that's our deal. Give me an hour. Most. I just need to— Oh, god—" He bolted from bed to bathroom, old terry-cloth robe flying, and Becky fled before she could hear anything.

On the highway, Becky knew exactly when and where to twirl the dials for music, sometimes switching from WXTV to WMMR and back again in the space of a single song. Why wouldn't they play anything other than Crystal Gayle, for Christ's sake? Or Kenny Rogers? She kept both hands tight on the wheel and eyes locked on the road lines, never went a fraction over 45 mph, not that their old truck wanted to. Nobody passing on I-50 gave a ninth-grader a second look, but she knew what to do if she was pulled over: start to cry right away, say that her boyfriend got dead drunk and she'd been scared and she was going straight home, swear to god, and she never would again, Officer, promise.

"Won't save me a ticket but might keep them from arresting me," her father mused, when he'd told her how to say it.

It was two exits, one roundabout, and four lights from the farmhouse to the showroom, and she sweated through each one. Worst part was the left turn across traffic into the showroom driveway. Becky hung there forever, blinker on, foot hovering between brake and gas. Eventually she made herself go, eyes half-closed in the turn, and bumped down the gravelly gully, *Jesus Jesus Jesus, thank you.*

One other truck idled in their small lot, facing the road. Shit: they were already here. Becky hopped out and let down the tailgate. She could only carry two boxes, would have to come back for the rest.

"Hello?" she called.

The Traskers ran their own farming equipment store outside Rockford and were here to buy up inventory as cheap as they could get it, then turn around and sell it at markup, a profit too ugly to think about.

"Vultures," her father said, with a show of cheer. "Picking us dry."

They all did it. A few years ago, he had been the one to drive out to Minter's to sort through what was left.

"We'll get it back," he kept telling Becky, "in the summer."

He used to say *in the spring*. Before that, *it'll pick up in fall*.

"Good afternoon," Becky sang out to the two men getting slowly out of the truck, a father and son, it looked like. She'd never opened the showroom on her own before, but had helped her father dozens of times. She unlocked the doors and used the boxes to prop them open, ran ahead to the fuse box and hit the lights for the office and front section, where the harvesters were proudly parked in a neat row, on the diagonal.

"I'll put the coffee on—" she called back, staying ahead where they couldn't see her. "Or there are sodas in back. Dad'll be here any minute."

The son was kind of cute. Becky took off her cotton pullover and checked to see if she'd sweated rings on her tank top. She should go sit in the office, she knew, in that lit-up glassed-in box where invoices and catalogues were stacked up, spilling across the desk, the chairs, the metal file. But instead she tracked the men, admiring the curls poking out from under the son's cap, his thumbs stuck in his back pockets, the mostly clear skin on his soft cheeks. Becky fluffed her bangs and was so busy working on something clever she could say to him that the older man's sudden presence made her jump.

"There you are," he said low. Short and burly, bald head like a crop circle.

Becky caught a whiff of minted chewing tobacco. "He said to, um, show you the spreaders. I mean seeders. They're just over—"

"Yeah, show me." He grabbed her elbow and pulled her toward him. Becky grunted in surprise. "Oh shush," he said, and the combination of his tone—*don't be silly*—and her fear that the son might see or hear her (being silly) kept her quiet, even as he groped her breasts and ass, quick and rough, under the cover of the dark aisle full of pipe lengths and electrical cords. In less than a minute it was over, she was pushed away with a friendly sort of thump on the back and the man turned the corner alone, calling to his son, "This the only cultipacker, or do they have any better brands?"

Later, when her father had arrived and taken the man and son into his office, Becky watched through the glass. The son sat down before her father did. Her dad's heartiness, his larger gestures, the other man's crossed arms and unresponsive back . . . Becky had to look away.

For a long time she sat on a stack of wood pallets, picking at a scab on her ankle. A creaky old fan spun slowly up by the dusty rafters. "Bec? Hey, Bec?" her father called, leaning out the office door, unable to see her. "Grab two sodas for us, okay?"

Slowly Becky walked to the back, returning with the cold cans in her arms. In the dark she took one of the Dr Peppers and peeled off its tab. And then she coughed, and coughed, and dug back into the cavities of her nose and throat so she could hock one perfect glob of phlegm into the soda.

Opening the office door she stamped a smile on her face and felt powered up with love for her daddy. And for how little he knew.

Early the next morning Becky stared up at her bedroom ceiling and thought that they were stuck: her father wouldn't admit to her how bad things really were, and she wouldn't force him to because she knew she was supposed to be reassured. Would it be different if her mother were here, if the cancer in her breast hadn't burst its bounds and spilled into other parts of her body, killing her when Becky was six? Maybe her mother would have been the one to size up the situation and say it straight: Hank, we need to do something else. There would have been a "we," someone for her father to share his fears and strategies with, someone from whom he would take counsel.

Though thank god he'd never married any of the loud-laughers Becky knew he sometimes bought dinner for at the Black Owl, and probably went home with for a few hours when he thought he wouldn't be missed. What they really didn't need around here was a hysterical second wife flailing about when the electric was shut off or the bank called, making visible what they were all supposed to ignore: Daddy's business, circling the drain.

Becky kicked off the unbearable covers. She'd been fighting to pretend a hot nauseous pain hadn't been growing in her lower belly all night. She pulled a sweatshirt over her nightgown and let herself out the kitchen door into the predawn chill, breathing fresh air into her lungs. The fading moon, a thick lemon slice, hung low over a clump of horse chestnuts separating their property from whoever had bought the Hinmans' place.

It was freezing, but at least she wasn't about to puke. Becky found a pair of old rainboots on the cluttered porch and walked circles in their mostly dirt yard. Cars were beginning to flow on County Road M, and a lone crow yelped once overhead, and then again from farther away.

If they lost the house, she supposed they'd try to get one of the rentals in town. Maybe a long-term efficiency in the Rose Suites, just off the highway; how much were those? Her father would get a job, eventually, at someone else's store. Becky guessed she'd have to drop out of school, go full time as a waitress. She recoiled, thinking of how her father would paper it over: *for a little while. Start you up again in the fall.* And season would slide into season, year into year, and she'd turn into one of those hatchet-faced diner lifers with varicose veins and dead eyes.

Cold but afraid to go inside, Becky went to the barn, where a stack of boxes—blades or spades—had been dumped after delivery, and left out or forgotten. She tugged open the sliding door, nudged the boxes in with her foot, and then sat down on them. The haphazard collection of inventory in progress was loosely arranged according to a system only her father knew. Becky held her stomach and bent over, a rolling pain built of nausea. No denying it—she'd caught that damn flu and now she'd have to do all the sheets and towels again.

And how dare that bald pig grab at her like that? Right in her father's own showroom! She wanted to torch that whole place, combines, office, and all. Burn it down with that fat fuck locked in.

That's when the idea came. The first idea, the one that led to a chain of other ideas, spreading into a yearlong series of changes that would eventually turn everything around for them. For her.

The idea was—*Wait,* she begged her nausea, *give me a minute to think.* She lurched up and took a full circle to see all the boxes and the unused space and the strong beams and the warm familiar wood smell—*Do we need a showroom anyway?*

Becky threw up then, spattering the rainboots, and did it a dozen more times that morning. But between bouts she huddled in bed with a pen and a pad and all the financial records she could find at home. Later that night, her father brought in his most recent files, bewildered by her vehement phone calls. By then Becky had run the numbers so many times that she shook with excitement and fear as she raced to explain the plan to her tired father. Drop the showroom, save 14K rent for the year. Clear out the barn and use that instead. Save on gas, electric, heat, security. Reduce inventory by half but keep up wholesale orders for longtime customers. Stop sending receivables to Manheim Accounting— Becky herself would do the books. Market the whole idea with the slogan "We Pass the Savings On to You."

Hank Farwell told his sick teenage daughter to take a can of ginger ale and get back in bed. But he sat up late with the scribbled pages. Becky's plan got put into action over the next six months and by the end of the year all of Pierson was talking about Farwell Agriculture Inc.'s miraculous rise from the dead. How it just went to show that one of their own (they meant Hank) could get it done with some grit and quick thinking.

All year Becky supervised the rebirth of the business. She reorganized the barn and ordered a FARWELL AGRICULTURE INC. sign directing people where to turn off Route 4. She threw a "Thank

You for Your Business" lemonade party in June that raffled off a John Deere tractor, their last, and gave twenty-five percent off new standing orders. She read up on accounting and took the bus to a one-day small business conference in Rockford, flummoxing the organizers when they realized they had registered a high school sophomore. By winter, Becky was friendly with all the suppliers on the phone, and handled all orders, often combining shipments and suggesting discounts that were impossible to refuse. Her father took care of what he'd always done best: talking wary locals through every angle of a purchase.

One Sunday evening that winter, the Farwells hosted a small gathering in their home. The local Rotary Club, after snubbing Hank for years, had welcomed him back into the fold after the business made its one-eighty. Several men now called up to a week ahead to make sure he would attend the next meeting.

Pierson men had a subset of the Rotary, an unofficial club for those in agribusiness. Hank was now avidly pursued to join these evenings as well. The habit was to hold a bimonthly get-together at someone's home, rotating around the farmhouses of the members, usually on a weekend evening after dinner. A nominal subject would be set for discussion—price of seed in the Rock River area, for example—but the two-hour sit-down was mostly gossip (who was slipping), politics (Reagan and subsidies), and laughter among a handful of men whose thickened hides and long workdays didn't offer much opportunity for that.

That Sunday, the first time Hank hosted, the men entered the property under Hank's new plastic sheet sign flapping in the night wind against two fourteen-foot metal poles: WE PASS THE SAVINGS

ON TO YOU. They went by stakes marking out a barn extension for smaller handheld tools. The winter had been cold but dry; the men hardly had any snow to knock off their boots before finding seats in Hank's warmly lit living room, with its new TV set and new double-pane storm windows.

It was the unspoken custom for the host's wife to provide coffee and some kind of sweet—a nut cake usually—and then to immediately withdraw. The men fell quiet when Becky brought in the tray. Later, they would all become accustomed to her at every business meeting or social event or club date that had to do with agribusiness in the county. They'd hardly remember a time before she was a part of it all.

On that first night at the Farwells', though, the men fell silent and uneasy one by one as Becky put down the tray, then pulled up a chair and sat down. They glanced at Hank, who acted as if it was nothing strange.

Becky regarded them all kindly, stirred her mug, and smiled politely. Then she said, "Thank you for coming. Ready to begin?"

2

Pierson, Illinois
1981

PIERSON, ILLINOIS, WAS A SMALL Midwestern city about two hours southwest of Chicago, split by the Rock River. The town spanned the width of less than a mile, and its central feature was the low-head dam that stairstepped the water to a gushing froth before it flowed on west under Pierson's two bridges, the Galena and the Sauk. Like most river towns in the area, it was named after an early European settler who mounted a ferry system and profited from nineteenth-century traders and travelers. And like most small towns in Illinois, Pierson claimed a vague but definite connection to Abraham Lincoln, who led a company in and around the area during the Black Hawk War. On the south river promenade a bronze statue of Lincoln surveyed the storefronts facing the water: a tanning salon, the Chamber of Commerce, Piccadillo's Bar. The local history museum, in a building that used to be the old high school, hedged about Lincoln but went deep on the town's one dramatic incident: the "Pierson Disaster."

For Becky's seventh-grade history report, she told the story of the Pierson Disaster—an 1806 riverbank crush accident that caused several drownings—from the point of view of a lame saloon-keeper who watched it all unfold, helplessly, from the banks. He hated how conspicuous he was, dry, with his cane, made unmanly by the surrounding furor of accident and heroics. But instead of acting, he observed. He saw it all, from that first innocuous shoving: how the men's hands shot to their hats as they toppled backward; the horses and women screaming; the dark bodies dragged onto land.

Becky's teacher, Mrs. Nagle, held her back after the bell. "Incomplete," she'd written at the top of the front page.

"Who is this man?" she asked.

"I don't know. No one." Becky was annoyed; now she'd have to do it all over.

"Did you use the research sources?" By this Mrs. Nagle meant the endless flapping loops of microfilm in the dim projector room of the local library.

Becky admitted she had not.

Mrs. Nagle paged through her report, pointing here and there at poor Mr. Sam Smith's reminiscences of that awful day. Then she took a pen and wrote two more words at the top of Becky's paper: *Fiction. Fact.* "What you wrote was *this*." She tapped one word. "And the assignment was *this*." Tapped the other.

Becky redid the paper and never again did she stray outside the lines. In truth she was surprised that Mrs. Nagle had taken the time to challenge her. Most often Becky's compositions received As and Bs with no more comments, no matter what she had written about. In a school where the graduation rate hovered around fifty percent and there was no funding to separate out advanced classes, being a high achiever just meant that you'd fly under the radar.

Only Ms. Marner, in senior year math, pushed Becky. She never let up, this tall and bony taskmaster whose first name was Diana and always insisted on "Ms." ("*Say it with me, class, 'Mzzzzzzzz Marner.' Not so hard now, is it?*").

Ms. Marner made Becky's tests more difficult and wouldn't listen to any complaints. She mimeographed pages of extra work and expected Becky to return them to her faculty mailbox within two days, no exception. She insisted that Becky join the Mathletes club (Becky was the only girl, and the only senior) and she brought her books from an out-of-state library, a videotape once even, that lurched ahead into the origin of numbers, the ideas behind the domains, vast overarching concepts.

Becky loved the mimeographs, the challenge and puzzle of each one, but she couldn't understand why Ms. Marner was so into theory—it was dense, barely comprehensible. Becky was into math for the calculations. A mental arrangement of digits, the slotting in of value and function, seeing the total in her mind's eye as clearly as it would then be printed on the page. She couldn't explain to anyone, even Ms. Marner, what that inner game felt like: how the symbols *click-click-clicked* into brain-place, like the sound and feel of the colored wooden pegs in Chinese checkers.

One Saturday Ms. Marner drove Becky and two of the boys two hours each way to Peoria to compete in a round-robin state math tournament. She ran from corner to corner of the crowded gym to watch their various matches. When Becky won a prize there she heard a single hoot that rose above the rest of the polite applause. On the way home, Ms. Marner played show tunes on her tape deck, smoked Virginia Slims, and took them for burgers at a truck stop diner. Later, Becky realized that her teacher had most likely paid for all of it herself, the tournament registration, the gas, and the burgers.

One Thursday afternoon Ms. Marner waved the freshman boys out early and made Becky do what she couldn't bear to do: talk about colleges. "IIT, is what I'm thinking. Obviously, U. Chicago is your moon shot. But I don't know what the counselors have told you about aid . . ." She glanced up at Becky over her readers; when Becky didn't respond she went on, "Anyway, IIT has a phenomenal department. I know the chair, slightly, from way back and I thought I could give him a call."

Becky shrugged. "I mean, thanks, but . . . There's a lot of stuff going on with my dad. It can't happen."

"So maybe you do a year or two closer to home. And then you transfer. Your options go exponential then."

Becky bent to her backpack, fumbling with its zipper and straps. Talking about what you knew you could never have only made things worse. "I have to go."

"If this is about money, there are all sorts of scholarships and loans. You're not the first student to need—"

Becky hurried out of the classroom without saying goodbye. She couldn't explain it to Ms. Marner. How much her father depended on her, how much the business did. Just breaking even took everything the two of them had. She couldn't leave. When she got home, her father was sitting in his chair, TV on. Patient, happy to see her.

"Little late tonight," he said.

"Yeah." Becky went over to turn on the oven for their meal.

■ ■ ■

Sometime after that interaction, Becky stopped attending Math-letes. She avoided Ms. Marner's gaze in class and when her teacher tried to talk to her after class, she muttered excuses about being busy. She *was* busy, caught up in a shipping snafu that ended up costing several thousand they didn't have.

After graduation in June, Ms. Marner found her in the gym, where parents and purple-gowned seniors milled around and drank punch. "I hear you're a working stiff now, like the rest of us."

"It's just an entry-level thing," Becky said. "Mostly paperwork." The truth was that her new job at Town Hall thrilled her. She'd applied on a whim after convincing her father that she could still do his books. What she didn't tell him was how much they needed the paycheck.

"I have something for you." Ms. Marner handed her a small gift-wrapped package. "I've missed our extra assignments. Come visit me sometime. Since you'll be around."

Becky's eyes were hot but she pretended they weren't. "Okay, yeah."

"Good luck, Becky. Congratulations."

Becky thanked her, and escaped.

Later that night, she opened the gift, which turned out to be one of those little books of wisdom for graduates and a long typed letter. Becky read the letter as fast as she could, skimming it, unable to take in all that Ms. Marner had written: how much she valued Becky as a student and a person, and how gladdening it was to see her succeed. That she hadn't meant to get pushy and was sorry if she had offended. That Becky reminded her of herself at that age, and perhaps seeing the potential in such a talented female math student had caused her to get overinvolved. She wished Becky all the success in the world.

Becky folded up the letter, put it in the silly gift book, and tucked both in the bottom of a drawer under a pile of jeans. She didn't throw either away until years later. But she only ever let herself read the letter that one time, on graduation night.

3

Pierson
1983

WHEN SHE CAUGHT THE DISCREPANCY in a refund from Golden Fuel & Oil on a Friday afternoon in September, Becky paid attention. She was the sole female employee in Bookkeeping and the only one under twenty-five—she'd been technically seventeen when they'd hired her but a tacit silence on this was agreed by all—so mostly she strived to fit in, to hide her natural affinity for columns of numbers. Every once in a while, cued by a sudden pause in the droning *chunk-chunk* of Freddie's machine on the desk facing hers, she would even waste several minutes tapping buttons with the eraser of her pencil, the way she'd noticed others doing it.

$542. She knew instantly there was no need for this refund. Although occasionally a company would credit Town Hall a future month on the rare chance they paid ahead by accident, most preferred to refund, to keep the books even. She herself had filled out this particular amount on the oversized pale green watermarked check sheet for Accounting to sign off on, one of dozens of payments she and Freddie processed every day.

Still, Becky pulled Golden's accounts and paged back, comparing months of charges. Golden had had the town contract for years—not only the schools and library, but also Community Bank and the Historic Center. No doubled payment that she could find. So where was this $542, marked "Paid to City of Pierson," supposed to go?

Becky took the check and the current Golden book down the hall to Accounting. She hesitated outside her boss Jim Frantzen's door, which was closed, emphatically closed and not balanced ajar on a half-latch, which meant *technically here but for Christ's sake don't come in*. Who else could she ask? No to Bob P., *definitely* no to Gary—last week he'd fingered the hem of her jacket and whispered that a tighter fit flattered a girl more—and no to nice white-haired Mr. Kaplan, unfortunately, who had apparently left early for the weekend.

Becky completed a lap of the offices on floor three, painfully aware of the secretaries who eyed her uncertain progress and said nothing, stuck at their desks until five even if their bosses had already gone. Finally she turned into the break room. Dingy Formica counters, a wheezing fridge, the permanent odors of burnt coffee and tuna fish salad. To her surprise, one of the two HR reps—Mr. Fine, who had processed her hire—was at the single round table, turning newspaper pages. Becky hesitated a moment— Mr. Fine had been at the staff presentation last week and hadn't seemed pleased with her after—but then she forged ahead.

"I'm glad to see you," Becky began. "Can you help me figure out who I should—" She fumbled to unfold the check sheet and to find the right page in the account book, but before she could finish Mr. Fine scowled and slapped his paper shut. Ropy strands of colorless hair stuck to his bulbous head.

"Ask your supervisor."

"I would, but he—"

"Miss Farwell, I was under the impression that you were mature enough to handle the simple responsibilities of your job. Input the debit, input the credit. Calculate the difference. Balance the books. Are you saying that's too difficult for you?"

Becky tightened her hold on the check. "No."

"Well, then."

The gleam of ice in Mr. Fine's widely stretched smile made Becky back away. She was almost at the door when he called her.

"A word of advice, Miss Farwell? No one likes a Goody-Two-shoes. Think twice before proposing 'A New Method.'" Becky flinched at the title of her failed presentation. "When the grownups have had things pretty well in hand since before you—"

"Absolutely, Mr. Fine. I appreciate it." Her arms tingled, but her back was straight and her voice was steady, reassuring, complicit. This was no different from her years of dealing with patronizing agribusiness suppliers on the phone. She knew what threatened looked like, how it smelled.

She smoothly tucked the check away, out of sight, then pinned Albert Fine with a merciless smile, held the eye contact an extra beat. His bony ringless hand, his lingering in the break room at 4:45 on a Friday. The careful hopeless combing of his disappearing hair . . . Becky took it all in, so he could see, and let pity soak through her smile until she could feel his soul shrivel. Then she turned sharply and left.

She could barely hear herself going through the "goodbye, nice weekend" routine with Freddie and a few other coworkers over the Klaxon fury in her head. Still, she managed to straighten her desk, cover her typewriter, replace the Golden ledger on its shelf.

And tuck the mystery check under an extra sweater in her bottom drawer.

The next morning, Becky woke before dawn, listening to the repeated four-note song of the mourning dove. Although she'd repainted in soft peach with cream accents, there was no disguising her childhood bedroom. Her books stood on the shelves where her dolls had once been propped, and her blouses and skirts hung on the splintery wood dowel that still held traces of her junior-high-era perfume. Through the gap in the curtains she watched the top branch of the front-yard cottonwood wave in the same motion and at the same cadence as it had the last eighteen years.

A terrible thumping came from the stairs. Becky went cold, couldn't move. But then she heard a strangled cry and raced from the room. Her father sprawled sideways, his robe askew and one arm twisted behind his back.

"Holy god, Daddy. You gave me a heart attack." She strained to right him, arms around his waist. They sat on the stairs, her father breathing hard. "You okay? Yeah?" She swiped a piece of his hair back, relieved to see his mild smile return. He was abashed, and so at least a little aware.

The strokes had come in tiny rapid bursts, the first series last winter, undetected except for slightly increased confusion, forgetting—keys put through the dishwasher, the lost name of a church pastor. The next two events had been unmissable, bringing about as they did stumbling, a frozen right arm, and a loss of language that bordered on muteness. He did okay at home, for the most part, but Becky wondered for how much longer. And then what. When she pictured a fall like this morning's on a weekday when she was gone—and him with a broken leg or back, in agony for hours, alone . . .

They were due in Champaign-Urbana for an 11 am appointment. "So now we have something to tell the doctor. How about some eggs before we go?"

The appointment itself was shockingly unhelpful. As far as Becky could tell, no one could give her any sort of guidance on what to expect or when to expect it. This time, for the first time, she took the brochure titled "Area Facilities for Long Term Care."

Now, in the west parking lot of UIUC's campus, her father safely deposited at the barbershop in the hospital's lobby where he'd get a shave and a nice long cut, Becky folded the pages in half and wedged them into her purse. The Datsun ticked for another minute, engine cooling, while she sat there casting into the future. There were savings to get her father through a year or maybe two at one of those places. That was if they sold the farmhouse and the business, which had dwindled steadily since his decline. If only one of those doctors would be straight about how long they expected him to live!

Becky got out of the car and began to walk, fast, without a direction. The campus courtyard stretched wide from one tan cement building to another, paved pathways crisscrossing all over like a corn maze without the corn. She slowed to match the tempo of the enrolled students, wishing she had some books to carry.

"Oh my goodness, Becky Farwell?"

Becky froze. Sarah Meakins, wide-eyed with friendly delight. Shit. How could she not have guessed this would happen? There must be at least a dozen Pierson High grads at UIUC.

Pleasantries gave way to Sarah's recounting Becky's high school career to her unimpressed friend. "We called her 'Baby'— remember that, Becky? Because no one had ever taken pre-calc as a freshman before."

"Are you a transfer?" Sarah's friend asked. She was pulling crumbs off a muffin wrapped in a paper napkin and eating them one by one.

"No, I—"

"Oh, Becky's holding down the fort at home." Sarah turned to Becky. "My mom told me you're working in Town Hall!"

"I deferred Notre Dame." Becky blinked as a ray of sun bounced off a roof's corner right at her eyes. "And Case Western." This was true, and the offer of a full ride at Case had particularly stung. "I also got in to U. Michigan, Northwestern, U. Chicago, Carleton . . ."

Sarah's friend stopped picking at the muffin.

"Well . . . that's great, Becky." Sarah spoke slowly, half-smiling.

"Though I'll probably go to Johns Hopkins. Quality-wise, it might as well be an Ivy, but with more scholarships. They said I'd probably qualify for the business school by next year, depending on how many credits they offer."

Now Sarah and her friend were silent. They exchanged a quick glance.

But Becky couldn't stop. "Johns Hopkins is in Baltimore, though. And when Georgetown brought me out they made a good case for why you'd want to be in a major city like DC, not plunked down in some farm town, ha, for college." None of that was true, but Becky could have gone on for hours.

Wow, Sarah's friend mouthed. She took a real bite of muffin and stepped back on the path.

Sarah reached out to touch Becky's forearm, a light tap. "Say hello to your dad."

Then they were gone, bookbags jouncing, heads close together, moving into the massed line of other students.

Becky burst into tears. First for her own stupidity and humiliation and then—so dumb, so hopeless—for the stupidity and humiliation of crying. Head down, she pushed into the nearest building, ignoring the die-cut SCHOOL OF ART on its glass door.

Becky spent several minutes in the ladies' room, and when she reemerged her blouse was retucked, her red-blond hair reclipped into its tortoiseshell barrette, and a new slick frost of lip color drew attention to the set of her slight angry smile. As she marched toward the door, intent on getting back to her father and the hell out of UIUC, a tubby man with a crew cut materialized behind the desk in the cool rotunda and called out, "Brochures are up here."

Becky came forward and took one. "The Space of Place: Regional Artists on the Meaning of Home."

"Are you a first year? This is our gallery area, where—"

"Yeah, okay, thanks." Now she had to take a look around.

At first, Becky made dutiful circles in the small white-walled rooms. Nodded occasionally, although she was the only visitor: very nice, yes, interesting. Would her father be done with the hot-towel shave? He loved to be tipped back in the chair and they'd let him stay that way, angled toward the TV, until she returned. She thought about whether they'd need gas for the ride back—$3.50 a gallon, Jesus—and how much deposit was required by the nursing homes listed on that folded sheet in her purse. Were fees like that negotiable? Was there a payment plan?

And then a visceral urge to back up cut through her mental calculations. Becky reversed past the last three paintings until she came to a stop in front of a framed picture in oil, hung at her exact eye level. She inched closer.

Hadn't she seen a painting before? Well, of course. The junior year spring trip into Chicago, which had included a stop at the Art Institute, the still lifes rotating through Barner's Restaurant on Second, where she and her father went regularly for meat-and-three on either Wednesday or Thursday, depending on when they had ham loaf. (Barner's still lifes were sourced from the manager's mother's home for the elderly, which put out residents' depictions of a bowl and fruit—same bowl, different fruit—each week on Visitor's Day, priced to sell.)

I've seen paintings before, Becky argued to herself. But it didn't feel true, compared to being in the presence of *this* painting, the physical result of however many possible permutations of pigment and brushstroke and horsehair and vision and canvas and flaking nail-joined wood. Five minutes passed. Fifteen. Her arches ached, her purse was on the floor. She reached out and unhooked the piece from its hanger and for a brief moment studied it in her arms, the shortened plane of its image a whole new—

"Whoa, whoa." The man from the desk was at her side, gently but immediately taking the painting away, his face dark with displeasure.

Becky was caught off guard. "You can't hold them?"

"No, you can't 'hold' them. Christ."

Well, she hadn't known. "All right, I'm sorry." Her impulse had been only to more closely examine it, the way you picked up a single high-heeled pump off the shelf at Rudy's. "It's for sale, isn't it? Wait—why is it for sale? This is a museum."

"Yes, but we include gallery sales in our rotating exhibit twice a year. If you want, you can sign up for our newsletter." Still holding the frame to his chest, the man nodded toward the front desk.

"Can I . . . Please. Just a bit closer?" Becky held up her hands and then clasped them behind her back.

A flash of amusement, then the man extended his arms. Becky hung her face over the painting as if steaming her pores. The man started talking, although she wished he wouldn't, about the deceased artist, his stellar career that flew under the radar, his influences included Hopper, of course, but also the modern gestural work of . . .

Becky tried to memorize every inch of the canvas, knowing with a sick sadness that her time was running out. She had to get back to her father.

At last, having finished his spiel, the man carefully rehung the painting. Tactfully stepped back—but not far—so Becky could pick up her purse and leave.

Becky gave one last regretful look, then began to turn away. Stopped, her eye caught by a small circular sticker next to the painting on the wall. "Hey. What's this?" She tapped the number printed on the sticker.

"That's the price of the piece."

$540. Becky's heart started pumping. For a moment the nearly matching figures, here and printed on the check buried in her office drawer, seemed manifested straight from her own mind. *Don't be crazy*, she told herself. She waved at the man without looking at him and hurried for the door.

Waiting in line at First Federal, Becky thought about the Pierson Disaster, how most of the town had unreasonably blamed the bank for those drownings on the morning of its opening ceremonies, and that a faint hint of guilt and apology still hung in the air, eighty-plus years later. She hoped it might work in her favor.

It was a late October afternoon, and she was fourth in line along the dusty velvet rope. She'd timed her visit for the afternoon "rush" of storekeepers making deposits before the close of business. She had chosen her outfit just as carefully: new cream-colored boatneck sweater, pulled down over the pinned waistband of a thrift shop jersey skirt one size too big, and her favorite thin-heeled pumps, the ones she knew would tap smartly on the bank lobby's polished flagstones.

Now third in line. She smiled back at Mr. Fornet as he touched his baseball cap. Repeated versions of the same old lines with the lounging security guard as she had on every bank visit she'd made in nine months on the job. *Weather's turned. Sure has. With our luck, there'll be snow by Halloween.*

The teller waved Becky up to the counter for her turn. "Where's your coat?" she asked.

Becky made a shiver motion and set the forms and checks on the worn brass surface, a chest-high counter.

"You're crazy," the teller declared. "I even wore mine on a smoke break!" The bank was a long quarter mile down First from Town Hall.

"I'll jog back. In my heels."

The teller snorted. "Don't kill yourself for them."

Becky had studied this woman for weeks, had chosen her for a certain disdainful quality, a punch-out-and-get-the-hell-out attitude. She didn't know her name but could picture her at Ladies Night with a group of fellow working girls, voice rising above the hubbub as she held forth on the latest idiocy of her pimpled creep of a manager. Becky leaned an elbow on the counter and watched the woman's formidable mauve nails detach deposit slips, stamp checks, and tap on the keyboard.

An ancient fan slowly stirred the air a dozen feet above them. Becky made herself look away from the ring of lit windows lining the balcony, where the manager's office must be.

The teller was processing the mistaken refund by now. Becky lounged against the counter and pinned her eyes on the Golden check—receipt separated, $542 added to a list on the teller's screen, and set to the side in a growing pile. Wait, she told herself. Wait. One agonizing check more and then—

"Holy crap." Becky slapped a hand over her eyes. "I can't believe I spaced on that."

"What?"

Becky reached over to tap the withdrawal form in front of the woman. "Getting that signed!" "Petty cash," she'd filled out, as neatly as ever.

The teller picked up the form and studied it. "You'd think they'd put you as a signatory by now."

Becky motioned for it impatiently. "I gotta run back up there before—" She glanced up at the clock and the teller mirrored her action, then winced.

"I'm screwed," Becky moaned. "I was supposed to get it yesterday, but . . ."

"Nah," the teller said, in a low voice. She scrawled something along the bottom of the slip and detached its receipt, putting the original on top of the pile of checks. As she opened the cash drawer, Becky whispered over the counter, "You're saving my ass."

"No worries." The teller gave her a smirking wink that said it all: *us against them.* She started to hand over the piles of receipts to Becky, including the envelope of cash, and then paused, studying the amount. "Five hundred, huh. What are they going to do, go crazy on toilet paper and Sanka?"

Becky leaned in. "Hookers and blow." The woman laughed outright and gave her the money.

Thank you, Becky mouthed, and backed away from the counter.

Her new evening routine, that next month, was to switch off the overhead and turn on her bedside lamp. You didn't need to look directly at a painting, she found. In fact, sometimes it was better to move around in its proximity while pretending you had forgotten it was there. They weren't the same, but she remembered the same delicious charge she'd once gotten from slowly, so slowly, pulling her trig text out of her locker while Cal Hartman eyed her. Turning a few pages, cocking a hip. Replacing that book, stretching up to reach a notebook instead. Her back to him, her whole body covered in sparkly invisible ions from his gaze. (Cal Hartman himself, though: bleh.)

Tonight was Thanksgiving, and Becky sat on the front of her bed in a turtleneck sweater and jean skirt, filing her nails. Her insides felt thick and sodden from the three-course "banquet" at the Palace Diner out on Route 4. With her father near silent the whole meal, there was little to do other than eat steadily from the thick white platters of food that covered their booth table: turkey and gravy, potatoes and green beans and two kinds of stuffing. Three slices of pie, one extra because the waitress was fond of Hank and counting on that big holiday tip. Which Becky had added to the bill.

She filed and burped and waited for the painting to work its magic. The office was closed for the next few days and the streets were full of noisy students home for break, but Becky's room stayed the same—drafty, scuffed at the baseboards. For a moment doubt flared: not at what she'd done, but why she'd done it. What if it wore off?

"Daddy?" she yelled, not looking up from her nails. The late-night TV movie was the second Indiana Jones, and she could follow every chase or torture scene by the strangled sounds coming up through the floorboards. "You asleep?" To her surprise, the TV sound cut off, and her father's heavy steps—same as always, even after the strokes—sounded up the back stairs.

Becky met him in the hall. "C'mere for a second." She drew him in and gently settled him on the foot of the bed beside her. "All they did was wrap it in brown paper," she mused out loud. "Secured it with plain old Scotch tape. I was expecting some big production, like . . . big box, thousands of those Styrofoam peanuts. But no."

The actual transaction had taken place in a back office at the UIUC museum. The female clerk—no sign of that first man—hadn't blinked when Becky produced her crinkled envelope of cash. Becky had had a whole story plotted out—*my grandmother's seventieth, we all chipped in*—but in the moment of truth she forgot it all.

"I was so dumb," Becky said to her dad. "She held it out to me and I didn't even take it at first. I thought maybe someone else was supposed to carry it to the car. And, like, tell me how to transport it." Or approve her setup, at least. She'd stuffed a lot of pillows in the back seat, including the ones in cornflower print behind them on the bed right now.

"It won't bite," the woman had said, with a dry single laugh, a little impatient. She'd had a cold sore at the corner of her mouth.

"I know." But Becky hadn't even been sure how to hold the thing—flat like a pizza? In front like a shield? In the end she'd seized it any old way, on fire just to get out of there.

Here with her father, though, she was the expert. She rested a hand on his curved back, on the wool blazer she'd chosen for him tonight, and urged him to appreciate how different it was to have a real painting in the house, why it gave her regular old room a whole new feel. And that he shouldn't worry about the money. She was doing real well at the office. "Not everyone gets a bonus at the end of the year." She rubbed the slack muscles along his neck and shoulders.

"Storm."

"No, it's clear tonight." But he meant the painting, he was looking *into* the painting where the background's slate blue with scrapes of white did lighten to a summer-tornado shade of yellow green.

"That's a storm?"

Did he mean, had she spent five hundred and forty (diverted) dollars on a drawing of a gully washer? "Maybe," Becky muttered, a bit sulky.

The woman with the cold sore had insisted on rattling off facts about the artist's dates, influences, and methods while the painting stood propped on the office easel and Becky crushed the envelope of cash in her lap. *I said I'd take it*, she wanted to say. Was this a kind of test? Why hadn't she learned anything about the artist before showing up here?

"And of course, it's the silo image itself, both archetypal and reminiscent of the farm in childhood where the artist—"

"What is?"

"The silo." The woman stopped in her presentation. "The subject matter."

"Oh. Right." So that was what you called it, that part. Becky supposed she had registered the shape of a silo in the painting and now that it was mentioned, the forms of a sagging fence and a stand of cypress trees, but these images were somehow only tangentially related to the thing itself. *Subject matter*, she repeated silently. In all those fevered weeks of acquisition, she hadn't known what the painting was about.

Holding her father's hands, Becky stepped backward to guide him down the hall, then waited outside the bathroom until the flush, then shuffled him to his turned-down bed, where she'd laid out his pajamas. He could take it from there, more or less. She made sure to put his glasses on top of the alarm clock—the one he used to set for 4:40 am —and plug in both night-lights.

Back in her own room she hurried into her own bed. What did it matter if her father didn't see what she did in the painting? That old lava lamp on his dresser, that's what made him smile. Hell, even when he'd been fully with it he never cared about any kind of pictures, never remarked on one that she could remember.

So why this queasy sadness? She wouldn't cry. She wouldn't give in to the sudden images pressing down on her: no college, no boyfriend, no mother downstairs wiping up the last of the kitchen after tonight's family feast. Becky rocked herself fiercely and marshalled a barrage of new thoughts like a deck of cards rainbowed out for her mental pleasure.

There she is in the office, catching up the phone on its first half-ring. Turning in the week's report a full day early. Overhearing Mr. David say, *That new girl's shaping up to be a real powerhouse.*

Now she's slicing through a tangle of invoices, back straight at her own metal desk. Making Mrs. Harris's day with a pouch of shrimpy kibble for the tabby who lost part of his tail in a garage door mishap. Her neatly labeled record books, her own carton of yogurt in the break room fridge, the *good morning*s exchanged with everyone, even old Mayor Thomsic if she happened to pass him in the lobby.

Becky rolled onto her side so she could look at her painting. Hers, it was hers now, and who cared if anyone else recognized its power? Night winds started the cottonwood branch brushing, scraping. She clicked off the light. She lay in bed urging the painting along.

Go on, go on, *change me.*

4

Pierson
1984

ALMOST 9 PM AND THE server still hadn't cleared their entrée plates. Becky knew that her new boss, Karl Price, would insist on ordering a selection of desserts for the table—*To share! C'mon, a bite won't kill you.* Then someone would say, *All right, I guess I'll have coffee.* Then Karl would insist on a glass of "dessert wine," something horrible and sweet that nonetheless he'd spend half an hour sipping from and talking about. Who knew that the most tedious part of her promotion to assistant comptroller would be these endless restaurant meals? If you'd told her three years ago she'd get paid to eat steak and laugh at bad jokes, Becky would have said that sounded just fine.

Karl had a penchant for holding client meetings at restaurants, and by now, just a few months into her new position, they had cycled through all of Pierson's and most of the surrounding counties' "fine dining" establishments (steak houses or Italian). Tonight they were back at Mama Sofia's, where Becky had quietly reminded Karl not to order the fish. So he'd steered all of them, including the two reps from Malten Industries, specialists in municipal wastewater treatment, toward the lasagna. Becky sadly poked at her enormous amount of leftovers. Dad would love it, there was enough for two more meals, but she had a policy of no doggie bags. Karl took food home, and the reps often did, but Becky had her own standards.

"I hear you have a family business, too," Bill from Malten said, angling toward her. He'd gamely tried to turn the conversation toward work throughout dinner, even though Karl mostly wanted to opine about the White Sox. "Out on your place?"

"Yes. Well, sort of." Becky had almost entirely wound down Farwell Agriculture Inc. She'd stopped taking standing orders last year, stopped insurance, and finally had let go their half a dozen seasonal workers. The inventory was mostly gone by now, as were leftover building materials and pallets and shelving. Every night Becky parked in the shadow of the barn extension and wished they hadn't taken that on. They still owed nine grand on it, empty and beautifully painted.

"A lot of times," Bill said, his voice lower now, "we offer add-on residential or commercial services as a perk. With a town contract. Think of it as a bonus, something to hang on to."

Becky nodded tiredly. She hoped he wasn't going to say cash back or cash benefit or cash anything. This was about the time during every dinner when a rep would try to bribe her, with varying levels of subtlety. At least Bill stayed in his lane. Someone from food services once tried to give her a year's membership to Weight Watchers because "all the girls loved it."

"The council has final decision," she told Bill. "We're really just getting to know the people behind the names."

"But you make the recommendation," Bill countered. "Why don't I have someone come out to your property for a free assessment and a future credit? You can always cash it in later if you don't—"

"Excuse me," Becky said. Often it was the only way. "I need the ladies'."

In the hall outside the restrooms she tried her father from the pay phone. It rang eight times and then lapsed into the answering machine message, her own embarrassingly girlish voice. Becky hung up without saying anything—Hank barely acknowledged the machine—and then tried Mrs. Nowak next door. Again, no answer. Did this mean that her neighbor had already gone over to check on her father? Or had Mrs. Nowak fallen asleep again, in front of her own TV? For the fiftieth time Becky wished the old biddy would take the twenty dollars she tried to give her, instead of waving it off irritably and claiming no one needed to pay her to do a good turn for a neighbor. The thing was, it was hard to enforce a good turn. When you were paying, you could complain.

He'd be fine. He almost always was. And surely they were about to wrap up. The Malten people had to drive back to Green County, after all.

Becky went into the ladies' to check her lipstick. In the mirror she tugged at her suit jacket so the frayed lining stayed hidden. How would one cash in a wastewater treatment service? she wondered.

She flicked water at the mirror to obscure her reflection. She could act all high and mighty for not taking bribes, but she'd taken from Pierson, with that doubled check. Acting out like that had been childish, irresponsible. Not to mention incredibly dangerous. Even as she slid back into her seat—plates cleared, finally—Becky breathed a tight little prayer of gratitude, yet again, that she hadn't been caught. If only she could pay it back, that stupid $542. Even though the town accounts would never actually miss that mistaken refund.

She would never, never, never again risk so much for so little. A painting. Of a stormy day. In exchange for her job, this promotion, her new office: an actual office! (Shared.) Even these dinners became unbearably precious when viewed in that light. Not to mention the paycheck, which was the only thin wall propped against the bills bombarding their mailbox every week, every day.

The problem was—and here Becky's eyes slid automatically around the walls of the restaurant even as she smiled at Karl's "You didn't fall in, did you?"—paintings were everywhere. Art was everywhere, once you were awake to it. Not great art, granted, but even the weaker stuff held interest if you looked. These landscapes ringing Mama Sofia's, for example—fuzzy Mount Vesuvius from a dozen vantage points, each in off-putting shades of muddy brown and fake teal. Each with a perspective error, and a large, cheap-looking, gold-tinted frame.

The *Tribune*, the *Sun-Times*, even the *Rockford Register* ran articles about and reviews of shows in Chicago. Becky read these over toast and margarine at home, turning to sections of the paper she'd never before opened. The reprinted images were of terrible quality, so she had to squint at the ink, trying to remake the copy of the copy in her own mind, trying to see it for real. She heard ads for estate sales or gallery openings on public radio. Not that she could go to any of those. (Could she?)

The worst part was her own painting. How much she still loved it and how much it made her want another one. One night in a fury of guilt and self-loathing Becky had taken the thing right off its hanger and put it into her closet facing the wall. But by the next morning it was back up and even worse—she rehung it slightly to the right. Making room for something else.

"*Stop* it," Becky said. When the reps and Karl glanced up in surprise she pushed her fork away emphatically. "I swear if I take one more bite . . ." They laughed and continued to demolish the tiramisu and a piece of chocolate mousse cake.

Forty-five glacial minutes later Karl had signed the credit card slip, and Becky loaded up her arms with brochures and files and reports the Malden reps had pressed on them—Karl took nothing—and somehow managed to unlock her car, dump everything in the front passenger seat, and turn on the engine.

Then a face at her window made her jump. Bill. Christ, hadn't they had enough? The goodbyes and jokes and *let's set something up soon* had taken forever standing in the cold dark parking lot. He motioned for her to roll down her window.

"Forget something?" she asked, trying to keep the bitchiness at bay. Karl had already zoomed off in his Acura.

"Just this," Bill said, slipping an envelope over the glass ridge. "I didn't want to say anything to make you uncomfortable, but, well . . . it's a small world and we've all heard about how much you're doing for your father these days."

"Oh." She was caught off guard. But of course everyone knew everything in this place.

"Times are tough all over. We just want you to know that Malten cares about you." Bill smiled, still stooped over.

"I can't—"

"Yes, you can. Think of it as a boost from friends. Completely unrelated to everything else."

"Uh huh." Becky handed the envelope back out the window.

Bill stepped away and let it drop onto the pavement as his fellow rep pulled up behind him.

"That's the kind of company we are!" Bill called, getting into the car. "A community, not just a company."

Becky waited a long time after they drove off. Other customers exited Mama Sofia's, almost always with takeaway cartons, and walked slowly to their own cars.

After a while, she opened the driver side door. There it was, an unmarked white envelope, still on the ground. She picked it up and peeked in at the crisp fifties, ten of them. She placed the envelope on the topmost brochure ("Wastewater: What You Need to Know"). She would slip it into one of the accounts somehow. God knows, no one would argue against a credit. Then—her heart pumped—she and Pierson would be even. Dirty money from the rep's bribe to pay back dirty money she'd found for her painting; poetic justice, you could call it. In any case, she'd be clean.

The next day Becky leaned into Karl's office. As usual, she felt groggy from too much food too late at night while he looked exactly the same: crisp in a short-sleeved shirt and tie, well-shaped Afro, whistling a tune between his teeth.

"That was fun," she said. "They enjoyed it, I think."

"It was, wasn't it?" Karl beamed. Becky knew he relished this moment, so she gave it to him every next morning. "And we even got a little business done, before the tiramisu." He patted his belly. "Thanks to you, always keeping my nose to the grindstone."

Becky smiled. "I just need the receipts." The Malten visit had included coffee and snacks in the afternoon, beers at McSweeney's Grill, and then dinner.

"I gave them to you."

"I don't think so." He definitely hadn't and this wasn't the first time, either.

Karl patted around his waist pockets as if last night's dinner check would suddenly materialize in today's pants. "Got to be here somewhere." He lifted up a folder.

"I'll call Visa," Becky said. Again. It took three weeks for a copy to be mailed out.

"Foo. Just type something up and I'll sign it."

"Mrs. Shinner needs receipts for any reimburse—"

Karl waved his hand. "We been signing off on charges long before that lady joined the party. You'll see. Type up what you want."

"All right." Becky couldn't keep disapproval out of her voice. Did no one in this office share her meticulous habits?

"Just leave out that extra side of garlic bread," Karl said, "or I'll get in trouble with the calorie cops." He meant his wife, Cherie, who once told Becky to swap out all the break room sodas for diet and to make her the bad guy if it came to that.

Becky left Karl's office, bitterly thinking, *He who has all thumbs never has to lift a finger.* At her typewriter she rolled in a fresh sheet of letterhead and tapped out "Client entertainment: Malten Industries, two employees, two Pierson City employees, Thursday, September 6, 1984."

First coffee and pastries ordered in from French's Diner. She'd paid cash for that, she remembered. And had the receipt. She fished it out, entered $15.59. For dinner, she started to itemize the appetizers, carefully notating the antipasti they'd ordered. Wait. First there had been beers across the street. She should have added that in the first line.

Becky started to pull out the paper and then stopped. If Karl wasn't going to bother with specifics, then she wouldn't either. "Drinks," she typed firmly. "$60 for wine and beer." That would do it. Would be a little over, in fact. Next she listed dollar amounts for dinner (appetizers, entrées, dessert) and a fifteen percent tip. Make that twenty. She totaled the sum and created two lines for signature: Karl's and the office manager's, Mrs. Shinner's.

Then her phone rang, and Becky hurried to answer. The form she'd typed for reimbursement got stuffed into the worn plastic expandable labeled "Karl to Sign" and she forgot all about it until the check showed up in her mail slot: $425 for client entertainment reimbursement, payable to Accounting General. For Becky to deposit and reassign and withdraw, no one the wiser. *Temporarily*. The money would come out of Town Hall for a bit, and then go back in. *It's borrowing, plain and simple.*

It had gotten harder and harder to bring Hank anywhere, but the problem was, he still loved being out and about. So Becky took to driving him around the outskirts of town after church on Sundays to find that most regular harbinger of autumn: garage sales. Hank loved these; he'd putter through the tables, picking up items and setting them down, maybe manage a few words with neighbors or friends, or simply be able to wave back genially when someone called out to him. Often Becky would set him up near whatever appliances were out for sale: blenders, toasters, beat-up motorbikes, so that Hank could finger their gears and wires, take them apart with the big hands that never lost their dexterity. Mostly, though, they'd end each visit with Hank offered a seat in a lawn chair and a glass of iced tea while Becky browsed the tables herself.

Amazing, she thought, how people took literal junk from their homes and had the audacity to charge money for others to pick it up and take it away! The worst were the clothing racks and shoe trees. Becky thought other people's worn-out robes and jeans and bathing suits—yes, bathing suits!—so awful she made sure never to even look in their direction.

On September 22 the Langleys' house was the third they'd stopped at. It had a good selection, because the two Langley girls—Marissa and Joan, both married and moved away now—were serious about emptying out the home they'd grown up in before downsizing their elderly parents into a smaller place closer to one of them. Becky had set Hank up in a shady spot under an elm and left him listening to a Cubs game playing on the radio near the cash register while she flipped through albums, idly handled some china and cookware, and wished they could go home soon so she could change out of her church dress and scratchiest nylons.

"What about this?" a woman called from over by the side of the garage. "For that wall in the dining room."

"What's it of?" her husband called back.

"I don't know. Come look. They got lots of pictures and stuff over here."

Becky followed the man without any real excitement or interest. She watched as the couple discussed and dismissed a gaudily framed portrait of a woman in a light-green dress. When they left, she moved in and reached past that painting, and a leaning stack of six others, to pick up a small oil of a boy holding a book, a cat twined around the legs of his chair.

She couldn't have explained it to herself in words even if she'd wanted to. But she couldn't ignore the instinct that was screaming inside her like a heat-seeking missile.

The cash register was being manned by a bored dad more interested in the Cubs game than any merchandise. Becky grabbed a handful of kitchen tools—a scuffed plastic spatula, two wooden spoons, a pair of tongs—and set them next to the small oil near the register. "What's the score?"

"You don't want to know."

Her breathing accelerated while the man slowly added up her purchases, and she tried not to flinch as he turned the painting this way and that, looking for the price sticker. Squinting, he handed it back to her. "Can you read that?"

Becky pretended nonchalance. "It says ten, but I can go compare it to the others if you—" She waved back at the garage.

"Nah. Let's call it fifteen with the other stuff."

"Okay. I just have to . . . Dad, can I see your wallet for a second?" She could feel the man's eyes flicking to them, and away, as she maneuvered to get at the wallet Hank was sitting on. Finally she was able to hand over a ten (from her purse) and five crumpled ones.

"Bag? Receipt?" His tone said there was nothing he'd like to do less, and even though her nerves were tingling, urging her to get away with the painting under her arm, Becky stood her ground. Sure, why not. Yes, please. All right, Dad, we'll catch the last innings at home.

For the rest of the afternoon and evening she didn't have time to examine the little painting, or maybe she put it off on purpose. There was vacuuming to do, and potatoes to boil and mash, and towels forgotten in the washer that smelled moldy and had to be done again. Then Hank had an accident so she had to clean that up too.

But all her instincts at the garage sale were confirmed when the phone rang at 8:30: Marissa Langley, brisk and apologetic, sorry she'd missed them when they'd stopped by earlier, her husband had said how nice it was to catch up.

Uh huh.

Then Marissa explained, all in a rush, the mistake: a few items hadn't been meant for the sale. Some furnishings, some art, you know, nothing spectacular, but things that had held personal meaning for her family. Including, oh, that small picture Becky had taken home. She was sure Becky would understand. A friend of the family's had found it in a charming place in Europe. She'd always meant to get it appraised, but— Actually, she just needed it back.

"That's too bad," Becky said slowly. Gripping the handset.

Yes, Marissa agreed quickly. She could just kill her sister for putting it out with the other things. She'd be happy to run over now, if it wasn't inconvenient.

"No," Becky said.

"No?"

"I'd like to keep it," Becky said. "That is, it's mine now. I'd be happy to show you a copy of my receipt. I think it was your—or your sister's?—husband who made the sale and wrote it out for me."

"Oh, *him*," Marissa said. "He doesn't know anything about anything. That painting wasn't for sale."

"Well, I don't think you're suggesting this, but of course we could take it to small claims." Becky let that hang, then added, "I'm sure that this receipt states it all pretty clearly though."

The dishwasher gurgled and sloshed.

"You always did think you're so great, didn't you? No wonder you never had any friends in this town. Think you're so much better than—"

"Goodbye, Marissa," Becky said cheerfully, and hung up the phone. Hank had shuffled into the kitchen at the sound of Marissa's raised voice, audible right through the receiver. Becky gave him a big hug. "What do you say about ice cream? I think I'm in the mood."

It took careful sleuthing through the yellow pages and asking the right people at work (Mrs. Deedham, who was known to go antique hunting) to find out what an appraiser was and did, and how much one would cost. Nothing, as it turned out. Unless you wanted him to make a sale, and then he took a cut.

Linda Speer of Linda Speer Antiques and Art was much less interested in the painting than Becky would have expected, which suited her fine. She'd followed Mrs. Deedham's recommendation and driven the painting out to Joliet the first weekend day she could get someone to come over for Hank.

Linda rattled off specifics, pointing out the watery signature at the bottom (Becky hadn't really paid attention), examples of similar works by the artist and others of the time and era (lesser known French postimpressionist, 1890s), and features of condition that might affect market value (shitty frame, though that wasn't the way she put it, and slight discoloration along the upper left edging).

"We often see these in the low five thousands," she said. "But the cat might bump it up. It's new to me, that cat image. Maybe . . . six to seventy-five? If you get it cleaned up and reframed."

Becky nodded. The two of them looked at the piece propped up on Linda's desktop easel.

"But you're not selling."

"No, I don't think so. Not at the moment."

Linda nodded. "We'll give you a printout of the info in case you change your mind. No prices guaranteed, of course. But I can think of quite a few collectors who'd be interested. People love cats."

Yuck, Becky thought. "You mentioned framing and someone who could clean or . . . ? Can you tell me more about how that works?"

That was really the moment that the painting's true value appeared: Linda talked and talked and talked, not just about framers and restorers, but also consultants and specialists, movers and refinishers, liquidators and auctioneers. She talked until her next client showed up, and then she finished up with a quick, enthusiastic explanation of estate sales and directed Becky to a pile of brochures on a display table in the front hall. Becky took a few of the magazines, too: *Midwest Art* and *Art in America*.

On the way home, the brochures and magazines on the seat next to her, Becky found herself driving fast. Everything inside her was rushing forward, new ideas and plans, ambition she wasn't even sure she could qualify.

In the next eight weeks Becky found and pounced on four separate accounting mistakes that Karl or another accountant had made that resulted in overages and credits. She swept these funds aside and held on to them. Also she stopped correcting Karl, and others, when they rounded up for reimbursements or doubled something she had already paid for. None of the mistakes were big in and of themselves—most were in the tens of dollars, occasionally a hundred or so—but they accrued. Becky began to see the genial sloppiness around Karl's department as a built-in feature, one that she learned to keep her mouth shut about.

She began to roam around the counties to search out estate sales for art. The first one she visited was a bust—moldy upholstery and elaborately framed crap. At the second one—way out in Franklin Lake—she found what turned out to be an early Jan Westerman, and by the fifth trip she was starting to recognize and greet regulars on the circuit. One of those tipped her off to a retired Chicago gallery owner who now sold out of her home outside Springfield. By the end of the year there were five paintings hanging on Becky's bedroom wall, and one two-foot sculpture in the corner hallway outside the guest bathroom.

5

Pierson
1986

BECKY WAS IN THE NEARLY full Rockford MetroCentre, waiting for the Judds to take the stage, and annoyed as hell. She recrossed her legs, pinned against the row in front, unable to get comfortable in the metal seat. All she wanted was to quickly greet Ingrid Beanton, an old high school classmate who held a ticket for the seat next to her, and then move on to find a better seat down front. Alone. But from where Becky sat in Mezzanine G, the options a few levels down were narrowing every minute, no matter how anxiously she eyed them. She could, of course, go ahead and change her seat now . . . But then she'd spend the whole concert conspicuously not looking back here. And what if they ran into each other in the ladies'? Or if Ingrid spotted Becky's light-red ponytail in another section and put it together that she hadn't even waited around to say hello?

So, fine. She would wait around to say hello.

A rolling cheer went up from the arena as another stock photo of the Judds lit up the screen above the empty stage. Naomi's fluffy brown hair was swept to the side and her tangerine-lipsticked mouth opened wide, teeth a thick white. As usual, she came off younger than her daughter, Wynonna, whose heavier, straight-jawed face was pressed up against her mother's cheek. But Becky loved Wynonna more—all true Judd fans understood this—for her voice, of course, but also the sad awareness in those heavy-lidded eyes.

8:10. They'd go on any minute. Becky counted the dwindling empty spots in the level below. All around her moronic couples were loud-laughing and making out and saying incorrect things about the Judds. *Hope they play that "Rockin' with the Women." (With the rhythm,* Becky silently corrected.) *Well, they've had about five Number Ones already.* (Nine, including "Cry Myself to Sleep" this week.) *That first record's still the best one.* (Wrong. *Why Not Me* far outdid *Wynonna & Naomi* in songwriting caliber, instrumentation, not to mention vocal arr—)

"Hello in there," called a young female voice. Right away Becky recognized the tall pudgy figure of Ingrid Beanton (she would *not* call her "Beanie" the way everyone at school had) standing at the end of the aisle with a shy smile on her face.

Everyone in their row looked over to her, and then back to Becky. "Well, come on in," Becky called back crossly.

Ingrid wide-stepped over tight-jeaned legs in her own tight jeans. "Exsqueeze me. Exsqueeze me."

Becky shut her eyes briefly. Another roll of applause around the concert hall. When she opened them, Ingrid was beside her, expectant. Becky hadn't directly spoken with Beanie—*Ingrid*—in the two years since they'd graduated, and maybe not even in all the time they had spent in the same class of Pierson Elementary and then Pierson High School. Back then Ingrid had been a slightly chubby volleyball star who floated easily between the standouts, the burnouts, and even the theater weirdos. Now she was a softly rounded ER nurse in clogs and a faded denim jacket with a tight permanent Becky could tell she'd done herself.

"Straight from work?" Becky asked, meaning the ugly shoes.

"Good to see you too, Becky Farwell. Think they'll open with 'Rhythm'? I heard Wynonna did 'Tears for You' a cappella two nights ago in St. Louis."

Becky opened her mouth but just then the lights dropped and a general clamor rose as members of the band walked to their instruments. She searched wildly for available seats in the lower levels. Meanwhile, Ingrid took two quick snaps with the 25mm hanging on a strap around her neck. When the swinging bass chords of "Rockin' with the Rhythm" kicked in, she nudged Becky and winked. Wynonna came in with her guitar ahead of Naomi, who was serene in her petite beauty and easier vocal part.

"Can't wait for Wy to go solo already," Ingrid half-shouted in Becky's ear. Huh. Becky hadn't thought of that. Wynonna solo: that would be something. She tried not to notice how her and Beanie's shoulders were rocking in the same rhythm, right and then left, and then right, and then left. Along with everyone else in the crowd.

At work the tedious client dinners with Karl continued, two or three per month. Karl now also liked to take office teams on what he called "off-sites" for weekend barbecue "brainstorm sessions" in his spacious backyard. Becky estimated these events extended the actual completion of any work project by three or four hundred percent. But she attended, laughed, lingered in Karl's doorway the next day with gushy gratitude. Karl was fifty-nine with a history of angina and a paid-off second home in Lake Geneva. Becky could wait.

Because work had become just as much about what she thought of as her Activity, snatching up any invoice error or forgotten reimbursement or unused staff training budget and tucking the money away into accounts only she kept track of. In the past year she'd used $24,290 to purchase art, which often she resold for more. After repaying Pierson, whatever was left over was hers to play with. She couldn't tell which part of it pleased her the most: the pieces of magic hanging on her walls at home, or the fact that they had come from mistakes in the office only she knew how to spot.

It wasn't enough, though. The money or the art. Becky had her eye on something bigger, much bigger. The Activity needed to grow—somehow.

She wouldn't find those answers in the Art History 101 night class she'd been taking once a week at the School of the Art Institute in downtown Chicago. Becky had begun in high hopes. She loved the bad grilled cheese and burned coffee at the diner where she always ate beforehand, and at first she'd loved the thrill of the darkened auditorium as the part-time instructor—not a real professor; she had no illusions—clicked through slide after slide of ill-lit historical paintings and talked endlessly about the least interesting aspects of them: color, line, shape, form, texture. Only once had he mentioned the word *value* and when he did, Becky started up. There was a grimacing caricature on the screen, a George Grosz in browns and greens. Not that she'd ever want something like that, but . . .

She raised her hand.

"Yes?" The teacher squinted out at her, puzzled.

"How much is the . . . What is the price?" The length of the pause and the way her uncertain words hung in it let her know she'd made a mistake.

The teacher pressed her to clarify. Other students—mostly senior citizens—looked away. "I thought you said . . . what its value was," Becky mumbled.

"Oh, *value*." The teacher was relieved. "Value meaning lightness or darkness on a gray scale. If we notice the shifts in shading in Grosz's later work, we can clearly see how—"

Becky slumped down, grateful for the gradations of shadow in the auditorium. You weren't supposed to talk about the money. You were supposed to pretend it didn't exist.

"How much did you pay?" she called into Ingrid's ear. "For your ticket." Wynonna was circling the stage in an extended instrumental break, stopping by each band member to jam. Her mother, lightly toe-tapping at her standing mike, waited for this part to be over. "Donny told me it was face value but I feel like he scalped me."

Ingrid paused in her dancing. "You gave him money? That dipshit."

"He didn't charge you?"

"*I* bought these seats. He and I were supposed to go together."

It all came out at intermission, when they ate three-dollar hot dogs with their feet up on the row in front and shared a watery beer. Donny Wagner worked in management at Collins Stamping over in Palmyra. He had glossy tumbled dark curls and wore a puka shell necklace on weekends, out at the bars. It was rumored he'd been married before, a crash-and-burn with no kids, but no one had the real story, since Donny was one of the few people to have moved to Pierson later in life, where he lived with a cousin out on Kilgore.

"He had a few meetings with my boss," Becky said. "He kept calling me later. I don't know why."

"Because he's a dog in heat, that's why." A foam of beer hung on the corners of Ingrid's mouth. "No offense."

Becky shook her head, *it's fine*. "We went out once, last Thursday, for—"

"Wings night at the Canteen," Ingrid finished. "Did he spend the whole time talking to other people at the bar? Like, calling them over to your table?"

"*Yes*. Like he was running for office. And then he said he had an extra ticket and did I want it and . . ." Becky stared ahead at the audience milling around in the smoky glare of the halftime lights. For a full idiotic minute at the Canteen she'd thought Donny was asking her to go out again, to go *with* him to the Judds. "I don't even know why I said yes in the first place." Becky crumpled the paper hot dog wrapper.

"Because he's super cute, dummy. Still has a good flat stomach, not like most of the schlubs from school."

Becky shuddered. She didn't know anything about Donny's stomach, flat or not.

"We dated for three months," Ingrid said. "In all that time, guess who never bought one full meal for me. Get this: One Sunday he was supposed to come out to my folks' for a dinner. It totally was *not*, like, meet-my-parents—my dad was out of town, even! But my mom had made a full chicken thing, with real mushrooms, and like a dodo bird I even baked a cake. Duncan Hines, though, thank god." Ingrid chewed her hot dog meditatively.

"Uh huh," Becky said cautiously, not sure where this was going.

"So we wait and wait. My sister's husband starts eating in front of the Notre Dame game. Finally the phone rings and he says he's at the Sunoco down the road, can I meet him. It's, like, what the fuck, but I go. He's all smiling but squirrelly and says it's engine trouble and he can't make it out. But the whole time his truck was sitting over by the pump! No mechanic anywhere that I can see."

"He didn't make it for dinner," Becky guessed.

"That's not even the worst part," Ingrid whispered.

Becky smiled. "You gave him money for gas, didn't you."

Ingrid covered her face, and Becky was afraid she might cry. Then came a burst of laughter. "And I slept with him after that, like, four more times! Am I a dope, or what?"

"No," Becky protested. *Kind of*, she thought. "What about the tickets though?" The lights had dimmed again, Tanya Tucker on the PA system faded out.

"I mail-ordered them three months ago. Soon as they announced the tour. I was hoping I'd have . . . well, that I'd have a boyfriend by now. Then stupid Donny started sleeping with Kristine Looney and I pretended I hadn't heard about it, I offered him the ticket thinking maybe he'd change his mind. And show up." Ingrid looked down at her clogs.

Normally, a moment like this would have filled Becky with distaste. People were so needy, so unbearably undisguised! But now she only tipped the rest of her flat beer into Ingrid's cup. "I was the one who gave him thirty-five dollars," she said.

Ingrid's eyes fluttered. "Thirty-*five*?"

"How much did you get them for?"

"Eighteen each!"

Wynonna and Naomi stomped into a cover of "Girls Night Out" and the entire audience jumped to its feet, including Becky and Ingrid. Becky didn't even shrug Ingrid's arm off her shoulder later in the show, or protest when Ingrid held her camera high, twisted it around to face them, and clicked off several snaps.

"Those will never come out," Becky yelled.

"Oh stuff it, Becky Farwell," Ingrid shouted. She was sweaty, beaming. "We'll mail one to Donny."

"With a bill for thirty-five dollars."

This sent Ingrid into whoops of laughter.

Becky allowed herself to sing along with everyone to "Grandpa," which she usually disdained for its overdose of sentimentality.

The encore was "Why Not Me." Ingrid was in her own world, eyes closed and swaying her head left and right with the music. She was one of about three thousand women in the audience wholeheartedly buying into the song, nurses and teachers and homemakers and retail clerks, all of them crying out the question along with the Judds. To her surprise Becky too got swept up in the lyrics, noticing for the first time how the phrase went from plaintive to exultant as it was repeated. Wynonna sang like she was really feeling it, this single that had been on the charts since last summer. And even Naomi's fill-in harmony worked, calling out to all of them in the crowd, every person's longing. Making what they wanted into the best part of themselves.

6

Pierson
1986–1987

BECKY AND INGRID DIDN'T FALL in right away. After the Judds concert, Becky hurried away from Ingrid, grateful they didn't have to hug or anything like that.

But on a November afternoon, Becky was in a staff meeting when one of the secretaries leaned in and whispered loudly in Karl's general direction, "The fire department's here!"

Instant flutter of excitement through the sleepy room. Anything was better than a staff meeting.

"Oh oh," Karl said. "Who forgot to unplug the toaster?"

But it wasn't the truck and the guys in their gear, only Chief Edwards, alone. And he only wanted Becky. "Let's take a drive," he said, putting a hand on her back. "Your dad's over at County ER."

In fact, he was dead. Had died even before the ambulance got out to their place, called by Mrs. Nowak when she arrived to find him fallen halfway between the TV and the bathroom.

That morning Becky had unwrapped his midmorning coffee cake and shown him that the plate for lunch was where it always rested in the fridge: middle shelf, covered in tinfoil. He'd seemed no better or worse than most days and nodded when she reminded him Mrs. Nowak would be stopping by in the afternoon.

During the short ride to the hospital in Chief Edwards's personal car, Becky hoped and hoped she had remembered to hug or kiss her father goodbye this morning. She usually did, but sometimes when she was in a rush she didn't. Had it been a rush morning?

She thanked the chief when he dropped her at the front door. No, he didn't need to walk her in, she would be all right.

From the serious, calm face of the doctor who greeted her she knew he was gone. They brought her to his room, quiet and dark. His belly a rounded mound under the green sheet. His cheeks were sagging, brow with the same creases, eyes shut.

"Massive stroke," the doctor said, just as she reached for his hand under the sheet. Not warm, not cool. Rough in exactly the way she knew it would be. Instantaneous. He didn't suffer.

Becky leaned her hip on the bed, nudging Hank over a little so she could sit with him. She didn't want to let go of his hand.

"Here, let me get you a chair."

"Can I . . . Am I allowed to sit on the bed?"

"Oh," he said quietly. "Yes, of course." He helped her lift her father's body, to make room.

By the time she got home that night it was almost 8 pm, and there was an unfamiliar car out front. When she approached, she saw Ingrid's face, her brief burst of smile, and then a chastened look. Ingrid got out of the car first, her mother followed, and Becky awkwardly accepted hugs from both of them. She stood by the car, expecting they would leave, but Ingrid simply walked her to her own door and came in, as natural as anything.

Becky was too tired to object. "You don't have to," she said, however, when Ingrid went right into the kitchen to warm up the food they'd brought. And start on the dishes.

"I know," Ingrid said. "Here, Mom." She had found some cleaning supplies in a closet and now Mrs. Beanton was vacuuming the area of the hallway, near the bathroom where— Oh. Becky felt a little sick as she realized what Ingrid's mother was working to clean, and why.

She ate the chicken and rice Ingrid handed her, and drank a full glass of water rather crossly when Ingrid wouldn't let up about it. A few more cars arrived, and Mrs. Beanton brought in dishes for the fridge. When the phone rang, Ingrid answered, and took down messages, nodding and saying the right things. At some point Becky even went up to bed, following Mrs. Beanton to her own room, where the sheets had been changed. Becky fell asleep to the sound of Ingrid moving around the kitchen and when she woke in the morning she half-expected to find her there, even though the house was empty and still.

Over the next week, leading up to the funeral, Ingrid slid seamlessly into Becky's life. They both belonged to First Presbyterian so Becky understood the machine that now cranked into action: helping her arrange a service, a burial, a reception. People had loved Hank and went out of their way to assist, even with things Becky hadn't known she had to do.

The biggest surprise of it all was Ingrid. She came to the house and supervised food: portioning, labeling, freezing. Occasionally vetoing entirely: "Uh uh, that one goes straight into the trash. I've seen Mrs. Fremont sneeze into her open hands." She nudged Becky to order food for the reception, she made her get a hair appointment, she kept a list of all the incoming cards and flowers.

Becky got tired of being bossed around but Ingrid never picked up on hints like "Well, this has been a big help, so . . ."

Mostly Ingrid was just there. After dinner she'd show up with some kind of snack or a couple of light beers. Becky didn't feel like talking much and she certainly didn't want to cry or look through photos so mostly they watched TV. Stupid shows that Ingrid loved—*Dynasty*, of course, but also all the half-hour comedies about families with sassy-bratty kids and adults with wacky problems. Ingrid ridiculed every feature of these shows but seemed to enjoy them anyway. Becky got used to her being curled up on the other side of the couch, Keds off, beer in hand. Neither of them sat in what had been Hank's armchair.

The day of the funeral was cold and slushy. A raw sadness stabbed at Becky, underneath everything she did or said. She shivered through the service, her feet icy and numb, and only a few people came to the cemetery to watch Hank's dark coffin lower into the muddy grave. But the reception back at the church— coffee, deli platters, and many homemade desserts—was full of clients, coworkers of Becky's (including Karl and his wife), and parents of her schoolmates.

Ingrid came to all of it: the service, the burial, the reception. She stayed in the background but she stayed. Hanging up coats, clearing away plates, reminding people to sign the guest book. Becky had no memory of procuring a guest book.

Toward the end of the day, that longest day, Ingrid passed by her with an armful of wadded tablecloths and Becky snapped. "You don't have to stick around, you know. Didn't your folks leave, like a while ago?" Ingrid still lived at home too. "Nobody asked you to do all this." *We're not really friends. We don't even know each other. And we don't have to, just because we're the only losers our age still left here.* Becky managed not to say any of that out loud, but she knew it bled through her face and voice.

Ingrid only rolled her eyes and went off with the tablecloths. But later, when Becky peeked around for her, she was gone. By the time the last group of mourners left the church hall, the windows were dark. Becky needed four trips to carry the flower arrangements out to her car, the only one left in the parking lot. She didn't even want them but she didn't want to leave them for the janitor to deal with.

For a while she drove around. Looping back and forth along the river, crossing the bridges north and south. She slowed at the sight of Barner's Restaurant, realizing how shaky and tired she was, not having eaten all day. But her lips were chapped and throat sore, and Becky didn't think she could speak one more sentence out loud, let alone to someone who might have served her father his last plate of warm mashed potatoes drowned in butter, Hank's standing weekly order.

She might even have cried, then, a little or a lot, driving back home through Pierson. She might have given in to all the sadness, the confusion about what would come next. Why did she feel so young? She was assistant comptroller, not some little kid, not some *orphan*. She was twenty-two years old!

The first thing Becky saw when she pulled around in front of the house was Ingrid's VW bug. A blaze of gladness spread through her. She got out of her own car, stuffed full of lilies and gladiolas, and walked over to Ingrid, who was sitting in the passenger seat with the engine off and the overhead light on, flipping through *Glamour* magazine.

Ingrid rolled down her window. She gestured to the brown paper grocery bag on the seat next to her. "Ritz crackers and a

thing of that port wine cheese. Also Keebler cookies, the ones
with M&M's. Because I didn't know if you'd want salty or sweet.
Or both, because that would be the right answer. And . . ." Ingrid
rummaged on the car floor and pulled up a glass bottle. Johnnie
Walker Black. "Voilà. My dad's. He was saving it for a special occasion probably. So, you know."

Becky had to use both hands to tug open the old car's heavy
freezing door. Ingrid broke into a foolishly huge smile. "I can
just drop this stuff off," she said, grabbing up the bag and bottle,
scrambling to follow Becky to the house. "If you're not, like, up for
company."

"I'm never up for company," Becky said, holding the front door
open for Ingrid. "You pick whatever shows we watch, I just don't
want to talk. I'm sick of talking." She watched Ingrid kick off her
shoes and start tearing the wrapping off the booze. "Also I'm in an
incredibly grouchy mood," she added.

"Tell me something I don't know, Becky Farwell. Here's your
drink."

As wasn't uncommon in Pierson, or in other small Midwestern
cities, Hank Farwell's death triggered a wave of town love to carry
his only child through the difficulties that came afterward. Becky
had her pick of invitations for Christmas and New Year's, which
she celebrated as a guest in multiple homes for multiple dinners,
with the Beantons' as the main event. Hank's death propelled her
to officially and finally close Farwell Agriculture Inc., and it perhaps nudged along a surprise salary bump at Town Hall. Her soli-
tary circumstances, that tragic aura, and her *grit*—no quality more

admired in Pierson—all of it combined to plant her firmly in the town's psyche.

Theoretically, she could have gone off to college then. No one would blame her. But she knew it was too late. Every week Karl ceded her some new responsibility. By now she was overseeing the entire team of in-house accountants and had been asked to sit in on senior management meetings about fiscal planning. She owned—and wore in regular rotation—four skirt suits and a dozen blouses.

She and Ingrid had become—Becky could admit it now—friends. She bought a VCR so they could watch all the tapes Ingrid rented on weekends. She started stocking Entenmann's Danish rings and Diet Dr Pepper and Tato Skins. On the nights they weren't together Ingrid often called Becky on the phone, *just to talk*. It took a long time for Becky to understand this and then to come to enjoy it. They argued over the merits of WMMR (clearer reception, insipid afternoon DJ) versus WOHA (less likely to tune in, deeper cuts of George Strait and Randy Travis). They shared gossip about classmates, picking apart old high school beefs and infatuations. They compared stories about creepos at work. Becky got used to Ingrid's tendency to turn all topics toward the men she was interested in and a repetitive speculation about whether or not they would call her. Becky's role, she learned after an awkward bungling, was to insist against all evidence that yes, of course, fill-in-the-name would call. When Ingrid's yawns began to break into her every other comment, Becky would try to end the call but Ingrid never wanted to. She liked to talk when she was sleepy. Plus, there was always more to say.

Sometimes they went together to church, especially if there was a service project after coffee hour, like boxing up lunches for a shelter or tutoring kids in earth science or algebra. Both were hard workers and liked doing good for the town, especially if it came with lots of praise from others (Becky) or a buffet of baked goods (Ingrid). Pierson got used to the two of them together, and eventually Becky did too.

But the main reason she didn't want to leave—or leave yet—had to do with the Activity. Because of the holidays coming fast after her father's death Becky ended up out of the office for over a month. Each time she stopped by to check in, see if she could help out, Karl had turned her right back around and sent her away.

All right. If she couldn't be at the office, couldn't keep a steely eye on the receipts and the budget items, what she could do was learn. By now she'd grown past the local art circles, the estate shows, and the small-time county galleries. She'd thumbed through every back issue of *Midwest Art* in the library and now drove around to newsstands to seek out magazines everyone in town would have scorned as uppity: *Vanity Fair, Vogue, Bazaar,* and even some oversized European publications that cost nearly ten dollars each. Here, the coverage of art was blue-chip, New York–based. Becky picked up on names and trends. She spent long winter afternoons sinking deep into images of oil paintings and shiny tubular sculptures and—wherever she could find them—prices, auction sales, records, and results. She lay in bed—her own bed, in the same small room—and thought about art. Buying art and selling art.

7

Pierson
1987

TOWN HALL'S BASEMENT RAN THE length of the block-long building, was barely heated, and functioned as a damp chaotic storage space everyone tried to forget about. No one wanted to go down there, what with all the jokes about bodies buried and black widow spider nests. But people had to, for extra chairs and holiday decorations and to dump boxes and boxes of files they weren't allowed to throw away. Mostly staff begged the maintenance guy, Scotty, to do those jobs for them.

Becky used to scoff at all such wimpiness but now that she'd spent two hours sunk in the clammy gloom, she had to admit it was creep central down here. That hulking structure shoved up against the north wall, for example, the bulbously shaped thing eight feet tall and shrouded by a cracked blue tarp, what the hell was that? Why did she keep eyeing it every few minutes, when she was supposed to be maximizing the time she'd found to sneak down here?

Becky shifted her perch on the file box she sat on, angling away from the tarp-hidden monster. The lights buzzed and flickered, straight out of a horror movie, but that was why she had a flashlight. Clamping it under an armpit, she put the cover back on one box of files, made a tiny pencil hash mark to its lower corner, and shoved it over to make room for the next. If she kept a steady pace, she could get through two or three more before anyone upstairs noticed she was missing. Karl was out for the day, and the others thought she was delivering copies of the latest memo around the office.

The sheer number of bank accounts held by Town Hall—past and present, closed or dormant or active or some kind of combination thereof—would have daunted much more experienced accountants. It was a running joke upstairs that the tax firm who'd reviewed their books for decades, and hadn't flagged a single transaction since anyone could remember, didn't actually exist. Becky sized up the magnitude of this chaos—this subterranean tunnel of interlocked funding sources—and grasped instantly how it worked in her favor. She bought a small spiral notebook and began to carry it with her to every meeting, budget session, and client dinner. She filled it with notes tracking every account ever mentioned, and compared those with whatever she could find in the current books and bank statements. Then she asked Scotty to carry up file boxes from the basement, so that she could—as she put it to Karl, who shook his head at the idealism and foolishness—"Brush up on institutional memory." Get a handle on how things used to run. On her own time, of course. Personal career development.

Karl was completely oblivious to the inner workings of the budget—how the town's money got sorted and pumped through the various pipes and then shunted toward, or away from, categories of expenditure. He was a *people person,* not a *number cruncher.*

Happy to leave all those pesky details to Miss Farwell, if anyone asked. As long as the line items were accounted for in the spreadsheet he'd be a *happy camper.*

Soon, Becky stopped asking Scotty and began to carry up files herself, two boxes at a time, the way she used to when helping her father with inventory. Today she'd simply gone to the files themselves, small spiral notebook in hand. It was easier, more direct, even if she couldn't stop sneezing—from mold?—and jumped every time the ancient boiler hissed. Nothing wrong with being discreet, either.

Becky was searching for something. Had been for the three months since she'd come back to the office. Although she still scooped up any wayward funds that came across her desk via someone's stupid mistake, for the time being she had paused any real art buying or even shopping. The search had taken over, even though she didn't know exactly what she was searching for—a combination, a path, a recipe. She'd know it when she found it.

She was about to pack it in that afternoon—or was it evening by now?—when she glimpsed a file of records that looked different. Bank statements, like so many of the others, but these were from Midwest Credit Union. Huh. As far as Becky knew, those accounts had been closed. She checked her notebook, went back to lift the lids of a few other boxes. Town Hall's many accounts were held at several banks, officially on the theory that the more widely spread out the financials were, the better. But Becky knew the real reason was probably neglect and carelessness. It was an extra step to officially close an account; easier to just start using a new one.

The statements in Becky's hands held as little as sixty dollars in one account, a hundred and ten in the other. She couldn't remember seeing a current balance from Midwest listed on any recent budget documents. She couldn't remember if Midwest Credit Union was even still in business!

Whipping her arms in front of her as she went—horrible ticklish spiderwebs brushed her face and hair—Becky took the folder back upstairs to her office. The halls were quiet, everyone out at weekly happy hour. It was 6:30 pm—too late to speak to a customer rep. She dialed the number on the ancient statement anyway, holding her breath. After five rings, a machine picked up. "Thank you for calling Midwest Credit Union. We are now closed. Business hours are from 8:30 am until—" Becky hung up, energized.

Maybe, she thought. Maybe this could work.

Three weeks later she watched Karl present to the town council the "Streamlined Savings" proposal she'd carefully created. In a series of overhead acetates, with a color-coded flow chart, he pointed out how much money was wasted in keeping overlapping accounts. Karl—that is, Becky—had created a plan to realign them by subject area (Payroll, Building Ops, Park Security) and budget time frame (Tax, Reserve, Capital Development). With attentive research to which banks provided the best value, the reorganization could save an estimated eighteen to twenty percent on fees per year.

The council seemed pleased, if not dramatically enthused, and authorized Accounting to go ahead with the project.

"Don't think this means an automatic raise," Karl told her afterward, as they walked back to their corner of the office.

You're welcome, she wanted to say. "It's just a better work flow," she did say.

"Uh huh," Karl said.

So the realigning of accounts was her cover. It was clear that Becky was taking the reins of Town Hall's banking, and everyone seemed relieved they didn't have to think about that mess anymore. She made sure to choose the most inopportune times to press Karl for his signature on various changes: closing accounts and renaming other ones. Harried, he'd grump and sigh but did what she told him to do, without a lot of close attention. In this way, Becky added herself as signatory to almost all the restructured accounts.

At first, every account Becky set up or renamed was legitimate, and in familiar banks: Federal, First Bank, Chase. Becky waited for the secretaries to begin to recognize and nickname them, for the junior accountants to sigh loudly at the change (junior accountants sighed loudly at any change). She watched with pride as her new accounts accordioned in and out with money, a much smoother process than before. It was odd, the way she could still enjoy the well-performed functions of her actual job, when the job itself was already beginning to seem mildly beside the point.

Just goes to show, Becky wanted to tell someone, how much college is worth, how differently things operate in the real world. A page from her textbook in that Accounting 101 night class often came back to her. A colored sidebar titled "Prudent Protocols," in the chapter on financial controls. *Segregation of duties* was the upshot. The person who writes the checks is not the same person who deposits the checks.

But Becky was!

So much for all those professors, all that tuition people paid. After all, even if she hadn't been *stealing* (Becky never used that word, so unsubtle), she would have been the designated person for all those duties. She had seen the same names on all the receipts in the basement files, her ghostly predecessors. This was the way Pierson had always run the town business. Was it her place to raise a hand and say, "Hey, we ought to do things the way *textbooks* tell us"? In her mind's eye she saw the expression on her father's face, on the faces of all the farming businessmen she'd known: a snort, a flash of scornful pity for folks who didn't know how to pick up and get something done by their own damn self.

"Earth to Becky. Hello in there?" Ingrid snapped her fingers. They were in line at Hefeweisen's, and it was finally their turn to order.

"What. Oh. Uh . . . whatever you're having."

"Bratwurst for two, extra slaw." Ingrid shrugged. "What's up? You are out of it, lady."

They paid for their sandwiches and ate at a crowded counter, with two root beers. Becky had followed Ingrid from store to store this Saturday, trying on clothes without much heart. The problem of how to set up the Midwest account, the real one, without notice, had taken over her every waking moment. Should she slide it by Karl, like the others? What if he noticed the unusual bank, had questions about whether Midwest was even still open and why they still held accounts there? Why would Becky want to keep an account there, of all places?

Also there was the mail problem. Becky spent a day lurking around the office mailboxes, pretending to study some papers, to figure out the reason she'd never come across any of the Midwest statements. The postal carrier dropped off the day's mail around 11 am, with a *thunk* inside the ground-floor hall. One of the secretaries lugged the piles upstairs—taking her sweet time, Becky noticed—to sort into each person's labeled wood box. At the end of the sorting the secretary dumped a handful of mail down below the boxes, onto a messy shelf Becky had never paid attention to before. After the woman left, Becky moved in.

Return to Sender. Not at This Address. Forward. Redirect. Piles of mail addressed to names Becky knew hadn't been working in the office for years. Magazines with no specific addressee, office product catalogues, mailers and circulars, and . . . bank statements. There. She plucked out an envelope bearing Midwest's cheesy old logo and ugly font. "Mr. Theodore Reed, Financials," was mass-typed onto the envelope. Ted Reed hadn't been here since the seventies, as far as Becky knew. And they hadn't had a separate Financials Department ever. No wonder the statements had gone missing. The secretaries must have been dumping this monthly envelope into the junk drawer for years!

"Ooh, hurts so good," Ingrid said, crunching on the last of her salt and vinegar chips. "I either hate-love these or love-hate them."

"Disgusting," Becky said automatically.

"Oh shut up. Want to get a cookie at Brel's?"

"I don't have time. Can you drop me—"

"Fine, fine, after a couple errands, okay?" Ingrid loved to drive around Pierson with Becky, picking up a few groceries or stopping to check out a sale. *I have to get out of that house*, she would say, meaning her parents'. But she made no moves to get her own place, so Becky knew they really didn't drive her as crazy as she claimed.

Becky, who didn't actually have any particular place to be, let Ingrid take her all over town, waiting in the car while her friend went in and out of the pharmacy and then the bookstore. It wasn't until they were waiting for an oil change that Becky noticed the rubber-banded pack of envelopes and one *Country Kitchen* shoved up on the dashboard.

"What's this?"

"My folks' mail. Didn't I tell you? Assholes keep knocking over the mailbox at fifty miles an hour—I think it's on purpose but my dad sees the best in people. Anyway until they get something else set up they're doing 'Hold for Pickup' and *I'm* doing the pickup." Ingrid fussed with her sunglasses in the rearview mirror, pushing them up over her hair and then down again. "Let's see if Top 40 is over already."

"So you're renting a box or something?"

"They're way too cheap for that. No, if you ask, the post office will hold your shit, at least for a while. Gives me another thing to do on Saturdays, I guess."

Huh. Becky pretended to be interested in *Country Kitchen*'s recipe of the month, Southwestern Potato Tots, while she thought things over furiously. When Ingrid proposed milkshakes next, she said fine.

The next week, Becky caught the mail carrier on the stairs.

"I'll take that," she said, cheerfully reaching into the woman's corrugated plastic box to scoop up the armful of mail. "Heading that way anyway." Next day, she mimed a smoke break, lingering around the outdoor ashtray, and did the same thing. If the carrier minded, she didn't say anything. Why should she?

The fifth or so time Becky sorted the mail before the secretary could get to it, the woman asked if she had a problem with the previous system.

"Nope," Becky said. "It's just that I like to get a head start on balance sheets each morning. That way when I see Karl I can let him know the . . ." Here she went off on an ultra-detailed description of the most technical accounting tasks, including segues into the new banking systems. The woman visibly flinched at the onslaught of unnecessary information and Becky wrapped up by saying, in a singsong way, "So don't mind me, I'll be out of your hair in one sec."

And so the pattern was set. Becky Farwell, tedious overachiever, now wanted to get her mail first thing. It spread through the office, as she knew it would, causing annoyance and minor ridicule, but soon was accepted as status quo, the way most people's quirks eventually were. From there it was a short step to Becky's actually picking up the entire office's mail from the post office on her way in. As Ingrid had said, this was indeed an option on offer—especially in their tiny town, where the box of mail soon had a regular spot of honor in the P.O. foyer, set aside for Miss Farwell daily—extremely convenient for her to review all bank statements and set aside if necessary. Including the ones for an account newly renamed RF Capital Development at Midwest Credit Union, which began arriving in September 1987.

The branch location in Grantford, twenty minutes from Pierson, was a decent-sized one-story brick building scarred by a huge new false facade complete with plaster pillars and a clockface bigger than a car door. Becky stood out front, sweating in late summer's strong morning sun, and waited for the few employees inside to open up. Eventually one of them came over, flipped the sign, and unbolted the heavy glass door. "Morning!"

"Morning." Becky spoke fast and clipped, nervous as hell. Air conditioning did nothing to calm the red flushes along her neck and hairline. It was her first time in here, but you'd never know that from her swift and direct walk to the teller behind the counter. "I have a few deposits," she said, "to a municipal account that we recently . . . Yes. Here."

The teller, a pleasant chubby man in his fifties, took her checks over the counter. Becky bent to fill out the deposit slip, pressing down too hard with the ballpoint pen. She forced herself to say nothing as the man slowly, very slowly, went through each check. She wouldn't let herself look at them in his hands, even out of the corner of an eye, knowing each one by heart: the insurance payment made out to Accounting, one to Karl from Sandstone Repairs, and one Becky had written herself, out of the Water Management account at Federal. In total, $3,223. The symmetry of that number pleased Becky and was partly why she'd chosen these for her first deposit.

The teller took her deposit slip and compared it to the checks. He turned to his monitor and began to key in some numbers, using a pair of readers set way down on his nose. A few other customers had entered the bank by now, calling out greetings and asking questions. Two people queued behind Becky. She wouldn't let herself wipe at the cooling trickle of sweat on her nape.

It was over before she knew it. The teller gave her a brief smile and nod as he handed over her stamped deposit carbon copy. Becky thought she would almost pass out as she backed away and turned to go.

"Wait a second— Excuse me." His voice stopped her short.

The next person in line looked back at her, confused. Becky couldn't speak.

"Pierson, is that right?" the teller called over to her. Jesus, his voice, so loud.

Becky made some sort of motion with her head.

"You all still doing Petunia Fest? My wife runs a gardening club and she can't stop talking about it."

"Every July," Becky coughed out. "First week."

"Good to know," he said. "I'll be the one watching PGA in your finest pub."

She waved at him and managed to walk steadily out into the humid glare. Holding her breath, slamming her fist against her hip. She did it. She did it. She did it.

8

Chicago
1987

ON FRIDAY, DECEMBER 4, 1987, RF Capital Development held forty-two thousand dollars. When Becky arrived at Chicago's massive Merchandise Mart at precisely 10 am on the Art Expo's opening day she had in her purse a pristine checkbook, two pens, three forms of identification, and a new lipstick from Ralph's: Apricot Dream.

The international art expo—Becky had worked out the shorthand for "exposition"—comprised three days of contemporary art sales, panels, and exhibits. Becky wanted nothing to do with the latter two. She'd told Karl she needed a personal day and had been up until 1:30 am sorting through potential outfits, wishing she could ask Ingrid's opinion. In the end she decided to mix the daring (Sergio Rossi zebra heels, found on consignment in Rockford) with the tried-and-true (black pencil skirt that hugged her ass, silk blouse with a floppy bow), and after much deliberation she'd pulled her hair back into a basic chignon, a slightly dressier version of what she and Ingrid wore to Ballet Stretch.

Unfortunately, she'd had fewer options when it came to outerwear and the eighteen-degree temperature meant the big coat, no discussion: navy blue, but not in a good way, hooded, enormous. Even a woman with two inches on Becky would have been dwarfed by this thing, a mispurchase from last year that she regretted but hadn't gotten around to correcting. Her cheeks burned in line at the coat check and she held the wadded-up big coat under her arm like a bag of dirty laundry. Released from it, she felt instantly lighter, anonymous.

She paused briefly in the entrance of the main hall, fighting down a rush of anxiety under her breastbone. Before her stretched a space at least the length of a football field, divided into hundreds and hundreds of walled-off makeshift display areas, each marked with a sign flag stating a gallery's name and city. Aisles branched into sub-aisles, which split into cul-de-sacs and dead ends. Paintings were hung inside and outside each gallery's designated movable partitions, so close to one another it was hard to tell who was showing what. People passed back and forth, meant to circle around, took a wrong turn, and ended up fifteen minutes later on the opposite side of the convention center. Becky thought of the giant corn maze at Thigpen's off County Road N and just as quickly told herself to cut it with the hick town associations.

High above the echoing warren of art cubicles arced the hall's unfinished steel rafters and domed ceilings. Becky gazed at a large gorilla made of thousands of glittery beads, suspended from a beam and revolving slowly in the heights of the dust-moted air. Enormous, ridiculous, a bit lonely: the gorilla floated serenely over the mass of people and objects below, and no one else seemed to notice her up there.

Becky gripped the chain of her purse and set a course for square number 131, the Ferramini Gallery from New York. Three weeks of frantic research said they were bringing some Eric Fischls, and Becky was going to buy one—her first big-name piece. First time in the big time. Becky blew a tiny kiss up to the floating gorilla for luck.

The Eric Fischls were there, three of them, hung on their own partition at Ferramini. Becky didn't pause in her moment of relief at seeing them—this was only the first of many steps. Although she had run this transaction through her mind a hundred times, she hadn't banked on there being so many *people* around. Pressed shoulder to shoulder, jostling Becky, taking their sweet time in front of the works and blocking the painting—which one would it be?—that was going home with her. She pegged two gallery assistants, clerks, whatever you called them: a bone-thin sallow woman in a Mao-collar dress, and a handsome black man who was only as tall as Becky. She edged her way in front of the paintings—a small, medium, and a large—and had to stop herself from bouncing up and down on her toes.

"Do you have a price list?" she said, louder than she'd meant to. She'd memorized this phrase from *ARTnews*—or was she first supposed to ask "Is the work still available?" Shit. Too late now.

The handsome guy handed her a leather folder, like a menu. The figures were much higher than Becky had expected, but still within the range of RF Capital Development. Did she love these particular paintings? Maybe. Not really. It didn't matter. This was going to be a strategic buy, her first, to put her in the mix. Everything she'd read confirmed this was what you needed, a blue-chip trading piece.

The guy had moved on to help someone else, so Becky decided to plant herself at the elbow of the skinny woman, who was intently listening to a long story told in hushed tones, alternately, by an older couple in matching glasses. Eventually Becky's presence must have bugged her enough to hold up a finger to them and fake-smile at Becky. "Can I help you?"

"Yes. I want to buy one of the Eric . . ." Becky had to swerve away from pronouncing the last name, and instead gestured to the wall. "The medium one. I mean the medium-*sized* one."

But in response the gallery woman only smiled at her. A wide, pleasant smile, as if Becky had complimented her earrings. "I'll be with you in a minute." She turned to the older couple, who immediately resumed whispering their story. Becky stood there, uncertain and mute. What had happened? In her daydreams saying the words "I want to buy it" triggered a flurry of excitement and deference. She shifted from foot to foot, unsure whether she was supposed to wait here, adjacent to this never-ending conversation. Or maybe she should go over to her painting, claim it? Wasn't someone supposed to be giving her forms to fill out? Or a cup of coffee at least? For a sweaty confused moment she felt like she was wearing the big coat. Lumpy, uncool, out of place.

Eventually the woman double-cheek-kissed the older couple and gazed fondly after them as they made their slow way out into the crowded aisle. Then she abruptly turned to Becky. "Now. Let's sit for a minute, shall we?"

The sudden solicitous attention unnerved Becky, and she took a cautious place on an ottoman cube next to the woman, who introduced herself as Lori Levine.

"I'm interested in either the small or the medium—"

Lori waved that off. "Remind me how we know each other?"

"Well, I don't—"

"You weren't in Berlin for Roger's fiftieth. Wait, don't tell me. At the Fraelick show? Not at Bibi's, because I was in Milan for—"

"We've never met," said Becky firmly. "However, I'm ready to buy the Eric . . . ah, the Eric . . ."

"Fischl," Lori said, still musing. "You weren't at Larry's last month, were you? Or the *Artforum* thing, with the horrible food? I remember Eric and April went straight to Fanelli's afterward."

Becky, quiet, raced to catch up.

"You're local? Chicago-based? Because I don't recognize your name from our client list. Farwell. Far-well."

And now Becky began to understand.

"These particular pieces have been promised to certain collectors for months. As I'm sure you can imagine."

"You mean . . . all three? But they're not marked 'sold' or anything."

Lori flashed another wide, wide smile, and touched Becky on the knee. Signaling to her colleague, she said, "Trey can put you on our mailing list. I'm *so* glad you came by."

Her moment was slipping away and Becky panicked. "How much, um . . . What was the price, for the other collectors?"

Lori froze, face pinched in disbelief.

"Because I am prepared to offer ten percent more."

As soon as it was out of her mouth, Becky knew she'd made a dire faux pas. Even Trey seemed to edge away from her. Lori slowly stood up from their shared ottoman and moved to greet some other viewers as if ignoring what Becky had said was the kindest for all involved.

■ ■ ■

Two hours later Becky was drinking a second Bloody Mary at the café on the west side of the convention hall. Drinking it in hard fast pulls through a straw. One side of her chignon—probably it was just a *bun*—drooped and the stereo behind the bar played Madonna's "Cherish" for the second time in a half hour. Becky sat with her back to the expo, pointedly ignoring the loud-talking visitors who chattered on in German or whatever over cappuccinos or plastic flutes of champagne.

A man leaned over with a light tap on the counter to get her attention. "Buyer's regret?" he said, in English. "Or a good chance missed?"

Becky eyed him, straw in teeth. Tall, fifties, pin-striped. Violet pocket square and more than one ring on his fingers—homo, probably. "Little of both," she said, rattling the ice.

"Allow me." The man slid onto the stool next to her and waved for another Bloody Mary. "Sounds like you've had a day. Tell Papa all about it."

Becky snorted. Well, why not? "I thought I knew what I was doing but . . . there are rules they don't tell you, you know? One set of rules for some people, and another set for other people. Why is that?" Pinstripes held up his hands in mock surrender. "And who are you?"

"Am I one of them, you mean? Not really."

"Not one of me, though," Becky mumbled at her drink. She missed her old straw, the one she'd chewed to bumpy perfection.

"My name is Frederick Palliser." Did this guy pause, as if she was supposed to know him? *Forget it, buster. I don't know anything.* "But most people here call me Mac."

"Well, *my* name is Rebecca Farwell but most people call me—"

"Reba, I hope!"

Becky stared. He couldn't mean Reba McEntire, the country singer. Not here, not in this world.

"Well, you do bear a faint resemblance." He hummed a few bars of "You Lift Me Up to Heaven" that were remarkably in tune. Could this day be any weirder?

"Sure, call me Reba," Becky said. "So, Mac: what do you have to do to buy a painting that you really really really really really really really want?" She broke off, tearful, drank again.

"Ah." The teasing tone left Mac's voice. "What happened?"

So she told it all, in a ragged tumble of details and shame, and Mac listened closely, frowning, occasionally interrupting with a question or clarification. As soon as she said the name *Lori Levine* he murmured, "Oh dear." But when she got to the part where she tried to outbid the reserved Fischls he had to stop her.

"No." Mac put a finger to the bridge of his nose. "No, you didn't, my sweet Reba."

"I did," Becky whispered miserably. Mac put his hand on hers and she dropped her forehead to it, bonking an eye socket on one of his rings. "The way she *looked* at me!"

"You didn't know."

"Now I do. It's who you know, isn't it."

"Now you know me, sweet pea. Oh, come now. None of that." For Becky was blubbering, at least until Mac gently but firmly pulled his hand out from under her wet face. He gave her a pristine and scented handkerchief (after dabbing at his own hand). "Just think of all the money you *saved*, darling! Between us, our Mr. Fischl is a bit, well . . . what's the saying about fish and visitors after three days?"

"I may have had a little too much to drink," Becky announced.

"But now you can go find something else! Oh, let's go do that. Buying well is the best revenge."

"I can't!" Becky wailed. "I already spent it all!"

"On what, you crazy girl?"

Becky sniffed and pulled a crumpled receipt from her purse. Mac studied the image stapled to it. "It's . . . nice. There are some nice things someone could possibly say about a piece like this." Then he flipped to the receipt, stamped PAID. "Sweet Mary, mother of Jesus."

Becky said nothing. She barely remembered the transaction, the white-hot wrath in which she had smoothly signed away all the money in RF Capital, plus a good chunk from her own checking account, for a flashy piece that even at the time of the sale didn't do anything for her. All that work, all those months, the basement files . . . Gone. Pointless.

Mac exhaled. "Well. How about you come with me. I keep a place on Oak, and I need to let the catering people in. You can take a rest in the guest suite and—" He circled a hand at her face and hair. "Freshen up a bit. And then I'll introduce you to some useful people." He folded the receipt twice and slipped it into his inner jacket pocket. "And we'll sort *this* out."

Above them the glittering gorilla spun slowly, implacable. Crowd noise peaked, and a clutch of late lunchers vied for space in the café.

Becky accepted Mac's arm to navigate stepping down from the stool in her zebra heels. She felt depleted, emptied so far there was a new kind of space inside her—room to look around, room to make new moves. In sixth grade she had first grasped the concept of negative numbers in one widening tumult of realization: sinking below zero only revealed more options! A mirrored infinity of values. Underneath the placid surface of zero lay an ocean of possibility.

Walking with Mac through the Art Expo—a slow procession, since he had constant greetings to exchange—gave Becky that same unlocked sensation. She carried deficits—the blown money, Lori Levine's shaming pity—but the equation wasn't complete. Not yet.

"I have a big coat," she told Mac, on their way out.

"Of course you do," he murmured.

What followed were two days and nights in the wild swirl of Mac and his coterie. That afternoon while Becky lay on his Memphis chaise longue with her shoes off and a glass of Alka-Seltzer in hand, Mac worked the phone: first an old client, then a friendly dealer, then a rival dealer. In thirty-five minutes he had unloaded Becky's painting—later to be referred to only as "The Horrible Mistake"—and turned a slight profit too. Which stayed with Mac, no discussion needed.

"I think I'm in love," Becky said, with a gentle burp.

"Aren't you sweet." Mac spread an afghan over her legs. "I'm going to speak with Maria about canapés."

Becky closed her eyes and drifted in a vodka haze on that strange and expensive sofa. She wanted to stay awake, she wanted to memorize every detail of the layout and furnishings. A woman in an honest-to-god black-and-white *maid* uniform had brought her the fizzing glass of Alka-Seltzer. On a tray! But her stomach was heaving, and she couldn't even focus her eyes enough to see what Mac had hanging on his walls. *Canapé,* she whispered to herself, savoring the word.

At Field's the next morning she and Mac were the first ones in. On his instructions she bought a pair of jeans so dark and fitted she had to lie on the dressing room floor to zip them up. She bought a poppy-colored dress with skin-tight long sleeves and sharp shoulders pushing up toward her ears, a pair of heels, and a droopy cashmere cardigan that cost so much Becky had to look away quickly when the sales girl rang up its four-digit price tag. She'd put it all—plus a three-pack of Hanes—on her Visa, and held her breath until the charge went through.

Over the next two days Becky walked the art fair with Mac, shadowing his every move as he compared, whispered, shook hands, and made deals. She had never felt more awake, more *centered.* "Are all of these for you?" she asked, after he closed on two Wegman prints, a small Joan Mitchell oil, and a series of sketches by Dominguez.

"They're for me now," Mac said.

She soaked in his counsel, his side notes, the amount of minutes and seconds he took to view paintings. The way he circled back, or led out a long lead time, or moved in fast to get what he wanted. Who was who; whom she should cultivate, whom she should AAAC (avoid at all costs); the drinks she should order and who should pay for them; how to pronounce "Biennale," "Ruscha," "Benjamin" (as in Walter); when to pay a flat fee, who gets a commission, who gets tax-deferred; names and numbers for the right guys to crate, ship, insure, and install. It was everything she didn't know she'd needed to know.

The only piece he didn't try to teach her was how to have an eye for the work itself. "You were born that way," he told her. "Some of us are, kid."

Becky didn't try to fake modesty at this. She knew she had found her people.

"Then again," Mac went on, "we all make the occasional stinker." (The Horrible Mistake!)

There was a price for all this, of course, and Becky paid it during the socializing hours in the bars near the expo and especially at the all-hours gatherings in Mac's apartment. It wouldn't do for her to spend any quiet time in his beautifully appointed guest room, she understood, even if that would be a way for her to make some feverish notes or even to calm her racing mind. No, she needed to be out in the mix, circling Mac with all the others and paying court. Becky could tell she wasn't the first odd duck he'd taken in under his wing. He liked to provide; he liked to preside. A motley crew flowed in and out of that sumptuous condo on the forty-third floor overlooking Lake Michigan: spectators, wealthy widows, bargain hunters, and hedge fund dilettantes. Becky allowed herself to be the naif Mac painted her as; she even played up the *I'm just a girl who cain't say no* routine to prompt more lessons from him.

Late into Saturday night Becky sat up with the hardiest of Mac's coterie, hungry for every gossipy story, every scandal recounted, every bangle on a woman's arm or silk striped sock on a man's ankle. She drank copious amounts of champagne but if anything the liquor clarified her, woke her up. Pressed against her in the tiny love seat was a European dealer named Sven something who whispered that Chicago girls *gave him the hard one*. Becky only laughed. Later in Mac's guest room she'd discover that Sven's hard one was in fine form. Thanks also perhaps to the white powder he snorted up on a rigorous schedule, every forty-five minutes. Each time he proffered the lines to her first, with utmost courtesy, and each time she passed he said, "Okay, no problems."

Mac, looking on as Becky rested a hand on Sven's thigh, pursed his lips in pretend judgment. Becky winked at him.

Only a few hours later and she'd crept out of the apartment, leaving Sven asleep amid tousled silky sheets. She found a pen in the magically spotless kitchen and wrote Mac a note of gratitude and a promise to call him later that night. They'd already discussed half a dozen galleries she had to visit—with him, of course—and people he had to introduce her to. Becky propped her note against his gleaming espresso machine, and tiptoed out to the hall elevator, shoes in hand.

She drove back to Pierson barefoot, with last night's makeup still on her eyelids and her crotch aching from Sven's heroics and her new super-tight jeans. She found the country countdown and sang along loudly to Conway Twitty and the Oak Ridge Boys and even Ronnie Milsap, all the songs she knew they'd never listen to, Mac or Sven or Lori Levine. Or Eric Fischl. Who cared? She was by herself and she was young and smart and had a thousand good ideas and all the energy in the world to try them out. One or two paintings she'd bought before Mac she knew now—only slightly sadly—had to go. Could be sacrificed, to pay back what she'd taken. She thought about what she wanted to buy next, and how and when she would do that. She made a list of names, people to call next week. She cranked open the window farther to let in more of the cold fresh air.

She couldn't see going to church but Becky thought she'd let herself into the office for a few hours instead, to get caught up. She hadn't been in since Thursday and strangely she missed it. *I can get a head start on the monthly income statement*, she thought, looking forward to the way her desk would look in the quiet of the Sunday afternoon, every light off except for hers. *Then maybe call Ingrid. Go out for nachos.*

9

Pierson
1987–1989

THUS BEGAN A YEAR OF driving. Back and forth from Pierson to Chicago, Becky motored her little Datsun on I-88E and W. She racked up mileage and gas credit and learned the finer points of every truck stop in western Illinois: which had the most reliable coffee, the cleanest bathrooms, the least skeevy gas station attendants.

On the front seat she kept a pick comb and a giant bag of chocolate-covered raisins, and she kept herself awake with sugar and teasing up her bangs. Those drives let Becky review everything she had learned from the evening's events. Which paintings she'd seen at which galleries, and for how much. Dollar amounts, buyer's premium, and who she could push for a discount. Mac said ten percent was standard to whoever knew how to ask, but Becky thought she could get a bit more. She had learned how to ask.

As the miles ticked by, she would also catalogue names and faces and proclivities, chart the friendships and backstabs and double crosses. Navigating people and their weirdnesses was apparently as essential as recognizing a genuine Stella.

More and more, artists were joining Mac's group for the late-night meals at Yoshi's or the Berghoff. *We pay them surprisingly little attention*, Becky mused. *You'd think we would bow down, or at least show a little respect.* But the raucous one-upping and vulgar jokes and endless gossip never abated—it merely swept over the mid-level artist picking at his frites. Maybe that'll change, Becky thought, when it was Schnabel or Baldessari she was having drinks with.

The drinks. Always more drinks. Becky had a delicate task to manage her intake or what appeared to be her intake, mindful of the two-hour drive that followed every gin-soaked night. (She tried not to take Mac up on his generosity too often, his routine insistence that she stay in his guest room. He was exasperated by the very existence of her car.) Champagne, of course, champagne like water in between the rounds of Fuzzy Navels and Kamikazes, B52s and Cuba Libres. Mac insisted the bartender at the Berghoff make something he called a Slippery Nipple that involved sambuca, but one sip—or nip—had been enough for Becky.

When it came to picking up the tab, someone usually did before she could figure out how to maneuver. On their first day together, Mac had made tentative reference, in a questioning voice, to the source of her funds . . . her capital by inheritance? She had performed a modest shrug. Say no more, he commanded. You're in fine company.

Weeks and months passed in her car. She grew sick to death of the Nitty Gritty Dirt Band, learned to take off her bra with one hand on the wheel. She bought snow tires and a backrest, could scoop up the exact toll in coins, $1.45, without looking. The

Datsun's trunk began to hold a rotating collection of shopping bags: thick soft ropes for handles, beige and cream tissue paper surrounding their contents. She loved those bags, from Field's and Carson Pirie and appointment-only boutiques on the west side of the city, almost as much as what was in them: Lacroix, YSL, Alaïa, Herrera, Ferragamo—and Chantal Thomass under all of it. If only she didn't have to make selections based on what would wrinkle least from hours in the car!

And by what she could squeak by on credit cards that, to be fair, had expanded their limits exponentially based on her growing spending activity. But Becky had hit her stride on financing her new life with a combination of diverting funds at the office and re-selling art pieces she snapped up at a bargain, the latter a technique she learned from Mac and perfected with her own good ideas and careful research. Borrow, buy, resell, repay. Repeat.

One Saturday just before noon she pulled into a spot on lower Wacker and nodded to the security guy at the loading dock. Healthy tipping led to all sorts of parking strategies in the city, if you knew what to do. She took the cement stairs up to street level and almost lost her scarf into the river when a gust of autumn wind came off the lake. Becky knotted it firmly on her purse strap and strode quickly to the looming hotel complex that bordered Jackson. Why did Mac want to meet here? The east side was dead in terms of galleries.

The Renaissance Hotel had a sweeping half-circle driveway out front, jammed with cabs and doormen pushing wardrobe racks. Becky swerved nimbly between all of it and hurried in out of the wind. She pegged Mac and a guest having coffee in the lobby and could tell, even before she had circled through the revolving doors, that his companion had nothing to do with the art world.

"Hello," Becky said, eyeing the stranger while Mac popped up and double-cheek-kissed her. "Am I late?"

"Not at all," the woman said, smiling mischievously. "I'm getting caught up on all things Reba."

"This is Marcy Patterson from By the Lake Properties. I told you about her, darling."

Becky shook the woman's hand and said *No you didn't* through her teeth to Mac, who ignored her. All things Reba?

Before she sat down, Marcy handed Becky a glossy packet of brochures. At a glance, Becky knew she'd been shanghaied.

"It's time," Mac said. "I won't take no for an answer. Marcy has your specs and a full slate of condos to show you. Don't worry, I've already briefed her on our need for wall space."

"Our?"

"*Mi casa es su casa,*" Mac said brightly. "Or however in reverse. Now if you'll both excuse me, I have to be at Spiaggia at—"

"I'm very sorry," Becky interrupted, pushing the brochures back to Marcy. "I'd love to find a time to call you about this, but a move isn't in my near future." She wanted to kick Mac under the tiny café table.

"Oh I know that!" Marcy laughed easily. "My firm specializes in second homes and weekend properties—"

"*Pieds-à-terre,*" Mac put in. "Not to be too too."

"I don't think so." Becky glared at him. He'd told her lunch with a dealer in from LA!

"You know what?" Marcy held her smile, but her eyes slid back and forth between them. "I'm going to visit the little girls' room and then you two can see if we're all on the same page."

Mac launched in before the woman was even ten paces away. "Do you know what I had to do to get this appointment? She's doing a huge favor for me!"

"I can't," Becky said. "Things are stressful at my job right now. There's a big shakeup underway and I can't overextend my—"

Mac scoffed. Becky rarely brought up Pierson—all she said was she worked in town government—and god knows Mac was anything but interested. "Do you want to be a player or not? You know the deal: deals are made at a handful of downtown restaurants, and purchases are to be displayed, no exceptions. Do you think someone's going to drive out to the prairie to take a look at those nice Clemente sketches you just bought?"

"I'm not selling those," Becky said, a bit sulky. They were in fact propped against a wall in Hank's bedroom—she had to stop thinking of it that way—and it was impossible to imagine collectors or speculators viewing them there.

"Aren't you just a touch abashed to never reciprocate, always the guest and never the host? Time to grow up, sweet Reba. If you want to be in the game, you got to have skin in the game. Now look what you've done. I made a sports reference."

Marcy approached. Becky whispered, in a panic, "Fine. Fine! But I can't afford whatever someone like her charges to—"

"All clear?" Marcy said. She didn't sit down.

"All clear." Mac rose, tugging Becky up to standing. "Forgive me for being gauche, but I was just explaining that a broker's commission—"

"Is paid out by the property management company," Marcy put in. "Never the client."

"I can't buy a condo," Becky blurted. Even the thought of filling out mortgage paperwork and submitting bank statements made her hands go numb.

"Of course," Marcy said, kissing Mac goodbye. "Remember, I have all I need about your search criteria and price ranges."

"Ta ta," Mac said. "Be good." This last was directed at Becky, who scowled at him.

Over the course of the next three hours Marcy whizzed Becky in and out of half a dozen rentals in "luxury properties" in River North, Streeterville, and the Gold Coast. As soon as Becky got over the way she'd been set up she began to enjoy the hunt. By the time they'd looped back to where they'd started, she'd accepted the idea of taking a lease. More than accepted—was galvanized. A place for her art! A place to have people over, the right people! Where she didn't have to hide paintings or crowd them in a crappy bedroom or see them leaning against each other on the floor. She could install proper spotlights!

The peak of Becky's excitement coincided with Marcy's showing her a thirteenth-floor two-bedroom in The Pointe, a modern high-rise overlooking the lake on Randolph. She almost said yes before they were fully inside the unit. The cool gray tones of the carpet, the sleek fixtures, and the impersonal near-industrial blankness of the high ceilings . . . *Reba*, she said to herself. *This was where Reba belonged.*

Becky had to use all her self-control not to react when Marcy read out the monthly figure, plus first and last deposit, plus maintenance fee. Plus parking. Plus several move-in fees, one time only, of course.

"Is any of that a problem?" Marcy asked, as she pulled the paperwork out for Becky's perusal.

"It won't be," Becky said. She'd make this happen.

She had fallen behind in paying back Pierson, just a bit, less than a thousand or two, over the past few months. Not that she'd actually admitted it to herself, officially. Now she foresaw how that gap would spring open further, what with first and last month's rent, security deposit, furniture, moving expenses . . . Well, it wasn't ideal. But what business didn't hold on to at least some debt? It was a perfectly valid expansion strategy.

Although the town paper dutifully covered the mayoral "election," it was mostly a baton handoff and everyone in Pierson knew it. Mayor Thomsic had presided for so long, most people had a story about meeting him as a little kid and then introducing their own kid to him on some visit back home. Even his grandkids were having kids now, so when he announced his retirement it both made perfect sense and seemed earthshaking.

To Becky particularly. Before she could think through what this change would mean for her Activity, which had run so smoothly for the past year, those shunted-away sums added to RF Capital twice monthly, never too much and never too little, Karl called her in and announced he'd be heading out too.

"I'm too old for this shit" is how he put it, having heard from the council how much would be expected of him in Pierson's "new era" as they helped get the new mayor up and running. "You wanted this, didn't you? Well, now you can have it."

Not exactly the grateful and praise-filled moment she'd imagined but still, there it was: at the end of the next quarter, Becky would become CFO and town comptroller. She was not yet twenty-four years old.

Ingrid stuffed an enormous "balloon bouquet" through Becky's front door and insisted on champagne when they next went out to dinner. *Sparkling wine*, Becky thought but did not say. She had only recently learned the difference.

"Second in charge," Ingrid said excitedly. "Of the whole enchilada."

"It's more of a mini taco." Becky didn't know how to sort out her feelings of pride. Self-deprecation was the standard in these parts, of course, but she couldn't help being thrilled by this achievement. She'd stockpiled a small stack of the newspaper that included a front-page article about her, headline "Pierson Grad to Be City CFO."

"Comptroller. Comp-troller." Ingrid rolled the syllables around. "Sounds like a made-up job name though, doesn't it? Or something from *Star Wars*. What's wrong?"

"Nothing." Becky's cheeks were on fire. She'd just realized why she'd set aside that stack of copies. For Hank. He'd have laminated the article, like her high school top GPA award, and put it up with the pizza-shaped magnet that was still on the fridge at home. He would have handed it out to every client who came in the shop, every person he met in town. She would have been mortified, and euphoric.

"Well, anyway," Ingrid said. "What do you hear about this new guy? Is he as hot as he is in the photos?"

"Gross. Who knows. I don't think he's supposed to be around Town Hall until after the election. I have to have a one-on-one with him pretty soon."

"A new era for Pierson!" Ingrid said, echoing the *Gazetteer*'s favorite headline.

All Becky knew was that it would be a new era for her Activity, and the uncertainty about how the Activity would be affected was keeping her up at night. Terrible timing, when she'd been socking away even more than usual for the new apartment costs and when she was at least $15,000 in the hole for Pierson. This new mayor, Ken Brennan, was a committeeman from Springfield and had a picture-perfect family. Probably the worst thing that could happen to Becky was an eager-beaver young gun who wanted to actually know what went on down the hall from his office.

Becky swigged some more of the sour-sweet sparkling wine, now flat. Ingrid didn't seem to be enjoying it much, either. To soothe herself, she ran down a list of numbers: the funds she'd taken in the past two weeks since signing the lease on the Randolph place with Marcy: $2,800 from Water Management; $800 (twice) that should have been put to Human Resources; $5,000 from Infrastructure; and $740, $600, and $1,560 out of Buildings. These amounts were nearly double the rate she'd been depositing into RF Capital for the past year. It seemed like a lot, if you viewed those amounts—$12,000, set aside in just a few days!—but Becky had transferred so many other sums back and forth between the many other (legitimate) town accounts during that time, subtracting and refunding and paying back, that her own money was nearly impossible to see in that snowstorm swirl of transactions. Or to miss.

But could she keep it up? Not at this level, not forever, of course. She'd ramped up hard because of the apartment. And because Karl's leaving brought an added layer of cover for her in the chaos of transition. How long could she push it this time? Should she ride the edge for another week or bring the Activity back down to what she thought of as its regular pace—a few thousand here and there, paid back within a week or two, almost entirely. Modest, stately.

In all these calculations Becky failed to realize Ingrid had sat back and was watching her with a strange and quiet little smile.

"What?"

"I'm pregnant."

Now Becky sat back too. "In what sense?"

"Becky."

"And you're sure it's . . . Neil's?"

"Becky!"

"What? Sorry. I didn't know if you guys were still serious." She didn't particularly like Neil Yesko, who'd been two grades ahead of them in high school. (Not that she ever particularly liked any of Ingrid's boyfriends.) He'd played ice hockey all through school and still did in a semi-pro league somewhere. Was in a group of dolts who bragged about any and all sexual activity and got in trouble senior year for making T-shirts that said "Pierce One High" with a bawdy cartoon. Ingrid said he'd straightened up and he'd moved up to management at the big-box electronics place. But still. Neil Yesko? For Ingrid?

Ingrid was still looking at her, across the table. Waiting.

"What?" *Pregnant?* Jesus Christ.

"Aren't you going to say something? Try to talk me out of it?"

"Not my place to say. What do you want to do?"

In response, Ingrid slapped her left hand onto the table, next to the bread basket. There was indeed a chip of a diamond glinting out of a shiny new gold ring.

Becky's throat squeezed. "Are you happy?" Suddenly it was all that mattered, that Ingrid be happy with this and every other thing that would come to her in life. "You're happy about it, aren't you? Do you want this?"

"Becky. What's wrong?"

"Nothing! I just—" Hot tears gummed up her throat. Too much newness, too much rushing forward—this new mayor, her apartment in Chicago, Ingrid leaving her for Neil Yesko . . .

"Yes," Ingrid said softly. "I want this and I'm happy. He's a good guy. You'll see."

Becky groaned, and wiped her eyes hard. "Do I have to?"

"Everything will stay the same. Except now there'll be three of us. I mean, four."

10

New York City
1989

TEN DAYS BEFORE INGRID'S WEDDING, Becky drove to O'Hare and parked in the windblown long-term lot. She dragged her suitcase onto the airport shuttle, checked in quickly, and was at her gate three and a half hours before departure, time which she spent reading *Art in America* and then *ARTnews*, in between intense study of every gate agent and disembarking passenger. At precisely forty-five minutes to boarding Becky carried her luggage into the largest stall of the women's room, where she rapidly changed out of a boat-neck, gathered-waist jacquard print dress, pearl string necklace, and open-toe bowtie pumps. She folded these and expertly repacked them, including her nude hose. When she exited the stall, slightly red-faced, she wore high-waisted black silk slacks and a cropped zip-up thin black leather jacket. She dunked her head briefly under a rushing faucet and then immediately patted her hair dry with a small hand towel produced from her purse. Six brushstrokes and a squirt of hairspray and that perky bouffant was now a modern, slicked-back fall. Makeup she'd deal with on arrival.

Back at the gate, a boarding delay was announced. Harried stewardesses conferred, a long line formed at the counter. Lightning flared about the grounded planes. Becky asked someone where the cafeteria was and got a blank look. She ate a carton of yogurt while sitting on her suitcase and read headlines at a newsstand.

At last the plane boarded. Becky didn't notice the uncharacteristic quick movements up and down the aisle, the curt intercom announcements—all business, no jokes—or the thwacking gusts against the rising plane. She was slightly disappointed when no carts of food or drink came by, and only a little startled the time they hit an air pocket so hard that her view of the cabin bounced, and several overhead bins slammed open. This wasn't much different from riding in the pickup bed; whenever Hank went over a road rut she'd popped into the air.

"I'll help you with the oxygen mask," she told her seatmate, a college-age boy who had slept through the safety presentation, and was now clutching his Walkman.

He just stared at her. Oh well. Becky went back to *ARTnews*, glancing up only when another wave of gasps interrupted her. When they touched down, once, and then again, a hard slam, she cheerfully joined in the applause, thinking it was too bad the thick storm clouds had blotted entirely the New York lights.

Becky stepped quickly past the captain's area on her way off the plane, where one stewardess had her arm around another, crumpled and crying. She hurried around the slowpokes on the jet bridge, unable to contain her excitement any longer. Flying on an airplane for the first time had been interesting, but now Becky was in *New York*.

Although she had assumed her host would be long asleep—

after the delays and the taxi line, Becky didn't reach the third-floor walkup on the corner of Thirtieth and Park Avenue South until after midnight—Fernanda Ebersole yanked the apartment door open just as Becky fumbled quietly with the keys Mac had given her. Giant wineglass in hand, music blaring, Fernanda ushered Becky into a living room where half a dozen people were smoking, arguing, and in the case of one couple, passionately kissing. Even over the course of the next three days in Fernanda's guest room Becky never quite got the full story of how Fernanda and Mac knew each other. When she wasn't hosting late-night dinner parties Fernanda was on the phone in Italian or Portuguese or French, pulling the long cord with her into the bathroom or kitchen, tangling it on armchairs and toppling lamps.

Whatever Mac had told Fernanda about her, Becky was able to come and go as she pleased, with no other requirements than to join the living room party as often as she could, as a source of witty remarks and an appreciative audience of catty gossip and fashion world scandal. (Fernanda did something in PR for one of the Italian houses. At first sight, in her sweeping floor-length caftan and silk turban, Becky would have pegged her for early forties. Making coffee in the late morning, first cigarette between her lips . . . fifty or upward, for sure.)

On her way downtown that first Friday morning—it wasn't even 9 am and she would find that no galleries opened before 11— Becky reflected that, on the whole, no matter how friendly her host seemed, she would rather have stayed in a hotel. That delicious anonymity, the chance to be alone and drop the thousand minute arrangements of face and voice and body position, the ones she had to instantly assume for other people. The chance to be away, for a few expensive hours, from other people!

But Mac had insisted, because Fernanda was an essential acquaintance for Becky. There must be a benefit to him, Becky speculated, in her staying there. So she had acquiesced, as she acquiesced to almost all Mac's directions. Not that he approved of her going to New York. Overpriced, overhyped. Why bother when one could scheme a beautiful collection right from the shores of Lake Michigan? Had she never heard of a fax machine, darling?

There were more and more barbs in Mac's assessment of Becky's purchases, her deals. And the whole "I made you, sweetheart" routine, with its required deference, was getting old. It was a relief to be away from that, Becky thought now, reversing direction and walking quickly back along the same block. She hadn't yet figured out the subway, and she'd be damned before she'd be a rube asking for help, so her MO was to walk swiftly and confidently in the general direction of where she wanted to go, even if that meant missed turns and repeated changes of course.

On her map, the map in her purse that would *not* be brought out, Becky had used a ruler and colored pencils to grid the area bounded by Fourteenth and Canal, Greenwich and Avenue D. At least ninety galleries worth visiting clustered in that space, so thirty a day, about four hundred twenty minutes viewing time (once she realized operating hours), meant she had fourteen minutes allotted to each space. Not including bathroom breaks.

Except Becky spent nearly three hours in the very first gallery she entered that morning. She couldn't resist, she refused to check her watch, even as her face got hot and her inner voice screeched that she was making the rookiest of all rookie mistakes: falling in love with the first thing seen. Because Becky had fallen in love with the six canvases—oil, pastel palette, abstract images of boxes on top of boxes. Every physical indicator was going off like an alarm: shallow breathing, prickly armpits, the inability to stop pacing. She just wanted to look at them, to look and look and look.

Becky summoned all her acquired skills as a collector when she sat down with the owner to learn about the pieces and the artist. All of what she heard only added to her conviction. The artist, as the gallery owner explained, was Peter Wand, a fiftyish classically trained figurist based in Zurich, who had been on the outskirts of the Ab Ex movement, had one solo show in Lausanne (not that that mattered), used to be married to Patricia Nadal (again, irrelevant). Poised for a breakout. He'd delivered this series only last week, no promises but the *Voice* had been considering a major profile and space was already lined up for a quarter column ad buy in *Artforum*.

Becky drank deeply from her glass of Perrier. For less than ninety thousand she could buy all six works. Ship them home, sell four—already her mental Rolodex was throwing off potential buyers—and watch Wand's star go up. This was *it*, the find. The one she'd make her name on.

"May I use your phone?" How was her mouth so dry? The owner graciously set her up at his own desk and then excused himself.

It took Becky three tries to dial the right number. She couldn't see straight for the sheets of pastel bricks raining down her mind, and the dollar calculations, and her brute force of want.

Mac was cheerful, at first. Happy to hear of her excitement. He claimed he'd even heard of Peter Wand, and listened to Becky spew all her disjointed thoughts and plans. He waited until she was finished, and then he gently, very gently, dismantled every angle of her idea. Becky had to grip the strange desk to absorb the blow: Mac's utter dismissal of Peter Wand's worth and work. How limited the market was for late Ab Ex, the way the line and color screamed Twombly derivative, a dozen more reasons a buy of that magnitude was premature, a bad investment, off the mark.

In an instant Becky saw all her idiot enthusiasm for what it was: naïve inexperience. How far she still had to go to catch up with someone like Mac, who could call on decades of deals and trends before putting a play into action. Who did she think she was? Thoroughly chastened, she tried to thank him. Mac brushed it off. Even, perhaps, forgiving her for going to New York, without him.

The next afternoon Becky took a seat in a bright second-floor library at Swann Auction Galleries on East Twenty-Fifth. She'd been downtown all morning trying to make up for yesterday's folly, cramming in as many galleries as possible, and she'd take another taxi back to SoHo afterward. But for now, she tried to take slow calming breaths in the peaceful space, the rows of folding chairs slowly filling in, the light-wood lectern awaiting the auctioneer. She didn't know what to do with the paddle, white card stock printed with the house's blue *S* logo, that she'd been handed after checking in. Hold it on her lap? Dangle it by her side? Sit on it? Becky noticed one woman fanning herself with casual aplomb.

As soon as the auction began, however, she forgot her unease. Staff set up each work—from the lot "Selected Sketches, 19th Century"—and carefully adjusted the lighting before the grandly mustachioed auctioneer rapidly detailed artist, style, background, quality, provenance, and highlights. Whistler, Bellows, Lewis, Léger. Becky craned and peered, trying with no success to see behind the curtain to the next work. Finally, finally, the small page was set up for all to see. The drawing was exactly as perfect as in the catalogue where she'd clocked it over a month ago. It hit her all over again: the insouciant curve of the line, the spiky end of one charcoal edge, the ideal balance of white space and plain coal-colored sketch.

"Mary Cassatt, early study for an unfinished drawing, mother and child theme. Initiating bids at ten, do I see ten thousand—"

Becky's hand shot up. Without her paddle, which had slipped to the floor in her excitement. Keeping her hand up, arm extended, she groped down. The man in the next seat bent and retrieved it for her but she had no time to thank him. The bids swept ahead, eleven and now somehow fifteen, she kept raising but so did at least two other paddles. And why did the auctioneer keep glancing to his side? Who was . . . Oh. An agitated younger man taking orders from a telephone, one of several set up on a plain light-wood table.

Becky held her ground. *Up*, she lifted at eighteen thousand. She'd promised herself twenty would be the max, had to be the limit. But then there was still one paddle and the man on the phone and she went up again at twenty-two.

The very first time she'd laid eyes on the image she'd seen Ingrid in the drawing. Ingrid's tired night-nurse tenderness in the easy way the mother held her baby.

Up, she flipped her paddle, answering the auctioneer's look. Twenty-five. A long moment, would the other paddle . . . No. The room let out a soft sigh. Becky almost hovered on her seat, alight in every nerve.

Twenty-six, yes from the phone.

Twenty-seven, Becky's paddle up.

Twenty-eight, a longer pause. The man on the phone covered

the receiver with a cupped hand. His nod, to Becky's eye, was one millisecond slower than it had been.

"Twenty-nine thousand dollars," she called out, putting up her paddle before the auctioneer could turn to her again. That did it. When the man on the phone shook his head, face drawn, warm applause broke out in the room.

Becky nodded tightly to those in her row who leaned over to murmur congratulations. She had to hold it all in, bursting elation, body-rocking adrenaline that made her want to shriek with triumph. The underlying ripple of fear about how much more she'd spent than she'd wanted to, how very much deeper she'd dug into the hole.

Ingrid, though. The thought of Ingrid. That's what carried her through.

Becky managed to learn the subway: people exited through the same turnstiles for entering, and sighed loudly if you dithered even a moment with your token. She fit in openings and retrospectives and ate a hot dog or a pretzel from a street cart every few hours. She even mostly recovered from the gentle sting of Mac's correction, with those Peter Wand paintings. Becky did what Becky did best: put it behind her and hurried forward.

She redoubled her efforts at self-discipline: she checked off every gallery on her map grid, she took extensive notes, she made introductions and pacified a jealous Fernanda (*You never here! I have all these for you!*). She kept her mind off her bank book, which was drained because of the Cassatt. Focused instead on listening, learning, taking it all in.

On the last night she went to an event in the Puck Building

on Houston Street, a dark-red structure that loomed high over its corner, marking the essential division between SoHo and everywhere else. Becky wasn't sure who was being celebrated—a tenth anniversary for one of the nearby galleries, perhaps—or how she'd made it onto the list, but she'd changed into a Betsey Johnson black-and-purple-flowered frock, slicked back her hair on the sides, and milled around the crowded loft space holding a plastic cup of tepid chardonnay. Her feet hurt so much she couldn't feel them anymore, and smiling enigmatically at people she didn't know was leaching away her last bits of energy. How long ago had she eaten her last hot dog? Why couldn't the stereo system play something other than David Byrne, David Byrne knock-offs, or David Byrne parodies? She had to find some food.

A few turns in the halls adjacent to the main room led her to a kitchen, where at first Becky thought she was alone. Alone with *food*, platters lined up on a long metal table—untouched mini quiches and grapes and cubes of Brie. She found a napkin and piled it high.

"You're supposed to wait until they bring it out." The voice came from a young boy, unnoticed until now, sitting on a dish counter and kicking his heels against the metal below.

"Aren't you supposed to be in school?" Becky spoke through a mouthful of quiche.

"It's six thirty," the boy said.

"In the pm," another voice clarified, this one from an even smaller girl, with matching brown bangs, intent on a coloring book spread open on an overturned white bucket.

"In the pm is when grownups get their food." Becky wondered if it was time to push on to the Fleshman opening, which started at seven.

"We got pizza already," the little girl said, frowning at her drawing.

"Can you bring me a 7UP?" the boy asked Becky. "From out there? *She* forgot again."

Just then the swinging kitchen doors blew open, and in came a very tall woman in a white tux shirt and twisted bow tie. Her exasperated glance fell on all of it—the children, Becky's full napkin, the banging of heels on a metal counter.

"Go," she said, pointing to a back room.

"But Mom, we—"

"No ifs, ands, or buts. We had an agreement."

"She took food," the boy pointed out.

"Hey!" Becky protested.

The tall waitress gave Becky a quick once-over. "Would you do me a solid?" She tucked her tray under her arm and began to repin her hair, a pale fuzzy cloud. "You're a gallery girl, right? Help them get set up in there with like a game or something?"

"Uno!" the little girl cried. "I can do my *own* hand."

"We have Battleship too," the mom said firmly, cutting off the boy's objection. She pushed the platter of food toward Becky. "Did you see David Armstein out there? Or Patel what's-his-name?"

Becky was distracted by the tall woman's whirl of action: put down her tray, wipe her daughter's nose, peer out the door's porthole, muttering to herself. And how did this waitress mom know the names of two top dealers, whom Becky herself had been hoping to sight?

"Ten minutes." The woman wheeled on Becky. "Take the food with you. I just need one shot at . . . Half an hour, tops. Kids, show this nice lady how to play Chutes and Ladders. In the *back*."

"We could take this whole platter?" Hmm, not bad.

"*Mom.*"

"Paul. I *will* bring you a 7UP, I swear by all that is good and holy. Give me just a few more minutes." With that, the ostrich-like mom took up her tray with a flourish, and backed through the swinging doors.

The girl tucked her coloring book under her arm and waited expectantly. The boy—Paul—arced himself off the counter. They were both so much shorter than Becky expected.

"Chutes and Ladders is the dumbest," Paul said. "Let's play Uno."

Because she was still hungry, because she had time to kill before Fleshman, and mostly because she wanted to sit down and take off her heels, Becky ended up playing an hour of Uno—no real Spanish was required, it turned out—and beating the kids an average of four games to one. They ate all the quiche and the cheese cubes, and then the girl—Frieda, five—put the lettuce on her head for a hat. Becky learned they lived in New Jersey but their father was in Colorado, they had a pet guinea pig named Franklin because the other guinea pig (Francis) had died in the summer but they couldn't bury Francis in the backyard because it was shared with the other townhouse residents and Mom said they couldn't. Also—Paul crawled over to whisper this wetly—some of them had dogs and a dog would probably dig up a buried guinea pig and—

"All right, I get it," Becky said.

Their mom worked in an office sometimes, doing something (her children were weirdly ignorant about what), and also waitressed for a catering place. Their babysitter had bailed at the last minute—"Because she's a *space cadet*," Frieda reported gravely—and so they'd been dragged a long way in the car to the event tonight.

"That's not fair!" Paul exclaimed. Becky had played a well-hoarded Draw Four.

"Completely fair." Frieda had wandered over to her stack of art supplies, so Becky was playing her hand as well. Paul grumbled, then took his turn. She stopped his move. "Save that one. Wait for when I'm closer to Uno, and then use it."

"Oh. Yeah." But then he leaped up, scattering the pile. "Frieda! What are you doing, dummy? She's going to kill you!"

Instant tears, a sudden tussle, and more noise than Becky could handle. She separated the children, soothed Frieda's wailing—how did parents *stand* that sound?—and eventually found the source of the problem: the five-year-old, coloring with her crayons (*scribbling*, Paul spat), on papers she'd pulled out of a black, ribbon-tied portfolio. Becky gently removed them from the child's sticky grasp. They were copies of a résumé, she saw. And stacked behind those in the portfolio were photographs of photographs, thumbnail images and blown-up shots and installation views, all of which Becky immediately removed, lifting them high above Paul's reaching arms. "It's okay, I'm allowed. This is your mother's? She's an artist?"

"She taked pictures of me too," Frieda insisted.

Becky sat on a radiator and paged through the acetate sheaths. The photos were staged stills of men and women, utterly ordinary suburban types, clothed in robes and holding strange objects as if they were scepters. Posed against garage clutter, country kitchens, all with mesmerizing ambiguous expressions: resigned, lightly humiliated, shyly proud.

"That one's my soccer coach," Paul said, breathing into Becky's ear.

"How large does she print these? In what editions?" Both kids stared blankly—of course—so Becky rummaged to find their mother's CV (her name was Tracy Moncton), skipping past a carefully typed and Xeroxed artist's statement ("At the juncture of domestic realism and fantasia, my work seeks to uncover hidden conflicts in hierarchy and chaos, gender roles and the Green World, structuralism and—") to skim the relevant info in her bio and background. Hunter College, then a year toward an MFA at Columbia, unfinished, group shows at UMass, RISD, and a church on Staten Island.

Becky went back to the photos and was holding one up in the weak overhead light when Tracy Moncton herself reappeared in the kitchen.

The kids ran to plow into their mother, who had a coat over one arm and two glasses full of amber liquid pinched in one hand. She kissed the tops of their heads, glanced at the open portfolio in Becky's lap, and handed her one of the glasses.

"Lagavulin. I owe you several, but Ahmad could only slip me two. All right, gang, let's get this stuff picked up. I'm Tracy, by the way. The total stranger who had you babysit my kids."

"Reba," Becky said. "Are these—"

"And all for nothing," Tracy went on, nudging over the stack of Uno cards with her foot. "Nobody out there. Low men on the totem pole." She took a big drink. "Where do you work again?"

"No, I . . . Who's your dealer? What kind of lab do you use?"

Tracy laughed tiredly. She took the portfolio off Becky's lap and put it in a bag, along with picture books and reusable water bottles. Frieda clung to her arm, sucking her thumb and whining softly. Becky checked her watch—too late for Fleshman.

"How about some dinner?" She saw Paul's eyes light up and added, "My treat. I'm only in from Chicago until tomorrow and I collect . . . Well, I don't have any photographs yet, but I'd love to learn more about your process."

Tracy, squatting on her heels, gave a sharp look up. "My process, huh."

"How about pizza?"

"Yes! Pizza!"

"We have to get back. It's late, and the bridge traffic will be a nightmare."

"Mom!"

But Tracy wouldn't hear any protests, from either Paul or Becky. Who couldn't stop staring at this frizzy-haired waitress, her long limbs and practiced movements, the way she scooped up kid debris and deflected Frieda's tantrum and drained her scotch. She was so—so—*regular*. She could have been any mom in front of Pierson Elementary, sharing a cigarette with a friend and keeping an eye on the time. Working the second shift at Smiley's Diner. Where did she come up with these visions? The soccer coach under a dulled ornate crown, a Wiffle ball balanced on his wide-open palm?

Becky ran through all the artists she'd met—for no more than a minute or two—at Yoshi's in Chicago, those Mac and his crowd tolerated but mostly ignored. Had any of them been this normal? Had any of them been *moms*?

"Do you have a card?" Their coats were on, and Becky's energy surged.

"Ha." Tracy produced a postcard from a tote bag full of them. "Take three. Take thirty! God knows I couldn't give them away out there. Come on, kids. Thanks again, um—"

"Reba," Becky supplied, scanning the postcard announcing open studio dates and hours. When she looked up, they were gone.

That night, her last in New York, Becky waved off the cabs lined up on Lafayette and began to walk north, crossing all of Houston's lanes and wandering side streets near NYU until she figured out how to get to Third Avenue. From there, it was only a mile or two back to Fernanda's, and Becky barely felt the heavy night wind pushing her this way and that, block after block.

A fantasy bloomed. What if she stayed? What if she started over here in New York? What if her art buying and selling could sustain itself, without the constant tension that came with the Activity? Without the Activity?

Becky walked fast past shuttered storefronts, paint stores and health food stores and nail places. She avoided the crazies talking to themselves, the garbage blowing up and around the curbs. Traffic swept past her and blew her hair forward.

God, what would it be like. To live only one life. To just be . . . who? Reba, she supposed. No more Becky Farwell, Pierson protégé, star citizen, beloved small-town wunderkind.

Maybe, she told herself, pausing to study the inscrutable menu in the window of a Chinese takeout place. A single breeze of possibility blew through her mind. She caught its scent, what life here would be like: light and free. Excited, she kept walking north.

That energy was partly why she went to bed with Fernanda later, acceding to the woman's frank need and smooth arms and murmured Portuguese endearments. It was easy to give when you were caught up in a dream.

It was also why Becky took one additional step before heading to LaGuardia the next day. She rode all the way out to Tracy Moncton's small shared studio on the far west side of Manhattan, having carefully prepared her pitch. She looked carefully at the woman's work, past and present. There were a few others there for the studio visit, presumably for wine and cheese, but Becky ignored them. It didn't faze her that Tracy's studiomates were amateurs of the worst landscape kind, or that Tracy herself had overdressed in a sadly desperate suburban-housewife style: pumps and silvery stockings, turquoise acrylic sweater. Becky studied the woman's equipment, her portfolios; she used a loupe to go through slide after slide. She shut Mac's warning voice out of her head and questioned Tracy closely about her rent, lab, film.

At the end of the visit Becky put forward her proposal. She'd heard of arrangements like these but never thought she'd be interested herself. A few minutes later the two women shook hands on a deal that would have Becky—Reba—fronting a thousand dollars a month for overhead (including babysitting, which Tracy insisted cost ten dollars an hour; highway robbery, if you asked Becky), in exchange for first option on any new work and a fifty percent discount. As Becky carried her suitcase downstairs, mindful of the Cassatt treasure wrapped snugly within, she heard Tracy shriek with jubilation.

Becky made it to her flight just under the wire, but this time she knew what to do. She held Mary Cassatt securely on her lap and watched the metal-colored Long Island Sound tip sharply and recede beneath her window. In the quiet of climate control the numbers she had committed to came back with icy clarity, standing out in relief against the grayish clouds: now one thousand more per month to her overhead. Add that to one mortgage plus one rent, her car payment, the impossibly high but necessary entertaining costs, and the hundred other fees and expenses that came with collecting. Becky traced the figures on the inside of her window with a fingertip.

Say she did sell everything she had. Even the best-case scenario resale of all her pieces wouldn't set her up for more than the smallest fingerhold in the New York scene. And then what? She'd stand around galleries, not buying, not dealing, while the invitations dwindled and the opportunities evaporated. Would she have to live in *Queens*?

Becky shook her head and held the Cassatt closer. Numbers never lied. New York was impossible. Even if she could guarantee her past skimming would never be uncovered, how else, *where* else would she be able to fund her art collection, keep it going? No, back to Pierson it was.

11

Pierson
1989

IN THE PHOTO, HANK FARWELL stands so straight he's pushing his chest out farther than his chin. Beside him, Jean Dore is calmer, more at ease even with the round bouquet she has to hold. One side of her hair is tucked behind her ear, a casual mistake perhaps, given the formality of the photo, but Becky always loved that detail. She wished the photo wasn't in black and white, so she could examine the exact coloring of her mother's hair at that age, twenty years old, and compare it to her own at almost twenty-five.

Hank had kept this photo framed on the mantle, but he also had a crumbling white satin book with a dozen other photos from their small, family-only wedding in 1959, at a church in neighboring Dixon, where her mother had grown up. As a girl Becky used to page through the stiff curling photographs, searching for hints of what her mother had been like. The smiles were so forced, the poses so standard, that it was impossible to tell.

Hank used to say that he could instantly distinguish which photos were from before the service and which after. "Pale as a ghost," he'd say, pointing to his face in the earlier ones. Becky didn't really see a difference. "There, see—by then it was all official and I got my color back." The new Mrs. Jean Farwell had the same smiling complexion in every photo. But only in the one on the mantle had she unthinkingly tucked back her hair in that girlish gesture. So this was the one that Becky now kept at home on her dresser—in Pierson, that is, not the Chicago condo.

Now, this October Sunday morning, Becky and Ingrid were midway through the reception for Ingrid's wedding to Neil "She Actually Said" Yesko (as was piped in frosting, under a busty rendering of Ingrid, on his bachelor party cake). Becky was crammed next to the bride in the ladies' room of the Amber Gate Banquet Hall on Timber Creek Road, west of Brinton. She held up layers and layers of itchy crinoline and slippery satin, her eyes shut as demanded.

"Don't look," Ingrid snapped again. "Don't look!"

"It's not the looking," Becky mumbled.

"Shut up! I can't help it! That's so mean!"

"All right, all right, I was just kidding."

Silence again in the bathroom. Through the walls they could hear the raucous talk and burbled bass from the reception.

"When they say 'morning sickness' they make it sound so petite and dainty," Ingrid complained. "And all anyone ever admits to is throwing up! Nobody but me gets the trots, apparently."

"Mm-hmm." Becky had heard this speech before. It was their third emergency rush to the bathroom since the service. Ingrid claimed no one knew the reason for the suddenness of the date, and her parents had been happy enough to save money with a brunch reception, so Becky kept quiet about how the other bridesmaids had guessed the truth right away.

"Neil's haircut looks nice, doesn't it? I like it longer in back like that."

"Sure."

"Could you tell my aunt was avoiding my mom the whole weekend? We *told* them there'd be a champagne toast. It's not my fault they're all born-agains."

"The groomsmen have been pouring shots of Jim Beam in the coat room."

"I'm sure Aunt Christy'll do penance for all our souls." Ingrid let out a sigh, her forehead on the heels of her hands. Becky, who had opened her eyes, adjusted her friend's tilted headband, silk flowers on elastic. "All right. I guess we can go." Ingrid stood and the two of them began the process of rolling the girdle back up her thighs and stomach. Muffled in a face-full of dress, Ingrid said, "Also, Mayor Ken Doll has probably sent a search party for you. Ow." The band on the Wonder Shaper had snapped back.

"Sorry. What are you talking about?"

"Following you around like a lost puppy. 'Becky, I need your opinion on what house to buy.' 'Becky, I need your opinion on what pants to wear. And don't mind my wife over here at table three, or our twins at home.'"

"You're the one who invited them."

"They weren't supposed to come! Jesus H., as if I didn't have enough stress without worrying which relative is going to say something to insult brand-new Mayor Ken Doll Brennan. Mayor Bren Kennan!" Ingrid laugh-burped, washing her hands. Becky knew she'd had a bit more than the "just for toasting!" pink champagne. They met eyes in the mirror.

"'He was like the country he lived in,'" Ingrid intoned, quoting one of their favorite movies. "Come on. You know it."

"'Everything came too easily to him.'" Becky obliged with the rest of the line from *The Way We Were*. "But Redford is a stretch, even with the hair."

"It's not the hair, dummy. It's the golden boy aura. Okay, it's the hair too."

"Hmm."

In truth, Becky didn't want to talk about the new mayor, an eager-beaver type who had already cornered her twice during hors d'oeuvres. She was stretched to the limit at Town Hall right now, between the increased focus of her new promotion and trying to make up the difference in several accounts she'd borrowed from too heavily in the past two months—to furnish the new Chicago apartment, to transport and install her many pieces there, and to throw several open houses aimed at cultivating top-end buyers and dealers. She was fighting to put back as much as she could, not knowing how closely this new mayor would be scrutinizing the finances.

Ingrid had been studying Becky in the mirror above the sink. "What about Adam Murphy? He is at your table, after all."

"Murph plus three other horny single guys. I wonder how that happened."

Ingrid began a lilting "Well, you never know . . ." But a fierce look from Becky shut her up. They left the ladies', Ingrid's dress squishing through the door. "Just be careful about him, okay?"

"Please. Murph wouldn't know how to—"

"Not Murph, Mayor Ken," Ingrid hissed. "He's got his eye on you and I don't like it."

For a second this caught Becky off guard. An anxious flare

sounded deep inside her, a kind of muffled sonic boom. Had she underestimated golden boy Ken Brennan? Was he smarter than he seemed? She mustered a smile and found a distraction.

"Before we go back in, I wanted to give you this in person." Becky steered them to a long draped table covered in gift-wrapped boxes. Ingrid lit up, even though she'd been stopping by Sears daily to check on her registered items and therefore knew what almost everyone had bought her. Becky moved presents around to find the package, 11 inches by 17 inches, covered in plain white paper. No card.

Ingrid sat on a nearby bench and opened one taped flap. "Should we get Neil for this?"

"What?"

But Ingrid ignored her own question and went right on unwrapping. Becky took a deep breath when the drawing was revealed. The child's tiny fingers, curled around one of her mother's. And the woman's relaxed posture, all that warmth and strength vibrating through the few lines on the page.

"Oh, wow," Ingrid said, her pink-chapped hands gently bracing the sides of the frame. "This is so sweet."

"Do you like it?"

"I *love* it. Love love love. Of course I can't put it up until, you know, the cat's out of the bag." She patted her belly. "It's going to look great over the—" With one arm Ingrid thrust the picture out to squint at it. Becky reflexively jumped, ready to catch it if it fell. "No. Too small. And we're thinking Neil's Zeppelin tour poster will go there. But I'll find the perfect place." Ingrid stood and propped the Cassatt back on the gift table. "Thank you!" She enveloped Becky in a hug.

Becky eyed the sketch leaning against the toasters and blenders. She felt reasonably sure no one here would give it a second look.

As they entered the reception room the DJ had just cued up Garth Brooks's "Friends in Low Places" and everyone was screeching for Ingrid to join a front-of-the-room sing-along, which she happily hurried to do.

"Hi again." Ken Brennan, suddenly at her elbow. "Got a second for me?" He held up two plastic flutes of pink champagne, and his ridiculously handsome smile did its work even as Becky saw right through it. Told herself she saw right through it.

The wedding progressed from Ingrid and Neil smushing cake into each other's faces to line dancing led regally by Ingrid's mother and her friends: the Picnic Polka, Louisiana Hot Sauce, Tush Push. Becky watched it all from a table with Ken, who talked and talked. Mostly he told her about his misadventures in area real estate, an epic saga of his family's move from Springfield that involved plot twists and reversals and a nearly lost deposit and a corrupt moving company . . . Becky picked at her slice of cake and tuned out. As the wedding dwindled, new Mayor Ken only seemed to pick up steam.

"It was a little too much house," he finally sighed. "And way, way, way too much money."

Well, obviously, Becky thought. She knew what Mayor Ken's new salary was, and a third-grader could have told him not to even bother.

"They want us to go under," Ken said, pushing aside the table centerpiece, his voice suddenly serious. Becky tuned back in.

"Who?"

"Listen." He leaned close to her, elbows on knees. "For the last eighteen months I knew I wanted to get out of Springfield. That place makes Chicago pols look like Girl Scouts. But they kept bringing me along, this committee, that committee, *hey Brennan come by the club*, or *how about a round this Sunday—*"

"Which club?" Becky cut in. Damn. She *knew* the real deals got made in those stupid cigar and scotch sessions. Maybe she could get Ken to—

"What I'm saying is, I was listening." His eyes, greenish brown, were intent on her. "I saw the budgets, I saw what they actually have while they're telling you they don't. Remember last year when you put in for road repair on the . . . I can never remember which bridge is which."

"Do I *remember*?"

"What came back? A quarter of the ask? An *eighth*?"

Becky stared. "We got nineteen hundred, on a bid that came in around twenty grand. And some line about waiting for more research on a new form of—"

"Macadam," Ken said at the same time she did. "A new form of macadam that would solve all your problems. Did you ever hear about that macadam again? Meanwhile, do you know about how much Greenland County got that spring for an eight-mile lane rehab? Twenty-five thousand. Right off the top."

"Those fuckers," Becky said. They'd closed the bridge on Galena three times last year because of dangerous conditions. She'd narrowly avoided a fourth by selling off one of her very few—and very much cherished—pastels, a mid-level Roger Hilton. She'd made the sale swiftly and sloppily, trading speed for a good price, and poured that money into Pierson's Roads account. *Becky always finds a way*, is what was said around the office, after she put out a vague story about squeezing some funds from one place and shifting funds around from another. Obviously they knew she didn't always find a way, but she tried to patch the most obvious and glaring holes and when that happened, the praise rolled in.

Every time she drove over the crumbly but still-standing Galena bridge, though, she cursed a little bit in honor of that lost Roger Hilton. It had been a great piece.

Ken went on, citing memo after memo where Pierson had gone to the state for funds and been denied. Becky fumed. They'd looked like *chumps*, she and Mayor Thomsic. They'd been laughed at, fobbed off with stories she couldn't believe she'd fallen for. And they'd never once pushed back. Just think what she could have done for the community with that money from Springfield. Just think what she could have done for the Activity!

"Thomsic always had a positive spin," Becky said sullenly. "Said he had people there, said it would be our turn someday."

"That's where you went wrong," Ken said. "They counted on that. His wanting to keep up a good front, make it look like he had things in control. But I have a different— Listen, do you want to get out of here?"

"What?" She hadn't noticed, but now the dance floor was empty and the DJ had packed up. Around them servers were whisking off white tablecloths to reveal the scratched wood tabletops. "I can't, I have to . . . Where's Ingrid?"

There she was, in the lobby, changed into a shiny rose-colored dress with her hair freed from the elastic band of silk flowers. A group of women surrounded her, laughing and tossing confetti, shepherding her out into the chilly afternoon. Becky watched her go, love and melancholy welling up.

Luckily, Ken Brennan kept pulling at her attention. "I know a good place for beer."

"How do you . . . Where's your wife?"

"Went home a while ago, set the babysitter free. Come on. The end of a wedding is so depressing."

"Beer in the middle of the day isn't depressing?" But she took the hand he held out. Let him hold her coat, open the door of his car for her, of Fitz's when they got there.

From the booth, watching Ken as he went up to order their drinks, rolled sleeves and bare forearms resting against the bar, Becky could see his appeal. She'd been hoping, she realized, that someone she knew would see them together.

Perhaps it was to cut off those feelings that when Ken returned to the table Becky said, "Listen. I'm not sure we should make any major waves in your first year." She was only looking out for him, after all. *She* could take the heat from council and residents, but he'd probably want to keep his nose clean.

But Ken wouldn't hear of it. He was one hundred percent in, one hundred percent with her on helping this town get back on its feet. He didn't care about optics, he cared about results. And from what he knew, she was the only person who could spearhead real change. "Don't you see? That's how we're going to get them. That's how we can win."

"Shame them," Becky said slowly. All those promised state grants that never came through: for demolition of old properties, for roadwork, pension help. For repairing the riverwalk! God, how many times had the state sent out inspectors and environmental teams and financial assessors. She'd walked them up and down the riverwalk dozens of times, she'd followed up diligently. Nothing ever came back.

"Point out every way they're failing us, every dollar missing, everything Springfield owes us."

"It'd be ugly. In town, I mean. Thomsic kept it—*we* kept it—pretty optimistic." So that the constituents wouldn't know the full extent of their helplessness. So he could get reelected.

"That ends now." Ken shrugged. "I can take it, and so can you. They *love* you. You can convince them, I know you can."

"Sure, because I'm the one who'd be the messenger. You'll get to shrug and say, 'I tried my best for you, Pierson, but when it came budget time Becky just couldn't get it done.'"

"Bullshit," Ken said. He reached across to take her hand, as if they were shaking, but instead just held it lightly on the damp bar table. "I will never hang you out to dry. Whatever you say, I'll fall in line."

She withdrew her hand from his. This could be the cover story she'd been waiting for: Springfield. They were in the hole because of Springfield. And if Ken backed her, the town would buy it. Wouldn't they? If the state was shorting them already, who would notice another hole within the hole?

It would be a risk bigger than any she'd taken: to ride her Activity on Springfield's back. And on Ken's. But also, and this was the weird part, she believed in Ken. In his smarts, in his passion. He reminded her of her. So if he went to bat against the state and won more for them . . . Becky won too. If she could take what she needed *and* Pierson could be fully operable? The ultimate dream.

"All right," she said slowly. "I'm in. Let's shake things up."

Ken sat back against the high booth, then sprang up. "Wait here. Don't move." He returned minutes later with two shots. "Johnnie Black," he said, passing one to her. He clinked his whiskey against hers. "To not getting rid of us."

Becky nodded once and sent the Johnnie Black scorching down her throat.

12

Pierson
1990

DATE	RECEIVED	NOTES
March 31, 1990	*$45,000*	*J.W. Roof Service and Repair*

IT WASN'T HARD TO DO. Becky had logged so many invoices in her years
of bookkeeping that she had a veritable mental album of Accounts
Payable: dozens of templates, fonts, misspellings, dropped digits,
and unimaginative company names to whip through. She mocked
up an invoice, at home usually, on one of four flea market typewriters, rotating through different kinds of paper (cream to dead
white, in varying weights), and gave it a fake service date and amount. In the beginning, she worried about the bill itself, and
would go to great lengths to simulate the crunch of post office processing by crumpling, then smoothing the bill, folding it in thirds,
at times flicking it with dirty dishwater and leaving it to dry on
a tea towel. Then she just dropped the fake invoice into the wire
baskets for Accounts Payable along with the real bills she sorted
from the general mail delivery.

Payments rolled out with no questions, funneled into the spiderweb of accounts and sub-accounts and sub-sub-accounts that she herself set up and managed, closing and instituting accounts so often that everyone in the office was grateful not to have to understand the big picture, grateful she was there to tell them what to do. No one had a better memory than Miss Farwell. She could call up details on the past four rounds of tax code revisions without batting an eye (if you'd been so unlucky as to ask a tangential question)—and would reel off numbers and years and acronyms, on and on and on, smiling brightly at you there by the water cooler, until you could thank her, nod as if you knew what she was talking about, and flee back to your desk. *Thank god for Becky,* so commonly muttered around City Hall, was a kind of shorthand everyone understood. It meant *Thank god someone else knows that mess so I don't have to get my head around it.*

Money moved in and out of the accounts, including RF Capital Development, one of a half-dozen dedicated "RF" funds, and Becky made sure to supervise numerous payouts for bills from all of them. At times she even let RF Capital empty out—though she hated to see it that way—just as the others did, to keep them all alike. Then once a month she would pay her credit card bills using RF Capital. She often paid city cards that way too—they were transitioning to credit for many services—and also she ostentatiously "paid back" to City Hall any personal charges, i.e., meals without clients, using her own pale pink checks stamped *Miss Rebecca Farwell, 140 County Road M, Pierson.*

So much money shunted in and out of that one artery, RF Capital Development, and yet Becky could put the total in the account to within a few dollars at any time. Not to mention she kept detailed notes—stupid, she knew—logged in the meticulous bookkeeping manner that was her second nature. By the end of the 1980s she was taking a hundred thousand a month and putting back into Pierson maybe a quarter of that. Her annual salary was a respectable fifty-nine thousand, plus benefits.

DATE	PAID	NOTES
October 9, 1989	$140	United Airlines (NYC)
	$300	Le Cirque (NYC).
October 16, 1989	$199	United Airlines (NYC)
	$695	Casa Bella (FRANK M BROUGHT FRIENDS!!)
October 25, 1989	$180	United Airlines (NYC)
	$80	CATS tickets
	$400	Four bottles Château Mouton Rothschild
October 26, 1989	$580,000	Wired to Frank M, via Beate Gallery, full payment for Thiebaud, ICE CREAM CAKE 1979
October 26, 1989	$14.99	Pierson Fantasy Florals (Mrs. Fletcher, Happy Secretary's Day)

By early 1990 all of Pierson knew that Becky loved "pictures." For her twenty-ninth birthday, the city council surprised her with an ornately framed oil rendering of Rock River, commissioned by esteemed area painter W. Marlon Rinman, who presided gravely over the ceremonial unveiling of his work, accepting Miss Farwell's gushing astonishment with mere nods of acknowledgment. Later, several members of the council wondered at the way Becky chose to hang this beautiful piece, so relaxing to look at, right next to a couple of other pictures, small brown things with squiggly lines. Like stuff your kid made.

But if only she had someone! Women in Pierson would inevitably gossip.

I heard she was dating Ted Thompson.

Oh, she dumped Teddy two months ago—but he won't say a bad word about her.

What about that commissioner from Rock Falls, the one she brought to the tree lighting last year?

He could light my tree.

Who knows.

Men can't handle strong women. They don't like it when they're not the one wearing the pants.

Nothing Becky can do there—she's always going to be the one wearing the pants.

Thing is, even if they have it all, some women—at this, everyone sighed—*just aren't lucky in love.*

Ingrid laughed every time Becky did this routine over the phone at night, cranking up her voice into her best nasal flat-vowel accent, making up what *they* were all saying. *Who?* Ingrid demanded. *You know who,* Becky said. *Them.*

Fuck them, Ingrid said through the receiver, and Becky smiled. Sleepy-phone protective Ingrid was one of her favorite Ingrids.

DATE	RECEIVED	NOTES
June 9, 1990	$140,000	Mapplethorpe, SHADOW BLOCK, sale to Monk Gallery, LA

DATE	PAID	NOTES
June 10, 1990	$499,999	Hockney, STUDY 2 (Ghent Gallery— NEVER AGAIN!)
July 4, 1990	$1,900	Marilynne's Pony Parade (July 4 town party)

DATE	RECEIVED	NOTES
July 21, 1990	$4,000	Doherty video
	$45,000	Auerbach, PROFILE
	$19,000	Bill, THREE SQUARES sale to Adira Khan (via Mac)

DATE	PAID	NOTES
July 30, 1990	$35,000	Marden, SKETCHES FOR COLD MOUNTAIN
	$43,000	Sherman, UNTITLED NO. 102
August 1, 1990	$1,000	Tracy Moncton, monthly
August 7–10, 1990	$9,000	Bergdorf (Ungaro, YSL, Perry Ellis)

Council meetings took place monthly, on Tuesday evenings, in the first-floor conference room in Town Hall. Budget season was May and October, so during those months Becky and Mayor Brennan held more frequent sessions for various city services to come plead their cases for funding. Later, the published budget would be released to the local paper, and a public hearing traditionally took place in one of the church meeting rooms.

Council members, many of whom had been elected and re-elected for decades, could barely remember a harder time than the present year, although they often tried to: the Carter administration crisis . . . the mid-sixties drought . . . the early-eighties subsidy squeeze. But no one could successfully argue Pierson had seen it worse before.

And it was clearly taking its toll on Miss Farwell. Each meeting, stretching past 10 pm, deepened the violet shadows under her eyes. Look at her tonight, shaking her head even before Police Chief Vessey finished reading his statement. It had to be hard, to be the one always having to deliver bad news.

"I wish we could, Jim."

"Now wait a minute. We were told if we held off until fall we could—"

"It just isn't there." Becky brushed at the binder in front of her. Several council members nodded, or shook their heads, meaning the same thing. "I would go to Busch Municipal on my knees if it would do anything. They're screwing us, Jim. Excuse me for putting it that way." Her voice caught.

Mayor Brennan began to speak, something conciliatory, but Chief Vessey shook it off. "You said fall," he told Becky, exhaling hard. "Training, operations, patrols, ballistics. Can't be done on ninety thousand. We've waited. Now it's goddamn *fall*!" That last shouted word startled everyone, but none so much as Miss Farwell, who flinched, both hands flying up to her mouth and nose, pressed together in front of them. She swiveled to turn her back to the table. Was she—?

Brennan called for a break. Vessey hovered, uneasy, until a council member drew him away. Miss Farwell stood, shielding her face, and walked quickly out of the conference room. In a short time she was back, though, in the same chair at the front, her face freshly washed and her eyes shining and steady.

"Next item," Becky said. Voice clear and almost entirely calm.

DATE	PAID	NOTES
November 20, 1990	$650	Groceries
	$1,300	Wine delivery (Thanksgiving here with I's parents and two aunts, JESUS GOD)
December 10, 1990	$1,400	Resurface HS gym floor
	$500	Food, drinks, decorations (HS Winter Ball)
December 15, 1990	$1,299	(Franklin Furs—Mrs. F)
	$4,500	(Swarovski—office staff)
	$850	(Blackhawks VIP pkg—Ken)
	$2,000	(FAO Schwarz delivery—TJ)
	$32	(necktie—Ken)
	$13,300	(Davis Jewelers—Ingrid)

"What the shit," Ingrid said flatly. At Becky's door, 9:45 Christmas morning, dangling the emerald pendant necklace from her gloved fingers. She pushed past Becky in her robe, bringing cold air into the house.

"How did you know I was here?"

"Because, you dummy. I drove by last night on my way home from church and saw your lights on! You lied to me!"

"The flight was canceled last minute!" Becky wrapped her robe tighter, naked underneath. She'd been upstairs having espresso, opening her own gifts to herself: a rare small Barnett Newman oil and two photographs from Tracy Moncton's latest editioned series. She'd had to fight to get these from the woman's new big-name agent who only reluctantly allowed the sale when Tracy insisted, still honoring their deal. The artworks and all of their discarded packaging were now strewn across Becky's California king–sized bed.

Guilt after the nightmarish series of budget meetings had worked its way through her, and the past several months she'd pulled back hard on the skimming. She'd moved money around to return some to various accounts, and she'd covered as much as she could for the town out of her own pocket (secretly, as far as she could). That meant denying herself the fall art shows and half a dozen serious deals that made her fume with longing and regret. So these purchases were extra special.

"Why didn't you call? We have so much food!" Ingrid stalked the living room, her fleecy pajama bottoms tucked into winter boots. Then she stopped, suddenly quiet. "You don't . . . Do you have someone over?"

Becky followed Ingrid's pointing toward the stairs. She laughed, immediately igniting her friend's ire again.

"I knew you weren't going to the Florida Keys. I told Neil, *I call bullshit*. Since when does Becky go sit on a beach for vacation? Since when does she *vacation*! But I can't believe you lied to me."

"I lied to everyone. Do you want a coffee?"

"No, I have to get back. My in-laws will be expecting a festive brunch on top of tonight's roast beef extravaganza." Ingrid collapsed onto Becky's leather sectional. "And what the hell is this?" She swung the emerald necklace around her fingers.

"You're welcome?" Becky curled up next to her friend, whose wide pale face looked more tired than ever. She'd had to quit being an ER nurse after TJ was born in order to care for him full time. After a series of bewildering seizures, and multiple tests, he'd been diagnosed with an intellectual disability. Ingrid dealt with all of it—finding doctors, researching treatments, and now her own lack of income—with brisk good cheer. Becky wasn't sure what it meant for TJ and never really knew what to say. "Did he like the electric car?"

"Oh, Becky." Ingrid's face lit. "I don't think he's gotten out of it since six am. He can barely sit up in it but he's driving it all over the house, ramming it into everyone's legs, making all the right car noises . . . We're going to go broke for that thing's batteries." She grabbed Becky's hand, but then scowled. "But *this*? And don't tell me it's paste. What are you thinking, spending that kind of money?"

"I thought it would go well with your eye color."

"With my jelly-stained sweatsuit?"

"I'll exchange it for you."

Ingrid let the necklace fall in a silky metallic heap onto the coffee table. She stared at it, not Becky. Becky made herself wait. She wouldn't think about the two pieces on her bed upstairs. She wouldn't look toward the one painting she allowed herself to display down here, a 6-inch-by-6-inch Matisse oil. Pretty enough to escape anyone's notice—Ingrid had never commented on it—it was worth several times the house and property lot combined.

"You could tell me, you know." Ingrid pushed back a tendril that had escaped her scrunchie, and smiled. "If there's . . . someone. Like, a guy. Or a girl!"

Becky laughed, and so did Ingrid. "I'm just saying!"

"Nothing's going on, Beanie. I'm sorry I didn't call. Tagging along on other people's family holidays can get me down, that's all."

Ingrid weighed this as she was now weighing the necklace coiled in her pink palm. She had no response, which startled Becky, who realized that what she'd said about tagging along had more truth than she'd planned.

"Well," Ingrid said at last. She handed the necklace to Becky, swiveled away from her, and waited.

Becky needed three tries with the clasp, her fingers brushing against her friend's nape. "What do you think?"

Ingrid turned and held down her bulky acrylic scarf so they could see the pendant, half-hidden in her pajama top.

Becky burst out laughing. "Okay, I'm an idiot. Give it back and I'll—"

Ingrid put a hand over the emerald. "No way! I'm going to wear it on every trip to the FastMart. And the pediatrician. And story hour at the—" They tussled, shrieking, until Becky slid off the leather couch onto the carpet. Ingrid gave her a hand up. "All right, let's go. I'm already in the doghouse."

Becky put her hands on Ingrid's shoulders. "You head back, and I'll be half an hour. I'll get doughnuts from that place by the gas station."

"My in-laws are the worst, you'll go crazy," Ingrid said happily, giving Becky a long muffling hug. "We'll start drinking at noon."

"We'll hide in the kitchen with a bottle of wine." Becky breathed in the sugary scent of Ingrid's melon shampoo.

"It's a Christmas miracle," Ingrid sighed. Still hugging her.

13

Pierson
1991

BY EARLY 1991, CRISIS GRIPPED Pierson. Although the financial situation was nowhere near as bad as it would become in a few years, the budget-cut pileup had reached critical mass—broken playground equipment and mail gone missing and forced police retirements—at least in the eyes of the citizens. The local paper's editorials grew more pointed, and although they generally followed Becky and Ken's script by blaming Governor Thompson and the Illinois legislature (even, at times, Mayor Daley or President Bush), suspicion was tightening around even the beloved "Pierson Pair."

The tipping point was petunias.

Ken, still enough of an outsider, had little compunction in canceling the annual Petunia Festival. When you couldn't afford new textbooks or toilets in the elementary school, who cared about flowers?

"Aren't they kind of garish, anyway?"

Becky shot him a warning *don't go there* look across the conference table. Too late. Aggrieved council members spoke over each other, praising the petunia's hardiness, its long bloom phase, the subtle differences in shading from grandiflora to milliflora to wave variations. Becky knew what the bottom line was, under the committee outrage. The Petunia Festival wasn't just a time-honored summer tradition, it was the main tourist attraction of the year, bringing in an annual average of four hundred thousand in visitor business. Merchandise, food sales, entertainment. But what did that matter if they didn't have the funds to outlay for the mammoth necessary preparations: bids for landscape firms, the tools and contracts and equipment and inevitable overruns.

Doodling a petunia in her notebook—anyone raised in Pierson knew one when she saw it—Becky thought about money too. Her Activity account was out. Run dry, scraped clean. For the past few months Becky had been on a buying binge. Art world prices fell by the week, and she scooped up everything she'd ever had an eye on. She knew she should rein in her spending, but she couldn't. Everything was so cheap! All the names, every phase, every dream buy now a possibility. In the past six months she'd acquired pieces from artists who were laughably out of her league. She bought early works and canvases with paint still drying. All you had to do was hesitate for an iota, and a seller would lop off another ten percent. In fact, the hardest part was getting a hold of anyone. Gallery after gallery shuttered; dealers disappeared, their answering machines so full they weren't accepting any new messages. Friends, other collectors, warned her to stop but if the whole system was going down in this market "correction," then for the sake of sweet baby Jesus, Becky *would* own a Rauschenberg. If only for a short time.

The other problem was space. A lack of cubic square feet. Crated art all over her Chicago apartment, when the condo was where she was supposed to view the art, to show it. She could keep pine boxes in Pierson, for Christ's sake. But she was maxing out: both bedrooms, the combination living room/dining area, the small foyer, and even the kitchen were all covered with paintings. She'd even had to slide stacked canvases under both beds. Only minor works, a lesser Kline and a Barrett add-on from a package deal earlier in the year—but it was still far from ideal. Her cocktail party guests laughed when they saw the crammed space, joking they had the same disease, but she knew that all these wealthy collectors—acquaintances, business contacts, all of them calling her "Reba"—displayed their own works throughout giant suburban estates.

How long could she sustain this? She owed six thousand to her condo management, and the dunning letters left in her mailbox were getting serious. She should stop opening those.

"Maybe our superhero will rush in and save the day at the last minute." This voice, sing-songy and nasal, belonged to Phil Mannetone from PR and Communications. Overgrown Neanderthal mouth-breathing Phil. Always in her business, acting like he was in on some kind of joke. Across the conference table he gave Becky a long, loaded smile. "Becky, you always seem to find funds somehow. Somewhere."

Ken snorted. "If anyone can price out what's needed from *this* quarter, they're welcome to try. But in lieu of any—"

"I'm not talking about the budget," Phil smoothly interrupted. "Not the official one, anyway. Just wondering if Becky could work her magic and find a little extra somewhere."

"If only I could," Becky said. *You fucking nitwit, don't you think I would?* She hadn't sold a piece in months, so there was no magic to be worked. No "miracles" of "juggling the accounts" to come through for Pierson, and without those regular infusions of her payback, people—like Phil fucking Mannetone—were obviously starting to notice. If only the market would come back! If she could just buy a little time, art sales would resume—they had to!— and then she'd be able to keep the worst at bay.

"This isn't on you, Becky," Rhona Lear said, and shot Phil a dirty look. "It's on all of us."

"Thank you," Becky said. "But Phil does have a point. Maybe there *is* a way. I'm spitballing here, but what if we . . . did it ourselves?"

Then she was off and running, the other council members eagerly taking up her idea and fleshing it out. What if they reclaimed the Petunia Festival as a fundraiser for the town? Leverage petunia nostalgia into a do-it-yourself planting weekend this spring. Start a pledge drive for planning logistics. Lean on small businesses for donations for publicity. Bring in the League of Women Voters, the Girl Scouts, the local press. Who needed landscapers when nearly everyone's neighbor was a proud gardener with years of experience? True, it would be nothing like past years and the revenue would certainly be smaller . . . but there would be petunias. And concessions.

Becky's cheeks grew warm as she worked, up at the whiteboard scribbling down all the ideas and plans and numbers and dates. With all hands on deck they could just about pull off a "planting day" event with a kickoff in early April, to make sure this summer's Petunia Fest would happen. Phil Mannetone sketched out press releases and a pitch for local TV, the picture of enthusiasm, but Becky knew there was trouble. He was trouble.

Three months ago, she'd come in late one morning to find him strolling around her office in front of her desk. He had some pretense of a letter he wanted to get her opinion on, but he was looking at the things in her office—her leather coat and her *objets* and the fresh flowers delivered weekly. And then at her, in a way no one else did: speculative, interested. What was it he'd said? "Someday you'll have to show me how you do it, Becky Farwell."

The council meeting rushed ahead with plans and decisions, infused with positivity for the first time in months. Only Becky grew quiet, glancing up now and again at Phil Mannetone. Sorting through what she knew about him outside of this room, his family, his home, his routines and habits.

Three weeks later she was standing in the freezing wind on a makeshift press stage while Ken wrapped up his speech for the two press reps and a smattering of citizens, more than Becky had expected for a March Friday with snow in the forecast. "Why didn't we do this in the auditorium?" she hissed at Ingrid, who needed her full attention to hold back the thirty kids onstage—a Boy Scout troop and some matching local Brownies—from playing their part too early.

"You wanted that big finish," Ingrid whispered. "Graham, if you're going to rip the bag you can't hold it. TJ, hold my hand. Here's my hand."

"Petunias," Becky called into the mike, as soon as it was her turn, after the cheers for her had finally quieted. "Are one of the country's most recognizable flowers. And although they are known to be the most beautiful"—unfortunately this set the small crowd into applause, muffling her point—"they are one of the hardiest, too!" She hurried on to the plan: reclaiming the annual Petunia

Festival as a fundraiser for Pierson, using volunteers for the planting and maintenance and a local pledge drive to boost the summer tourist business.

"We thought about cutting it—as I know you know, Pierson has been going through a hard time lately—but like I told Mayor Brennan, Pierson doesn't need pity . . . it needs petunias!"

This line killed, of course. It would headline tomorrow in the paper. Ingrid fought valiantly to hold back the troops while wrangling her giant toddler. She gave Becky a look: *Jesus, hurry up.*

So instead of outlining what it all meant dollar to dollar, or how next month's "Planting for the Future" event would kick off a town cash drive to repair or replace services—it was all in the press release anyway—Becky gave the nod. More or less in sync the kids tore open their decorated brown paper lunch bags and began to toss handfuls of seed—bird seed, not petunias, but the effect was the same—in the direction of the rutted dirt behind a park bench.

It worked. Warm murmurs and genuine applause spread through the crowd, and Becky stepped away from the mike filled with pride from a thought-through plan well executed. Mayor Ken smiled and waved, bird seed in his hair. Ingrid gave her a long one-armed side hug and Becky didn't pull away. People still cheered, even the reporters.

Who needed Springfield? Becky thought, face flushed in the cold. *Why should anyone count us out?*

Forgetting, for one moment, that without Springfield she had no enemy for the budget shortfall. Without Springfield, and the political strands of truth and untruth and half-truth she wove together, she would have nothing, no money in the secret account, and no way to cover up what she needed to do. (It didn't matter that she currently didn't have any money in the secret account.)

Becky watched the gritty seeds skitter off into the cutting spring air. The levers in her mind worked frantically to balance guilt with energy, recognition with effort. She herself was the cause of the pain she worked so hard to remedy. But who could say where the town would be without her? All the work for this planting fundraiser: the idea and the number crunching and the late-night planning . . . it was exactly what she would have done if the town was truly in the hole. Which it was! Couldn't one make up for the other, karmically or morally or whatever? Like a kind of equation where one complex function Xs out another and replaces it, after a lengthy series of twists and reversals?

"You okay?" Ken said, when she took a wobbly step back.

Sure, sure, of course. Becky smiled for the cameras.

One week later, Becky held the door of their cab for Monty Dubner, some jackoff from Connecticut who owned a part-share in the Tremen Gallery in the West Loop. Only after significant name-dropping—and hints that they could come to some other arrangements without Tremen knowing—had he agreed to come to her place in the city to pick up the Caulfield oil she was selling to him at a ridiculous fraction of the nine grand she'd paid for it last year.

So intent on managing her unaffected business mode (desperation had an odor and she was, in fact, desperate to sell), Becky didn't notice the way Ronan at the door didn't look at her when he buzzed them in. If she'd been half a second faster off the elevator, Monty going on about his kid's snowboarding camp in the Alps, she could have seen the new fixture on her door first, and at least had a chance of bluffing it off.

But instead they were taken by equal surprise by the padlock and corresponding orange notice (like the ones the city slapped on cars getting the boot): SEE MANAGEMENT FOR ACCESS.

"Fuck." Humiliation blared in Becky's ears.

Monty reached over to flick at the ugly, cheap padlock. "Technical difficulties, huh."

"It's a mistake. I've been having an ongoing disagreement about a board policy that . . . Just stay here for one minute. I'll get it sorted."

"Stay here?" Monty laughed, glancing around the narrow condo hallway.

"You're right, I'm sorry. I'll meet you in the lobby in five minutes." She strode back to the elevator and slapped the down button.

"My next appointment is in forty-five."

"There's coffee downstairs," Becky said smoothly. There was no coffee, as far as she knew. They rode down silently. As soon as she pointed Monty toward a configuration of black leather couches, Ronan hurried around the doorman kiosk.

"Miss Farwell, I wasn't supposed to—"

"Ronan! What the fuck," she hissed, crossing the lobby.

"I know," he said miserably. Last Christmas she'd given him—and each of the other guys—five hundred in an envelope and a bottle of Courvoisier.

Right then a short pants-suited woman came striding out of the property management's office, calling her name. Becky went to her in an icy fury, hoping that Monty was far enough away not to hear. "Unlock my apartment right now! Can't you see I have a business—"

"Please follow me," the woman said. A security guard appeared behind her and Becky whipped past both of them into the office.

For eight or ten trying minutes she beat her head against the joint stupidity of the woman, the property company, and the rent-a-cop who stood around like his numb presence meant anything at all. Why couldn't they see that if she could get *in*to the apartment, she would be able to sell a piece (or three) and get the money to *give* them for the piddling back rent everyone couldn't shut up about! A man with a checkbook was literally waiting in their overdesigned lobby and— They were going to hear from her lawyer. Today. In an hour. But for now if she wasn't given access to—

Changing tactics suddenly, Becky stormed out of the office. Ignored the woman calling her name. At a glance she saw Monty riffling through a magazine, so she had some time. Maybe.

"Call Jorge for me," she whispered to Ronan, who'd certainly overheard all of what had gone on in the office. "Tell him to meet me upstairs."

He paused, but nodded.

In the hallway outside her apartment, Becky paced. Counting down the minutes she had—fewer than what she needed, likely—before the office woman and the guard found her. Counting up the possible dollars she could get from Monty.

Finally! Jorge, with a bolt cutter. She scrounged the only cash on her—fifty bucks—and passed it to him after the one hard *clunk* that snipped off the cheap lock.

"Not me," he said, when she tried to thank him. He backed away fast to the freight elevator.

And then she was in, rushing through the darkened rooms and the furniture covered with sheets to protect it from sunlight and fading. She didn't have long. As if the place was on fire, Becky raced through it, making snap decisions based on split-second calculations: price paid, price possible, what she could carry in her arms right now. She gathered paintings and shoved them into a grocery bag. She threw a T-shirt over a forty-pound galvanized-steel sphere and hoped it wouldn't break her purse. Voices from the hall made her freeze, but they faded past her door. Hurry, hurry!

She left with the door carefully closed and the broken lock dangling. Took the side stairs down three flights and then the freight down to the basement level, after which she jogged up one full flight, weighed down with art in bags and under both arms, and peered through the cracked lobby door over by the mailboxes. Surely she'd be able to catch Monty's eye and direct him to—

But the lobby was empty. Ronan caught sight of her and winced. *Get out of here*, he mouthed.

But where's— She motioned toward the leather couches.

He shook his head. *Gone*.

Becky wilted then, legs buckling. She had to rest against the door jamb so she wouldn't drop all the pieces onto the floor with a clattering thump. Why couldn't anything ever be easy? Why was she living life backward, with all the room in the world in her empty home out in Pierson, and this tiny overflowing treasure chest locked away from her?

Monty never returned any of her calls, but Becky caught a cab and managed to sell whatever she could to whoever she could find at a loss she couldn't think about. By next month it was all smoothed over with the property managers. Back rent paid, fees paid, three months' advance rent paid, plus a thousand-dollar donation to the office "slush fund" to compensate for "any inconvenience."

She'd skated through. But for how long? In the back of her mind all through that late winter Planting Festival work, Becky knew it couldn't continue. Her apartment as an art safe house, this racing in and out of the city, the juggling of funds, the placating of idiots who could nonetheless bring her down. Something had to give.

14

Pierson
1991

"FOUR MORE COUNTS ON THE out breath," Ingrid said, nodding *yes* in response to Becky's wild-eyed *no, I can't*. "Carbon dioxide is what's making you feel like that, so— No, don't gulp in, you need to breathe it out."

"I—can't—" Becky sat on her office couch surrounded by flyers that read Planting for the Future, knees clamped together, shoulders hunched. Tiny specks flared in her darkening vision and she felt like a vise was clamped on her lungs. Only Ingrid's warm hand on her back kept her from losing her mind. That, and the awareness of Mrs. Fletcher right outside the closed door.

"Heart attack," she gasped. Hot tears squeezed from the corners of her eyes.

"You know it's not," Ingrid said. She put two fingers on the inside of Becky's wrist. "Better already. Now ten more breath cycles. Four on the in breath, eight on the out breath. Go."

The first two times this had happened, Becky had promptly driven herself to the ER, convinced the unbearable tightness in her chest had to mean a cardiac implosion. But the tests all came back negative, which then led to an unendurable encounter with a doctor who gently introduced concepts of "life's general stressors" and "taking it easy, day by day." When's the last time she took a vacation? What about a relaxing hobby? Did she have anyone with whom she could talk about difficult feelings?

So now Becky just called Ingrid when the warning signs started up: buzzing deep within her ear canals, and then a dry-heaving sensation as if her innards needed to forcefully expel something. If she was lucky, Ingrid would arrive before this, the worst part: chest locked up so tight Becky felt like she was breathing through a straw. A spitball-plugged straw.

Now, as before, Ingrid blithely ran through everything that was happening physiologically, spiking heart rate, over-oxygenation, irregular muscle freeze. "Textbook anxiety attack."

"But I'm not"—breathe out—"anxious." It was true. Never were these "anxiety attacks" prompted by thoughts or fears about her Activity. Hadn't one of the worst, for example, kicked off in the middle of the night? Waking her out of a perfectly deep sleep? Ingrid could throw around "stress reaction" and "panic symptom" all she wanted, sounding all too similar to the on-call dopes in the ER, but those were for chumps who couldn't handle their business. Not Becky. No one had the slightest clue how much she had to cope with, the entire art market still going ass over teakettle. Newspapers had trotted out the bursting-bubble metaphor in every article this year, like stuck robots. Meanwhile she dealt with it day and night, constantly on the phone to antsy collectors and dealers, fielding calls from her artists themselves, who only now poked a head out of the clouds to survey the shit-strewn apocalypse and ask, "Wait, prices are down?"

Becky had it handled, though: the art plunge, the losses she held on pieces worth a fraction of their cost, the new filing system in the office making it hard for her to keep track of Activity invoices, the incoming day's mail she had to get to first before some eager-beaver junior accountant asked, "What's the RF Capital account connected to?" And she *wouldn't* think about Mac. How she'd called him yet again, just before this lung-squeezing attack. Was he ducking her? And could it be true, the rumor going around that he had somehow engineered a coup for the ages, buying up all of an unknown's early work and parlaying it into a future show at the Gagosian? That the name of this unknown soon-to-be supernova was Peter Wand, the artist whose pastel brick paintings had entranced her years ago in New York? Which was worse, the anxiety of the rumor or the idea of confronting Mac with it?

"You didn't make an appointment," Ingrid observed, dropping Becky's wrist.

"Like I have time to rehash my childhood for some cut-rate Dr. Freud. Especially when he's not even a doctor."

"Social workers are perfectly—"

"Unable to write prescriptions. All I need is this." Becky shook the bottle she'd been clutching in her lap like a talisman. But frankly the Valium did little, even at a double dose, once a surge erupted.

"Have it your way." Ingrid stood up and strolled around the office, rubbing her lower back. She was pregnant again, and happy about it, even in the midst of taking care of all that TJ required. Becky fell back against the couch, lungs loosened, grinning. Ingrid picked up a Pol Bury cylinder, chromium-plated brass, 1969, worth eight to nine thousand (in a normal market). "I hate being your dealer." Although Ingrid now worked catering at the Golf

Club in Lincoln Heights she still had enough connections to get prescriptions. Which she'd agreed to only because Becky refused to see a medical professional.

"You love me, though." Pleasantly sleepy now, Becky curled her legs underneath her. "Want to go to a matinee? No one'll miss me for a few hours."

Ingrid thunked the Pol Bury back on Becky's desk. "I can't."

"Not even for *T2*?" They'd already seen it once. Becky put on her best Austrian Arnold cyborg voice: "'I know now.'"

"'Why you cry,'" Ingrid finished, her accent much better. She sighed. "No, I got to pick up TJ. Hey, did I tell you our exploratory committee finally met?"

Becky flinched. "You don't want to take on the bureaucracy, trust me. What's wrong with what's-her-face?" Ingrid had a mild obsession with bringing a special-needs program to Pierson Public Schools. She'd gotten other parents hyped up and they were reaching out to other area schools, attending conferences.

"She's costing you a fortune, is what's wrong!"

"Pssht." It was true the woman's rates seemed astronomical, but if that's what it took to have a retired child specialist, MD PhD, come to your house three times a week, Becky was happy to pay it. Happy to put it on her credit card, that is.

"No, it's insane and we never should have let it go on so long." Ingrid hugged one of Becky's expandable folders to her chest. "If we get matching state funds, by the time TJ is in first grade—okay, maybe second or third—this program could—"

Becky sighed, chest still aching. "You say that like you haven't heard me place a hundred hexes on every Springfield official! Besides, it'll never equal what TJ gets from Dr. . . . Whoever."

But Ingrid was off and running about community and public investment and studies showing that mixed classrooms benefited *all* kids, those with and without special needs. Becky kept quiet, wishing Ingrid would stop worrying about the bigger picture and just focus on TJ. Who was getting the Cadillac of private therapy!

To distract herself, she thought about resale. It was all anyone talked about right now, how to unload pieces and where and who might be buying. Becky had run through all her contacts and started over again in widening circles that went nowhere. With the Activity stalled because of Pierson's dire straits she needed income from art. But this shit market meant no big or steady sales. Without funds from either she'd end up losing the apartment, and that would be that.

Or she would get caught, she reminded herself. She thought of Phil Mannetone's horsey wheeze-laugh, the wiry black hairs thickly covering his pale arms and the back of his neck, and repressed a shudder. She chose her moments with Phil carefully, effectively. Lingering with him out in the parking lot next to her car, having called him over on the pretext of a quick question about one of his "masterful" press releases. Lightly touching his forearm and tossing her head back with a laugh. Deliberately lowering her voice so he'd need to lean down, closer to her.

Last Friday she'd called him late in the afternoon, asked him to drive her to the county office of the Illinois waterfront historic society. She could really use his communication magic to convince them to rebuild the site of Pierson's primary visual appeal. The office turned out to be closed when they arrived at 5:04, oh shoot. Well, how about a friendly beer at this out-of-the-way pub on their way back into town? Phil's uncertain face, the way Becky'd had to coo over wallet photos of his mousy wife and bucktoothed kids. Her foot under the sticky bar table, lightly brushing his calf, once, twice.

Bile pumped up her throat and she shook her head, willing it back down. *Nope*, she told her own train of thought, the sense-memories of Phil Mannetone, the aftershock of panic. *Nope, nope, nope.*

Out loud she said to Ingrid, "I wish you'd stay with the doctor. For TJ."

"Just wait until you see our proposal," Ingrid said. "We've got this pro bono education lawyer, it's going to be airtight."

"Fine, sure. But what TJ gets from—"

"Becky! I am not an idiot, okay?" Ingrid stamped her foot, though it fell muffled onto the carpet. "You think if there was any other way I'd take all this help from you? You think I don't know it's not right, how you can pay for all this and how much I need it? Neil says don't look a gift horse in the mouth, but Jesus."

"It's fine, Beanie, you don't have to worry." Under the Valium swirl, a pinch of throat tightness. "How much have you been . . ." How to ask this. "Talking to Neil? About stuff?"

There was a long cold minute while the question hung in the room.

"Because it's no one else's business, all right?"

"I'll see if I can get you some Xanax." Ingrid put her hand on the door. "They say it's better than Valium, for long term."

"Don't go yet."

"I have to run."

"Did I ever tell you you're my hero?" Becky couldn't let Ingrid go without seeing her smile again. If that meant breaking into one of their favorite cheesiest movie songs, so be it.

"Becky."

But she got louder, swooping her voice up to match lyrics about soaring like an eagle. Hitting some but not all of the high notes.

"Oh my god." There it was, one glimpse amid Ingrid's exasperation as she left.

Becky's chest eased even more. Now that was real relief.

15

Miami
1991

TWO WEEKS LATER, BECKY FLEW to Miami on a Hail Mary. With only days to the Planting Festival, Ken was either too busy or too discombobulated to confront her about why she wouldn't be at the Saturday walk-through. She started applying sunscreen on the plane and kept it up for the entire thirty-six hours of frothing international art fair madness. Pierson needed approximately two million dollars to climb out of its perilous debt. If she could sell nearly her entire collection, Becky could possibly close the gap. But all of that depended on Emi and Josh Robb-Tenner.

Becky started chasing the Robb-Tenners as soon as she landed. Impossible, of course, to find them in the fair's main tent, where she was in any case distracted by dozens of people who wanted to chat with her, even more she needed to avoid, and a barrage of art she couldn't afford. The couple's one announced panel—"Future/ Text/Image," whatever that meant—was so full that even though Becky thought she'd arrived early she couldn't see a thing over the heads of those standing in front of her. At that night's parties she "*just* missed them" or "they're supposed to stop by . . . at some point?"

She was hardly the only one chasing them. Emi's work, subject of an *Artforum* profile and a solo show at the Getty, was having a moment. "Encounters," the artist called them: semi-staged inter-actions between viewers and hired actors impersonating viewers. Tense know-nothing gatherings of people in empty-walled galler-ies, studying each other, wondering—out loud, eventually—where the art was. Sometimes Emi inserted herself into the encounter, feigning boredom and bewilderment, although she did that less now that her photo regularly appeared in *Vogue*, Musto's column, and *Page Six*.

The whole thing didn't do much for Becky, but then again Emi wasn't the prize. That was Josh, founder of the Tenner Gallery in London, a scrappy hip place in a shitty neighborhood that every-one was talking about, after two dazzling shows last year. Tabloid photos of Matthew Broderick leaving the gallery and Julia Roberts rushing in, shaded by a security team, cemented Josh's reputation.

"Reba!" On her second night, her last night, Becky's own party's cohost rolled in two hours late, barely bothering to cover up the fact of having been somewhere more important or interesting. "Look at all this gorgeousness! And I did nothing. You hate me."

"No more than usual." Becky did the double-kisses against Dani DeStefano's mock-pout cheeks, hardened with fillers. In fact she had practically killed herself all day getting the suite's pool area ready and could have used a hand, even one of Dani's.

But if her one Miami contact came through, all would be for-given. This was her last and best chance to snag Josh Tenner, and Becky had gone all out. Four cater-waiters for a party of twenty. Platters of ceviche on every surface, a dozen baskets of moon lilies floating in the pool, and a pleasingly sullen trio warbling Irish folk-punk flown in this morning—an early profile she'd dug up on Josh had mentioned that he loved the live Dublin music scene.

Dani sideswiped a ground arrangement of ankle-height votives with her stiletto. "Oops! Fire hazard! Yes, champagne please. Lighting these must have taken you hours."

"It was nothing." Becky couldn't waste more time on pleasantries. "Are they coming?"

"Hmm, it's so *buggy* out here, though. Who, darling?"

She wanted to take away Dani's champagne flute and bash her with it. "The Robb-Tenners!"

Dani looked at her. "They're here."

"What?"

Dani pointed, not nearly as subtly as she might have, to the clutch of six or seven people near the bar, sitting sideways on chaise longues, huddled up in a low conversation. Sure enough, now that Becky actually examined faces, she recognized Emi's Asian features, Josh's dark sideburns. But—but—that group had been here for at least half an hour. Emi was in jeans and a button-down . . . and so was Josh. Their sneakers weren't even couture!

Jesus, she'd missed them? Could they have come in during the four minutes—six, max!—that she'd run to use the restroom? Both Becky's arms went numb with panic. She was going to kill Dani. But first, she gripped Dani's elbow and marched her over to the nondescript group, instantly affecting warmth, generosity, welcome. As Emi rose to kiss Dani, Becky wedged herself into the empty space next to Josh, setting her foot on the low table rung to cordon him off from whatever loser he'd been talking to before.

"So, what'd I miss?" She put on a huge, complicit smile while frantically eye-signaling a particular server. "Is there any more news about Darras? What a fucking nightmare." Everyone was talking about the empty booth where one of New York's top galleries was supposed to have been, before last week's stunning news of its collapse, the owners pulling out at the last minute.

"It's bad," Josh said.

"Bad? It's an incompetence tsunami. You'd think someone would have—"

"We're pretty upset for Paul, actually. Emi has two good friends who show with him and now—" He spread his hands.

"And that's the hardest part," Becky said, smoothly downshifting. "Where it leaves the artists."

"Yeah, well, I've known Paul for years and I'm sure he'll do right by those guys." Becky watched Josh aim this reassurance at Emi, now perched on the arm of someone's chair.

"Of course he will," Becky murmured, slapping a mosquito on the back of her arm. "Oh good. Here's a little treat. We could all use a pick-me-up, am I right?"

With less of a flourish than he could have made, the server leaned over the group and placed on the table a glass tray holding three straight razors, a bank-new twenty, and a Bayer's aspirin bottle holding a quarter ounce of high-grade Cuban cocaine.

Astonishment and delight from the hangers-on, but Josh only said "Um. Wow." He looked around, but Emi was deep in conversation with two women and his other friends were snorting lines like pigs at the trough. Becky felt a sharp thrill of satisfaction; she had him cornered.

"So. Secondary market, huh? How's that going?" Tenner Gallery's move into resale had made headlines.

"Well, thanks." Josh's tone was warily polite.

"Good, because I have a deal to propose, and I hope you won't be too modest when I say that Tenner is the only shop I'd consider placing my—"

"Sorry, what? I'm having trouble hearing you." Josh winced as the Irish troubadours shifted into a loud cover of—why?—"Mr. Bojangles."

Becky spoke fast, going in for the kill. She explained her proposal: Tenner's handling the sale of her entire Chicago collection, immediately, in exchange for which she would host a Happening, or an Encounter, or whatever it was called, for Emi's first Chicago exhibit, at whatever venue—

"Anything like that," Josh interrupted, "is for her reps. I don't have anything to do with—"

Chicago's art market, Becky said, straining to be heard, has such potential for— Sensing his displeasure, she switched tacks: she'd had a ton of interest in her own collection, as a whole, (not true; everyone had scoffed at the idea of such a short sale in this market) but she had a feeling that Tenner was— Of course, totally, no one should talk business on such a gorgeous night but if he'd only take a quick look at some images—

That's all you got? She heard Mac in her mind, disappointed and just a tiny bit amused. *Time to nut up, buttercup.*

"Is anyone else getting eaten alive?" Josh said, only a little desperately, slapping the back of his neck.

"I'm not," Emi said, and Becky could have kissed her. Her own skin, thanks to a Herve Leger bandage dress and its stupid cutouts, was covered in bites.

"I think it's all the candles," someone else said, tipping his head up from the coke.

"Well, I'd rather not bring home malaria," Josh said, landing his hands on his thighs.

She knew it was desperate, but Becky didn't care. She pulled out a slide sheet. "Look. This Diebenkorn is part of the same series you have in your catalogue."

Josh looked. He nodded.

"And I have two De Staëls from the same period. Plus an André Derain, the one of the bridge. You said you'd always hoped a good Derain would—"

"How do you know that?"

"That it could hook a buyer into Fauvism who would then—"

"No, wait. Where did you hear I said that about a Derain?"

Becky bobbled, her pitch thrown off. Josh stared hard at her, annoyed. How had she known about his desire for a Derain? Honestly, she couldn't remember. She'd pumped Dani for info, although that was spotty at best. She'd done hours of research on the Tenner Gallery, their financials, purchase history, forecast trends, party attendees. Made calls to the Robb-Tenners' associates and acquaintances, pretending various levels of closeness to Emi and Josh in order to keep the conversation flowing. Well, and there was the time she'd paid a freelance art installer to end up with one of Josh's exes at the end of a long Tribeca late-night bash—she'd never specified what he had to *do* with her in those hours!—and to report back in the morning with everything he'd gleaned.

By now Josh had stood, disentangling himself from the chaise and the coke table and Becky's leg. She started up again, "Forget the Derain, you're right, let me show you the numbers I ran on—"

But Josh had backed away enough to get a bead on Becky and the rest of the scene. He took in the lilies, the acoustic faux-Pogues, the circles of bare skin running up the side of Becky's electric-blue dress. Then it all collapsed. As if in concert, led by Josh, the others rose too. Even Dani, who was the only one to thank Becky and kiss her goodbye. Flustered, Becky began calling after people, urging them to the raw octopi, the silver tequila. They could throw the candles in the pool! Or move inside—

Josh and Emi slipped away, arms around each other, into the palm tree shadows lining the property. From the back, in their matching clothes, they looked like two brothers consoling each other, or plotting revenge. They turned a corner, and were gone.

Becky sat down on a chaise and scratched her bug bites until they stung. What would Ken Brennan say, in this moment, on this patio? Becky visualized him: pleated khakis, loafers, no socks, mustering an *oh well* smile for her. He would've said the coke was a cheap shot, which it was. He would have said that she gave it her best, that Tenner was overrated, that there had to be another gallery. That tomorrow was another day and he had faith in her.

She was so, so tired. And so broke. This ridiculous last-ditch party. A second opinion on TJ's neuropsych evaluation. The private investigator who'd been on her payroll for less than a month. He'd done well, she admitted, he'd gotten her almost everything she'd asked for, and he'd asked no questions.

Tomorrow's flight was at 5:45 am, and by 10 she'd be leading a presentation on the final Planting Festival numbers at the council meeting. Easel pad, markers, bad coffee, bad jokes, her Rockport Total Motion comfort pumps. She'd come so close to fixing what was broken. What she'd broken. But she'd failed, misjudged a hundred social cues and made a fool of herself. Now they'd all have to soldier on with more platitudes and hard work, good Midwesterners to the end.

16

Pierson
1991

ON PLANTING FOR THE FUTURE, that first one, it was seventy-four degrees, full sun, light wind. The most perfect May Saturday in the history of Pierson, in the history of the world. *We lucked out,* everyone said. *Sometimes your number comes up.* Underneath the weather talk Becky knew what people were saying. *Things are finally turning around. We might catch a break yet.*

Becky raced all over the riverfront—she'd been out since predawn—in the pale-yellow Town Hall T-shirt all the volunteers were wearing. She had a clipboard, she had a walkie-talkie. She answered a million questions: Are there any more gardening gloves? Do you know why the hose on Galena isn't working? Where's First Aid? Somebody told me to tell you one of the speakers shorted out.

Everyone had turned out: families, seniors, whole squads of Brownies and Boy Scouts and VFWs and Rotarians. Kids wandered the food tents, spending all their cash on corn dogs and popcorn and Diet Sprite. None of the Memorial Day or July Fourth parades had had this kind of turnout—not in years. Five hundred, six hundred people at the fullest part of the day, and if they weren't seeding beds they were paying for rides on the Tilt-A-Whirl or the Gorgon's Head; they were listening to a local band and eating hoagies from a cart.

Becky stopped by a gaggle of women who'd claimed one of the biggest planting beds. Old hands, they'd brought their own padded gardening kneelers. They praised her for getting the numbers exactly right: enough seed packets, hoes and forks, porta potties, coffee urns and packets of creamer. "Your dad would be real proud," the most gray of the gray-haired women said.

All of a sudden Becky's eyes watered, and she had to pretend to need to rush off. She did have to rush off, of course, there were a hundred other things that needed her attention. But the mention of Hank got to her. A few moments later she found herself wandering away from the crowds.

This is where he would be, in this patch of grass behind the Ace Restaurant. Not planting, but enjoying the day, the hustle-bustle, his girl running the show. He'd have been in a metal folding chair with plastic strips. A Packers hat on his head and white zinc on his nose. He'd have a magazine in his lap but he wouldn't look at it; instead he'd have his eyes on the river ahead of him. Not noticing the patched-up unsightly riverwalk, that constant reminder of all that the town couldn't get done.

Becky stood in the warm grass. Alone and not alone.

"Pretty nice," Hank said, smiling up at her. "Check out those seagulls."

A dozen birds floated on the green water, just north of the Galena bridge. Every few moments a couple shot up straight vertically, hovered in air, then dropped again to the water, plunging down, flapping like crazy.

"What are they doing?"

"Diving for fish, maybe. This warm weather's got everything going."

For a while they just watched the water, the wide eddying flow as it shunted south from Ash Hill State Park, poured down the cement breaker in a mini waterfall, and turned foamy against the rocks under the bridge. Little sloppy waves pricked up like scales, flashing sunlight back in wavy glimmers. Pages on Becky's clipboard fluttered. Bass rumbled from the band covering "My Girl," occasionally pierced by a feedback squeak.

Her walkie-talkie blared. "Anyone seen Becky? Registration needs her pronto!"

"Yep," she said, holding down her button. "On my way." By the time she turned back to Hank, he was gone.

As if she didn't already see Becky approaching, a secretary waved frantically at her from the registration tent. Her name was Joni and she fit the type for one of Town Hall's dozens of cubicle dwellers: short curly salt-and-pepper hair, bristly wide-eyed attitude. She wore her yellow Planting for the Future T-shirt over a lumpy blue windbreaker.

"We have a problem." Behind the table with Joni, Marcia Knox nodded in urgent agreement.

Becky saw what she meant. "That's the opposite of a problem."

Cash, buckets of it. Crammed into the raffle bin, overflowing several banker's envelopes, hundreds of small bills handed to two government workers with nothing but a card table and a flapping sign: ENTER THE RAFFLE (WIN A YEAR OF FREE PARKING), DONATE

TO THE FLOWER MAINTENANCE CREW, SPONSOR A TYPE OF PETUNIA IN HONOR OF A FRIEND OR LOVED ONE. CASH ONLY.

"What about this?" Marcia whispered, half-rising off her chair. A gray metal cash box, stuffed overfull, held mostly closed by her butt.

"Now that's a nest egg," Becky said, but neither of the women laughed. "All right, don't panic. Later on I can—"

"I'm not *comfortable* being in charge of this much money," the first secretary said, with a meaningful loaded look. *Oh for Christ's sake*, Becky thought. *Do I have to do every goddamn thing myself?*

"Fine, give it to me," she said. With palpable relief Joni and Marcia immediately shoved the cash box and the banker's envelopes into two canvas tote bags, then emptied the raffle bin into a third.

After fruitlessly looking around for someone to drive her, Becky began a slow heavy walk uphill to Town Hall. Maybe she could steal a few minutes in her office. In the cool quiet, with a few red licorice strands she'd stashed in her desk.

Instead of waiting for the terminally slow elevator she took the stairs, sweat cooling on her skin, forearms aching from the weight of the tote bag straps. The safe was kept in a filing room on the other side of the hall, but the light was on in her own office. Becky stopped. A figure was moving around inside.

Phil Mannetone. When Becky burst through the doorway he didn't move to hide what he was doing—bent over her desk, searching through papers. Instead he casually looked up with a sideways grin. "I'm the only one who sees it, aren't I? What you're doing in plain sight."

"I don't know what you're talking about." Becky knew she needed to think, to get control of the situation, but all she could feel was a white-hot fury at this ape with his paws in her things. She stepped toward him and he quickly moved to the other side of the desk.

"About three months ago one of my underlings got ripped a new one for messing up the copier, again. Yelled at by one of *your* underlings, who said that seven visits from the tech service guy was way over the line and if he couldn't photocopy a memo he had no business in our office."

Becky felt her throat tighten. What to do. How to get around this.

"So I comfort the little shithead, tell him I'll take care of it. Who knows, maybe we do need a new copier. But then . . ." Phil held a smile. "I looked up the invoice. And checked the dates. I bet you know what I found, Becky. No tech came out on those dates."

Becky dropped her bags one at a time, soft *thunks*. Twenties and fives and wads of one-dollar bills spread onto the carpet, a messy pile. She went over to her file cabinet, took out a key and unlocked it.

"Don't try to sweet-talk me," Phil said, his voice wobbly. "I'm not playing any of your games again. I never wanted to—" Becky ignored him, pulled out the manila envelope, and took out the 8 x 11 photos. "What are you doing, what are those?" She set them out on her tidy desk, one at a time, giving each ample space. Then she simply stood back and waited.

Phil approached gingerly, hands behind his back. Eyes scanned one and then the next, and then the next. His face worked hard, clenching and chewing, mouth moving without sound.

The PI's long lens had captured decent shots of the most incriminating interactions—in black and white, blurry in closeup but still definitively the two of them. The first set showed Becky pressed against Phil with his back against her car. Her face buried in his neck (she'd had to stand on her tiptoes), his head tipped back, eyes closed. What was great was how his hand was caught right smack cupping her ass cheek. He'd done that only for the briefest of moments, right after she'd gone on about their connection and his constant flirting, before yanking it away in horror and sliding out from her grasp. But it had been enough.

The next set of photos was even better. (Or worse, depending.) Becky, through the back windshield of Phil's car, blouse ripped open and lacy bra exposed (she'd done that herself). The two of them in a clinch—three seconds, max, before Phil pulled away. The PI had even caught a gleam of wet on Phil's mouth, and his *smile*—she forgave the hack his exorbitant fee for that alone. Phil must have been in the process of nervously apologizing, declining the offer although he was flattered, don't get him wrong—but of course what he said wasn't visible in the photo.

"You bitch," Phil breathed.

"Here's how this is going to go," Becky said. She hadn't fully prepared, hadn't guessed today would be the day, but was nothing if not ready to step up. "You're going to resign. You're going to take a job way out in Freeman County. Lucky for you, there's an opening in the Comms Department, and even luckier for you, your supervisor is willing to write you a glowing recommendation *and* pull a favor to get you hired."

"You can't do this," Phil said. But his eyes were on the photos and she knew she had him.

"It'll all be very amicable, just a change of pace, blah blah. Maybe you'll even want to sell that two-bedroom ranch that you and . . . Karen, is it? That you and Karen bought. Maybe you'll upgrade to—"

"Don't you fucking—"

"Or these go to Karen," Becky hissed, swooping in close. "They go to Mayor Brennan, they go to your new employer, any new employer you ever get, wherever that might be. If you even think about stuttering out word one about my business about which you know *nothing*—" Even she was surprised by the fury in her voice. "I'll make it my mission to shred your high school sweetheart marriage into a billion miserable pieces."

Nearly there. Nearly there. Becky had closed many a hard deal and she knew how to wait it out. Phil was crumbling but she knew he'd make one more weak-ass stand.

"I'll tell the council, I'll send an anonymous—"

"And you'll watch your boys grow up with another father."

Her ugly words hung there, and Becky saw them finish the job. Phil nodded, gaze cast down.

Becky smiled brightly and clapped him on the shoulder. Swept up the photos, filled the air with details and promises. His resignation on Ken's desk first thing Monday. The great middle school out in Freeman County. How smart he was, she always knew he was smart, despite what everyone said. Look at him, taking care of his family as only a true man knew how to do.

Once Phil was down the hall and out of sight Becky gagged once, twice, then gained control. She'd give herself ten minutes, she told herself. In the cool, in the quiet, she collapsed on her couch. Maybe she'd even try one of those stupid four by four breathing exercises. Before she freshened up, straightened her shoulders, and went back down to plant more petunia bulbs.

17

Pierson
1991–1993

THIS WAS WHEN SHE COULD have stopped. Cut her losses and gotten out. In the aftermath of almost being exposed by Phil, Becky felt an exhilarating relief, an almost holy sense of having been spared. Anyone knew a gift like that was the final one, a sign to hang it up and be thankful. That, plus the fact that the art market was still a smoking cratered wreck.

Not to mention then the overwhelming triumph—temporary, but nonetheless—of Planting Day, the town's buoyant spirits, the high-fives in restaurants and even church . . . She'd done it, she'd shored up Pierson (if not the riverwalk), and did she mind the constant congratulations, the tangible results of coming through as the hometown hero they all wanted her to be? Not in the slightest.

One summer evening in late July of 1991 she arranged for a surveyor to come out for a few hours, to walk the property behind her home, taking measurements and soil tests and knocking stakes into the overgrown grass. They went around and around Hank's old barn, grasshoppers bouncing up and down in the dry heat. She broke the lease on the Chicago condo, paid fees, boxed her art, and transported it all to County Road M, leaving it stacked in as many unobtrusive places (basement, laundry room) as she could find. She told Mac she was looking for something better, and he bought it. He was too busy with his own drama—sales halt, inventory overload, fights with longtime friends—to care. Becky took bids on rebuilding her barn, and pined for the art that had to be hidden away—for now—and waited.

Ingrid gave birth again, a girl this time, named Rachel. Becky bought too many diapers of varying sizes, came over all the time with takeout, and let TJ wreck her nerves with his screeching and banging (Ingrid and Neil seemed immune by this point).

"Don't say it," Ingrid groused. Walking Rachel around and around to get her to sleep. Becky folded baby laundry and mimed a zipping motion to her lips, but really: what had they been thinking?

"One time! One lousy time he didn't pull out. And I—"

"Okay," Becky said. "You can stop right there."

"You," Ingrid sang to her baby, "are a terrible mistake." But she was blissful, fooling nobody.

If Ingrid noticed that Becky was more willing to come over in those first crazy newborn months, or wondered why her friend wasn't as busy as always, she never mentioned it. There was too much to do and too little sleep on which to do it.

By January 1992, Becky's architectural firm had finished plans for the remodel. They'd need to wait to begin excavation until spring came, but that was fine because she barely had money to cover the drawings and blueprints anyway. All of it, this crazy Art Barn dream, was loaded onto her credit cards, whose sky-high limits had been built over years of outrageous art world charges and payments. She still read *Artforum* the day it arrived and she still went into the city for openings and parties, but it was merely to keep a hand in. She hadn't bought anything in a million billion years. Six months, that is.

Hiring freeze, she and Ken announced. Town Hall staff took it with the same numbness they'd received the news about the ban on holiday bonuses and the hold on raises. Ken kept the biweekly Friday bowling nights but only Becky knew he'd begun to pay for them himself. The swimming pool went dry for the second half of the summer. Hours shrank at the community center, the rec league, the senior center. Tree roots buckled sidewalks, garbage went uncollected. Becky drained her own personal accounts, left bills unpaid, and tried furiously to hold the rickety structure together, week by week, month by month.

One curling yellow Post-it on a corner of her desk read only: "Riverwalk." As if she could forget. Nearly every day calls came in from residents: yet another pothole, yet another rat spotted. But no matter how much she schemed, she couldn't figure out how to fund any improvements that would be worthwhile—that would even be *visible*. With the art market in the gutter, Pierson's hopes were pinned on grant applications and state help. Each time she and Ken proposed a tax increase to fund the riverwalk's repair the council roundly voted it down, and who could blame them. Their tax base was tapped out. So they'd all have to put up with it, the cracked and damaged slabs fronting the town, mud slopping up worn-away steps.

Life without chasing art was as boring as Becky had guessed it would be. She tried to enjoy magazines and TV, but not being able to buy any of the fashion she coveted made her too frustrated.

She read the news, idly followed the debates between Clinton and Bush. She worked up an opinion about Mike Tyson's conviction for rape, since everyone else had one. She and Ingrid went to see *The Silence of the Lambs* on one of Ingrid's rare nights away from the kids, and while Becky hid behind her hands and shrieked at every jump scare, Ingrid downed popcorn unfazed and critiqued the dialogue.

At least when Ingrid's special-needs proposal came to Town Hall with three earnest parents none of them was Ingrid, home with a feverish kid and miserable about having to miss the presentation. Becky sat in on the meeting and rejoiced—the ask was so out of reach that even the parents themselves seemed a little relieved when Ken gently held up a hand to stop them. After all, he and Becky explained, they couldn't even get the elementary school's regular teacher aides back this year.

"We're not quitting," Ingrid shouted on the phone, later, over TJ's joyful shrieks. "I've got a line on some private donation sources. We'll regroup, we'll hit you up again when things are better."

Of course, Becky said, dying inside but only for a few bad minutes.

All the while her barn transformed, bit by bit, in secret. From the outside it was the same structure it had been since her birth and long before that: midsized pitched-roof granary, with top sliding doors, repainted occasionally over the years in classic dark red. Half the homes in western Illinois had an identical version out back, in various degrees of falling down. Mostly they were used now as garages, extra storage for lawnmowers and snowblowers. Occasionally people would do a small to medium renovation of the kind teenage Becky had convinced Hank to do: flooring, partial shelving units, maybe electrical. But no one, her contractor kept saying, had done *this*.

Only once in 1992 did Becky leave town, for the April weekend of Tracy Moncton's new show in New York. She was so out of practice that she'd forgotten to set up a story about why she'd taken a personal day for the Friday, and when she'd called to check her messages, more out of habit than anything else, she found that Ken, after leaving several unanswered messages on her machine, *had driven over to her place.* There were all these trucks parked in front and out back, guys clomping right across her sod, did she know about that?

"Goddamn it," Becky muttered, into the blank receiver of a pay phone. Now she'd have to come up with a home improvement project to cover the construction. She hung up, staring at her reflection behind the silver buttons.

"If it has to do with teenagers, I'll see your 'goddamn' and raise you a 'fucking hell.'" This from an impeccably dressed woman behind her in the hallway outside the Stone Gallery.

"Sorry," Becky said, moving away from the phone. "Go ahead."

"I'd much rather hear about your crisis than risk hearing more about my own," the woman said. Her name was Jessa McGown; she had a slight Texas accent but an Upper East Side address. She was forty-eight, the mother of two rowdy prep schoolers, and a collector specializing in mid-century photography, mostly photo cards. They chatted on the way back into Tracy's show, which was a knockout, so packed that they could barely see her on the other side of the room, huddled with her agent and some others in a small group. Becky had turned down Tracy's obligatory offer of a drink the night before—or scratch that, maybe breakfast? No . . .

how about a coffee around 9:50 am?—when she understood how furiously overscheduled the artist was. It had been a few years since they'd mutually agreed to terminate that original agreement, once Tracy had vaulted high enough to make many times over what Becky had once paid her monthly. But polite and prompt invitations still came for every show and event, and Becky knew that if she were to make an offer on a piece in today's show—god, she wanted to buy something, anything—Tracy would instruct her people to give her at least part of the old discount.

Was this nostalgia? Becky wondered, as Tracy unsmilingly posed for a photograph against the wall next to one of her works. She was happy for her, even as their paths were diverging.

Meanwhile, Jessa chattered on, asking all about Becky's interests, what fields and eras. They shared the stories all collectors had, of near misses and disaster deals. Jessa had a gentle, sly wit and wasn't afraid to skewer some of the big names without first ascertaining how close Becky was to them, as was the usual custom. To her surprise, Becky spent over an hour talking with her, and accepted a ride back to her hotel in Jessa's car. They exchanged phone numbers and agreed to get coffee the next time Becky (Reba) was in town, or at the very least to find each other at Basel.

Kicking off her shoes back in her room—the Radisson on Eighth Avenue, for budget reasons—Becky realized that she'd honestly enjoyed the woman's company. Without wanting or needing something from her. That was regular old friendliness, right? For Christ's sake, was she getting soft? Was she getting *old*?

"Twenty-seven is not old," Becky told herself firmly, pinching the tiniest bit of skin at her middle. Maybe she should start doing that *8 Minute Abs* video again. Then, as she always had, she flopped back on the hotel bed and called Ingrid. With enough well-timed questions about the kids, Becky could keep Ingrid talking about herself so that she didn't ask, and Becky didn't need to tell, where she was.

The Art Barn construction entered its last phases in early 1993. All around Becky the art market giants had shattered and fallen, but Becky had burrowed her way underground where she couldn't hear any of it. Just as spring approached—you could smell the difference even in the cold air—she began to bring paintings down into the new space. She especially loved to go down into the half-finished galleries late at night, after the workers had knocked off, a huge dark-purple goblet of Barossa's Signature 1992 in hand. (She was up to Syrah, subset Australia, in her "Wine for New Connoisseurs" course.)

To enter the lower level, Becky had originally wanted a trapdoor leading to a hidden set of stairs. The contractor balked, as did the installers, so she settled on a descending ramp, and planned to block the view of its entrance with something—a sprayer, a round baler—once construction was complete.

Underneath the barn—one full story down, she'd fought the architect for this depth—the space opened to a small front rotunda where sketches would go, then narrowed down a hall off of which lay three adjoining rooms: two smaller spaces across from each other (10 feet by 14 feet), and at the end a white-walled real gallery with a high ceiling and—at some point, Becky thought—a top-of-the-line lighting system that wouldn't be out of place at Pace or Gagosian.

Tonight, it would be Hartung. Oil on canvas, the width of her chest and one extended arm. She carried the piece across the room and set it on the floor, leaned it against the wall in the precise center—this took several adjustments—as flush as she could, given the risk of it toppling forward.

And then, looking. As much as one could in that unlit subterranean space. In the chair, squatting on her heels, or her face an inch away. She thought about Hans Hartung, his deceptive technique—how the slashed and curved lines across the canvas appeared haphazard but were in fact painstakingly considered, arranged. She didn't linger long here, though, because thinking about art was the least interesting way to experience it. The difference between reading the recipe and spooning in a bite of trembling lemon soufflé.

But Becky did think about collecting, the work of it. Deep underground at night she arced out plan after mental plan, considered every angle of her body of work. Where it could go, grow. Works she wanted in her collection, works she could let go (theoretical until the market returned). Mentally sliding pieces in and out, evaluating, calculating. The question of her photography holdings, options to focus on subject matter, technique, the context or history. Depth versus breadth: the essential conundrum.

If she had accomplished this much before thirty, imagine what she could do in twice that time. Would she have twice that time? In the chair, eyes on the painting, Becky steadied herself and went to the worst place she could think of: getting caught. How it might happen, who might be the one. The Phil scenario, or another just as bad. What Ken would say. What Ingrid would do. She strained, she goaded her imagination into worst-case scenario, all the while staring at the Hartung until—panic aching in her chest—one perfect bloom of love for the painting erupted in her heart, for the fact that it was *hers* and here she was and here it was.

Light-headed, fingers numb, Becky crated the work. She stumbled up the ramp, forgetting her wineglass, forgetting the wine. Not for the first time, she wished she had someone to talk to. Not another collector, not even another Mac or a new friend like Jessa. What she wanted, what she wondered about, was what it would be like to talk to someone else who had an Activity. Who stole as much, who feared as much. One single hour of *that* conversation, she thought, could bolster her for years.

18

Chicago
1993

MAC'S APARTMENT WAS FROZEN IN time. Except for the art, all furnishings were exactly as Becky remembered them from her first visit six years ago, and every visit after that. Music piped in from his giant Sansui hi-fi was just as she'd guessed: heavy on the bossa nova, "ironic" show tunes, and endless varieties of prog rock. Even the menu hadn't changed; Becky dismissed again the waitress's proffered platter: California rolls, mini quiche bites, spears of something wrapped in prosciutto. So many things wrapped in prosciutto.

She'd copied this down to the final detail—god, how she hated *lounge music*, ironic or not—for her own cocktail parties. Back then she'd thought everything Mac said and did was *au courant*. Only now could she see the faded edges, the subtle straining for relevance.

Not that she had much time for anthropological reflection. She'd been swarmed since she first set foot in the place thirty minutes ago: Garrett Marshall pressed his card into her hand, with a crossed-out phone, his personal number written over it. Then

Leon from Cavendish Gallery cut in to say he needed a word, if she could—but Zoe Lang signaled frantically across the room, and two other dealers she recognized hovered nearby, waiting for a chance to break in.

It's been forever, they all said to each other. And: are you all right? After the shock of the crash and the tentative beginnings of—knock on wood—a rebound, parties like this were more about reconnections, showing one's face, rather than any real deals. But the way Becky had gone big right up to and into the implosion meant that her holdings were strong and broad. Word spread fast, and the calls to her private line had begun to multiply. People wanted to buy now, for the first time in a long time.

As soon as she could, Becky excused herself. She had come for one reason, and for that she needed to case every room. Passing through the crowded foyer, through the sitting room and dining room, pretending she was on her way to speak to someone—*I'm sorry, I can't but I'll be right back!*—she avoided the beseeching calls—*There she is! Reba!*—as she checked every wall, every painting, every carefully spotlighted piece.

But Becky knew where it would be, if it was here. Mac's office, that small back room off the kitchen, door closed and the usual sign taped up: THIS IS NOT THE POWDER ROOM! FIRST LEFT OUT OF THE FOYER.

Becky let herself in.

Fuck.

So it was true.

By the time Mac himself came in, muttering about uninvited plus-ones and boring ones at that, Becky had been sitting behind his desk in the darkened room for some time.

"Jesus, Mary, and Joseph, you startled me!" Mac made a big

to-do about holding his hand over his heart, then fanning himself. "Darling, why are you *lurking*?" Then he squinted, for show, scanning her black-ruffled Perry Ellis granny dress. "And so *gothic*. Is that what they call it? Well, to each her own."

"You weren't going to tell me?" Becky said. Damn it, her voice was a little wobbly.

"Tell you what?"

Silently, Becky pointed. To the painting directly ahead of her, alone on the wall, in what she knew was the place of honor despite the dust and the clutter of this small space.

Mac didn't look. He didn't need to. Peter Wand's *Wall, Number Nine*, a large-scale oil on canvas in shades of peach and gray. Blocks on blocks, a blurring sheet of repeated pastel images. Just as thrilling as when Becky had seen it hanging in that no-name gallery in New York, on her very first buying trip.

"You told me not to make an offer."

"That's right." Mac was smooth and calm.

"Juvenilia. Underproduced. Color derivative."

"I changed my mind once I looked into it. Darling, don't let's make this a *thing*."

"You knew at the time. When I called you that day, when I asked for your advice. You planned it then."

She'd gotten the rest of the story from mutual acquaintances: Peter Wand as Mac's comeback, the international bids eighteen months in advance of the show, how quietly Mac had managed to buy and hold on to all the early works, all throughout the collapse. Everyone said it was the coup of the decade, and that only one man in Chicago had the eye and the balls to pull it off.

Mac had stayed silent, waiting perhaps to see if she'd make a scene. Wanting her to, a little.

"Okay," she said, breathing through her nose to ward off crying. She couldn't look at the Peter Wand painting anymore. "Okay, I get it."

"Oh, Reba," he sighed. "There are so many things you still—"

"Fuck off, Mac."

He didn't try to stop her when she shoved past him and left the party.

The whole drive home she gripped the wheel and lashed out at herself for being naïve, for being a fool. For wasting a killer Marc Jacobs ready-to-wear on the washed-up denizens at Mac's. For where she could have been, right now, had she trusted herself that day in New York.

It doesn't matter. It doesn't matter. (It did matter.) Mac was passé, he was a bitter old vampire, he thought no one noticed his pancake makeup. Mac was her past.

I'm over it. (She wasn't, not even close.) Becky listed out loud all the gallerists who'd practically stood in line to talk to her tonight. Everyone who'd called her in the past few weeks, the past few months. They'd wait on images from her, they'd buy whatever she wanted them to. What did she need a Peter Wand for? She'd build her own Peter Wand coup, a bigger one, a better one!

After some time, Becky quieted. Turned on NPR and let the news wash over her: standoff with fundamentalist crazies in a place called Waco; Oscar winners and losers and Billy Crystal's best lines; clean-up continued on the Eastern seaboard after the storm of the century. But she didn't hear a word. She'd come back from this, of course. She could already see how it would fuel her. But right now she still had more than an hour to go, to drive her burning self home.

19

Naperville, Illinois
1994

BECKY TURNED DOWN YET ANOTHER Toys R Us aisle, assaulted anew by the flat, bubblegum pink that coated every doll box no matter the brand. Rachel, Ingrid's almost four-year-old daughter, charged furiously ahead, then skidded to a stop in front of a display of fist sized stuffed animals. "No! He's not in there."

"You haven't even looked," Becky said, coming up behind her. "There's the cat, and the squirrel . . . Is this a—sloth?" She scanned the shelves. Rachel was right; the panda wasn't here. *Fuck.*

She'd been sure if they drove far enough they could find a county where kids and their parents hadn't yet scorched the earth buying up every one of these tiny animal collectibles—called, horribly enough, "QT Pets"—but she saw now that her instincts had been wrong. Of course the fad had swept through here already. Now that hour's drive was moot, and she'd be listening to more kiddie sing-along music on the way home.

But it would give Ingrid the rest of the afternoon, and that was the point of these excursions. Becky had been taking Rachel out more and more often, on weekends and school holidays. TJ had come to need more and more treatment: physical therapy, social groups, appointment after appointment after appointment. Becky didn't know if he was getting worse or if Ingrid just couldn't stop searching for the best way to help him but god knew she'd rather drive to every toy store in the state than listen to Ingrid read her the latest research study on speech delay in the intellectually disabled community.

"Maybe you should get another deer," Becky suggested. "Trade with a friend for the panda."

Rachel shook her head. "No. Just panda."

"You know this is a merchandising tactic, right? They underproduce certain products to manipulate the market so you'll keep . . ." She took a deep breath.

Little Rachel stared up at her with that uncanny mini-Ingrid face.

"All right. Sorry, let me think." Becky steered the girl back out into the main aisle, where she spotted a restock clerk, in the store's telltale green apron. "Hold on. We're not done here yet."

"Becky," Rachel whispered uncertainly.

A few clipped sentences exchanged with this nimwit got Becky the location of the stockroom. There, lingering in the doorway, she managed to find the right man—older, jovial, on break—to flirt with enough to get them to the loading dock, where Rachel bounced up and down while Becky switched to sweet-talking two men unloading cartons. Whether the girl saw the cash exchanging hands Becky didn't know. (She hoped not; Ingrid's one condition for these outings was that Becky spend nothing other than a small amount for lunch or ice cream.) But less than half an hour later one of the men motioned her over, slit the box with his X-Acto, and their small crowd bent over it, sorting quickly until Rachel's cry of delight made them all laugh. Back they went to the floor clerk, who price-stamped the toy. In line at the cash register, clutching her panda, Rachel was stunned quiet with happiness.

Becky was so proud of her triumph that she automatically said yes when Rachel caught sight of a restaurant named Jungle Jelly as they walked to the car in the enormous parking lot. Jungle Jelly sounded disgusting but Rachel wouldn't stop talking about it, so what the hell.

Jungle Jelly turned out to be a cavernous shrieking hellhole where adults were shunted to one side and fed fourteen-dollar plates of nachos and congealed cheese, while hordes of kids tossed themselves into ball pits, climbed alarmingly high net walls, and disappeared into plastic tubes along the drafty dark ceiling. Becky lost Rachel immediately and figured this was another part of the excursion they wouldn't need to be specific about when recapping for Ingrid. She abandoned her table with its untouched food and strolled up and down a kind of catwalk set up alongside the play space. How did parents deal with the gruesome amounts of noise children produced?

"Reba?"

For a split second Becky didn't recognize the name, its connection to her.

"Reba!"

There, on Jungle Jelly's catwalk, like an apparition beamed in from another planet, stood Helen Jonson. Co-owner of Thread + Wax Gallery in Chelsea. In New York City. Becky's mind spun with nausea. Helen was in her mid-forties, less a player herself than embedded in a very tight-knit top art scene. Becky had bought about four major pieces from her over the past six years (including a Bleckner canvas she still owned), and once attended a charity dinner at Helen's table, where she'd donated a thousand dollars to the cause, something about funding the first museum for gay and lesbian art.

Helen pushed her thick black-rimmed glasses up into her salt-and-pepper hair. "Holy god, am I dreaming?"

Becky matched her smile and went in for a smooth double-cheek kiss. In an instant she sized up Helen's look—dark jeans, boots, casual-but-expensive oversized cardigan—and prayed her own ensemble could pass muster. Boxy cotton sweater—from L.L.Bean, oh god!—decent vintage-type pea coat, nondescript corduroys cut tight, thick-heeled loafers from last year.

"What are you doing here?" they both said. Helen pretended to rub her eyes. "Reba Farwell, this is my sister Annabel. She lives in Naperville."

"Unfortunately too close to this nightmare." Annabel, rich blond highlights, slim and sleek, terrifying. Her hand was cool and smooth. "You're in Chicago?"

Becky dodged the question. "Oh, I *know*. I've been trying to decide which is worse, the noise or the food."

The women laughed. "Apparently they serve margaritas in giant sippy cups," Annabel said. "Although the sugar content is probably, you know."

Helen leaned in toward Becky. "So, Reba, are you—"

Just then Rachel whizzed by and smacked the plexiglass below them. She motioned to Becky, *Watch this, watch this!*

"My niece," Becky said, for once grateful for a child's interruption.

"Oh, how old? Annabel has a girl in fifth and a boy in kindergarten."

"Rachel's in preschool." Becky felt proud about that answer.

"Where does she go to—?"

"Jason, *stop* it. Okay. That's one." Becky and Helen paused respectfully to let Annabel shout and gesture across the play space. "Two. I said two! That's two, Jason!" She took off toward the slide area, hair flapping behind her narrow shoulders.

"What happens when she gets to three?" Becky murmured.

"I frankly don't want to find out," Helen said. "To be honest, I'm three days into the visit and already thinking about having my tubes tied. You don't have children yourself, do you?"

Becky watched Rachel climb up a rope, squeezing it between her thighs. There was a pulsing wet warmth in both of her own armpits. "Nope," she said. How to get out of this? "Well. I should probably—"

"I've been meaning to call. Do you have a quick minute? I'm in the middle of this nightmare deal that's hit the skids and . . . Our table is right over there." She cocked her head and smiled sheepishly.

Rachel was slithering through a tube with several other screaming kids. Annabel nowhere to be seen. Becky nodded. "Sure, I have a few minutes."

A forged Balthus painting. Helen had images in her bag and Becky kept her hands remarkably steady as she took what was handed to her, one by one. Helen explained it all, while Annabel and her kids came back to the table and noisily resumed eating cold nachos. She'd been asked to handle the estate sale for an important client's friend and had said yes, sight unseen, as a favor. One of the paintings set off all her alarm bells: a purported early Balthus, sketchy provenance papers, coloring scale all off. Even the client wouldn't vouch for it, despite his obligations to the friend's family. Helen paid for three separate expert evaluations and all agreed: slim to no chance it was a real piece.

"So there you go," Becky said. She hated having the glossy photos of work in front of her, here. What if someone else from Pierson saw them, saw her with them? Also, where was Rachel?

"Unfortunately, that's only the beginning." Helen scooted her chair closer. "I have a buyer who somehow got wind of it during the presale, and he wants it."

"Even though he knows it's a fake?" This was Annabel, who was apparently not ignoring them as Becky had hoped. "What a tool. Go for it. Buyer beware, right?"

"It's not that easy. Reba knows."

Becky nodded, straining to catch sight of Rachel. "You can't have your gallery on that sale record."

"Yeah. It'll come back to haunt us. I can't touch it with a ten-foot pole."

"So call it off." From down the catwalk, she could see Rachel approaching, a bit shy. She tried to smile at the girl.

"God, I wish." Helen took off her glasses and scrubbed at her tangled bangs. "He's made this other sale contingent, and I'm wrapped up in that with about three other galleries. If I pull out I will seriously piss off some big people. Like a round robin of disaster."

Rachel was upon them. "Here's Rachel, so," Becky said, half-rising.

"Wait, here's another chair," Helen said. "Are you hungry, honey? We have tons. I just have to bug your aunt about some business stuff, which is so lame of me . . ."

Becky tried to object but soon Rachel was busily sharing a plate of mini fried cheese sticks, Annabel had included her in another round of lemonade orders for the kids, and she was trapped. She hoped the girl hadn't picked up on the "aunt" comment.

"Duh, why would anyone *want* a fake painting?" one of Annabel's kids said. She reached into the pile of photographs to pull out a blowup of the dirtiest looking one—Balthus's typical awkwardly sprawled preteen girls. Crotch shot centering the image. Rachel craned her head to see, chewing her cheese stick.

"Uh uh." Annabel took the photo away and snapped it back toward Helen. "But yeah, why? Either he's a pervert or it's for the money, I'm assuming. Wants to buy it, then unload it onto someone else, someone unsuspecting."

Helen took back all her images and put them away, slowly. She spoke without looking up. "Maybe, hard to say. There's more at stake than just money. There's prestige, there's leverage, there's the chance to say you made a deal with so-and-so gallery—"

"That's you, my big-city sis."

"Sometimes I think people in this business can't help themselves."

Suddenly all the noise from Jungle Jelly receded into a faraway roar. Becky's arms tingled as Helen continued, now looking around the table. "Something takes hold of someone, like an obsession or a mania. They begin to believe they can and *should* get a particular piece, no matter what. That they of all people were meant to own it. As if they're the only person the rules weren't made for." Helen shrugged; Becky couldn't speak.

"Becky," Rachel asked, tapping her, breaking the moment. "Can I have my QT Pet?"

"Becky!" Helen laughed. "That's cute. Is that what you call your aunt?"

"It's in the car," Becky murmured. She stood up unsteadily,

tugging at Rachel. Tried to form goodbye sentences in the usual social niceties but her voice echoed loud and fake in her own ears.

She avoided Helen's eyes and tried to give some money to Annabel, who refused. Nodded yes to all of Helen's *call me, we should catch up, this was the craziest small-world thing!* Dragged a startled Rachel to the exit.

Not until they were on the highway could she slow her breaths, gain a normal sense of perspective. She hadn't looked too crazy, there at the end, had she? Of course Helen Jonson hadn't tracked her to Jungle Jelly for the explicit purpose of scaring her. Naperville was a wealthy suburb and Becky's art circle was enormous; this had been bound to happen someday. But when would it happen next? She imagined worst-case scenarios of her secret life barging into Pierson: a fellow collector stopping by for poker night with Ken, her New York tailor arriving for a fitting at a Pierson coffee shop, arms full of Versace.

"That girl showed her underwear." Rachel, from the back seat, playing with her panda.

"What?"

"In that picture. She had no pants on."

"Yeah, well. The painter was a dirty old man, and that's what he liked to paint."

Rachel considered this. "Can I get a smoothie?"

"You can—"

"Yay!"

"—*if* we agree that we don't tell your mom about Jungle Jelly. Or the . . . picture you saw." *And the people you met*, she wanted to add, but maybe that was too much? In any case, the kid in this back-seat car seat was happy to agree to any terms for her smoothie.

Rachel soon went back to singing weird little songs to her new stuffie. As Becky made the turns from freeway to small highway, approaching Pierson, she couldn't stop checking the rearview—as if Helen Jonson and her rich housewife sister would have followed her. But it did feel like her own car was pulling a vapor trail, an unwanted trace of that uneasy encounter, into her hometown.

Always coming home to Pierson had seemed safe, impenetrable. Like a floating castle only she could see. But now Becky understood that she had twice the work to do. The way Helen Jonson, of Thread + Wax, had passed a plate of fries to Ingrid's daughter, the angle of her head as she'd spoken the phrase *like an obsession* . . . Becky had never considered the possibility that anyone from New York would find her here. What did Pierson, Illinois, mean to them? Why would they care who Reba Farwell was or where she spent her weekends, as long as her bank drafts cleared?

Stupid idiot. She'd forgotten about plain old curiosity. Nosiness. The bigger she got—and last month's deals had tallied somewhere in the high six figures—the more people would be interested. And if dealers and owners and artists were ever suspicious of her, of where her money came from and whether it was clean, they'd drop her cold. No matter how much she had in RF Capital Development.

20

Pierson
1995

THE DAY BECKY'S ERIC FISCHL arrived she had the gallery assistant who'd accompanied the piece from New York leave it untouched in the Barn's main level. The painting stayed there, crated, for almost a month until a new set of workers and their van came to pick it up. Gone in a resale deal she completed without thinking too much.

The catch to finally getting a Fischl, it turned out, was to completely lose interest in it. Its only value, Becky told herself, was in the name and context, a blue chip that was fading now anyway. What she could keep was the real reward: a more mature sensibility. The type Mac had always touted. That's what real players had.

I should congratulate myself, is what I should do, Becky thought. Standing in the space where the unlooked-at painting had been.

21

Chicago
1996

BECKY GOT SO MANY VOICE messages on the answering service she kept only for art business that she had taken to listening to the most recent one first. She could usually figure out what information she needed for the deal or the issue or the contact without needing to listen to all the recordings that came before. But she listened to every call that came pouring in on October 10, frozen at her desk in Town Hall.

"I can't believe it, even though I knew it was only a matter of time."

"Reba, you were always so dear to him. So, so dear. And if he could only—"

"—meet for coffee. Fuck, even a drink, on a day like this. What he would've wanted, right?"

She hung up and called her service right back, this time punching buttons to find the first message received. It hit her hard, straight in the middle.

"Reba? Mac's gone. Sometime last night, I think. Apparently

203

it was peaceful, so—so—that's something right? Reba, call me. I'm a mess."

Becky slowly replaced the receiver. Mrs. Fletcher called for something, but she was too stunned to respond.

For the rest of the afternoon, she went about her business at the office as usual. She returned a few calls to council members, went down the hall to remind Ken about a memo they needed to revisit, even held a scheduled meeting with Accounts to look over the projected budget for the first quarter of next year. And yet throughout the day the knowledge of Mac's death ribboned through her, a disconcerting blend of regret, sadness, and anger.

The weirdest thing was that she kept picturing exactly how Mac himself would have responded to the news of his own death. "Devastating," he'd say, impeccably mournful, "absolutely *gutting*." But then one flash-second later he'd have that wicked twinkle, ready as ever to get into the gossip, the juicy stories, *the good stuff*. Oh, Mac.

Four days later she was at Four Farthings in Lincoln Park, some kind of ye olde pub that Mac's crowd had never frequented, as far as she could remember. Becky had assumed there would be a reception in the funeral home afterward, where she would stay for a pro forma cup of coffee and then escape. But a mass pilgrimage was hastily organized, even though the old places—the Red Lion, Katerina's—had closed or reopened under boring new management. After the service, a grim affair in a west side funeral house, everyone had hurried out to the sidewalk, bundled up and shivering dramatically in the October chill. Shouting confusedly across open cab doors. Somehow, Becky was swept up.

Now here they were, twenty or so of Mac's cronies, the good-time gang. They drank gin, they drank the cheapest red. They told and retold all the old stories. Becky sat a bit apart, nursing one whiskey. Across the street was a small corner park with a crumbly stone fountain whose pipes were still somehow working in this early cold snap. One gusher of water flung itself up and up, never reaching higher than a foot or so.

Andy Morse, of the Pape Stewart Gallery, tall and stooped and curved down toward her like a floor lamp, had planted himself by her side and wouldn't stop talking. People were selling again, buying, big deals and bigger offers. Last week the starting bid on a Jasper Johns actually began at the reserve *and the whole room applauded*.

He wasn't the only one here tonight marveling, nervously laughing about the near disaster. They were once again moving art and money, if in a newly superstitious way. *Too bad Mac would never know how it came back,* they said. Hoisting a rare somber glass.

He'd known, Becky thought. Even though she'd heard he'd been foggy, in and out of the hospital for months, he would have known that the market would come back.

Andy talked on but Becky was thinking about Mac's funeral, toward the beginning of the service, when those in attendance had finally stopped whispering, began to pay attention to the priest at the altar. Becky, though, in her back row, was still craning her neck. Mel, Christophe, Annette, Jon and Allan, Wayne, even Carole P. All there, dressed to the hilt, faces suitably downcast. A full house. So why did she feel like people were missing? Extra chairs had been set up in the aisles, each row filled, flower arrangements the size of small trees on either side of the polished casket.

Mac would have been pleased by the handful of young men—or men shooting for young—with wet faces and heaving shoulders, bravely holding back their sobs. What was this nagging unease?

It wasn't until the third Latin prayer that she realized no one was missing, and that was the source of the strange feeling. Gone was that curious watchful tension, a constant waiting to see who would next push through the door at Yoshi's Café. Or, later, into her own lost Chicago *pied-à-terre*. Nobody's name to learn, no angling for a way in. No gossip, no backstory, no fear she'd embarrass herself. No more delicious hope each time the doorman called up.

As the priest intoned the phrases of a dead language Becky sat back against her pew and considered the facts: One, it was possible to become bored by this very group of people she had once desperately ached to join, this glittering appendage she'd assumed would be as endlessly fascinating as their art. Two, she was bored.

Huh. She'd been right to pull the plug on that condo. On Chicago. Though at the time she'd thought her problem was the money. To distract herself from the skitter of fear edging the feeling of boredom, she examined the program in her lap. "In Memory of Frederick 'Mac' Palliser, Beloved Friend, Brother, Uncle." Handsomely produced, the pages included not only the schedule of readers and hymns, but quotes from friends and colleagues praising Mac as a bon vivant, an art appreciator with a world-class collection, a generous mentor to countless bereaved followers. Becky skipped over all that. The last two pages displayed some of Mac's "favorite works" and artists he'd "championed," leaving as his legacy the discovery and nurturing of talent that would have been otherwise overlooked.

There in the middle of the page was a reproduction of Peter Wand's *Wall, in Blues*, one from the series that had shown at the

Gagosian, sold out instantly. Becky studied the image and waited to see if the hurt would reemerge.

They had still seen each other after the confrontation in his office, of course. At shows, at parties, even at the same dinner tables sometimes. At each encounter Becky was ferociously friendly, hailing and dismissing Mac in a firestorm of fast-talking energy. By then he was more and more a minor part of her circle, which had spread to other networks and other cities with other flamboyant figures at their centers. And over time the pain of that first betrayal lessened, under the armor of her furiously smiling facade, until Mac might have guessed that it had evaporated.

In the funeral home, staring hard at Wand's *Wall, in Blues*, Becky could just barely feel it there. Shellacked by pearly hardness, but a grain of hurt inside, nonetheless.

"I've been thinking about your Picabia sketch," Andy Morse said, as if casually. He meant the piece included in the most recent packet of photos Becky regularly sent out to her mailing list, offering works she was ready to sell. "Forty by twenty centimeters, is it? I have—"

"Forty-four," Becky corrected. Two people walked quickly along the sidewalk, arms linked, passing the fountain without a glance.

"—a client who is very interested in the Transparencies series."

"I'm listening." Did those night walkers notice the fountain, wonder why it was still on this late in the season? What did they think of its water's perpetual *bloop bloop* upward thrust, never quite making it high enough?

Andy Morse, pleased, started at four thousand. He'd love to do more, but without the client's prior knowledge he couldn't— Not that it wasn't a lovely picture, but the composition of woman and horse didn't have quite the same— Also she must have noticed a slight fading near the—

Becky said eight. Morse protested gallantly. She let him do more of his pitch, work up his giant exhaling effort about where he could top out—presuming client's approval, of course—knowing all the while what she'd take and what they'd end on. He said $4,999, she said eight. They shook on $7,400, Morse much less happy to do so than Becky, who'd paid five thousand for the sketch less than a year ago. All her deals went like this now, a win for her and a loss for the other party. Wait until they saw what she had planned for next year. Or the year after, if she could wait that long.

Becky clinked her glass against Morse's—"To celebrate!" he said, and then, chastened, "to Mac, rather"—and thought about her profit. She had gotten two thousand and four hundred dollars of pleasure from the small piece, yes, in these months it had hung on a side wall in her Art Barn, next to a funny Botero oil and above a Franke 3D wall piece. But what she'd gained was potential for a much greater degree of pleasure, the one she was tasting now: thousands of dollars of possibility, of other pieces, future works, the unknown.

Becky shivered. Her untouched drink was melting icily against her cold palm. For some reason she couldn't bear to look at that fountain anymore.

A burst of shouts and laughter from the group in the banquette. She met eyes with Morse, both of them acknowledging the impropriety, and the inevitableness. "It's awful of me, doing a bit of business on a day like today," he offered. He was decent, she knew.

"He would have approved."

"True. I'd better be off." They shook awkwardly. "Oh. Right." Andy paused. "Are you set up for getting e-mails on your computer? A bit poncy but—"

"Just leave a message on my service. I'll call you back."

"Well, for the invoice I mean. We've moved to routing all billing through the computer. Vanessa swears everyone is switching over."

Becky forced herself to let go of the cold glass.

"Much easier to keep track, apparently." Morse put his own glass down on a nearby radiator. "All the dollars, where they go, et cetera. Or so they tell me. I'm an old fart. Lovely to see you."

E-mail. Over the next few minutes as Becky extricated herself from the group—endless maudlin goodbyes and *we never see you anymore*—the term pinged her brain. E-mail. E-mail?

Becky stalked the tiny corner park, forcing herself around the small loop over and over in the cold and dark. She tried to remember what the computer repair guy had said some weeks ago, in the office, half-hidden under Mrs. Fletcher's desk, connecting the cables for her new IBM. Something about how they could send messages back and forth to each other, from Becky's computer to Mrs. Fletcher's new one. That's interesting, Becky had said, wanting him to get on with it. As if she and her sixty-year-old secretary needed to type each other computer letters! Mrs. Fletcher hovered, deeply unhappy about the man poking around under her desk, that dark secret cove where she kept her ancient slip-ons.

E-mail was supposed to be a tedious new feature of the office, of Town Hall, like a rearranged filing system or a change in the staffing schedule. She hadn't thought twice about it after the repair guy plugged everything in and left the bill. Pape Stewart would e-mail a sale agreement to her?

"But they can't," she said out loud, over the witless fountain gurgle. She didn't have e-mail! Or would it just show up on her computer screen at work, right in the middle of her notes for the budget meeting? "I won't get it," she told the fountain. But of course she would. With a sinking heart Becky saw the inevitable encroaching of computers, giant calculators that would never forget a number. How this would delight Ken, who always bragged about his car phone, and how soon enough all the computers, his, hers, and even Mrs. Fletcher's, would be linked up together.

Goddamn it goddamn it god*damn* it. Why did everything have to get harder, all the time? She'd hung on through the worst of the art market plunge, losing values on all her best pieces, losing her condo . . . Those shitheads still inside Four Farthings whimpering about flat prices had no idea what she'd had to do! Could they gather here in the cold fountain spray and comprehend even one percent of what she had accomplished against the odds, the massive undertaking that was her reinvention of what *ARTnews* called "a surprisingly stellar private collection," did they even have the ability to understand what kind of heroics and magic and nineteen-hour days it had taken to turn things around, financially and logistically?

Becky screamed, a wordless howl, and attacked the fountain. Kicking at its crumbling stone, slapping the foul-smelling water with her Fendi purse.

Anyone with half a brain cell would admit that what she'd done, go from art world nobody to settled perch with fresh capital, all on her own, no stable of assistants, no backing or insurance or advice from trusted elders, no *men*, was miraculous. Couldn't everyone just get out of her fucking way?

"E-mail?" she screeched. Hitting and kicking and splashing. A crowd was gathering at the window of Four Farthings. "*E-mail?*"

Hours later, from the Marriott on Michigan, she described the scene to Ingrid, minus, of course, Mac's after-party, Andy Morse, and the person who shouted from a condo next to the fountain park, "We just called the cops." Actually, all she told Ingrid was that an unbearably long management conference after-party had ended up at a bar in a neighborhood she didn't know. And that some banker jerk stole her cab right in front of her—*Dick*, Ingrid whispered sleepily—so she momentarily went off on a park fountain. Ruining her purse. Her thousand-dollar purse, she did not say.

In truth, once she could collect herself she'd scuttled over to Lincoln and found a cab like magic. Shook with cold all the way to the hotel, where her gold card member status made checking in after midnight—with no luggage and sewer-splashed hair—swift, no questions asked. Becky had let her fear and frustration drain away in a hot shower. She made tea with the tiny plastic hot water machine and then did what she always did when she felt small and embarrassed: called Ingrid.

Now under the covers in the dark hotel room, she curled on her side and listened to Ingrid's yawn-filled recounting of her day: horrible kids' party run by horrible mom who made everyone take off their shoes in her house and only served one small square of pizza per kid, nothing for adults except iced tea, and whose daughter's cake was *whole wheat*, I mean who does that? We were all eyeing each other like, this girl's headed straight for an eating disorder.

Becky expressed sufficient outrage in *hmm*s and *ugh*s. Every sentence from Ingrid a balm for her anxious brain. She could picture Ingrid's exact facial expression as she prodded the slice of dud hippie cake with a plastic fork. Soon there were long gaps in Ingrid's part of the conversation, a steady slow breathing that sounded like sleep, but Becky, wide awake, didn't want to end the call. She kept the receiver close to her face, a thin invisible tether to a world so much farther away than the hundred miles between them. So many things she wanted to do for Ingrid. A new car to replace that rattletrap Hyundai. A massage at the new day spa in town. Or a "salt scrub," whatever awfulness that was. Spanish tutor for Rachel, extra art classes that Ingrid always had to say no to. And whatever would help with TJ. This was the trickiest area: Ingrid kept such a lockdown on his treatment and education, cutting Becky off at every turn when she made the slightest suggestion for private this or big-city that. Worst of all was her banding together with all the other moms whose kids had similar conditions, organizing to demand more from the public school, coordinating campaigns to push for accessibility, privacy, acceptance. If she'd only let Becky take care of things her way!

After a while Becky softly hung up the phone. It was nearly 3 am but she had a new kind of clear energy, a returned confidence in her own wiliness. She didn't know about the World Wide Web but she knew one thing: Andy Morse and his computer mail sure as shit weren't going to be what brought her down. She picked up the receiver and dialed Ken at the office, waiting impatiently for his voice mail message to finish.

"Hi, it's me. Few thoughts, we can discuss on Monday." She

left messages like this frequently, on her own machine as well as others, an all-hours to-do list that probably wasn't anyone's favorite habit of hers. "Let's push the Springfield call to later in the week. I heard Grigson's out of town until midweek and it's pointless to talk to anyone else. About the situation with what's-his-face, I agree, it isn't working out. Let's have Barb meet with him once more, making sure to document the—" On and on she went, pretending to list items in random order, tossing off solutions as they came to her. Then, when she thought she could say it in sufficiently casual tones, she threw in: "Oh, and I've been kicking around some more thoughts about technology in the office. You may be right that we need to make a move here." Easygoing, happy to help out, Becky offered to form an exploratory committee—she'd head it up, of course—to investigate Internet options, get some pricing plans.

She moved on to a few other quick matters, scooching down farther under the covers and sliding the towel off her now-dried hair. Getting involved never failed. Enough of a flurry of proposals, agreements, ideas, and plans could always deflect attention from what she didn't want others to look at.

She couldn't know in the Marriott that night the exact way she'd adapt the Activity to the Internet, but Becky as usual could see the vague shapes of a future solution to a present problem. In this case, she would end up keeping the basic structure of invoices and diverting, only what used to be "paperwork" would become bills created on Becky's home computer and e-mailed to herself, via a series of fake addresses, from a separate server. Once you got the hang of it, it was the same as everything else she'd handled. Bank drafts would feed into RF Capital smoothly, and she'd make sure to link enough government business stops in between so that by the time the money reached its final destination it had been swished clean. She would pay her credit card bills by check as long as she could, but even when that switched over to online, she'd make sure her tracks were as covered by the computer as they had been by typewriters.

"Fine, then. See you Monday." Finishing her voice mail to Ken, she hung up with a satisfying *clunk*. Now she could sleep. They'd have to use more than new-model computers to take her down. She was Becky Farwell, quicksilver, out-thinker, king.

22

Pierson
Milan, Paris
Pierson
1997–1998

KEN WAS NOTORIOUS FOR HIS attention fluctuations. Though no one at Town Hall doubted his energy and commitment, at times he visibly wilted under the strain of the job, the deficit, the constant barrage of bad budget news.

"Golden boys weren't meant for this," was Ingrid's take.

"It's the twins," Becky said. "Can you imagine coming home to that amount of whining, crying, the noise and the mess and the—"

"Gee, Becky. No, I can't possibly contemplate what that kind of challenge and exhaustion would look like."

Becky subsided.

Sometimes in meetings you got the sense that Ken was only half-present, listening but not really, adding oddly off-tone filler phrases like "now you're talking" after an underling delivered some boring update. You could catch him twirling a pen for minutes on minutes, in a helicopter way he must have perfected in junior high school: flicking it with his forefinger to spin around the base of his thumb. It drove Becky crazy.

But she could never get comfortable with his dreamy out-of-it mode because the other half of the time he went super mayor on all of them: bursting with energy, revisiting plans and projects from months ago, remembering details and asking for revisions. Aides would scatter, the janitor sigh. Everyone stayed late, doubled their output. No one was safe when Ken revved his engine full speed.

One thing Ken never interfered with was Becky's careful sorting of the mail. By now she'd been picking up Town Hall mail for years, letting everyone believe it was a kind of quirk, part of her rock-solid morning routine: super-sized coffee at Smiley's, post office as they were unlocking, pulling into her Town Hall spot by 9:30 latest. No one saw the essential step in between, where she culled the mail for any Midwest Credit Union or any other bank envelopes related to the Activity and swept them into an unmarked beat-up accordion file that lived under the passenger seat of her car. Currently she owed Pierson around three million. But holding steady! And she would close it, thanks to a plan in the works that would actually take advantage of the art market's plunge and recovery.

Around this time Becky began to get up earlier and add more driving to her morning rounds. She liked it. She liked spiraling in widening circles through town, through the outskirts along Route 4, even picking up interstate connector 52 to go by one of the southeastern farms by the airport. In town she'd drop gears mid-turn, because she knew before it came into view how steep the hill on Nachusa was, or the way the pavement had tree-buckled on Brinton Ave by the river. She could do all of it, shift and decelerate and meet a stop sign with one perfect beat of motionlessness, before zooming on, while she sang along with Pam Tillis or Trisha Yearwood. Silently she'd run through a kind of tour monologue, touching on one house or the next, remembering for herself who used to live there and who before that, and what church they went to, and which kids had raised hell and where someone's pickup had run right over someone else's flower bed on which year's July Fourth, make that early-morning July fifth.

As if someone else were in the car with her (no one else was ever in the car), hanging on her every word, the scandals and the sorrows. Becky peering above the steering wheel or craning her head back as the landscape flashed by. At times muttering questions and then correcting herself, occasionally laughing when she lit on a particularly juicy anecdote.

Every so often she'd wind up back at County Road M, pulling up in front, two wheels in the gully. Get out and stand against the open car door, arms and chin resting on the roof panel. The sun would be pushing up from the wide empty field across the roadway behind her, warming her shoulders and neck, glinting opaque off the farmhouse's front windows.

On these drives she passed dozens of barns owned by neighbors and strangers: tall prairies, low milking, double level, hay door, livery style. How many, Becky wondered, still held mowers and seeders bought from her father?

Even parked directly in front of their property—her property, she still had to remind herself—she couldn't get a sightline on her own barn. It pleased her to linger out front anyway, on those early mornings. Reassuring herself of what couldn't be seen or known or even guessed at. Just another barn. After a few moments she'd tap her car, *all right, so that's that,* one more errand ticked off the list. Time to pick up the mail and start the day's work.

Jessa took Becky to the European fashion shows for two weeks at the end of February, 1997. Becky told Town Hall simply that she was on vacation out of the country—Ken was too frazzled to inquire much further, and in any case the office was getting used to Becky's odd hours, often away for days at a time, then working straight through several weekends. To Ingrid, she told a closer version of the truth: Europe, with a friend who also liked art, on her dime.

They were in Milan for Gucci, McQueen, Margiela—plus a host of smaller group shows—and then went to Paris for Dior, Balenciaga, and a Comme des Garçons set that included other-worldly garments by Rei Kawakubo, stuffed in odd lumps and elongated in strange places, that seemed made for beings other than humans. Jessa grimaced and sighed throughout, but Becky was so entranced she had tears in her eyes.

"That show was ridiculous," Jessa said crisply, over tea after. "Those clothes were a gimmick and anti-woman." Jessa didn't drink, not a drop, and not because she was in AA either. She just couldn't stand the stuff and never had. So in Italy they sampled espresso in every hotel and café, and in Paris Jessa brought Becky to exquisite, jewel-box teahouses where they drank tisanes from paper-thin bone china.

"Don't you wonder what they would feel like, though? To

wear?" Becky's head was still swirling: the model swathed in a fire-engine-red sheath with a pillow curving around her hip. The one in marigold with a stuffed tail!

"No, I do not. And I'd throw myself in front of you if you tried to buy something from that line."

"Oh, *buying*," Becky scoffed. You couldn't actually *buy* those pieces. (Could you?)

In terms of buying, she mostly lived vicariously through Jessa, who came regularly to "the shows" and was one of those women who bought "for the season"—a series of shockingly well-made outfits for day and night, for every occasion. Becky followed her to fittings and showings and underwear measurements, she took deliveries at their hotels and hung bags on top of garment bags in her own closets when Jessa's overflowed. She herself bought sparingly but expensively (it was impossible to buy other than expensively): a pair of softly gleaming McQueen boots that came to just above her knees; a Prada trench in muddy green; and a white pantsuit by Ann Demeulemeester that made her look, Jessa said, like an angel in a rock-and-roll band.

The other thing Becky liked about Jessa was that she never once tried to set her up. In fact, they rarely talked about love or sex at all, which was fine by Becky since those topics made her squirm. And she detected a slight pain in Jessa every time her husband came up, so she steered the conversation quickly away whenever that happened.

Midway across the ocean on their night flight from Paris, Becky woke next to Jessa frowning in sleep, shoulders hunched and arms tightly folded. She quietly unlocked her seat belt and reached into Jessa's bag on the floor, then carefully draped the pashmina across the older woman. Jessa gave a breathy sigh and turned her head the other way.

Pierson High School's track was a disgrace: pitted, torn up, hopelessly out of compliance with the sport association's requirements. So on Memorial Day weekend, Becky led a twenty-four-hour relay to raise awareness and funds for the track team—after quietly seeding the initial $10,000 herself.

They had a good crowd throughout the day, and even the first part of the night went smoothly: the teenagers loved running laps in the dark, hooting across the track, and chowing down on snacks in between turns. But as it got later, people slipped away. Flashlights dropped to the grass, the volunteer who was keeping track of laps on a borrowed whiteboard disappeared to the porta-potty and didn't come back. Becky, fueled by coffee in a thermos, went around nudging drowsy teenagers in sleeping bags, cajoling parents who were over it, and—worst of all—taking turns with the baton herself. Huffing around the track at 3 am was not how she'd envisioned this night.

Luckily, by dawn some energy returned to their small group, thanks to reinforcements by parents and younger siblings who showed up with hot chocolate and boxes of doughnuts. The kids set up some quickie 4 x 100 relays, which sped things along. And as Becky had arranged, the local photographer came for the big finish at noon, complete with about half the school band (on summer practice hours), a bunch of donated hoagies and Gatorade, and a grateful speech by the high school track coach. All of it raised a couple thousand more for the leveling and resurfacing. They really needed a new set of stands too. So Becky would still quietly need to make up the difference later.

Still, it was good for morale. There would be a nice article and some great photos. And she even might have lost a couple pounds, given all that running. Becky lounged on the grass with an ice pack under her achy Achilles tendon, watching little kids race each other down the home stretch, straining like Olympians to break the tape.

In November 1997, Becky took $27,000. In December, $38,550. And in January 1998, she took $52,243.

Pierson's deficit in 1997 ran to $532,000. Additional cuts the council announced over two budget seasons included Police Department K9 purchases ($6,000), Sewers and Sidewalks ($10,000), Fire Department radio equipment ($1,000), and the park cemetery ($2,000). The local swimming pool stayed dry for the third year in a row.

It couldn't be helped. Still, it hurt Becky to see the blows Pierson kept taking, and in a bizarre way it hurt her when no one figured out what was going on. Did no one love this town the way she did? Enough to pay attention, to dig deep for answers? Every budget they didn't investigate made her disappointed—angry, even—on their behalf.

She had created a series of private rules, a form of tithing. For every dollar she took, ten percent had to go back into the town in some way—through profits she made, or through her own personal account, or through time and energy and her own ingenuity. Also, if any of her acquired pieces shot up in value, ten percent of that had to go back into Pierson, even if she didn't sell. (That was a killer, given the market rebound.) Whenever Ken had that look—that beaten-down look—she took on extra work to lighten his load, and she had to find a way to pass the credit on to someone else. Whenever a storefront closed on Main, she redirected all her spending to the other businesses on that street, buying unused tanning hours and all sorts of hardware products she didn't need. At the end of every Friday she checked the total in RF Capital and whatever the cents number was—sixteen, ninety-four, thirty— that's how many good deeds she had to do the following workweek for coworkers and neighbors. Compliments, advice, plum assignments, picking up tabs at restaurants and bars, even leaving anonymous bags of groceries on front porches.

But this piecemeal approach was nothing more than a finger in the dike, she knew. If she could only catch her breath and have some time to *think*, she could finish putting it together, the big plan—the major sale, the deal of all deals—that would let her pay it all back. New York, it was going to happen in New York. One fell swoop, and it would be over.

23

New York City
1999

BECKY WALKED INTO BALTHAZAR THE biggest winner of the night, and everyone knew it. She'd arrived on the late side, half by design and half because of some consignor paperwork and conversations with officials at Christie's. In the cab ride downtown from Rockefeller Center she'd had plenty of time to revel in her success and also to practice, in the darkened back seat, the exact faux-modest tilt of the head she'd execute as congratulations burst forth from all quarters of New York's hottest restaurant.

Her entrance didn't disappoint. One well-judged pause at the host stand allowed everyone in the bar to turn and see her: Reba Farwell, in a YSL black silk suit and four-inch Jimmy Choos, her shining red hair swept to the side and tumbling down to one shoulder. The art crowd was well into the night's dissection of auction minutiae, and several people at the bar did, in fact, break out into light applause. Gratified, Becky waved them off. Quickly, the maître d' ushered her toward the back of the room, where a large group buzzed anxiously around a table. She took her time, though,

223

in that glorious walk across the golden-lit restaurant, lightly touching red leather banquettes as she passed them, glimpsing all the beautiful people doubled in burnished mirrors tipped from the walls. Heads turned, gazes lingered appreciatively, voices murmured. Becky soaked in every iota. She wanted that walk to last forever.

When Becky finally arrived at the table full of top dealers and collectors, Waverly Brant announced, "Holy shite-a-mighty, the conquering hero." Her hoarse British accent lifted above the fray. "Now we know who gets the bill!"

People laughed and lifted their champagne glasses her way. One was thrust into Becky's hand. Two young blondes gushed about her shoes, obliging her to lift a silky pant leg so they could get a better look. David and Joan, art advisers for Merrill, called out warm congratulations. Sebastian from that Luxembourg consultant firm, Gail and her husband (buyers from LA), and that one TV producer whose name Becky could never remember were all effusive with praise. Also crammed in their banquette area were dealers and collectors Becky knew by face but had never met, and some whom she recognized from the front section tonight at Christie's. These people watched her curiously, half-smiling, not as effusive as Becky's friends.

While she went through the double-kisses and breathless thank-yous and reciprocal compliments, Becky eyed out further into the room. Where were the other pockets, the more exclusive groups, the deeper sources of power? She thought she caught a few other potentials: smaller groupings, sedate, mostly male. Too secluded and far away for her to determine exactly who they were.

"You topped out over five hundred," Waverly said, yanking Becky down to a seat next to her. "Did you or didn't you?"

"Oh, well," Becky demurred. You didn't spill that easily, in front of this many people pretending not to listen.

"Six hundred? Did you make six hundred percent, you bloody bitch? Do I even want to fucking know?"

"You don't want to fucking know," Becky said, grinning. Her eight works tonight had each nearly doubled their reserve, and all had topped out far over the maximum estimate. She'd bought them in fall of 1990, at the market's nadir, for about five hundred each. Given tonight's nine hundred percent profit, and after the seller's commission and various fees for things like transportation and insurance, Becky's net tonight was just under three million dollars. It was going to set her free, that glorious sum. Pierson would get it all and her great and ongoing debt would be canceled.

As the champagne went around again, and their group swelled and thinned, the talk was mostly of the single mega sales, the O'Keeffe oil on board that went for nearly a million, the puzzlingly comparable two Robinson Leigh lots with wildly differing outcomes, and, of course, the night's meteor moment, an Andrew Wyeth tempera that hammered at six million, three hundred thousand, after ten full minutes of agonized bidding. The room had erupted at that, of course.

Becky—*no, she didn't need a menu*—took it all in and reflected gratefully that her own big night was carefully submerged under these standout moments. As usual, the urge to trumpet her successes from Lafayette Street to the goddamn Hudson River fought with the need to stay under the radar. This inner circle knew what it meant to resell at nearly one thousand percent and Becky had to be content with that, even if the conversation had by now flowed on to failed sales and who was slipping.

Plus, not everyone looked kindly on what she'd done tonight.

"I hadn't realized you were collecting in Minimalism," one acquaintance had said to her just as they were taking their seats at the auction. The woman had spoken pleasantly enough, but had leaned over to speak in a way that read as pointed. Becky's lots, four paintings by Susan Tillman and four sketches by Tony Smith, stirred talk after Christie's reproduced them in the catalogue and several preview reports had mentioned the "little known and unseen" works that added surprising fresh value to both artists' oeuvres. The works were unseen because Becky had held them for nine years waiting for this peak moment. She'd bounced two checks in the process of buying them, but the dealers, so grateful at the time for any little pittance, let her scrape up the money and come back. Over the years she'd carefully monitored sales and figures for Minimalist work, she'd read articles and visited galleries and kept tallies of who was showing where. Often, she'd been tempted to break up the groups and sell the pieces separately, especially in the dicey years of building the Art Barn, when her bills threatened to swamp her. Once she'd even said yes to a particular offer for one of the Smiths, only to call it off the next day, raising the wrath of a pissed-off buyer who hadn't done business with her since. But Becky ultimately heeded her inner call to wait, to hold on, to keep the pieces together. She was nothing if not tough and patient. (Also mutable and recklessly impulsive.)

If only Jessa were here tonight. The only one who'd known for some time what Becky was planning, she was off to St. John for most of the winter, though she'd had an orchid delivered to Becky's hotel with an attached note reading "Git 'er done & then we celebrate."

While Waverly told a long story about running into Jeff Koons's ex-wife (and art partner, and former porn star) in a restaurant in

Rome—most of them had heard this one before, many times—Becky scanned the room, then pretended to step away to check her phone for messages. If possible, the restaurant was even busier than an hour ago: waiters slid nimbly between tables, lifting high trays loaded with glassware. Women's laughter rippled across the room, everyone hunched over giant plates of steak frites. Becky vaguely recognized one of the sleek petite stars of *Sex and the City*, a show she never watched and a phrase she found annoying. Also a musician, young and bald, whose electronica hits were all over the radio, even in Pierson. She caught the invisible glow around them, the hovering servers, the vibrating awareness of nearby diners.

Becky took a roundabout way to the ladies' room, all the better to see and be seen. The powder room was crammed, and after washing her hands Becky had to elbow her way to some mirror space. Annoyed at the way her jacket tugged at her arms when fixing her hair, she shrugged it off, to instant gasps and shrieks of approval from the row of women: As per the stylist's firm instructions, Becky wore her YSL sheer blouse as designed—with no undergarments whatsoever. She laughed appreciatively and did a little shimmy in response, then, jacket on, she made herself go back to her group. A thread of disappointment unraveled—was this to be it, then? No one else to find? There had been talk of John Currin and Rachel Feinstein, and their people, coming tonight. But it appeared only the usuals were here. Had the evening's peak already passed?

Back with her rowdy group, Becky drank more and listened in and stewed. Darker thoughts began to descend: nine hundred percent profit was something, but why couldn't it have been one thousand percent? *One thousand percent*, now that had a ring to it. Also, as far as she could tell, the buyers of her lots weren't anyone of note, and the auctioneer had rushed to hammer on one of the Tillmans. Could have squeezed another ten percent for sure.

She also had a shaky developing awareness that her windfall wouldn't be enough to save Pierson. Not yet, not entirely. The cash she'd acquire in exactly thirty-five days, as stipulated in her consignor contract, would first take a brutal percentage hit for taxes, devastating no matter how good the deal. Next she'd have to take care of several of the Art Barn's builders who had allowed her a line of credit, now long due. Also American Express Gold had called twice last week, which meant that the other cards were full and at their limit. She'd bought pieces on agreement, there were bills for shipping, and certainly half a dozen other pressing claims on the money. All of that took priority over Pierson, Becky realized. For her own safety.

After that, what was going to be left? At the end of the last quarter, Pierson's total deficit was at nearly three million dollars. Becky had imagined she'd plug so much back in from this win— carefully, strategically—that she could bring them up to even.

For some time a woman's voice had been building, over and above the restaurant's din. Becky became aware of it only when she realized the woman was talking to *her*. Or at her. Shouting, almost, in a half-laughing way that bordered on hysterical: "And she just *sits* there, la di da, acting like nothing. Like nothing!"

Becky stared up in shock. "I'm sorry, do I—"

The woman was in her late fifties, well dressed but clearly drunk. Red-faced and wet-mouthed. Pushing back at friends who were desperately trying to tug her away. "What did you want with those pieces? You flipped them without a—"

A male companion took the woman's arm, spoke sternly close to her ear.

"I don't care. I don't care!"

"Oh dear," Waverly murmured.

One of the woman's friends leaned past the fracas to whisper to Becky. "One of her good good friends owned Madcabout Gallery, where you bought the Tillmans. They closed the next year. Anyway, I'm very—"

"I didn't flip anything!" Becky said this first to the woman accosting her, and then to the table at large. "Those pieces—"

"Don't explain yourself," Waverly exclaimed. "Piss off now, darling."

"I hope you're happy with yourself," the drunken woman spat. Some people laughed.

The maître d' arrived, the woman was drawn away by her friends, and Becky tried to calm her thudding heart.

"Bye bye," Waverly sang. A sympathetic stranger leaned over to ask Becky if she was all right. The maître d' came over to apologize. *I'm fine. Please, it's fine.* How had her triumphant night gone awry? Everyone was now staring at her, but for the wrong reasons.

After a few jokes—*That lady had forty pounds on our Reba, it wouldn't have gone one round!*—people moved on. The party swallowed up the moment and soon it seemed as if it had never happened.

Except Becky felt she sensed a change. No longer was her group waiting for her comments, response, insight on whatever the topic was. They'd split apart into twos and threes, gathering on the bench or standing nearby. Were they talking about her? Were they reflecting that she had, in fact, flipped those works in an ugly way? That she was a speculator, an investor? Or worst, an outsider.

"Horseshit." This from grizzled Jimmy Roth, who dragged a chair up to her. "Hope you weren't taking any of that seriously."

"No, I don't think so. But—"

"Nobody likes that kind of resale profit. Doesn't look good for everyone who came before. Don't worry if you get the cold shoulder. They'll come back around."

"All right," Becky said uneasily. Who did he mean by *they*?

"I gotta push off. But I'll call you, next week. Couple ideas we can maybe get together on. Will you be back at Christie's next month for the Continental silver? I'm hearing a lot of talk about the preview. Why don't we take a stroll through it, put our heads together on a few offers?"

"Continental silver. That's . . . antiques."

"Bet your ass it is. Furniture and decorative arts, that's where the real money is. If you know what you're about. I'll call you."

Jimmy Roth patted Becky on the shoulder and snaked his way out of the restaurant. For some time Becky couldn't move. He thought she wanted to buy and sell turn-of-the-century tea services. Snuff boxes. Grapefruit spoons.

When she came to herself Waverly was gone and the table was filled by people she didn't know. Becky caught herself tearing up, woozy from lack of sleep and all the champagne. And from hunger; she hadn't eaten all day. Not a single entrée had come for this table, which didn't surprise her; she knew that power move of never eating in front of people you did business with. She'd used it a hundred times, showing up for lunches and asking only for water with lemon.

"Excuse me," she called sharply, stopping a waiter in his tracks. "Menu, please. And can you lay a place setting . . . there." She pointed to a round corner table with a view out the window.

As soon as she was resettled, water and silverware, a fresh napkin snapped out and laid on her lap, Becky began to place her order. First she wanted to hear about the oysters, Blue Point and West Point and Du Jour. Half a dozen, please, with an icy martini, gin, twist.

Out on Spring Street couples passed by, going east, going west. A man lounged against the bodega and smoked cigarette after cigarette. People came up from the subway stop, went down into the subway stop.

Becky ordered wine, ordered salad, ordered the braised short ribs. She cut careful bites and chewed slowly. She had cheese with the last of her wine and a glass of Muscat with her caramelized banana ricotta tart.

She paid the check and added a thirty percent tip. And then she stood, took off her jacket, and walked the length of the restaurant in her see-through blouse, nipples hard against the soft sheer fabric.

Outside in the windy New York night, she reluctantly put her jacket back on. In the restaurant's small foyer had been a basket with cellophane-wrapped cookies and she'd rifled through to find the best-looking one. She planned to eat it in the cab.

24

Pierson
2000

"THIS IS FOR *FLATS*," BECKY told a middle-schooler, yanking away the bin before the girl could dump in an armload of buckled low-heel loafers that someone should have purged from her closet a decade ago. "Don't you know what flats are?"

"They're like party shoes?"

"They are not 'like' party shoes, you mean they are a *type* of party shoe. But flat! These have a heel." Becky took away one of the girl's horrible old-lady loafers to show her. "And they're not party shoes. Put them in women's casual." She pointed with her elbow to a table across the room.

Ingrid looked up from a mountain of tangled dirty sneakers. "Pretty sure we don't have to subdivide by kingdom, phylum, species."

"If we do this, we're doing it right." It was a gloomy October Saturday, their second year organizing the Sole2Sole shoe donation drive, and both Becky and Ingrid only now remembered why last year they'd sworn not to do this event again. A low-level smell filled the church basement, made worse by the humid rain smacking at the few and ancient windows. Ingrid had brought muffins, but even the kids turned them down. Senior citizens and PTA moms grimly dumped out box after box of used shoes into a growing hill in the middle of the room.

TJ whirled from bin to bin, carrying one light-up sneaker protectively. As he came close to Becky she fished around in the sneaker bin, found the matching shoe and held it out to him. TJ took it with a grin that made Becky reflexively smile back.

Becky felt uncharacteristically lighthearted. Last year's Christie's money was long gone. Had flown away with startling rapidity. Still, after taking care of the expenses she couldn't put off, she'd had 75K to slip into the pension fund to make her feel, if not clean or absolved, at least a little bit better. Now she was back to basics on a smaller scale: take some, buy and sell some, plug some back in where she could. Keeping it tight to the line.

Which reminded her, all day yesterday she'd meant to drive into Chicago, pick up a check that would cover what was a pretty ugly hole in the town's Operations account. An oversight. She wasn't usually sloppy. But with the shoe drive, one thing and then another kept popping up at the office and she hadn't been able to sneak away. It would have to be next week. She could drive up Monday, get the check deposited before Tuesday's finance meeting.

"Five o'clock, okay?" Ingrid said, more cheerful than the host of a nine-year-old girl's surprise sleepover should be. "You promise? Neil'll be wrangling the grill and what are the odds this sketchy magician shows up shit-faced. Oops." She glanced at a nearby retiree. "I really need help with the food. And the favor bags. And the games."

"Isn't Rachel too old for a magician?"

Ingrid yanked one Velcroed tennis shoe unstuck from its mate. "I don't think some rent-a-clown is going to knock her socks off, but it's the best I could do. With all that's going on, I want to make her feel special."

"Makes sense." Becky snapped a plastic lid onto a box filled with sorted shoes, hoping Ingrid wouldn't trip into the latest in the school funding saga. Most of the other families Ingrid had joined up with this time weren't even from Pierson! Ingrid had a knack for borrowing other people's troubles.

"Wait a minute. You brought these, didn't you?" Ingrid held up a pair of high heels and waved them at her. She had recently taken up knitting—*it's supposed to be soothing*, she said, *for fuck's sake*—and now went everywhere festooned in an acrylic scarf, no matter that it hadn't dropped below fifty degrees yet and most people still had potted plants outside. Today's scarf was extra-long, brown and cream, made with a loose sort of weave, so that the whole thing resembled a fisherman's net tossed over her friend's soft rounded body.

"These aren't even worn, you dummy," Ingrid said, examining the slingback Manolos. "They must have cost, what, two hundred?"

"Hardly," Becky said, walking around the echoing gym to flip on the hulking fluorescents. She'd paid four hundred ninety, retail. "They're duds, they pinch."

"Take them to the consignment place!"

"Should we have people start on the—" But when she turned around Ingrid had put the shoes on and was stepping around in circles to show off, arms outstretched, chinos pulled up over her knees. She danced up close to Becky, swinging the end of her scarf around in circles, and started singing the intro to Madonna's "Vogue."

"Come on," Becky said, but Ingrid lassoed her with the scarf and now they were bumping together in a silly grinding way, Ingrid laughing each time she toppled off a heel. Others were watching with smiles. Becky looked down and saw her friend's sturdy calves, carefully shaved below her rolled-up khakis, a faint green line roping down behind a knee. Varicose veins, brought on by Ingrid's new double shifts at the horrible giant Polish place out on 52, where one table of cheap old biddies could keep her running for ice, butter, lemons, and then tip less than ten percent. Becky could murder every one. But Ingrid was sweet to them, helping one lady to her car, chasing after another with her forgotten pierogis.

This big dummy. Becky's eyes filled, and in horror she gave Ingrid a hard hug. Ingrid, surprised, hugged her back, and then when Becky released her Ingrid took off the heels and rolled down her pants, and soon they were back to sorting piles.

After a while another volunteer mom strolled over, coffee in hand, to lean a hip against Ingrid's table and chat. While she and Ingrid talked about a school event or maybe a party Becky hadn't been invited to, not that she would have wanted to go, Becky pretended to be absorbed in her mound of shoes while subtly studying Ingrid.

"And then with the long weekend, we were going to drive up to Kevin's parents' place in Waukegan, but Sarah has a fever, so—"

Becky hoisted the box of shoes. "What long weekend?"

The other mom, whose lips were lined two shades too dark for her lipstick, glanced over with visible distaste. "Columbus Day," she said flatly. "Just when they get into a routine at school, the holidays start."

Ingrid nodded sympathetically.

"Columbus Day?" Becky's brain and speech couldn't catch up.

"Monday," the mom said. "Aren't you all closed, at Town Hall?"

"No. Yes." How had she not known? It all clicked into place, the half-heard comments she hadn't bothered to pay attention to: Ken's annual fishing trip with a childhood friend; Mrs. Fletcher's "see you in a few" instead of her customary grumbling about Monday coming soon enough. Sheena asking what plans Ms. Farwell had for the weekend. "Shoe drive," she'd muttered, thinking it was a bit much how underlings wanted to know everyone's *plans*. When she'd started at Town Hall you didn't even let on you knew your superiors had weekends, let alone breezily chat about what they were doing with them.

But Monday couldn't be Columbus Day, because that meant a bank holiday. And if Monday was a bank holiday, the check she had planned to deposit first thing—the check she wouldn't have until late tomorrow—wouldn't transfer through the accounts to hit the city's Operations fund before Ken carefully reviewed it for their 10 am finances meeting. She needed Monday. She'd counted on Monday!

It was 8:51 am.

Becky started sorting shoes in double time. She heard nothing from the moving lips of Ingrid and the other mom, she didn't even hear herself explain the sorting system to the new volunteers. She counted shoes, stacked boxes, fixed a broken packing tape dispenser one of the kids handed her, but all the while a calm and desperate reckoning took place behind her eyes. Hours, mileage, dollars; what she'd say, do, wear. The instant all of that slotted into place, a plan with a hair-thin margin of success, she began to move.

"I got to be somewhere," she called, running past a stunned Ingrid, slowing only to grab up the pair of Manolos, her Manolos, for her wild flight to the car.

"What? What?"

"I'll call you!"

It was 8:59 when she hit the gas in the church parking lot.

10:42. Becky's face against the glass door of the Stemen Gallery in River North, Chicago. OPEN AT 11 read the sign, but surely someone must be in there somewhere, in the back office? She'd never had to pee worse in her life.

10:43. Caught sight of a police officer writing her a ticket across the street. Ran back to the car, disagreed vehemently about whether four inches of bumper sticking out into a tow zone really mattered—her damn flashers were on!—but ended up with a ticket for $140 and a stern order to move the vehicle, now.

10:56. Circled the block three times before finding a spot on Randolph around the corner. Ran back to Stemen, Manolos on cobblestones, to find the gallery girl balancing a giant mocha latte while unlocking the door.

11:14. Argued with the gallery girl—after politely requesting the employee restroom—about the status of her account, her need for a check today—now—and whether it was possible to call the owner, yes, at this very moment, which was definitely not "the crack of dawn."

11:36. Finalized negotiations with the owner, trading a painful and outrageous fifteen percent cut on what she was owed for the ability to take a check now. Gallery girl took revenge by pausing midway to give detailed directions to a lost delivery guy who poked his head in, looking for a furniture store that used to share the building.

11:41. Ripped another ticket from the windshield, this one for not feeding the meter, $65, and drove ten blocks in the wrong direction trying to find the entrance to 209 West.

12:07. Inched up to seventy-five miles per hour, eyes locked on the roadway. One cop going the opposite direction near DeKalb sent her back down to sixty-nine. Fingers of sweat formed under her hair and collar and there was a tightening cinch around her middle rib cage imagining Ken's puzzled smile, Tuesday before the financials meeting, when he was unable to square the account's discrepancy.

12:51. She did it! Sauk Valley Credit Union, a majestically squat beige standalone, with all the free parking one could want in the mall's lot behind. But inside, check in hand, Becky got flattened. "Oh no, I'm sorry," the teller said. "The branch manager already left for the day and we're just finishing up the—"

Where. When. Where did he—

"Well, he usually picks up lunch on Saturdays, doesn't he, Jo? Panda Express."

12:52. Becky ran across the grass divider, up onto the macadam, swerved around pissed-off cars and grocery-cart moms who yelled *take it easy*. She hit the glass door of Panda Express with so much force that the paper-hatted workers all looked up in unison. She pegged the branch manager at first sight and immediately did two things: pointed out the time, 12:54, and laser-beamed into his young fleshy face every iota of Farwell magnetism she possessed. Also she'd buy him lunch. Back they went to the bank for her deposit.

1:14. Becky sat in the stuffy driver's seat of her car and cried. Half-cried, half-whooped. To think that broccoli beef and an order of cream cheese rangoon was all that stood between her and discovery—how could anyone not laugh to the point of nausea? That baby-faced manager in the poly-blend suit, short-sleeved dress shirt—*he* saved the day, saved the two Rothkos, her one Klimt, and several Bonnards, the Miró sketches and . . . Had he ever seen a piece of art, real art, Branch Manager Mike Dobbin? Because he may have single-handedly preserved the integrity of a collection worth $300 million. By processing the deposit of a $1,700 check.

Later in the day—she didn't know how much later, sunk in the Art Barn with a bottle of Château Latour—one of the many sucking-up gifts regularly arriving at her P.O. box—Becky regained her calm. Ingrid would be pissed at her, but when she got home the first thing she'd done was send over one of the girls from the office temp pool with the promise of twenty dollars per hour for as long as Ingrid needed her. Tacking up crepe paper and icing cupcakes weren't Becky's forte, even Ingrid would agree. And Becky was too exhausted to take on another project.

When hunger forced her aboveground again the sky had darkened. She sang along to Tanya Tucker while microwaving some broccoli cheddar soup, then curled up on the couch with a stack of personnel reports: it was annual review season. Before bed, she'd have half a sleeve of SnackWell Vanilla Cremes and play the next section of Rosetta Stone's conversational Italian.

But she couldn't shake a keyed-up mood, an uneasiness. Why hadn't Ingrid called back? Not once, not on Becky's cell or her answering machine. She gave up on the SnackWells and got in the car. "It's the perfect time for me to show up," she argued aloud. The kids would be watching their movie, and the bottle of Cab she had on the passenger seat would soothe Ingrid by the time the cork was pulled.

The Yeskos' house was quiet and dark when she pulled into the driveway. No balloons tied to the metal porch railing. No shrieking pack of kids thundered to the sound of the doorbell. Becky waited, then went around back and let herself in through the mudroom. In the kitchen the lights were off, dishwasher thrumming. An open can of Pringles on the counter.

Becky followed the muffled noise of the TV down carpeted steps to the basement, where Neil Yesko was on the couch watching the game, one leg thrown sideways, beer in hand.

"Hi, Becky. What a super surprise."

"Where is everyone?" Becky tried to avoid addressing Neil's crotch in its green sweatpants. "The kids, the party . . ." She gestured to the darkened house. "Your wife?"

"Huh." Neil glanced to the TV and back. "Well, my *kids* are upstairs asleep, Jesus Christ God willing, and my *wife* is at a hotel in Iowa City, and as for a party . . . you're looking at it."

Becky sat on the basement stairs. "But she—I was supposed to—" Did he say *Iowa City*?

"Yes, you were, Becky Farwell." Neil muted the TV in one stabbing gesture. "You were supposed to come over here middle of the day, and pop the champagne that's upstairs in my fridge, and get in our car where you'd be driven two hours just in time for the opening acts at the Country Bash Fall Festival. Which is on my credit card as we speak, two all-weekend passes and a non-refundable hotel."

Becky couldn't catch up. "She didn't tell me."

"Yeah, well, that's how surprises usually work." Neil put the volume back up and turned back to the screen.

Then Becky saw her own suitcase, set against the wall near the garage door. Ingrid must have used her keys, and she knew where to find all Becky's clothes, her cosmetics. The image of Ingrid's thrill at sneaking in to pack a surprise overnight bag flooded Becky with such wretchedness that she shut up her mind and made herself review, instead, if she'd left anything suspicious out at home (a receipt, a piece of packing material). But Ingrid—Becky knew this utterly, with a throb—would have been too excited about her own plan to care or snoop.

"How was she?" she asked the grubby beanbag chairs, unable to look at Neil.

"Before your little hired help showed up, you mean? Or after?"

Fuck. "Why didn't she call me?" Becky burst out. "Or *you* could have!"

Neil said nothing for a long moment. "She didn't want to go, but I made her. I tried to get her to ask someone else, anyone, of all those hundred goddamned girlfriends, but she wouldn't. So she went by herself—"

Becky squeezed her hands over her ears. "Which hotel."

Neil raised his voice. "—And god knows I hope she's living it up with Garth Brooks, my wife who hasn't taken a day for herself in over three years, who sits up at night each time TJ can't sleep, which is every night, and who wanted a couple of days to party and sleep in, have a good time, maybe order late-night room service with the person she *calls* her best friend—"

"Neil, just tell me where!"

"But let's be real, she's not going to any concert tonight, is she?" He got quiet, forcing Becky to look up. "She's watching the same crappy TV we always do. Alone in the double queen room that cost extra so you two wouldn't look out onto a parking lot."

"I'll drive there. Right now."

"She doesn't want to see you."

"Please," Becky said.

Neil studied her for a long time. "The Hilton Garden downtown."

Becky took the stairs two at a time, bumping her suitcase against the wall. From the car she called the hotel, got through to Ingrid, who was, as Neil predicted, watching TV in a sulk. It took nearly an hour, Becky flooring it along I-88, to cajole her out of her funk, but she did it.

Late that night, sweaty dancing and drunk with relief, Becky marveled at how close she'd come. How it had all almost unraveled for real, for good. Instead of handcuffs and a jail cell, here she was in a dive bar at 1 am with a happy Ingrid waving her up onto the karaoke stage for the Dixie Chicks' "Wide Open Spaces." They could do the harmony by heart.

Rachel's tenth birthday was in June. When it came time for her party, Becky was there early to tack up streamers and keep TJ away from popping balloons, and help Ingrid pour out pop and slice cake.

Becky struggled mightily not to go overboard for a present but ended up giving the girl a framed poster of her favorite band, five prepubescent boys, signed by each one—"Rachel, you're the reason we make music! XOXOXO, Robbie." "Rachel Y, all my love, Miguel." "HUGS, R!" Getting this done—those stupid teens had shark managers—had taken as much effort and money as procuring a Philip Guston, but Rachel's literal tears upon unwrapping the poster made it worth it.

While Rachel read out each inscription, shaking with delight, Becky thought about QT Pets. Rachel's once-prized specimens were now gathering dust on a dresser and would eventually end up in a box, in a closet. But Becky remembered the avid hunt to gain a full set, the feeling of completeness when the panda had been placed on the shelf beside the fox and the dog. Maybe she should try something new with her own collection. One last play.

25

Pierson
September 11, 2001

ALL DAY, ALL OF TOWN Hall stayed crowded in one conference room, where a TV replayed the planes cutting into the Twin Towers. Everyone except Becky. She was in her car, in the parking lot out back, with her cell phone and a notebook. First she called every relevant party in any current deal, nailing down who and what and how much. Then she worked international contacts, waking them up to reassure spooked Euro gallerists and Asian businessmen that her funds were liquid and in play no matter what. Every few minutes another dealer or collector would call her, wanting to share in the shock and fear of what was happening, but as soon as she could she got off the phone. Later was the time for *can you believe this* and *I just can't believe this.* Now was for clear thinking and quick acting.

The last set of calls was to her artists, the four or five she kept in supplies and with living expenses, the ones who gave her peace of mind when the sheer strain of her transgressions threatened to engulf her: *These people are making their work (and eating), because of me. And my Activity.* She made sure the New Yorkers were safe and accounted for; most of them had still been in bed when the attacks occurred. She got addresses for studios in SoHo, Tribeca, anything south of Union Square. *I'll take care of it*, she said over and over, to the painters and sculptors and filmmakers, stunned and afraid for their work and supplies, for colleagues and friends, for the meaning of art in the face of such a horrific, global event. Bit by bit Becky's calm steadiness, her willingness to see to all the details, let the artists gather their wits. *Okay*, they eventually said, breathing out. Distracted, watching TV throughout the conversation. *Okay, thank you, okay.*

Be safe, she told them. Call me anytime.

The only non-art call she made was to Ingrid. They had a two-minute conversation of the kind people all across the country were having, and for the first time Ingrid hung up first, wanting to get back to her kids.

When Becky finally went back inside, only Ken and a few others were still there. Still contacting surrounding counties, in discussion with Springfield and Chicago. Were further attacks a possibility? What emergency protocol, what statements were needed? Becky slid into her usual seat, exchanged one notebook for another. She jumped right in with questions for Police Chief Myerson, new in the job this year. Ken watched her and said nothing but she could feel what he didn't ask, what he never asked her: Where have you been?

26

Pierson
2002

UNDERGROUND IN THE ART BARN it was impossible to know the weather. Or care, frankly. Tarek mentioned something about rain, though Becky hadn't really listened; Tarek tended to talk while he installed.

Becky sat in the only chair, reviewing the paperwork for her new acquisitions. Tarek went about his business with the usual not-unpleasant accompanying soundtrack: squeaking drill bore, scrape and brush for paint touch-ups. Every so often Becky would look up over her drugstore readers to check his progress. Today he was removing and crating two larger oils to make room for three plexiglass-framed photo collages by Lolly Macnamara, to go with the two she'd bought months ago. All five together comprised the artist's entire body of work in the photo collage medium.

Lolly Macnamara was in her eighties. Always about to be rediscovered. She'd recently come to photo collage, a kind of work she hadn't made since the 1960s, apparently as a farewell tour of her previous modes. How nice it was, Becky thought, to see an older artist digging back into what she did well, instead of flinging herself into a last hurrah of some new and overblown technique, often tipping into melodrama and grandiosity, trying too hard. These pieces were tightly focused, subtle but rich.

She'd gone through half a dozen installers before finding Tarek and locking him down with a monthly retainer, enough that he'd be all too happy to bail on a job for his dad's cabinetry business when she called, as she did about twice a month. Tarek lived in Rockford with a sometimes girlfriend and her kids, had superior rough and finish carpentry skills, and couldn't have been less interested in art if he tried. He'd answered her (online!) ad for custom side work, shown up on time and aced her test job, matter-of-factly took the large sum of cash with which she'd paid, and gave her his cell number. She liked the way he fiddled with his work, adhesives and fasteners and mounts, breathing in exasperated huffs, until it was clockmaker-perfect to him. And how he shut up and let her look at the pieces he'd put up, sometimes for a long time, and didn't complain if she then changed her mind and asked for a rearrangement.

But today she wouldn't need a rearrangement. The Macnamara pieces looked good. More than good. The knowledge that she *had them all*, that there were no other Macnamara photo collages out there, in any other galleries or on any other walls, gave Becky the kind of thrill-shiver she hadn't felt in some time. Tarek stretched out on a paint tarp, eyes closed, while she walked back and forth, limping a bit because of the needly pain in her left buttock, now shooting down her leg.

All of something. This idea, born out of QT Pets, tested with these Macnamaras, now took hold of Becky so entirely that she began to shake. All of an artist's works in one medium, whether pencil or gouache or brass. All of an artist's work in one time period. All of the artists from one time period. Every piece that included an image of a diner mug, a dead person, an animal baring its teeth. You could slice the pie a thousand ways and still only be beginning. The collector determined the size of the field, the rules of the game, and what it meant to win.

"Okay," she said, loud enough that Tarek startled. "You can take down the other pieces in this room."

"All of them?"

"Yep. Also some next door, I'll show you."

"Big plans?"

But Becky was already into the next gallery, too busy with her thoughts to reply. It felt like starting over.

"*Bankrupt*," Ingrid said, her sleepy voice perking up with attention. "For real?"

Becky rolled over and shifted the phone to her other ear. "I shouldn't even be telling you this."

"I didn't even know that was possible. Towns, like, a whole town . . . can declare bankruptcy?"

"Not sure," Becky said truthfully. "The consultant said he'd heard of a couple municipalities downstate."

"So that would mean, what, all of Pierson's debts cancelled? Then what? We're under control of some bank? Or do the feds own us? What if they rename Pierson? What if they take over Town Hall and make you share your office?"

"Let's not get crazy. It's not going to happen."

"Mayor Ken must be wigging out."

"He is indeed." In fact, he'd gotten so disgusted with the consultant's digression about Illinois's murky laws on the matter, that it wasn't clear if Pierson would be eligible for Chapter 9, that he'd stood up right in the middle of the man's sentence and thanked him for his time.

Despite that awkward moment, Becky had been hugely relieved. The one or two times before this when Ken had brought up the possibility of bankruptcy as a solution for the town, Becky had successfully ignored it or distracted him. Then to hear from the consultant Ken brought in that there really was no clear path for this option should have been the end of it. Except she had a nagging feeling that Ken wasn't done with this idea, because she knew Ken. She would tread softly here—any vociferous pushback on his half-baked plan would likely cause him to ramp up in response . . . or worse, to get suspicious.

In response those next weeks, Becky funneled as much money as she could back into the town. Patching one leak after another, Band-Aids on a perpetual gusher. The way the corners of Ken's mouth had gone white during the consultant's presentation . . . the memory of that could make Becky transfer cash from RF Capital Development to a playground repair, a radio equipment upgrade for the fire department. The problem was, of course, that her new collecting plan demanded just as much skimming, if not (she hoped not, she told herself not) a bit more.

"Chicago-based collector Reba Farwell, in McQueen, consults with gallerist Paul Merkanen, at T+Go's Art+Design Fair in New York." *Town & Country*. "Museum director Chan Traylor and noted collectors Frank and Betty Linson dine with Reba Farwell after the show." *Vanity Fair.* "Reba Farwell, seen chatting with Liz Frederick, neé Rockefeller, at a private event held at Gramercy Tavern." *New York Times* Style Section.

Each time Becky saw herself in a society page photo layout she winced first, and scrutinized second. How did her hair look, her shoes—they rarely shot full body, which was a pity for her shoes—and why did her mouth make that strange shape when she was talking? Why did designers never think about women shorter than five foot three? Shorter than six foot three, for that matter? She'd get so caught up in evaluating her own image, one of many in dozens of thumbnail party shots, that she'd forget the real problem wasn't the way her jaw stuck out when she was caught faking a laugh at Dave Zwirner's boring story, but the fact that she was in the photo, in the magazine. In many photos, many magazines, more and more often.

It had a name, her new collecting plan, though she didn't hear the term *completist* applied to herself until much further into this, her next and biggest and most audacious phase. And it took a while for Becky to accept the label and then delight in the term itself, the way the word elevated collecting to a new level, the way it echoed *artist*.

Being a completist had the unintended and mostly unwelcome consequence of boosting Becky's visibility. Maybe some of it had to do with the way the art world, so insular and clubby in the past, now extended and crossed over into fashion, movies, design. Magazines and newspapers and new online forums seemed to care more about art events, keeping a closer eye on who was in attendance and naming them, increasingly, in their monthly society roundups. Jessa had been a fixture of these for years, of course, in photos with and without her odious husband, but Becky's appearance was relatively new. She realized that her own recent deals had propelled her up the chain: Farwell held all the pencil sketches from Calder's year before Paris. Farwell had bought all nine watercolors by some new artist before he was featured in British *Vogue*. Farwell had gotten there first, and cornered the market.

She took fewer calls, named higher prices, and sold by the lot. Or didn't, as she chose. This caused consternation and a fair amount of bitterness from some of her connections, but her own calls got put through right away. Invitations began to arrive with scribbled "Hope to see you there. xxxxxx," signed with initials anyone would recognize. Even more than her infamous sale at Christie's, this new approach turned Becky (Reba) into an art-world player at a level she hadn't been before.

Once a month Becky drove to the Barnes & Noble mall superstore on Big Hollow Road in Peoria, eighty-five miles south of Pierson, an hour and a half drive. Yes, it was stupid, and, yes, she did it anyway. She loaded up her arms with thick glossy issues and took them to a table, keeping her sunglasses on like a proper girl on the lam. Afraid to subscribe to any of these magazines, afraid that even having them in her home—in her town—would make her vulnerable. In its periodical room the Pierson library held *Vanity Fair* but not *Town & Country*, and obviously not *i-D*, *Artforum*, or *Interview*. No one she knew in Pierson took any paper other than the *Tribune*, the *Sun-Times*, or maybe *USA Today*. If—against all odds—someone from home saw one of the photos, she'd pass it off as a one-time thrilling adventure, this random invitation to big-city fanciness. If she was asked about the name Reba? Oh, well, you know those busy magazine editors were bound to get someone's name wrong. Just my luck it had to be me.

She ran mental drills for dozens of possible encounters, under her breath, there in the Barnes & Noble. Fine-tuned her voice for tones of pleasant surprise, patient explanation, abashed Midwestern humility. But still she hunched over her café table, covered the layout with her hand while she covertly studied the photos.

On the long drive home she amused herself with the photo layout those photographers could get of Becky, not Reba. Becky presiding over last week's contentious open hearing about cutbacks in the residential garbage pickup schedule. Becky passing out new copies of "Zoning Code Regs" after the first batch of copies (for "Future Unreg Codes") had an unfortunate acronym. Becky at Rachel's hip-hop dance performance. Becky, drinking Schlitz with old-timers at the VFW. Who was she with? Who was she wearing?

27

Milan
2003

BECKY WAS DEEP IN CONVERSATION with a German painter and his translator. The man wanted to switch to larger works—or was it that he *had* already switched? The translator didn't seem certain about tenses. Becky, interrupting in half-German phrases, set him straight. *Nein.* She had contracted for the full set of smaller canvases. She wouldn't take one if she couldn't have them all, and if he moved now to larger pieces she'd be forced to—

"Reba," Michel whispered, urgently, at her side. One half of the duo she'd spent the past two days with at the Milan Art Fair.

Tom and Michel were a twin-like NYC couple in their late twenties who seemed to spend their days drinking Campari and making up scandals and gossip. The three of them fell into an instantaneous best friendship, strutting through the galleries and the parties, texting each other good night at dawn. Tom's father—or was it Michel's?—was an SVP at Lehman's. Becky called them "The Babies" to their faces; they hung on Becky's every word, making purchase after purchase on her advice. It didn't hurt that they looked like Calvin Klein models and turned heads of every type and age.

"You must come," Michel said. Becky apologized to the Germans and extricated herself. She allowed Michel to take her arm and steer her through the twisting crowds and walled dividers. Around every corner another person to greet, fend off, promise to call—*I know, so sorry, we'll talk later*—in this thunderous gathering of money and power. And art.

Eventually they reached Tom, beaming, sweating under the display lights. He threw his arms open at the work, and Michel crossed himself. Besotted, they waited for her blessing.

Two nights ago at their suite at the Oasis—technically by then it was morning—Tom and Michel had invited the bellhop who brought up more ice to stay for drinks. And drugs. Soon they were cuddled close together on a divan, murmuring and touching, these three beautiful men. Tom—or was it Michel?—had asked Becky to stay, to watch.

She demurred, amused. Showed herself out.

Over *insalate puntarelle* at lunch the next day both Babies trembled behind their Tom Ford sunglasses, appalled at their bad behavior, and asked her to forgive them. Becky had just laughed and laughed. They were so grateful, so abashed.

Now she looked at the great discovery they needed her to sanction. It was a video piece, on a small TV monitor. A repeating loop of about four minutes of film: a woman (the artist), giving speeches as George Bush. She was slight, brown-haired, and dressed in a simple black shirt and jeans. But each clip had her at the presidential podium, or at Ground Zero, or in the Rose Garden posed exactly like Bush. Speaking his words, surrounded by his advisers, without a single knowing wink. Becky watched the loop once, and then again. She pronounced the artist's name in her mind, *Caitriona Molloy*, slowly, without speaking.

"Interesting," she said at last, in a loud but utterly flat voice, which had the desired effect of quelling the hovering gallery assistant. Then she drew Tom and Michel aside. She let them go on and on: the doable prices, the promising show in London, the way the piece mixed politics with humanity, how *funny* it was, how weirdly heartbreaking.

Becky heard them out. And then, as gently and thoroughly as she could, deflated their every hope. She named half a dozen other video artists on the market with similar projects, she told them the gallery was a bit player, a JV house trying too hard. She reminded them to build on their strengths, a parent's Barbizon holdings, a very nice Ashcan purchase, instead of chasing every whim. She urged focus in the face of distraction, and sure, if they wanted to they should make an offer but frankly she'd seen better work at a recent student show, not that they had to care about *her* opinion, of course . . .

No! They did, they absolutely did! The Babies were utterly chastened. She'd been ridiculously generous all weekend and they hated themselves for wasting even a moment of her time.

Becky held an indulgent smile, forgiving, understanding. What everyone needed was an Amaretto, was she right? She was right, she was always right.

After twenty minutes at the bar Becky excused herself. She doubled back and bought the Molloy piece for asking. She bought up the gallery's entire Molloy holdings—videos, a large-scale photo, comics, sketches—most of it sight unseen, hurrying the assistant, using two different credit cards and more than a thousand in cash.

That night she let Tom's calls go to voice mail, watched Michel text until 11:30, midnight, one. She changed her flight and went back a day early, collecting grateful messages from Molloy's agent, manager, and New York dealer, all of whom sounded a little stunned.

By May Caitriona Molloy had shows scheduled for later in the year in Tribeca, Toronto, and Berlin. *Artforum* ran a Top Ten column, and *Vanity Fair* posed her in Marc Jacobs, high-heeled boots hooked over a metal stool rung in a grungy studio. Becky sold selected works fast, to top collectors. But she kept every Molloy video piece, and struck a deal for first option on each new work. Stills sometimes reminded her a little bit of Tracy Moncton, although she'd heard through the grapevine that Tracy was now moving into feature films.

Becky archived all but one of the Molloy videos and for her own viewing displayed only *George Bush, C'est Moi*, streaming it on a perpetual loop against a bare space on the wall in between a decent Max Weber and a nearly photographic Richard Estes. She could look at it for long stretches of time, taking immense pleasure from the intelligence, the creativity, the vision, the Babies who found it for her intentionally forgotten.

28

Pierson
2003–2008

DATE	RECEIVED	NOTES
April 4, 2003	*$14,500*	*Lester Snow Removal*
	$9,440	*Lester Snow Removal*
	$33,000	*Lester Snow Removal*

WHY DID SHE KEEP THESE accounts? Why, after all the years and years of skimming? When she knew by heart the dozens of false companies she rotated through for made-up invoices? Becky didn't really know. She took; she kept track. She paid out; she kept track. Sometimes she told herself that this stupid accounting of her own crimes was to ensure she didn't slip up and double-bill by accident. A safety measure. But she knew that leaving such a clear record of the Activity was far more dangerous than the risk of messing up any fake company names or bills. Plus, no one noticed and no one questioned, not a single false invoice in all these years. No matter how obvious (to her) or how much she pushed the edge (they didn't even have that many snowfalls the winter of 2002–2003!). Sometimes, as comptroller, she had to shake her head. *Defalcation* was the technical term, which Becky had come across occasionally when she browsed issues of *The Journal of Accountancy* or *Accounting Today*.

Incredible, what a person could get away with. She wouldn't have believed it herself.

In May of 2003 she hung up a call and swiveled to find Ken and town council president Tyler "Ty" Rosario standing in her doorway, both smiling with anticipation.

"Uh oh, what'd I do now?" She stood as they came in, carefully closing the door against Mrs. F.'s peering nosiness.

"We'll make this brief," Ty said. "You've been very good to us, Becky." He handed her an unsealed envelope.

Becky looked to Ken, who was nearly bouncing with excitement. Before she could unfold the single sheet he burst out, "It's a three percent raise."

Becky's heart sank. She took her time studying the numbers on the page so she wouldn't have to look back at Ken. Sure enough, her annual salary, effective June 1, would now be $72,400. "Is this across the board? Is the freeze over?" They had been on a wage and hiring lockdown for the past eighteen months.

Ty shook his head. "Unfortunately, as you know, that isn't possible."

"I don't feel comfortable unless the whole team is part of this." But when she tried to hand the envelope back to him he held up both hands, *no takers*.

"You've got Mayor Brennan's full support. I hope you'll see it as a gesture of goodwill from all of us."

Becky bent the corner of the envelope and let its sharp point dig into her thumb. Probably Ken had forgone any bump so that she could have this. If only he wouldn't stand there beaming at her! $72,400. Blood squeezed from a stone. How much were the fake snow removal invoices she'd only last week submitted without a second glance? Nearly that.

It took everything she had to muster the right expression, which was the least she could do for Ken: taken aback, gratified, *oh but you shouldn't have.* You shouldn't have.

DATE	PAID	NOTES
February 19, 2004	$4,700	Round-trip airfare, business class, Japan Airlines
	$2,440	One night, Mandarin Oriental
	$23,000	Three Carrington map sketches, ink on paper, sizes various

During the thirty-eight hours Becky spent in Tokyo, her first visit to Japan, she ate two meals, the first a type of fried chicken at a stand-up lunch counter outside the private gallery—she saw what the businessman next to her was eating and pointed to that—and the other a steak, medium rare, ordered from room service. She didn't go to a single boutique or sushi place. She closed the deal for the Carrington works—which were even better in person—and opted out of a star-studded cocktail party in favor of an earlier flight back. As the formally polite stewardess began her welcome, Becky shook her head and asked for an eye mask and ear plugs.

In the time it took for her to fall asleep, her body thoroughly confused by the quick turnaround across time zones, Becky mused about all the art she hadn't seen in Tokyo. Nothing at Ishii or Arataniurano or Misako & Rosen, though she had contacts at each. No visits to the Hara or Mori museums, despite their holdings. Instead, her buying had taken place at a private home in a meticulously hushed and blank viewing space where the Carrington pieces she had expressed interest in were brought out one at a time, shown to her alone.

That was the thing about completism, she thought sleepily. The term made it sound like it had to do with *more*. But in practice it meant less. All she needed, all she was interested in, were the works that fit her predetermined categories—in this case, the sketches that Leonora Carrington used to develop *Map of Down Below*. The collection Becky was working on now was twentieth-century cartographic-like drawings made in preparation for fuller pieces. Not finished works but sketches, plans, maps for future maps. Several times gallerists had misunderstood, had wanted to show her oil paintings of map images, sometimes glorious works by big names. She had refused to even look. *Only* prep work, only maps, only twentieth century.

Now she had three of the Carringtons she needed. There was at least one, possibly two, still at large. She had leads, she'd find them. But right now she was at 35,000 feet over the Pacific, and her Ambien was kicking in.

DATE	PAID	NOTES
November 23, 2005	*$49.00*	*Office party sheet cake Schinkel's bakery*
	$50.00	*Office party sparkling wine and sodas Quick Bev-Mart*

Too much to hope that her fortieth birthday could pass quietly. She had to attend not one but two parties organized for her. The first Becky went along with because not doing so would have jeopardized a precarious deal in progress that depended on several people's goodwill—or at least what passed for goodwill in the art world: great shows of abundance (food, drugs, luxury abodes) cut with mean-spirited gossip and backbiting.

Becky never figured out how the Van Voutens found out it was her birthday, her "big birthday," as they kept calling it. But when they *insisted* she hop on their Gulfstream to Costa Rica, with twenty assorted others, she realized it really was insistence. What followed was a nightmarishly over-the-top four-day weekend in a Punta Islita villa with two private staff members for every guest, no Wi-Fi, and drunken Europeans being loudly naked in the pool all day and night. Howler monkeys woke Becky (Reba) at dawn, and the endless rum drinks gave her diarrhea. On day three she found a giant bullfrog in her toilet and so for the final fourteen hours she peed in the scrubby bushes outside the villa, praying that no snakes—or Europeans—would catch her doing so.

The second party, held on her actual birthday—the day before

Thanksgiving break—was in the Town Hall second-floor conference room, of course, where Becky was toasted with a long limerick-style poem whose line endings threatened to be risqué but mostly reverted to rhyming "Farwell" with "barbell" or "is swell." Paper banners and twisted streamers, decorative paper plates, and a Schinkel's ice cream cake (yes, ice cream in November)—every detail the same as not just Becky's previous office birthday parties but every other staff member's party, ever. Becky had managed to find out the one extra they had planned—sparkling wine to go with the soda—and called ahead to place the charges on her own bill, not the town's. But that was as much as she could do.

"And now . . ." Ken moved to the ominously draped item propped up on the whiteboard, motioning Louise from HR to help him.

Please don't let it be a painting. Please don't let it be a painting.

"Voilà!" Even before Ken and Louise managed to fully uncover her gift Becky could see that it was, indeed, a painting, 24 inches by 18 inches, possibly acrylic. She recognized it right away as one of the constantly rotated items at Prints Unlimited, a frame shop in a mall just outside town. This one was of a dog curled up asleep on a bed, on top of a white comforter. The modeling wasn't bad, but the artist was clearly enamored of his or her ability with chiaroscuro, because shadows fell on every side of the dog—east and west, front and behind.

"I know you don't have a dog or anything. We just thought this was the sweetest."

Becky gave Louise a huge smile. "It's really something. I'm so . . . wow."

"It's a Van Gogh!" someone shouted from the back of the room. Becky laughed along with everyone else, then, when the crowd quieted, said, "I'm so very touched. Thank you." She wondered how much each of them had chipped in. Five each? No more than ten, she hoped. "I know exactly where I'm going to put it."

By her side, Ken was still scrutinizing the painting. "Can't tell what breed that is," he muttered. "Huh. Anyway, it's bad training to let them sleep on the bed."

DATE	RECEIVED	NOTES
April 19, 2006	$64,200	South Elementary wiring repair
	$4,030	Cafeteria upgrade
	$500	Books and supplies
	$81,000	North Elementary playground reconstruction

DATE	PAID	NOTES
April 26, 2006	$10,000	Table, NYC All Stars Project fundraiser (J. Scanfield)
May 5, 2006	$5,000	Donation, Art Start (J. Scanfield)
	$3,000	Donation, Painting Promise (J. Scanfield)
	$5,000	Donation, Arts for All (J. Scanfield)
May 29, 2006	$19,000	CORN (c. 1935), Grant Wood, 9 1/2" by 7 1/2", graphite on paper, private sale (J. Scanfield)

■ ■ ■

Jessa's husband left her in February for a trust-funded preschool teacher who was twenty-eight years old. "I'm lucky," she said, "that he managed to hold it to that. Just one decade older than our son, maybe that was his red line."

Becky heard the anger and fear behind the statement, though. She tried to be chipper about it—Jessa would be better off! Hadn't this been kind of what she'd wanted, after all?

It turned out that this was not at all what Jessa had wanted. Her phone calls from New York turned desperate, agonized, especially once things turned ugly and public, with the husband screwing her from real estate to custody to assets. Becky, full of distaste for all things emotionally dramatic, kept trying to offer concrete solutions when it seemed like all Jessa wanted was to unload her fear and pain. *That's what your Upper East Side friends are for,* Becky wanted to say but didn't. Because one by one these society matrons edged away from Jessa too, afraid to take sides. Soon Becky heard that Jessa was struggling, whatever that meant in New York society, and couldn't keep up with her many social obligations.

"Thank you, darling. I didn't know what I was going to do."

"It's nothing." Becky held her cell phone between shoulder and chin, sorting papers at her desk in Town Hall. She'd purchased a table for some fundraiser Jessa was connected to and had hoped it would pass unnoticed, but Jessa had found out, had called to thank her. Becky *mm-hmm*ed through a long story about this charity's board members icing Jessa out at the last meeting, and then another about how the ex-husband was getting married in some bullshit barefoot-on-the-sand island wedding and any minute now Jessa expected to hear that her sons would have a new baby half-sibling.

"So anyway, I can't wait," Jessa finally wrapped up. "Don't even think about a hotel. We'll stay up late and eat all the calories afterward and I promise I won't make you talk to a single person not at your table."

What? Oh. "Actually, I can't make it in." When Jessa didn't respond, Becky hurried on, "I'm swamped next week, I'm completely swamped. But you know Julie Vrettos, right? Multimedia, won the . . . whatever it's called, the grant from Dia. She'll bring a great group, I'm sure. Liven up the thing, that's for sure!"

Becky hoped Julie's friends would keep it relatively tame for Jessa. Julie herself seemed tame enough—brainy, quiet, conceptual. Becky had been supporting her for less than a year. But who knew what kind of hangers-on she might round up for free food and booze.

"Oh, of course. Of course, darling." Why was her voice so tinny and small?

"I'll call Julie tonight. I'll tell her absolutely no drugs and no drama. And if I even hear one word about—"

"It doesn't matter," Jessa said, now crisp and loud. "That doesn't matter at all."

Soon, Jessa had to put her apartment up for sale. Becky watched through the industry news and gossip as she began to sell off piece after piece of her collection, even her beloved Regionalists. Becky continued to write checks whenever she found a charity Jessa sponsored, but the only thing she heard from Jessa was a prompt polite thank-you on a thick creamy notecard.

Becky waited to see what would happen with it, waited as long as she could, and then offered aggressively on the Wood. *Corn* was a piece she knew Jessa loved dearly, was one of the first she'd owned, had planned to give her son. Becky offered again, and again. She saw through the sales reports how Jessa's collection was decimated, scattered piece by piece in a way that made her cringe. The numbers alone told how bad things were; Jessa was selling everything she could. Except for a few holdouts, including *Corn*.

When Jessa finally agreed to sell she had a broker finalize the transaction, and Becky paid less than half of what the piece could have brought in over time, through a proper auction.

Becky arranged to pick the piece up a month later, when she was in New York. At Jessa's Upper East Side building, a young woman let her in, not Jessa (as Becky had hoped and feared) or either of her children (as she'd dreaded). The girl, harried and in dusty jeans, was overseeing movers, the screech of a tape dispenser echoing through the bare halls. She had Becky initial the purchase agreement and handed the piece over, tired, no flourish.

"Can I say hi?" Becky asked tentatively. "Is she in?"

"She's in Florida," the girl said. "I'll text her you were here."

Becky nodded slowly. She took in the apartment's empty walls. "Are the other works—the art, I mean . . . have they all been sold?"

The girl held her gaze evenly. "Is there anything else I can help you with?"

Becky took her cue and left.

In the elevator she untaped the cardboard envelope and peered in at the piece. Plain, dry, but strong. She didn't love it. She could maybe conjure up admiration. But she owned two graphite realistic pieces exactly this size depicting wheat and soybean plants (by nobodies) so to complete the set she needed corn. If it had to be this one, it had to be this one, no matter how overpriced, given Wood's name value.

Surely Jessa would understand. If she could only see the three perfectly matched pieces hanging in Becky's Art Barn . . . a *barn*, after all. Grant Wood himself would have appreciated that.

"Ma'am?"

Becky realized the elevator had reached the lobby; the doorman was waiting for her to exit. She sorted quickly through the torn wrapping, the tape, looking for something from Jessa—a note, her signature, even one of those fancy notecards with a scribbled "Fuck you." But there was nothing, only the art.

DATE	PAID	NOTES
April 9, 2008	$13,500	Pierson Junior/Senior Prom
	$15.90	Smoothie King (Ingrid)

Becky was on a karma high. Neither the school nor Town Hall had any idea that this year's prom would have been impossible if she hadn't covered it. Somehow they fell for yet another *I juggled the accounts to find extra*—which amazed her, because if anyone had the slightest inkling of how much these vendors charged, they'd never believe Town Hall could fund what she pulled off. More likely, they were all too grateful to closely examine what went into prom.

Becky didn't care. She wanted to do this for Pierson, dammit. Every outrageously overpriced item—even mediocre DJs made a killing this time of year—Becky happily took care of out of her own secret funds. Real flower displays? Sure. Laser light show? Absolutely. Giant piñata filled with candy and PROM 2008 spelled out in green and white, above a plastic rendering of a Pierson Pirate? Hell yes. The best part was cutting ticket prices—both individual and couple!—by fifty percent, ensuring that about twice as many kids got to go.

The Monday after the dance Becky was dying to hear how it went. She drove to Ingrid's around lunchtime and leaned on the doorbell with extra zest.

"*What?*" came a crabby shout from inside. When Ingrid opened the door, wearing fuzzy slipper–style boots and a hooded sweatshirt, she said, "Oh. Hi. Come in, I guess."

"Good day to you too, Mrs. Yesko."

"Don't mess with me, I'm having a day." Ingrid dropped onto the lower step of her staircase and put her forehead on her knees. Loud TV noises came from up above. "There was a mix-up with TJ's caregiver schedule so Roz didn't show this morning, so now I can't take my mom to the hair appointment I said I'd take her to, plus I said we could run her errands after, and I have to get to the store myself, we barely have any food in the house . . ." She raised her head. "What are you doing now?"

"Me?" Becky hadn't gone to sleep yet, after many hours of calls to Tokyo and Hong Kong, followed by paperwork in the Art Barn. Nothing on her schedule at Town Hall until 3 pm.

"Forget it."

"No! I mean, yes, of course. What's the plan?"

Several hours later they were still on the road, having crisscrossed town four times already. When Ingrid had laid out the itinerary—hair appointment for her mother, Costco out on Route 9, TJ's physical therapy—she meant to drive them all in her minivan. But Becky quickly convinced her that it would be more efficient for her to be the chauffeur while Ingrid did the shopping and ushering. (She also couldn't bear the idea of Ingrid's stained crumby van interior.) *Fine,* Ingrid said, tiredly.

Becky quite liked chatting with Mrs. Beanton, even if she had to shout over her shoulder at the little old lady buckled up in the back. And TJ was easy as long as he had his music and head-phones. By early afternoon they had returned Mrs. Beanton to her home, unloaded the groceries, and dropped TJ at his appointment at a therapy center in a strip mall on Gregerson Avenue.

Before Ingrid could get back into the car, Becky jumped out. "Want to get some lunch? My treat."

"It's almost two," Ingrid said.

"Coffee, then."

"We've been drinking coffee all day." It was true. They'd gone through the Dunkin drive-through twice.

Becky scanned the strip mall. "Smoothie King?"

Ingrid shrugged. "They're basically milkshakes, but whatever."

She perked up a few inches into her Strawberry Kiwi Breezy Blast with a Wellness Shot. Becky had the same thing except with an Awake Shot. They sucked out of the giant plastic cups and strolled under the dripping awning that ran alongside the store-fronts, Kay Jewelers, Frum's Cosmetic Dentistry, a copy center.

Finally Becky had a chance to ask the question she'd come over to ask in the first place. "How was Rachel's time at prom?"

Ingrid snorted. "That girl is grounded for the next two weeks and if she even looks at me wrong I'll double it. She got dropped home at *one am* by some boyfriend on the baseball team. No phone call, no nothing. We specifically said—"

"Right, but how was the dance?"

"I get it, she's got a rough deal in the family with all the attention going to—" Ingrid nodded her head toward the therapy clinic as if TJ could hear them. "But this acting out! It's a bad teen movie cliché! You should have *heard* what she muttered when her dad said she smelled like beer."

"Did the DJ do the thing where he—"

"Becky! I have no idea about the damn prom. I've been coughing for ten days, we got some crazy letter from a creditor when I know I paid that bill, I have the carbon check copy, and now my daughter probably lost her virginity in the back seat to some JV shitbox who plays second base."

Becky took a deep breath and refused to allow herself to make the obvious *second base* joke. "Sorry. I know how much you have going on." Her tired friend. No amount of prom magic could erase those faint purple shadows under Ingrid's eyes.

Ingrid tossed her near-empty smoothie cup into a metal garbage can. "No, I'm sorry," she said. "You've been so nice and I took up your whole morning. It's just . . ." She waved her hand at the therapy center. "I better get in there to check in with his team."

Twenty minutes later Becky was nodding off in her front seat. The rain had stopped and a gray fog had rolled in. George Strait's new mega-single "I Saw God Today" woke her up. She wondered if Ingrid thought it was too cheesy or if it got to her the way it was getting to Becky, annoyingly enough. She changed the station.

TJ emerged and stopped right in the doorway. Not wearing his headphones. Stubborn and grouchy in his baggy sweatshirt. From this distance he looked like a regular eighteen-year-old kid out for errands with his mother. But then he wouldn't move. Becky watched as Ingrid slipped past him in the doorway, motioned to him, coaxed him to keep going even as he stonewalled her, began to flap one hand against his thigh.

Was that Anne Murray on the radio? Becky straightened up. You never heard her anymore. This must be a new version of her cover of the Beatles' "You Won't See Me"; another woman's voice was alternating on the verses, aching and smoky. Who was that? Ingrid would know. They'd had a love-hate relationship with "Harmony" when it came out. Becky remembered Ingrid sobbing through embarrassed laughter during "It Happens All The Time."

She lowered the window. Ingrid had both hands in TJ's, talking to him calmly, occasionally touching the side of his face.

Becky turned up the volume, hoping that her friend could hear it.

Ingrid paid no attention. She took baby steps backward, softly leading TJ down the sidewalk in a slow moving dance.

DATE	RECEIVED	NOTES
September 29, 2008	$4,500	Community grounds maintenance, annual
	$6,080	Streetlight reinstallation
	$980	Computer equipment

Becky leaned into Ken's office doorway. "Ready when you are." They had an 11:30 with Accounts Payable.

"You following this?" he asked, so she wandered over to peer at the *Tribune* homepage on his computer.

"People get so worked up over these debates. Anyone in government can get up there and spout sound bites." Plus, Obama was going to win. She knew it, everyone knew it. There were plenty of McCain supporters in town—she saw the yard signs when driving her routes—but the groundswell of excitement for their Illinois rep dominated nearly every discussion in Pierson.

"No, I mean the Lehman stuff. The fallout. They're saying it's the largest bankruptcy filing in US history."

"Oh. Well, it's a shitshow all right," Becky said cheerfully. She hated when he went into a mope. It's true her art world colleagues batted around fears about the Dow plunge and mortgage-backed securities—probably some of them had even been at Lehman's!—but most of Pierson probably still had their money in treasury bonds and savings accounts with interest rates in the low single digits. If not under their mattresses.

"That's the tipping point for me." Ken swiveled away from the computer with force. Maybe it wasn't a mope after all. "I put in that call to the lawyer. If this thing gets worse, and all signs point to that, we can't be late to the show."

Becky stepped back. *Shit.* This couldn't happen. First because the whole thing was preposterous—no matter what outlier cases you could dig up, no court would realistically let them go forward with a claim to bankruptcy protection. But also it couldn't happen because . . . she would be exposed! The mere thought of a lawyer requesting back copies of her files and budgets and accounts made Becky's breathing speed up.

She kept her tone light. "You're saying we should try filing for bankruptcy, our fifteen-thousand-person municipality, because . . . a multibillion-dollar global financial firm might suck up all the available funds?"

"One bank or business will trigger the next, will trigger the next. It's a game of mousetrap, and everything's connected. The courts will be overloaded, the public will turn against the very mention of bankruptcy—if we have any chance, we have to do it now."

"I don't think the council will—"

Ken waved that away irritably. "We won't tell them anything until we know it's possible. Until there's a plan in place."

So his mind was made up. Okay. Okay, she would handle this. Becky edged back toward the door and made a show of checking her watch.

"Let's circle back to this. I'll do some asking around. Quietly, of course."

Ken nodded. They left together for the conference room and while Ken was quiet—resigned, determined—Becky's mind sped ahead with calculations. She'd research municipality filings right away—and there were at least three art world lawyers she could ask for confidential advice. She'd get ahead of it like she always did, through hard work and hustle. When threatened, Becky had learned to move toward the danger.

29

Pierson
2009

KEN TOOK UP DISTANCE RUNNING in a serious way the year that he and Becky tried to file for civic bankruptcy. They traveled to Springfield together a dozen times in the summer of 2009, and his routine became rock solid: upon Sunday night arrival at the Hampton Inn and Suites on Chuckwagon Drive—a name that stopped being amusing after three or so visits—he'd toss his bags in his room, change into exercise clothes, and hit the treadmill in the gym. (Becky learned to hide in her own room during this part, after catching sight of Ken in his short shorts and soaked T-shirt one too many times.) Monday morning he'd be up and out before dawn, jogging along the paved bike paths. In the car to and from their meetings downtown and on the Monday afternoon drive home Becky heard way too much about periodized training, heel striking, and—the worst, of course—*hamstrings*. How could anyone say that word without flinching with disgust?

Ken joined the Pierson Pacers, an unofficial trail running club whose off-roading excursions on Saturday mornings always finished up at Marty's Grill for steak and eggs. He took to stretching during meetings, streaming European cross-country meets on his computer, and wearing a giant gadget watch that recorded his every step, breath, ounce of weight. If asked what prompted all this running, Ken would slap at his middle—Becky saw him do this bit a hundred times—and make a joke about middle-age flab. In truth Mayor Ken Doll only grew more good-looking into his forties, as the silver-gray spread around his temples and the lines crinkled along his smooth forehead and the corners of his mouth. Becky, who compulsively tracked her own gray every morning and night, who spent hundreds every month on rinses and highlights, whose skincare routine involved sonic brushes and microdermabrasion and eye creams made from goat semen, found it infuriating.

Privately, all the secretaries worried about Ken's stress levels. They said among themselves that he was approaching Kenyan marathoner commitment, and that couldn't be good for a weekend warrior with a family.

What the secretaries didn't know, what no one in town knew, was the real reason Ken couldn't stop running. Filing for Chapter 9 would be everything he hated, asking for help, abandoning obligations, announcing to the state the full extent of their failure. *His* failure. But—he reasoned—what other option did they have? The town was teetering under a massive debt load. Fire and police pension funds had gone unpaid for two years. Public project bills were way past due. Vendors had been ignored, salaries barely covered. Fees were at their highest, while almost all services had been slashed or dropped.

"Stop," he begged Becky one night when she handed him piece after piece of paper documenting the full picture of their finances. "We don't need bankruptcy, we need a bulldozer. Nuke it all, and start over."

"It's always the darkest before the dawn," Becky said, getting up for more coffee.

They had stayed late at the office to prepare to meet the Springfield lawyer Ken had hired to put forward their case. What Ken didn't know was how much Becky had done of her own preparation. Over the past few weeks she had feverishly downloaded every piece of relevant case law. She dug up a connection at the Sidley Austin law firm, and had plied him with Negroni cocktails until the man spilled everything he knew about the hypothetical situation she presented him. Using a fake name she'd cold-called legal professors, journalists, and public policy experts. All of it coalescing into one clear conclusion: their case was bad.

When pressed for odds that a lawyer would agree to file on their behalf her Sidley connection had mused, "Thousand to one?"

Thousand to one. Becky could work with those odds. Now she just had to stay close to Ken as it all played out.

If only Ken wouldn't take the budget so much to heart. Like a personal shortcoming, or a fall from grace. It was just *numbers*. Shifted around from screen to screen, page to page. Sometimes Becky really hated how downcast these meetings made him; he'd get quiet and sad, mumbling one-syllable responses to any conversation she attempted. Jesus Christ, *he* wasn't the one simultaneously in a weeks-long four-way auction for Christo sketches that had gone from low to high six figures. *He* didn't have to juggle three phone lines, four secret credit cards, and a cover bank account so active that a branch manager once flagged it for potential fraudulent activity, sending Becky into a swirl of panicky action. Compared to that, Ken was practically on permanent vacation.

"The only other thing is . . ." She hesitated to bring it up at this point in the evening, but they might as well face the worst. "The riverwalk."

Ken put his face in his hands. "I know. I fucking *know*."

Pierson's beloved riverwalk had been degrading for years, decades even, and everyone involved had a different idea of how to fix it. They'd had engineers from local colleges run studies, they'd blocked off sections and done a quick-fix pavement smoothing, they'd priced out retaining walls and girders and steel mesh contraptions. Some helpful resident had posted to his blog a video of crumbling chunks of the sloped wall rolling down into the Rock River. At last count it had over nine hundred views.

"Maybe we can get it taken care of before filing," Ken mumbled. If granted bankruptcy, a new project of that size would be nearly impossible to get approved.

"We still need DNR's report," Becky reminded him. No new work could take place, even if they had the money, until the state finished testing for erosion and sediment control, and the fish people reported on how the fish would handle it.

Ken moaned some more curses into his hands and Becky dropped the whole subject.

All summer Ken insisted they leave by noon on Sundays so he could fit in a long run with his Springfield club before dark. He'd signed up for a half marathon on Labor Day and spent hours (it seemed like) in the car telling Becky how many miles he was scheduled to run every weekend from now until then. Becky let him ramble on, keeping quiet about the fact that she had no idea how long a marathon was, let alone half of one.

Their lawyer, Cynthia Merron, a black woman in her fifties, specialized in large-firm bankruptcy but had agreed to take on their case because she was intrigued by the challenge of whether a municipality filing was even possible. As Becky expected, she spent a lot of time describing how Illinois law was ambiguous on this point. According to the Illinois constitution, municipalities were prohibited from filing for bankruptcy, but a few downstate villages and suburbs had managed it recently, mostly because—as Cynthia put it—they'd been small enough to fly under the radar.

"We're small," Ken insisted. "We're that small!"

Cynthia exchanged a look with Becky. "Uh huh. Well, often it just depends on what evidence exists."

On that point, Becky was ready. She was the one who had prepared their documents for Cynthia, choosing exactly which financials to provide. Throughout the whole of this process she'd be the one to manage the flow of information, not that Ken had ever suggested otherwise. But Becky knew the success of this venture depended on her ability to thread the needle between the appearance of full compliance and the reality of what she needed to conceal.

Cynthia also encouraged them to continue to press lawmakers for funds. Their two contacts at the capitol were state rep Hugh Forbes, who sent an underling as often as he deigned to meet with them, and someone named Willa from the comptroller's branch office. Willa—short, white, and too young to have any authority— listened to Ken's spiels with aggressively noticeable attention, her eyes pinned to his mouth. Becky didn't bother. Unless they got a face-to-face with Illinois Comptroller Dan Hynes himself, it was all wasted air. Ken nevertheless prepared for these pitches to Willa as if they were in the fight for his life: color-coded tabs on obsessively rendered budget reports, photographs of every stalled project or worn-out public area in Pierson, not-so-subtle references to "our service member citizens" (he'd found out Willa's husband was an Army Reserves captain).

On the drives home Ken liked to repeat his best lines, in the same aggrieved tones, as if Becky hadn't heard the performance less than thirty minutes ago. It was 182 miles from Springfield to Pierson. Becky could do it in close to two and a half hours, although she knew Ken felt better when they kept it at the speed limit.

The week after July Fourth they managed to catch Rep Forbes on his way out to lunch. Ken chose to focus on pensions, which—Becky thought later—was a bad move.

Hugh Forbes only laughed when Ken showed him the numbers. "You all don't get the news up in Pierson? *Tribune*'s reporting two hundred billion, that's billion with a B, total debt."

Becky went a little dizzy from that billion-with-a-B.

"Because of . . . pensions?" Ken asked, in disbelief.

"State and local, all retirement benefits." Forbes pushed their folder back across the table. "We're neck-deep and that's for sure. You should know there's a move to cut costs from all downstate school systems. I'm not saying I'd go that way, but it's what I've heard. Bring some accountability back to local governments."

Ken sat back, stunned.

"What do you suggest?" Becky cut in, quickly. "We're underwater on both bonds and retiree benefits."

Hugh held up both his big hands. "Pray? Go back in time and

cast a spell on Cook County Democrats? Because those chickens are home to roost."

That night a tractor-trailer derailed on the Stevenson and Becky and Ken sat in traffic for over an hour. Ken was so down he didn't even complain about Becky playing the new Brad Paisley on repeat. Becky, though she tried to hide it, was elated. Who could pay too much close attention to their exploration of bankruptcy when the whole state was a financial mess? Forget about the national news—financial crisis, the Great Recession. Things were so bad in Illinois that their particular small-time disaster was like one star collapsing into the heat of a supernova. Who could tell which flames consumed what?

Ken ran eight miles for the first time. He ran four the next day and said it was harder than that eight. He got something called plantar fasciitis in his left foot—Becky refused to find out exactly what it was—and spent most of both drives with his shoe off, rubbing the sole of his foot against a golf ball on the floor of the car.

Cynthia told them one colleague advised her to pursue the filing, quick and dirty, and hope to jam it through based on speed alone. Another colleague thought it best to work slowly and carefully, testing the waters at every step. A third thought they had no case whatsoever.

They owed Cynthia $14,000 by mid-July.

On Sunday, July 23, it was still in the mid-nineties when they arrived at the Hampton Inn after dinner. Ken went down to the gym but was back upstairs to their adjoining rooms right away.

Rolling brownouts had caused fuse damage and all the electrical equipment was shut down until further notice. He looked so glum Becky couldn't even laugh. She shut her book—*Wolf Hall* by Hilary Mantel—which had been mailed from a friend in London months before it would be released in the US. "Let's go have a drink in the air conditioning."

"Beer is carbo-loading," Ken said. A slight smile flickered.

By 1 am they were lolling on the strip of grass behind the Hampton Inn parking lot. Ken had convinced the closing-up bartender to give them to-go cups of watery beer. Becky couldn't believe Ken could stand to drink it, warm and flat as it was by now, but he'd finished his and was starting on hers. Then again, he'd been drinking with intention and focus all evening.

"You're going to feel the hurt tomorrow. I mean later today." She lay back and looked up at the night sky. Orion's Belt, she'd always been able to find that first. Big Dipper, of course. Little Dipper. Which one pointed to the North Star? Becky raised a wavering arm—she'd had more than her usual too—and tried to trace a line from the cup's long handle to the right star, the way her father had taught her to do as a girl.

Ken put his hand on her knee. She let it stay there, on her jeans. Felt the soft grass under her bare feet and waited to see what would happen.

For a long moment he said nothing. He was lying on his side, facing her, propped up on one elbow. Big-wheelers revved and rumbled in the dark. At last he said, "I see that I'm going to regret this, but I'm not there yet."

"Maybe you won't even remember." She matched her tone to his: calm, light.

"Now's when you tell me I'm a fool."

"You're a fool," she said softly. But he didn't remove his hand. One of his fingers began a small circle on her knee, again and again.

"I always wondered why you never found someone. I think about it a lot. I think about you a lot. I always have."

So many women would kill for this moment, Becky thought. She could see why, objectively. Ken's throat, that hollow of skin where his top shirt button was open. The heat coming off his body, different in quality from the night's sticky humidity, but a part of that too. His sweetness, his beauty.

He leaned over and then he was kissing her, a sweet shock that had so much right, so much precision, that for a moment Becky kissed him back. Just for a moment, though. When she collected herself, made the micro-movements that would disengage, Ken pulled away at once. "Fuck," he breathed out. Rolled onto his back, away from her. "I'm so sorry. Jesus."

"It's been a long night," she said, wondering if she could make a quick exit to her room. "All those drinks, all the stress recently . . ." She wasn't sorry he'd kissed her but she really didn't want him to spin it into a huge drama.

"Becky. You don't need to say a word."

So she didn't. Eventually he pushed himself to standing and held out a hand to help her up. They went without speaking into the hotel and their separate rooms.

Ken pushed back or rescheduled the next three Monday meetings in Springfield. Becky drove out once by herself and spent three hours in a side office with Cynthia's law clerk going over spreadsheets, invoices, and receipts, with no visible results. Without Ken, she paid for a night at the Radisson, hoping it would be even one notch more luxurious than the godforsaken Hampton Inn and its dry cereal buffet. No appreciable difference, though.

Labor Day was windy and rainy but the whole office, and a good part of the town, turned out to watch Ken run his race in neighboring Sterling. Becky stood near the finish line, which had also been the starting line, for over two hours as one of the bookkeepers talked loudly on her cell phone the whole time. When Ken finally approached, smiling in pain, his twins burst onto the race course from under the barricade and sprinted the last stretch with him, pulling him along by the arms. Everyone from Pierson cheered so loudly they drowned out the announcer calling out finishers' names and times.

Becky kept a respectful distance while Ken bent over, hands to knees, his face a dark shade of red. When he finally stood up he started giving sweaty hugs and high-fives to the crowd of well-wishers, most of whom had contributed to the cancer research charity his training had raised money for. Becky, who had donated an anonymous thousand to the fund, made sure Ken saw her, gave him a thumbs-up, and headed for her car.

Ken took one week off from running after the race but the word was he'd already signed up for another one. Although his right hip flexor was tight.

They returned to Springfield on Sunday, September 23. Shortly after they arrived Becky holed up in her Hampton Inn room with a dossier about her newest obsession, a series of encaustics made to look like ancient funeral paintings: images and lists of provenance, show reviews and similar holdings. Ken thumped around in his adjoining room, but his door never opened. Was he skipping his running? She picked up her head and listened: a squeak of bed-springs and the low murmur of the TV.

When they met for dinner, green curry at Little Saigon, she held back from asking. Ever since the night he'd kissed her, Becky held back from everything, giving Ken the space and time to lead the way forward.

"Bailed on my run today," he admitted, poking at his curry.

"Oh yeah?"

"Stupid. I just felt lazy. Now I wish I'd gone."

"You can get it in tomorrow."

The TV in the top corner of the restaurant played soundless images of the Bears at training camp, huge men in helmets but no pads, moving easily through drills on a sunny field. They were the only ones in the restaurant, and thankfully the owner and server, knowing they were regulars, left them alone.

"I don't know." Ken glanced up and flashed one of his old smiles, a real one. He looked rumpled, as if he'd fallen asleep this afternoon. "I may need to dial back the running. Got a little out of control there."

"No!" Becky exclaimed. He gave a short laugh.

"Also I've been thinking. We need to tell Cynthia we're not going to pursue this."

"Really." She'd been waiting for this, for him to realize the fu-tility. And yet, the defeat in his tired face stopped any feeling of triumph.

"We have to call it. It's adding insult to injury, these bills. She can't even give us a guarantee we'd make it to a hearing!" Ken shook his head. "I'll own it. This was my fantasy, a clean slate. But it's irresponsible to continue, when the odds are so bad."

"Well, if you're sure."

Ken shrugged, staring up at the TV.

"I'm happy to call Cynthia, if you want."

Was he actually watching the game? Becky was antsy to get confirmation: this was over, *thank god*. Tomorrow, they would show up again to Representative Forbes, go through the ritual of asking (begging) for funds, get told no, and drive home. Maybe soon they could move on from this whole Springfield folly.

"Ken?"

"Yeah, fine!" he burst out.

From where he was leaning on the delivery counter with a newspaper, Little Saigon's owner looked up at them over his glasses.

"All right," Becky said quietly.

Ken tossed his balled-up napkin on the table, a kind of apology. They got the check.

The next morning Hugh Forbes gave them none of the false assurances of the comptroller aides and Becky had to admit this was refreshing.

Ken had decided that the environmentalism angle might move Hugh when it came to the riverwalk. He walked him patiently through data on forecasted water levels, and how getting ahead of global warming's effects by shoring up the riverwalk would not only be a major infrastructure win, it would look good to voters in advance of the midterm election. Hugh listened without comment while demolishing a cherry Danish. Becky sighed and got herself a blueberry muffin. At least they'd beat the traffic home.

Finally Hugh swept the photos of the crumbling riverwalk paths into a pile, handed the pile back to Ken. "It's just not there, friends. Possibly after midterms, if we can get movement across the aisle. I hate to say you made the trip in vain, because of course I enjoy the chance to visit." He brushed crumbs off his tie.

Becky filed away these comments, these mannerisms. The subtle glance he gave to the assistants: *Wrap it up, let's move on.* She knew what it was like to say no to budget requests for hours on hours too. For a moment she saw them all in an endless chain of asking and denying: federal to state to local.

One of the assistants passed Hugh an open file folder and pointed to something there with his pen.

"Hm? Oh, I see. Well, at least we got some signage for you, back in mid-August."

Ken laughed. "Those stop signs for the access roads off 52? No, still missing since . . . when was the prom, Becky? The kids had some kind of bet about who could pull down the most."

Becky smiled reflexively. But her mouth had gone cold and dry.

Hugh squinted at the paper. "Fifty-eight hundred, deposit received August 15. Signage."

Ken was relaxed, holding Becky's gaze, *Can you believe this guy?* "Well, I hate to break it to you, but we've had nothing for roads and repair since—"

"Ken," Becky said low.

"Our figures show—"

"And I'm telling you, there are no stop signs on our beltway roads, and it's a safety issue we've brought up time and time again.

One of the *many* safety issues . . . What?" This was to Becky, who was standing now, close to his chair.

"Do you need a copy of this?" Hugh said, confused. Looking back and forth between them.

"No," Becky said smoothly. The main thing was to get Ken out of the room. "We're good. We always appreciate any funds we can get, Representative."

Ken stared at her. She had to physically steer him out of the conference room, his body heavy and slack with confusion.

"I'll let you two get your stories straight," Hugh called after them, chuckling. "Always nice to visit, though!"

Somewhere between the conference room and the car he figured it out. "Fifty-eight hundred," he said.

In Becky's mind a voice screamed, *Yes! Only fifty-eight hundred!*

"You processed that deposit."

"Okay. Look."

"Fifty-eight hundred. It never went into Roads. We went over those accounts at the council meeting, last one of the summer. I remember because you did a riff, you said—"

"Listen, Ken—"

"'What did the stop sign say to the yield sign?'"

Becky said nothing.

"'I don't know,'" Ken recited slowly. "'They were talking in sign language!' It killed. Dumbest joke possible, and they all laughed. Then you told the one where, how does it go . . ."

"Don't. Let's just talk for a minute."

"How does it fucking go, Becky!"

She took a deep shaky breath. They were on the lower level of the parking lot. "A car slows down at a stop sign but doesn't stop. A cop sees him and pulls him over. The cop says . . ."

"What? I can't hear you."

"The cop says, 'Why didn't you stop?' and the man says, 'I slowed down, it's the same thing.' The cop starts beating him with his nightstick. 'All right, so now tell me if you want me to stop or slow down.'"

For a moment Ken just stood there staring at her. Becky held his gaze, nervously, but he only turned and walked fast to their car. Her car.

"You drive," Becky said. She handed him the keys, and pulled out her phone, hectically pressed buttons and the screen to load the bank website.

Ken jerked them forward and sideways out of the lot's turns and into the maze of streets hugging the capitol.

"Here!" Becky held the phone up to him. "See the transfer here? Fifty-eight hundred, right now. It says pending but it will be through by, by, Wednesday morning. End of day tomorrow, maybe!"

He wouldn't look. Straining over the steering wheel, cursing the one-ways only she knew how to navigate.

"It was a temporary thing. I just needed to cover . . . It will never happen again. Ken, you know I'm good for it. Ken! Where are you going?" They were heading the opposite direction from the highway entrance. Becky put her hand on the door handle. Was he taking her to the police station?

"I need to go back to the hotel," he said. Still wouldn't look at her.

"All right. All right. Good idea. We can talk it out. I can explain it, explain everything."

She tried to, a fast jumble of small truths and wide-ranging lies, a messy mix that came out nothing like the thousands of things she'd mentally rehearsed for a moment like this. (Although in all those practice scenarios she hadn't pictured herself thrown around her own car in the passenger seat while Ken drove like a madman.) Yes, she had diverted those funds. She would never do something like that unless it was an absolute emergency and—yes, she had always meant to pay them back. And she had, right now! But honestly, would that $5,800 have made a dent in the access road nightmare? No! He had to know that. She'd known it and that's why . . . She'd gotten in over her head. On a personal matter. An urgent personal matter. A mistake, she'd made a mistake. She would do anything to make this up to him. She'd double the re-payment. She'd fund those signs herself! He had to know she'd do anything for Pierson, anything!

As soon as Ken screeched into the Hampton Inn, he flung himself out of the car. Becky had to turn off the engine, take the keys. When she got into the lobby Ken was at the front desk, ex-plaining he'd forgotten something in his room, could he have the key card back, so sorry about this. Because they were regulars, the woman behind the desk didn't blink. Ken took off down the hall and Becky, grabbing her own key card, chased after him.

"Ken! Wait a minute. Ken, please!"

But he wouldn't wait, he wouldn't look at her. Slipped into his room and shut the door fast, in her face. Ignored her knocking, then her pounding. What was he doing? Was he calling the police? Should she try to run?

Eventually she went into her own room and climbed onto the still-unmade bed. Huddled there, ear to the wall. Nothing for a long while, and then rustled movements she couldn't parse. As soon as his door opened Becky sprang to her own door. Ken was disappearing down the hallway in his running clothes.

Becky slowly backed into her room. A gaspy, panicky laugh, relief, bubbled up in her. He was going for a run! The police weren't on the way if he was going for a run! She walked from the window to the bathroom alcove, and around the bed. Playing it out in her mind. He knew she took the money, he saw she returned it, and he was now out for a run.

Ken wouldn't turn her in. He couldn't because—according to his own moral calculus, which she knew almost as well as her own—he'd done wrong too. That night on the hotel grass, the way he'd leaned down and kissed her. He'd crossed a line, presumed too much. If he pulled the trigger, pressed charges, Becky knew Ken wouldn't be able to withstand all of the public fallout for her crime—her *fifty-eight-hundred-dollar* crime!—without also remembering his own misdeed. He might even convince himself that one had led to the other. And even if she never told anyone what he'd done, *especially* if she never told anyone, the fact of his leaning down and kissing her would drive him crazy with self-loathing.

When Ken got back from his run, Becky came out to the lobby and saw him slow to a stop in the parking lot. She raised an arm and after a moment, he returned her wave. Acknowledged her.

Right then, Becky swore to herself—the only person who mattered—that she would find a way to pay it back. This couldn't go on much longer. She was forty-four. Ken had had his glimpse. She would need to be more careful now than she ever had been. But she would make it right, for Ken, for Ingrid, for Pierson.

If she got this last set of paintings, she would have enough. And as soon as she had enough, she'd dismantle everything and pour all the money back.

30

Pierson
2011

IN THE LAST PHASE, BECKY worked harder than she'd ever worked before. She had two extra phone lines put in at the farmhouse, and the international deals had her up at all hours of the night, as she sold and traded endlessly in order to finance what she hoped would be her final big buys. In the Art Barn she had put together completed sets of works that focused on method and mode: preliminary sketches in graphite, in crayon, in ballpoint. She had sets defined by genre and image and era: every photorealist painting of a seated older woman who was a relative of the artist, completed in the year 1999. Textile wall hangings but only single-color by heterosexual male artists of the American South.

Becky had lived for the intensity of these searches, one-upping herself for every challenge she set. So much mental effort, so many variables to consider, so many hours and hours of research and phone calls and bids and failed bids and reversals and . . .

Sometimes she'd drive home from Town Hall in the middle of the workday, dizzy from fatigue, and fall hard asleep for an hour or more, shoes on, keys in the door. She ate three-course meals before dawn, drank four pots of coffee a day, and lost all sense of when a bowel movement might occur. Although her mind stayed sharp, the toll was taken on her skin: dermatologist after dermatologist couldn't cure the hives on her throat, the rosacea behind her knees, the delicate rash in the folds of her eyelids. Though meticulous facials and pricy skin creams meant she could hide most anything. Sometimes, clumps of red hair would come out in the shower, and that did scare her into a week or two of vitamins, brisk morning walks, spinach in her salads.

The chest pain, though, was what worried her the most, and therefore what she paid attention to the least. Others noticed, she could tell, when a wince seized her, cut her off mid-sentence. She took to knocking her sternum with a fist, shaking a bottle of Tums, which allowed people to commiserate about acid reflux. But it wasn't acid reflux.

Becky had come around to panic attacks in theory except— this was the weird part—now the pain in her chest sometimes started as a poker in her back, or a burning low sore throat. Her bad thoughts and feelings about getting caught, more frequent than ever since Ken caught her in Springfield, only sometimes overlapped with these pains. One type of distress might set off the other, or might occur a few hours later, and who could tell how, or if, they were related? Terror and chest pain chased each other night into day, day into night.

It was brilliant, what she'd made in the Art Barn, even if no one else would ever know. But it was time, more than time, to give it up. All she had to do was complete this last project. Complete the completing.

■ ■ ■

Miles Green, *Self-Portrait at the Docks*, 18 by 20 inches, watercolor, 1934–1935. A young black man, staring out of the canvas, cigarette lodged in the right corner of his mouth, its single smoke plume obscuring one eye. The other eye leveled straight at the viewer, giving nothing away. Behind the man, washy gray water, green-brown hulk of a crate, slats of a pallet. Ambiguous time of day.

Becky couldn't stop thinking about it. Night and day, she saw the man—Miles, as she thought of him—with his back to the Delaware, smoking, daring anyone to come for him. She wanted this painting more than she'd ever wanted anything, even that Eric Fischl at her first Art Expo, even the Caitriona Molloy she'd screwed the Babies over for.

For more than a year she hunted down the Green watercolor portraits, four of the five that existed. One by one she got her trophies, clearing a wall in the central room in the Barn to make way. There was much less interest in the watercolors than in Green's later oil work, but this group had been surprisingly hard to find and buy. Two retired dealers (New York and Paris), an African-American literacy foundation in Georgia, and the provost of Howard University: each had owned their Green watercolor since purchase. Each transaction took months, for Becky to procure the right introductions, get to know the owners, travel to and from various cities during negotiation.

Miles Green's later work, the 1950s civil rights paintings, were wall-sized oils in museums around the world, action scenes of horrific violence and chaos: clashes between protestors and police, tear gas, dogs, water cannons spraying with a heavy brutal sting. These were canonized works. They were studied in art history, history, social studies, black studies, cultural studies. Green's own story— son of Pennsylvania sharecroppers, self-taught while working as a postal carrier, worked his way into a long series of teaching appointments, met MLK, met RFK, loaned his images and time wherever they could help the movement, death by heart attack in 1981—cemented his reputation. The watercolor owners could ask what they wanted, and they did. She paid it.

But the *Docks* portrait remained at large. This stupid, maddening square of canvas, this missing piece, wouldn't let her go.

Greta Dreiser, the director of Philadelphia's American Museum, had declined to speak with Becky over and over, despite Becky calling in favors from every connection she knew they shared. When Ms. Dreiser finally consented to a phone call, she refused to answer any questions about *Self-Portrait at the Docks*: Why hadn't it been on display in over a decade? Could the museum show the terms of purchase? What would it take for an offer to be considered? At this, Ms. Dreiser simply hung up the phone.

The Green family was spread across the Eastern seaboard, and consisted of at least ten middle-aged sons and daughters from Miles's three wives. Most—but not all—were involved in the Miles Green Foundation dedicated to managing the artist's works, holdings, and rights issues. The foundation's executives coolly informed Becky they had no comment on the terms of purchase for *Docks* and in any case they discouraged museum sales whenever possible. It was impossible to approach the matriarch, Miles's widow: she was legendary for imperiousness, capriciousness, venom. And closely guarded by all her children. So Becky began to work her way through the Green siblings and grandchildren (writers, actors, one was an art director at ICP), traveling to New York, DC, Philadelphia, and the Connecticut suburbs at least nine times over a period of three months. She took them to dinner, to coffee, to baseball games. She learned their favorite foods, writers, their children's names, pet peeves, schedules, college teams. It didn't help that she was white, of course, while she tried to make inroads in these most elite black communities, but the Greens were familiar with the art world's asks.

She was absent from Pierson so much that a rumor started, which she didn't discourage, that she had a new boyfriend somewhere out East. When she was in the office she watched Ken carefully, though it didn't appear as though he meant to do anything different. He still ate lunch with her several times a week, sharing takeout in the conference room with anyone else who wanted to join them. She'd doubled down on all covert procedures, even making herself wait a long three weeks after Springfield before putting one dollar through the Activity. But she couldn't wait longer than that, and carefully, slowly, and thoroughly she restarted the fake invoices and diverted funds.

Corrine Green Garland, an exec at ColorComm, listened without judgment and said she had no interest in persuading American to sell any of her father's work. Gregory Green, an orthopedist and professor of medicine in Philadelphia, gave Becky twenty minutes in between classes at Perelman, and laughed: *I stay out of that as much as I can, nothing good can come from me in Berta's business.* Roberta Green had an assistant take Becky on a tour of the Green Foundation offices and gave a pro forma response that all museum holdings were to be treated under the original terms of sale. No, she would not care to hear Becky's pitch. No, she did not care to meet to discuss further. Jim Green couldn't be found; Freda Green Johnston was in the hospital from diabetes complications; Jan Green grew so suspicious of Becky she had a lawyer send a cease and desist.

She sent flowers and made donations to charities. She slept

with an ex-husband of one of the daughters even as she doubted his shady claims of influence at the Foundation. Becky knew she was pushing all the limits: she'd sold off as many other items as she could to fund this pursuit, she let all the other opportunities, other artists she might come to love, slip away. She stopped making the rounds, attending the shows, cultivating the future. One by one she burned through art world connections and influencers, and any dealers who might help, her biggest bluest chips.

You sure, Reba? She could hear the unspoken question behind every call, every searching conversation. These were the big players, people at Emmerich and Boone and Saatchi. It had taken years to build up these relationships and you only got one ask of this magnitude. *Green was a master, to be sure, but . . . all this for one lesser portrait? In watercolor?* Becky would laugh a bit, passing it off as whim, eccentricity. In any case, none of them could make it happen, and she'd cashed in every connection.

One evening in the United Club at Philly International Becky idly leafed through a left-behind issue of *The New Yorker*, stopping for some reason on what seemed like a medical article called "The Itch." Halfway through, with a growing horror of recognizing herself, Becky stuffed the magazine into her purse. She finished it on the plane.

The article, written by a surgeon, was about people who suffer from repeated, continuous itching in one spot with no apparent cause, a kind of neurological oddity. Nothing alleviated the maddening sensation, no drug or procedure. The sufferers exhausted practitioners, got labeled mentally ill, tied themselves up at night to prevent damaging their skin with endless scratching. One woman scratched at the side of her head so intensely that one morning she woke up leaking fluid from the area. The clinic doctor who examined her immediately called for a transfer by ambulance—the woman had scratched through her skin to brain matter.

Late that night Becky lay in bed and sobbed. What was it like to have just your one regular life and to be *content*? She was almost forty-seven years old and she had so much and it was never enough. Sometimes after she got a cherished painting up on her wall the sense of satisfied quiet that welled up inside, the only peace she ever knew, didn't last a week. Sometimes it didn't last an *hour*. Behind any happiness Becky could always feel the monster ready to awaken, ready to make her burn with longing and need.

It was Pierson that gave her the key to getting *Docks*. A Pierson wedding, one she never would have found time to attend if she hadn't been, in fact, the officiant. Mrs. Fletcher, now retired, had somehow extracted a promise that Becky would run the show when her son got married, if he ever got married. Becky had no memory of agreeing to this. It was half a joke; Robby was always falling in and out of love with one woman or another. But the joke was on Becky, because Robby found the real deal with an actor named Tim and on an October Sunday in 2011, there she was at the front of First Presbyterian reading out a short speech she'd come up with on a San Francisco red-eye twelve hours before. It was Pierson's first gay civil union, the church was full and buzzing, and Becky couldn't help smiling back at Mrs. Fletcher beaming with joy in the front row.

(She tried to repress the sting of the story about the photographer, who wanted to get shots of the happy couple and their families down by the Rock River earlier in the day, per Pierson tradition. By the time everyone had gathered at the Galena bridge, the photographer and his assistant had called it off. They'd taken one look at the abandoned riverwalk and determined there was no angle that could avoid its decrepitude.)

That was when it hit her, in the church, when her gaze slid across the aisle to Tim's family's side. His much more complicated family, sprouted along several divorce and remarriage lines, including his two stepmothers and his grudging father who had only recently come around to Tim's "lifestyle choice." Mrs. Fletcher had related the entire saga, the convoluted arrangements and reception politics, and what Becky had not paid attention to at the time but remembered now, looking at all the drama-causers, was one line: *That man's new wife gets all the attention but it's Tim's mother I'm going to give the best seat in the house.*

Tim's mother. Heart pounding, Becky's eyes sought her out, an older woman, unassuming, wiping her eyes. The first wife.

As soon as she could, she excused herself from the festivities.

It wasn't Miles Green's widow she needed access to, that imperious, well-guarded figure, it was his *first wife.* That's who would have sold the portrait to American!

Five weeks later, Tarek and Mrs. Green's chauffeur helped Adaline Green Remington into the Barn. They carried her wheelchair in but it was Becky who steered her down the ramp and into the gallery.

Mrs. Green—Becky knew that wasn't her name anymore, but she couldn't help thinking it—took her time settling herself. She was thin and straight-backed in her chair, a pale African American with dark speckles across her nose and cheeks, glossy hair neatly curled and pinned. Once she'd arranged her scarf and straightened her trousers, her hands lay heavy in her lap, pink palms up.

Then she looked at the work. Tarek had rehung the four portraits at Becky's precise measurements so they'd be at eye level for Mrs. Green in her wheelchair.

"Well."

If the portraits unsettled her, this woman who'd been married to Miles Green for only four years, no children, before the boom of his fame and fortune, she didn't show it. Becky knew she couldn't have seen these paintings since they were made in the drafty railroad flat the two of them had shared in the 1930s.

"So you really did. Get these together, almost all of them."

"I did."

"That one—" Mrs. Green pointed with her knuckles to *Self-Portrait, Pool Hall.* "You got it from that fellow in Canada?"

"Maybe," Becky said.

"He bilked you."

Becky laughed. "Probably."

"Let me see that one. The third one." Becky went to the painting and carefully lifted it off the wall, offering it to Mrs. Green with both hands. When it was on her lap, Mrs. Green breathed a long sigh. Becky crouched down and they both studied the exquisite little masterpiece.

For a long time they were quiet. Becky wondered what these paintings looked like to Mrs. Green, all these young faces of the man who'd left her for another woman, after many other women. That was so long ago in her full life. A private investigator had found her, married and comfortable, surrounded by kids and grandkids, in a Houston suburb. Becky had expected to have to woo hard, but it had taken only one heartfelt handwritten letter to persuade Mrs. Green to come see these pieces (all expenses paid, of course). Becky had offered to pay for her husband or son or anyone else to accompany her, but aside from the chauffeur arrangements, Mrs. Green had wanted to come alone.

At last Mrs. Green handed the frame back. "What does the Foundation say?"

"It doesn't matter. Your name is on the papers."

"And what's the museum say?"

"They wouldn't say much to me, unfortunately."

"But you want it, the one of him at the docks."

"Very much."

Mrs. Green was nodding slow and heavy. "You'd keep it here, with the others?"

"Right there." Becky pointed at the space reserved for it.

Mrs. Green laughed, a dry cough of a laugh. Becky didn't understand, smiled uneasily. "I don't mind," the woman said eventually, still chuckling. "I don't mind at all. Sure, put it here. Put him all the way down here."

Becky was afraid to clarify, but she stumbled through it anyway, the embarrassing need to confirm that it was happening, it was true, it was *yes*. Yes, yes, yes. She pushed Mrs. Green's unwieldy chair back up the ramp herself. Floated them both up to the waiting chauffeur.

The day Tarek hung *Self-Portrait at the Docks* didn't arrive for nearly six long months, as American dragged out all the paperwork and legal proceedings for the sale. But when he did, Becky was frantic, barely contained, barely breathing until she could be left alone in the room.

Miles Green, self-portraits in watercolor. A completed circle, completely perfected. Five strong faces, one face. Together for the first and only time.

Look at what I did. Oh look. Look.

Becky stayed down in the Art Barn with those portraits for as long as she could. She would make it last, this moment. As soon as she was up there again—out there again, in the world—she would have to think about the long strips of yellow caution tape strung along Pierson's riverwalk on both sides of the banks. The boards nailed to block the stairs that led down to what had been deemed a public hazard. She'd have to think about the op-ed that displayed a photo of the ugly damaged walkways next to one from thirty years ago, kids holding balloons and dangling their feet off the still-pristine concrete. *It's a shame*, everyone said. It did shame Becky, every time she drove across a bridge and had to glimpse the crumbled mess that ran the length of the town.

She couldn't fix the riverwalk now. The time to have done that was ten, maybe twenty years ago, according to the last surveyor team they'd had out. Their official recommendation was a complete tear-down, strip the banks and install blocks of mesh-wrapped rocks, a miserable low-cost retaining wall. Even all the money Becky had spent chasing these Miles Green portraits couldn't bring back Pierson's beautiful riverwalk. Time and the river's endless flow had eroded the town's shores irrevocably.

"Crumbled things from the inside," is how one of the engineers had put it.

But in her subterranean gallery was this small piece of perfection, these portraits brought together for the first and maybe last time. Becky had done that, so she would stay down with them as long as she could.

31

Pierson
2012

IT TOOK A LONG TIME for Becky to recover after completing the Green portraits. In fact, she never did recover in time. Just after the *Docks* painting arrived she fell ill with the flu and a high fever, spending two days at the hospital for fluids and another week in bed—the first time she could remember taking time off work for anything other than art business.

On a follow-up visit to her GP, the doctor took one look at Becky and ordered a full workup. She was visibly weakened and had lost almost twenty pounds from her already slight frame. There were sores in her throat and white lines on her fingernails she'd never noticed before. I'm fine, she insisted. Just need to eat more meat. She tossed the prescription for follow-up tests in the garbage on her way to the parking garage, but annoying health issues continued to plague her.

All that summer she often had to work from home, constantly on speakerphone with the office, having the junior accountants drive to and from with folders and paperwork and the mail, of course. She insisted that the mail be brought to her as usual, and as usual everyone accommodated this eccentricity. Mrs. Bucaro— who was covering Mrs. Fletcher's desk until Becky could fig- ure out how to replace Mrs. Fletcher (no one could replace Mrs. Fletcher)—boxed up stack after stack of get-well cards that had been dropped off by residents and vendors. Everyone wondered when she would be back "for good." Becky herself wondered. Some days she felt energy returning, but most mornings she couldn't will herself out of bed. Would end up bringing her laptop and phone into bed and doing as much as she could from there.

She couldn't even begin to think about tackling plans for a giant sale, dismantling as much of her collection as she could, the recoup of capital that would let her pour all the money back into Pierson's coffers. Right now that was too much, too hard. But she would. She'd get it back.

By the end of September Becky had made it into the office several days in a row. One morning Ken poked his head in first thing. "Hi," he said, staying outside the door. She saw him try to hide his surprise at how she looked: pale, wobbly, lessened, no matter how hard she'd worked on her makeup and outfit this morning.

"Thank god," Becky said, pushing one of four fruit baskets toward him. "Someone to help me eat my way to a clear desk."

"Just wanted to say, um, how're you feeling?"

Becky wondered if they would ever find their way back to the easiness of the years before, when their visions for Pierson were so aligned and clear, their goals and methods so closely determined. Used to be that Becky had literally been unable to tell who had written a budget memo, because over the years her language had become entwined with Ken's. All that had died with the Spring-field trips.

"I'm back." She smiled. "Want to come in?"

"No. No, that's okay. I've got the thing at eleven. Did you change things around in here?" He gestured at her office, where the quietly expensive furniture was arranged as usual. Only a familiar eye would have caught the difference: the art, almost all of it, was gone. Becky had pruned her collection down to the bone, first as a way of becoming a completist, and later in order to raise funds for the Green portraits.

"Just a refresh," she said, smiling at him.

"Anyway—you'll get me those edits? Any time this afternoon." He tapped twice on the doorframe.

"Listen, Ken?" Becky stood, but dizziness overtook her and she needed to press a hand against her desktop. "Whoa—"

"Are you—" Ken started toward her.

"Fine, fine." Becky waved him away. "I just wanted to say that I—"

"You should take care, Becky," Ken said quietly. "Take it easy today." Then he left.

November 29, 2012. Almost two months since Ken stopped by her office alone. When Becky pulled into her spot behind Town Hall she instantly noticed the drab brown Toyota out of alignment in the parking lot, engine running. She'd driven in from Chicago where she'd spent a night at the horrible Hilton on State in order to hand-deliver a piece to a German gallerist who—surprisingly—sold her on three new Luc Tuymans he had brought for a private showing. Becky hadn't been at all interested in Tuymans until she saw these in person. Two of the larger pieces were in her trunk now and one unframed sketch lay in the leather tote bag on the seat next to her.

Becky observed the two women in their strange car, their eyes on her, their Illinois plates. When she shut off the engine and stepped into the cold dry air they did too. They followed her at a distance of fifty yards as she struggled to open the building's rear door while balancing a box of yellow and pink frosted cupcakes. Padma Bedi was having twins and this afternoon was the office shower.

Becky didn't look back, although the women followed her up the stairwell, not saying a word. She felt them follow her into the long hall that led to her office, door open, no secretary in sight. Becky still didn't look back, even though by now she knew.

After that, things happened fast. Many people in her office. Men in FBI windbreakers, men in suits, uniformed police officers. Talking loud and hard to her or to each other. Her arms were relieved of cupcakes. Someone was very close, hands along her sides, her underarms, her thighs, the back of her neck. Her couch was tipped down and away from the wall, her bookcases emptied, her desk drawers broken open. She began to protest, not at the fact of what was being done, but its method. Couldn't they slow down? Couldn't they be more careful?

And then at last, the moment she'd feared and dreaded and imagined for nearly thirty years: "Rebecca Farwell, this is a warrant for your arrest on charges of fraud. You have the right to remain silent. You have the right . . ."

"I want to read it," Becky broke in, stopping the man's recitation. Close-cropped gray hair, unbuttoned suit jacket. "Can I—am I allowed to read it?"

Her arms were released, and she took the papers into her hands. Everyone in the room got quiet. Becky ran her eyes over the text, the embossed seal, the government heading, but the pages shivered before her and she only wanted the stolen moment to gather herself, to try to breathe through and around the heartbeats hammering at her throat, lungs, skull.

"All right." She handed the warrant back. "Go ahead." Becky could sense without seeing the consternation of a crowd building in the hall: assistants, secretaries, accountants.

How had it finally happened? What was the detail that snagged, that gave it all away?

Later she would learn that the cause had been her uterine biopsy, which her ob-gyn had insisted on when he discovered her erratic and often missing periods. Supposed to be a minor procedure but she'd had pain and a fair amount of bleeding, so she took two days off to recover. She hadn't informed the office of anything—none of anyone's business—but neither had she arranged for an assistant to get the mail; she'd assumed each day that she'd be strong enough to drive over to the post office at some point. But then the Norco made her sleepy and she put off calling someone to do it and eventually decided without actually deciding that she could skip that whole rigmarole. Just the once.

At the moment of her arrest, Ken was in his house. He had two FBI agents standing in his foyer, off and on their phones, plus a couple more in an unmarked car parked out front.

Ken sat at his kitchen table, doing nothing. Marie had taken the kids to her sister's in St. Louis. They wanted to make sure that the twins had as much peace as possible before the town exploded with the news.

Three weeks ago, Rosalind McInterye from Accounting had tapped on his door: worried, uncertain. He listened to her story with a sinking feeling. Earlier in the day Ros had gotten a call from her assistant who'd gotten a call from a temp, a floating temp they all liked named Trevor. Trevor had been on Becky's floor for the past few days, answering calls, filing, responding to letters. So he happened to be there when the postman called, surprised that Ms. Farwell hadn't stopped by that day, or the one before, to get the mail.

No problem, Trevor said. I got it. He carried the two plastic tote boxes into Town Hall and settled in to open and sort the mail. He used the wide empty surface of Mrs. Fletcher's old desk to open the bills and letters, arranging them into neat piles. *Make yourself necessary,* his mom always told him. So he organized the mail by department and delivered most of it to the right in-boxes. All well and good.

Except all the different bank statements were confusing. Some were obvious, but what about this Midwest Credit Union account, for example? Should that statement get filed with all the others, or should he put it on Ms. Farwell's desk? On her desk, he thought. But maybe he should check first.

So Trevor asked one of the accounting assistants to take a look. She asked her boss. Soon that woman came over and took away more of the statements—*messing up my piles,* Trevor thought—for further study.

Ken didn't leave the office until nearly three the next morning. At eight am, with two lawyers behind closed doors, Ken called the police. By the time Becky returned to the office two days later, the FBI had opened a case. For the next seventeen days they tracked her every move, meticulously uncovered her money trail, bugged her phone. And all the while Ken had to smile and joke and run meetings with her, and never let on.

His refrigerator had a cycle of noise about one minute long: hum, rattle, hiss, back to humming. Ken listened to it churn, unable to move, unable to ask the agents if it was over.

In the agony of the past twenty-something days he'd said the same thing over and over to the investigators: *I'll do anything.* He had no choice, of course. *I'll do whatever you need me to do. I just can't be there when it happens.*

Even though Becky Farwell had ruined his career and most probably was about to ruin his life, Ken Brennan recognized what was true about himself in his kitchen: it was him, failing her, right now.

Becky realized Ken wasn't there, even though she would have had a hard time sighting him through the melee of agents and police crowded in her office. She could feel that he wasn't there, even as she called his name. He wouldn't have been able to take this, she thought, as her arms were positioned for the cuffs.

Trapped, unable to move. Rising panic.

But maybe she still had time? For one last stolen moment?

"I have to go to the bathroom." Politely, clearly. Though they all still ignored her, preparing to move.

"Excuse me," she said, twisting to direct this at the female agent who held her arms. "I need to go."

It took a few exchanges between the agents and their boss, the

gray-haired man who'd shown her the warrant, but eventually it
was cleared. The female agent—Becky recognized her as one of
the two who'd followed her in from the parking lot—took off the
cuffs and led her out of the office. Her own personal restroom was
across the hall.

"But I need my bag," Becky said, voice wobbling. That was the
point!

"You're going to use the toilet," the woman said, not unkindly.

"Could you get it for me? The brown one, the leather tote?"

No answer. Step by step, she was being forced toward the bathroom. Wrong, all wrong! Now Becky became aware of others in
the hall, office workers gathered by the west stairs. Some dropped
their eyes when she saw them. One was crying. Most stood mo-
tionless in utter shock.

"Wait, please!" Becky cried. "Could you get my—ow—Wait!"
Someone else had taken hold of her arm, not gently, and together
the agents pushed her into the small powder room. One held the
stall door open, the other stood in the main doorway.

"Go."

"But I—"

"You have thirty seconds to urinate."

Shaking, stymied, Becky gave up hope. What a foolish plan,
to somehow get in here alone with her bag and have time enough
to take out the Tuymans, unwrap it, and hold that small beauty in
quiet, in private.

When she wept, it was for her own stupidity and because she
felt the full loss of that impossible last moment and because she
had to hike up her skirt and lower her underwear in front of two
strangers with guns, had to crouch, trembling, as they watched,

had to piss with both doors open, the stall and the restroom, had to piss in full view of the hallway where her coworkers had gathered, and she did, with wet cheeks and bare thighs, she cried and pissed and the agents were right there, impassive, unconcerned, and Becky understood for the first time what life would be like from now on.

32

Pierson
2012—2014

THE VEHICLES CAME AND WENT every day to the Farwell property—to what was still then, technically, the Farwell property: local and state police cars, SUVs with the US Marshals Service logo on the door, and unmarked sedans driven by FBI agents. They parked on the paved walkway, out back on the grass, anywhere outside the cones and stakes set up around the barn.

The police set up a barricade at each corner of County Road M and kept all media vans back a quarter mile. They turned away any curious onlooker, local or not.

They took the doors off the barn. Set up enormous light fixtures and power cords and plastic cones. Used ribbons of tape to mark off an entrance and an exit; carried boxes in, carried boxes out. Talked seriously in small groups: measuring, photographing, recording. Set up tarps, a folding table, a sort of staging area. Moved cars out of the way for a forklift.

After many months, the main operation was complete. FBI and federal marshals had removed all the art. Sometime after that, surveyors finished assessing the Art Barn itself—how it had been modified, the amount of construction work it had taken to build out the sublevel. Someone took away the tarp and pulled up the stakes.

What bothered Becky was that they'd never replaced one of the barn doors. It stayed propped against the opening, not attached back onto its top sliding hinge, giving the barn a caved-in look, like a mouth with its dentures removed. How Hank would have hated to see his good strong door now bowed in and weakening against the frame. If there was one thing he couldn't stand, it was people who didn't take care of their tools and their property.

Becky had many long hours to think about this, looking out at the now-emptied structure: the same red, the same wood, the same size as it had always been. If she was tired enough she could trick herself into thinking nothing had changed about her father's barn. If you ignored the ever-present cop car—and the tilted door—it was the same old place out of which they'd once run Farwell Agriculture Inc.

One morning toward the end time of house arrest, Becky sat up in bed, quietly but instantly awake. Thinking she must have heard something. She crept to the shades and looked down onto the front yard, the empty road: nothing. Except—there. Someone walking slowly toward the house. Becky gasped and flew to the stairs, her robe trailing open behind her.

She flung open her front door. "Ingrid!"

Ingrid came up the walkway. She put a hand up to shade her

eyes and saw Becky there in the door. She stopped and put a hand on her back, looked over her shoulder.

"Please," Becky said.

Ingrid nodded, after a moment, and came inside. Becky hadn't seen or spoken to her in twenty-two months.

"Did anyone follow you or . . . bother you?"

"No." Her tone was uninviting so Becky didn't explain about the cars that swept up and down the street at odd hours. Sometimes it was just to gawk. But sometimes it was to scream curses or dump garbage on the lawn or, once, heave bags of dog shit onto her front steps.

"I'm so glad you're here," Becky said quickly. "Did you get my messages, my letters? I didn't know if you wanted to see me."

"I didn't. I don't, really." Ingrid's voice was calm and dry. She walked a little farther into the living room, taking it in. Agents had combed through the house and taken anything of value. The carpet was ghost-lightened where furniture had stood. Bookcases were gone, and the dining set. Most of the cabinets and closets were empty.

Becky had waited weeks, months, for a letter back, before understanding it wouldn't come. Every day mail flooded into the house, letters and letters, infuriated townspeople, dismayed people from her past, anyone and everyone she'd ever met, or so it seemed. Becky rarely opened an envelope from the heavy piles, although one day a plain business-sized envelope with "D. Marner" written above the return address squeezed at her chest. Diana Marner, Becky's math teacher from so many years ago. The one who'd driven her to math tournaments, who'd smoked Slims, who thought Becky could have followed in her own path. Becky stood in the foyer and held that unopened letter for a long, long time before dropping it down to the floor with the rest of them.

"So," Ingrid said. She turned to gaze directly into Becky's eyes. "Are you all right?"

"Oh sure. I'm okay. Let me get you a glass of water, let me—"

"It's fine."

Becky hurried to fill one even though Ingrid waved her off. "Why did you walk, it's hot out already, it's—"

"Neil didn't want me to come, so I didn't want to take the car." Ingrid ignored the glass Becky held out to her. Becky wavered, then set it down on the kitchen counter.

"How have you been? How are the kids? Okay, Neil, too. See? Here I am, asking about Neil." Why was she joking around, for god's sake? "We can sit—here, I have these chairs." She dragged two plastic folding chairs from the utility closet and opened them facing each other where the dining room table used to be.

Surprisingly, Ingrid sat down at once. She was so much heavier than Becky had expected. She'd gained, it seemed, thirty or more pounds. The area around her eyes was swollen in the way it always was when she had cried. She wasn't crying now, though. "You have no idea, do you. Of how much harm you did. You think it's just about you."

"Of course I don't! It's not just about me—it was *never* just about me! The whole time, I was putting money back in. I was planning to put it all back! And I would have, if I'd just had more time."

Ingrid laughed, short and mean. "Oh please."

"I did things for the town that never could have happened if I hadn't taken some money. It's complicated to explain, but whatever money I used made *more* money, when I—"

"When you flipped the criminal goods you'd bought using stolen funds?" Ingrid slapped her hands against her thighs, once, hard. "Let me have that water."

Becky, caught off guard by the propulsion of Ingrid's words, hurried to get it and sat back down.

Ingrid gulped and wiped her mouth. "You did what was right for you. What made you feel good, so you could tell yourself you were the town hero. Instead of a fucking vampire, sucking us dry."

"I took care of you," Becky blurted out. "I did my best to help you out, didn't I? Every one of your needs, everything you'd let me do, was taken care of."

"Well, that's the worst part, isn't it?" Ingrid's eyes glittered, and her smile was horrible. "I know you did. So does everyone else. They all believed I was in on it."

"No!" Becky said, truly surprised. Not possible that anyone would see Ingrid in that way. "No one would think you—"

"You should have seen what it was like. Women shunning me at church, so I stopped going. Rachel got so many hate messages we had to close her accounts. Friends I'd had for thirty years wouldn't return my calls."

"Ingrid," Becky breathed.

But Ingrid was on a roll. "Neil left me. He's back now, but yeah, we separated for a year. We fought all the time, because he'd never liked my friendship with you, he never trusted you, and he didn't hold up well through the investigations. Rachel dropped out of school for a bit because she was worried about me."

Becky curved into herself, hands over her mouth. She could handle this only if Ingrid would stop using that bright hard voice. "I never—"

"What was worse than what everyone said, though, was what

everyone was thinking. That I knew. What you were doing." Ingrid stood up, walked around the empty room. "And you know what? I did. I didn't know that you were stealing millions of dollars from Pierson—from me, and every other taxpayer you've lived with your whole life—so you could buy yourself some fancy art collection. I didn't know the specifics. But I knew." She was nodding to herself, her back to Becky. "So many times I thought, this is fishy. Or, this can't be right. But did I listen to myself?"

"Please don't say that."

"Did I stop you, all those times you paid for things? Did I ever really make myself look at what felt off? No. I took money from you not just for me but for my kids. Which means I let them . . . I let them benefit from—" Now she was crying, and Becky was also. Ingrid stood and cried into her hands and Becky wanted to get up from her plastic lawn chair but she was afraid to go to her. How could she not have known how this would have played out? How Ingrid would take it on herself, absorb Becky's crimes as if they were her own?

After some time, Ingrid wiped her face, came back over to drink the rest of the water. But she didn't sit down.

"Ingrid." Becky's voice wobbled. If only she could make this better. "I'm so sorry, so sorry for . . . You are the best person I know, and I never ever wanted anything to happen to you."

Ingrid shrugged. "You know, the other night we were watching TV and something about you came on." Ingrid smiled, her old smile, and it pierced Becky. "Neil was about to change the channel but I heard the news guy say that you didn't get arrested for so long after they found out— It was a month, right?"

"Right."

"For a whole month, you didn't get arrested because the FBI

said there had to be someone else involved. A man. They thought a woman could never pull off that level of fraud by herself."

Becky smiled thinly. She'd heard this, too, from her lawyers.

"Neil switched it right off but I thought, *She'd get a kick out of that.*" She hesitated, then said, "I came today to tell you that I'm going to testify for the government. Next week."

The sentencing trial was to be held at a federal court in downtown Chicago. Becky had thought it would have come sooner, given her immediate guilty plea and complete cooperation—she provided information about the art, detailed specs on artist, price, provenance. Through her court-appointed lawyers she did as much as possible to aid with the seizure of assets for resale. The higher the auction prices, the better it would be for Pierson. Of course with the feds in charge of assets forfeiture it was sure to be a mess. She knew the art world must be in a frenzy, terrified of Becky's tainted pieces flooding the market all at once, dragging down prices and scaring away buyers.

"All right," Becky said. "I mean . . . I'm glad you are. If it will help at all, like . . . help you prove once and for all you didn't have anything to do with—"

"You think I'm doing this for me?" Ingrid said, her voice sharp again. "I'm doing it for TJ." She waited, and Becky's confused silence seemed to confirm something. "For TJ and all the others. Everyone who could have benefited from the Sunrise Program."

"The what?" Even as she said it, Becky knew it was the wrong word to say. But she didn't know what Ingrid was talking about.

"You honestly have no idea, do you. The Sunrise Program, the proposal you shot down, how many times? Winter 2002, and then summer 2003. Then again in a totally new format in 2005—"

"Okay, I'm sorry, I'm trying to . . . Remind me."

"The special-needs program! For the school! We had the law-yers, we had the specialists, we got the grant from NIH and all Pierson had to do was match the funds. Plus our group covered half of that with fundraising so really all Pierson had to do was take care of the other twenty-five percent." Ingrid paused, still gaz-ing down at Becky in her chair. "We did so much research. The stuff I used to tell you about. That integrating forms of treatment, neural, sensory, psychological—all in one group setting—works best. The kids learn from each other. They practice social interac-tion, they get prepared to be in the world. A program like Sunrise transitions them to assisted living, so they can be independent but still near family."

Becky only vaguely remembered the proposal, the discussion, something to do with social support for kids in the area, not even necessarily in the Pierson area. She'd shot it down easily, without much thought. What little money they had for the schools barely funded the basics. But she had never known how much the project meant to Ingrid. She hadn't paid attention, of course, figuring that what she gave for TJ's care was all that mattered. She closed her eyes, unable to look at Ingrid.

"I have to go." Ingrid came close and Becky breathed in her scent, baby powder and lemon. She felt one feather touch along her temple as Ingrid tucked her hair back behind her ear.

Then Ingrid moved away. The front door opened and closed. By the time Becky composed herself, got herself up, and went after her, Ingrid was past the yard and walking fast along the road, head down and arms holding each other. If Becky had had the strength to run, the ankle monitor wouldn't have let her. And if she'd had the strength to call out to Ingrid, it was too late.

33

Chicago
Dirksen Federal Courthouse
2014

WHEN THE JUDGE ENTERED THE courtroom, the packed room stood up with audible anticipation. Hundreds of people had crowded in behind Becky, and although she willed herself not to turn around she could feel their presence like a furnace of fury at her back. So many faces, so many voices she would recognize if she allowed herself to look or listen.

Judge Merida was in his late fifties, Latino, a pair of spectacles pushed up onto the top of his head as if they were sunglasses. He spoke to the lawyers, both hers and the prosecutors (all men), about motions and countermotions, exhibits, notices of intent. Becky concentrated on breathing slowly. She wouldn't break down. She'd let the process unfold.

Her hands, though, twisted violently against each other in her lap.

Witnesses for the government began to appear in the witness box. FBI agents testified to her method—writing fraudulent checks—and the numbers, which produced actual gasps from those in the pews: *For example, between April 2011 and July 2011, the defendant wrote thirty-two checks to total three million nine hundred fourteen thousand, which as you can see only sixty-nine thousand of which was for legitimate town business.* A worker from Pierson Streets and San—Callum Briggs, who smiled hugely at her before he remembered to look away—testified that the town pool went dry for three summers, that she'd denied funds for playground maintenance, tree pruning by the riverwalk, and cemetery repairs. Town council member after council member got up to testify to her malfeasance. The librarian wiped away tears while reporting how many fewer kids and seniors they'd been able to accommodate because of shortened hours. Ingrid testified, quietly and calmly, not looking at Becky. Becky held herself still during each person's testimony, kept her gaze steady. She had to work not to swallow too much; the dryness in her throat was a constant danger.

Those in the courtroom who were out for blood had a real disappointment when it became clear that Mayor Ken Brennan would not be appearing. Literal boos rippled through the room when one of the attorneys for the government began to read into the record Ken's pat statement, causing Judge Merida to call for order. Becky knew what they were thinking: *Can't show his face. He was in on it, how could he not be. All those years, he just left her with the keys to the candy store.*

In the years since her arrest, Ken had hung on to his job, but in name only. Editorial after editorial raked him over the coals. He was charged, then the charges were dropped. In May the town council unanimously voted to reverse-engineer the government structure to a "management plan," executed by a group of hired consultants. After Ken's term was up at the end of the year, he was out. From what little Becky had found out, at home in her ankle bracelet, he had put his house on the market and moved the kids to Rockford to live with his sister. No word on where Marie Brennan was.

Becky had waited to hear from him all those sleepless months, and no message ever came. She realized in her courtroom seat that she'd even been hoping to hear from him today, in some way. But the bland statement that disparaged her conduct and praised Pierson for its fortitude sounded nothing like Ken. Nothing like how he used to talk with her.

After that, the proceedings picked up speed. The government concluded its case. The only person willing to speak on Becky's behalf—of hundreds pursued by her lawyers, or so they told her—was Tracy Moncton, although she too declined to attend in person. Instead, she sent a video.

When Tracy's face and upright posture came on the screen of the monitor that was wheeled to the front of the courtroom, the place buzzed with murmurs and whispers. Over the past ten years Tracy Moncton had become a director of movies the audience had heard of, if not actually seen. Independent films with name actors, including one that took the big award in France.

"My name is Tracy Moncton. I'm a visual artist and a filmmaker. I understand that I don't need to take an oath for a sentencing hearing. I'm going to read a prepared statement." Tracy put on a pair of yellow reading glasses, low on the nose, and lifted one typewritten page. Her height made it easy to see most of her torso in the camera's frame: thin, long-limbed, in a loose black jacket over a black blouse. Her hair seemed the only undisciplined part of her: a wild and frizzy soft halo, shades of gray and blond. *"Boy with flag (version one),"* she read aloud. *"Boy with flag (version two). Emily in her kitchen* (editioned series). *Hero Lake* (artist proof). *Mika's yarn* (editioned series). *Going Underground* (film and print). *Going Underground* (installation)." Several minutes passed. Tracy read a dozen titles, twenty, fifty, more—no context, only the bare essentials of title and medium.

Becky's lawyers glanced at each other. The government's lawyers bent toward each other to confer in whispers. Judge Merida had a slight frown, looking down at the monitor. Becky alone understood. These were all the works Tracy had made during the years of their patron agreement. She recognized many of them, had owned several. They were in museums and collections around the world.

Tracy Moncton paused, blinked several times at the page in her hand. "I offer this list in lieu of what I was asked to prepare, that is, a more traditional statement of character. In lieu of a description of a longtime business arrangement whose origins were more important to me than I could explain within these circumstances. And in lieu of my gratitude for her patronage, and my misgivings about that now. I hope this list might be useful to Ms. Farwell in the coming years." Tracy raised her face then, and Becky watched intently as the artist's gaze blindly swept past her on the screen. With a quick motion, Tracy took off her reading glasses. "Thank you for including this statement into the proceedings." She nodded at someone off-camera, and the screen blacked out.

Warmth in her limbs, a tingle of energy. The first feelings of well-being she'd had all day. Becky tried to hold on to it, this inner strength, tried not to hear the lawyers and judge talking around and above her.

"Does the defense call any further witnesses as to character?"

"No, your honor. At this time, we'd like to allow Ms. Farwell to give her statement."

At the witness stand, Becky faced the courtroom audience for the first time all day. She brushed at her blouse, smoothing and tucking it, with fingers that felt thick and clumsy. In a surreal haze she saw suddenly that what she'd taken for an abstract print on the cheap fabric was actually tiny repeated ducks. Or loons, maybe. Hundreds of little black water birds cascading down her chest and stomach.

She realized she was delaying the inevitable: looking up at the people assembled to watch her be sent to prison. When she did, and felt the blunt force of their collective hatred, her will curdled.

"You may speak now, Ms. Farwell," Judge Merida told her.

"Yes. Thank you." She lightly touched the microphone to judge the right distance, a gesture she'd performed a hundred times before. For so many weeks and months, she had dreamed of this moment. Imagined giving a fully prepared performance: penitent, but eager to explain. She would weave in stories about all the times she had brought Pierson back from the brink—not just with money, but with her ideas, her efforts, her devotion. She wouldn't get into the weeds of art collecting, but would describe her perspective on everything they had heard up to now. She'd won Pierson over to her way of thinking so many times before, why couldn't she do it one last time? Make them *see*.

What a fool, she thought now. To think she still held that power. All her prepared rhetorical flourishes emptied out. She could no longer delude herself about the pain she had caused.

"Ms. Farwell. Do you have anything you wish to say to the court at this time?"

"No. I mean, yes." Her throat tight, her hands heavy weights. "I would just like to say that I'm sorry. I apologize to those I've hurt." She said it quickly and sat back.

Judge Merida denied the motion for self-surrender, denied the defense's motion for clemency based on cooperation with authorities, and explained why the upward variance in his sentencing was more than warranted by the scope of the fraud. She would serve twenty years. Bond was revoked and the defendant was to be placed in custody immediately.

Stifled gasps ran through the courtroom, a smatter of applause. Becky held on to the table's edge, shaking. From here to prison. One of her lawyers put a hand on her arm.

Judge Merida pushed his glasses up into his hair again, rested his forearms on the bench. He spoke to Becky and his tone changed, as if they were the only two people in the room. "The Bureau of Prisons will provide you with church, with classes if you desire. You'll get the chance to think about what you've done to this place. To your people. You will be incarcerated for most of the rest of your life, but—" Here the judge swept his gaze fiercely around the courtroom before coming back to Becky. "Your lifelong sense of civic responsibility and the efforts you made for Pierson—when you did make them—do not go unnoticed by this court. Good luck to you, Ms. Farwell." He banged his gavel. "Adjourned."

34

After

AFTER THE SENTENCING, PEOPLE FROM Pierson—especially those who'd driven in for the hearing and got hit with bad traffic on the way home—talked about Becky and prison. Prison would be different for Becky Farwell than it would be for pretty much anyone else, they knew. The ones who hated her the most delighted in imagining the hardships awaiting her: *Where's all your fancy pictures now, Becky?* And: *How'd you like them prison PJs?* Crueler jokes were about her getting beat up, and about how she'd be someone's bitch by the end of the first week. But those were few, and no one took real pleasure in them. For all that had come out, all she'd done, too many people had memories of Becky Farwell at the first Planting for the Future day, clipboard in hand, of her running lap after lap around the track at 3 am, of the DJ she'd finagled for the high school prom. Also no one could possibly imagine Becky Farwell, prison bitch.

"No visitors on family day," someone mentioned, in satisfaction.

"Doesn't have any anyway," someone else pointed out.

At some level, all of them understood that Becky was prepared for life in prison. It'd hurt her, of course—she was human. God knew she liked her creature comforts. But she'd always lived alone. And hadn't she overcome tough times before? Made the best of a bad situation? These were characteristics the town had always admired in her, after all. Everyone admitted that Becky's signature sturdiness would serve her well, incarcerated.

As it turned out, the first two years at West Virginia's Hazelton Federal were as hard on Becky as her most ruthless detractors could have wished. In later years she gave that period a name— Orientation—and then she tried never to think about it at all.

But in year three she answered a few questions about a fine in-stallment schedule for an inmate unclear on her restitution agree-ment. She settled a debate between two women about whether prison accounts bore interest, and which was a better deal for phone charges, postal money order or personal check. Soon she was helping people fill out dependent forms and asset forfeiture paperwork; she sketched out a monthly budget for a woman to send to her granddaughter; she did the math on Social Security reinstatement for a woman set to be released in 2028.

By year four, tired of overhearing idiotic opinions about money, Becky designed and taught a twelve-week extracurricular called Personal Finance 100. She'd originally named it 101 but quickly realized she needed to downshift into a more remedial mode. She illustrated what a pay stub looked like, detailed how to fill out a check, explained what kind of numbers appeared on a bank state-ment. This class—held once a week after dinner—was so popular that fights broke out over who would get the first row. Many of those enrolled had never held traditional employment, and they hung on Becky's every word and copied numbers laboriously into well-paged notebooks.

From there Becky branched out into Stock Market Basics, Retirement 101, and independent study projects for those who wanted to compare and contrast mutual funds.

She built a life in this way.

Whether or not people in Pierson learned about what she'd been doing in prison, they wouldn't have been surprised by it. Becky always had to be in charge, always had to be organizing people, bossing them. She'd done it for them for years. They'd wanted her to.

Becky never returned to art. She didn't open any mail from that part of her past; once, when a wealthy collector colleague applied to visit, she rejected the paperwork. Unclear on the exact nature of art's connection to her crime, other inmates called her "Picasso" for a while, which she tolerated with no visible reaction. To all appearances, Becky had easily given up her obsession for art—for chasing it, buying it, for being in its presence. The mania had released her.

At least that's what someone might think.

Becky was so good at lying. She could lie persuasively enough to confuse even herself about what was true and what was not. Over the years to come she built a lie strong enough to feel like belief.

I'm free, now. I'm free of all that.

When Becky did think about the past—because you had to, every once in a while; prison meant down time, hours of boredom—she went way back in time. Before all of *that.*

One day she returned to again and again was a trip Hank had taken her on when she was about eight. This would have been after her mother died, so Becky guessed that he wanted to get out of the house as much as possible. Get away from the sadness and also the reminder of their financial strain.

Why that day's outing included the school bus park, she could never figure out. All Becky remembered was running wild with another kid, either a girl or boy about her age, all around the property by themselves. Maybe Hank had a friend who worked there? Was having coffee in an office somewhere while she scampered around?

The day had been windy. Cold enough that she'd had on a jacket but she ran so much she heated herself up, shed the jacket, and kept running. They played tag, she and this other child, darted around and around the school buses. In her memory it seemed like hundreds but actually it was probably fifty or sixty, row after row of neatly lined-up mammoth yellow blocks. All empty, all impassive.

The magic strangeness of that space made them joyful, deranged, wild with freedom. Sprinting up and down the rows, a flash of a sneaker, a shout from up ahead. Becky could remember the exact pounding of her heart, the jumpy sensation of never knowing where the kid would pop out—right next to her, or dozens of buses up ahead. Hank not there but nearby. The way the wind ricocheted in and around the heavy vehicles, the way the sun's glare bounced off the chrome and metal. And her own happiness. Her shrieking, racing happiness.

If she thought about it enough, that day, she could let herself float around in the memory, and then she could pull up to an aerial view, see the school buses from on high: inch-long lozenges of that singular yellow-orange, row upon row of them, unending. The tops of the heads of two small figures flashing in and out of sight among the sameness.

Becky held that vision in her mind as long as she could. It would have made a good painting.

AUTHOR'S NOTE

DRIVING NORTH ON CHICAGO'S LAKE Shore Drive one day in 2012, I found myself captivated by a radio news report about the arrest of Rita Crundwell in a town named Dixon, Illinois. I wasn't alone. As more details of Crundwell's epic crime came out, the wider public was riveted by the fact that a government employee had managed to embezzle $54 million over 20 years—by herself— from a small township. But while news teams and investigators scrambled to find out and explain how Crundwell had pulled off what would turn out to be the largest municipal fraud in US history, I was more interested in imagining what it might have felt like for someone to do what she did. What kind of mentality does one need to show up to work every day, to interact with colleagues and neighbors and friends, while stealing from them year after year? What impact does sustaining a double life have on one's psyche? I was curious about how such a person might deceive others and how she might necessarily deceive herself.

From there my focus moved away from Rita Crundwell toward a main character I began to see in my mind: a woman with significant gifts of intelligence and drive, who lives in a tight-knit rural community, and is astonished by a sudden—and not entirely welcome—obsession with art. Becky Farwell came together as soon as I understood the nature of her all-encompassing desire: the way she has no context for loving art and for her ability to instantly suss out a good painting, growing up as she did without exposure to serious art. The way Becky craves paintings is inborn, as much of a surprise to her as to anyone else. As Crash Davis tells Nuke LaLoosh in *Bull Durham*, "When you were a baby, the gods reached down and turned your right arm into a thunderbolt." Once I developed this part of her character, I saw that the world of contemporary art collecting—with its inherent high stakes, big money, and class conflict—was a perfect arena for Becky to play out her complex relationship with the truth.

Beyond knowing the basic facts of Rita Crundwell's crime, I purposely learned little about the person herself. In making up the fictional world of *The Talented Miss Farwell*, I left myself plenty of space to create characters and a place I could develop from scratch.

My fictional town of Pierson shares topographical features with Dixon, but isn't meant to stand in for the people or businesses of the actual place. In the same way, Becky Farwell is not Rita Crundwell. What often happens for novelists is that the bare circumstances of a real situation quickly give way to an entirely different imagined story, and this was the case for me with *The Talented Miss Farwell*.

To those who are interested in learning more about Rita Crundwell, I recommend the documentary *All the Queen's Horses*. For background on the art world, I found the following books to be both helpful and engrossing: *Seven Days in the Art World* by Sarah Thornton; *I Sold Andy Warhol (Too Soon)* by Richard Polsky;

and *Collecting Art for Love, Money and More* by Ethan Wagner and Thea Westreich Wagner.

My title is, of course, in homage to the late great Patricia Highsmith, whose brilliant book was one source of inspiration for the life and crimes of Becky Farwell.

ACKNOWLEDGMENTS

THANK YOU FIRST AND ALWAYS to Alice Tasman, for believing in me and my work. Kate Nintzel made this a better book and me a better writer. Thank you to the amazing team at Morrow.

Carol Johns generously answered my questions about 1980s-era Illinois accounting office practices, and Nico Commandeur helped me understand more about white collar criminal prosecution. I'm grateful for their time and effort; all remaining errors are mine alone.

Special thanks to the good people and books of the Lincoln Park branch of the Chicago Public Library.

As ever, my writers group is indispensable when it comes to wisdom, enthusiasm, and laughter: Rachel DeWoskin, Gina Frangello, Thea Goodman, Dika Lam, Rebecca Makkai, Zoe Zolbrod. I'm thankful for skilled readers Liam Callanan and Valerie Laken. I couldn't be happier for the friendship of Lauryn Gouldin, Jenny Mercein, and Caroline Hand Romita. And thanks to the witches, who know who they are.

Most of all, thank you to my family—Alan and Betsy, Lowrey, Jocelyn, Malcolm. And to Courtney, Samuel, and Wendy, with all my love.

About the author

About the book

Insights,
Interviews
& More . . .

Meet
Emily Gray Tedrowe

Marion Ettlinger

EMILY GRAY TEDROWE is the Chicago-based author of the novels *The Talented Miss Farwell, Blue Stars,* and *Commuters.* She earned a PhD in English literature from New York University, and a BA from Princeton University. She has received an Illinois Arts Council award as well as fellowships from the Ragdale Foundation, Virginia Center for the Creative Arts, and the Sewanee Writers' Conference. A frequent book reviewer for *USA Today* as well as other publications, Tedrowe also writes essays, interviews, and short stories. ❧

A Conversation with Emily Gray Tedrowe

Q: What is your writing routine like? The Talented Miss Farwell is your third novel, has anything about your process changed from book to book?

A: I'd never done this before, but I wrote the first draft of *The Talented Miss Farwell* by hand. Using a pen and notepad. Often people are amazed when I tell them this, and I get it—it slowed things down considerably. And yet that was the point. I knew with this book I was tackling a much bigger project than I'd worked on before: a twenty-year time span, in-depth scenes from the art and finance worlds, and sustained tension that built to a dramatic ending. Removing the element of computer speed that we all know and love helped me quiet enough to sink deep into the story, one scribbled line after another. Writing by hand also gave me the sense of privacy, a knowledge that no one but me knew what the pages held. The freedom of that, and the chance to take my pages to a coffee shop or park bench, created a perfect bubble where I could play with Becky's story far from the distractions and temptations of the internet. Another benefit was that each time I typed up a chapter—piecing together my messy and crossed-out ▶

A Conversation with Emily Gray Tedrowe
(continued)

sections—I ran the story through my mind again, allowing me to understand its flaws and strengths.

Q: Were you interested in art before writing this book? How much research did you do on the art world? Was there anything particularly fascinating you learned?

A: While I've always been interested in visual art, I've never studied it formally (aside from one art history course in college). But I'm an avid museumgoer, and I tend to read biographies of artists. So I think you could say I had a medium amount of familiarity with the basics of the art world. For research, I sought out guides to art collecting, I read blogs and reviews, and I generally tried to approach all of this through the eyes of someone rabid for knowledge and impatient to understand everything—i.e., Becky. In terms of what I learned, I found myself most fascinated by glimpses of the social code inherent in the blue-chip collector world. For example, it's considered extremely gauche to attempt to outbid a piece that has just sold to someone else . . . so, of course, I had Becky do this. As with any subculture, there are hidden rules and protocols. I loved ferreting these out, and making them up.

4

Q: What was your favorite scene to write? What was the hardest to write?

A: I love this question because it reminds me how much I loved writing this novel. Yes, there were difficult moments, and yes, the revisions were hard work (revisions are always hard work). But I showed up happy almost every day I got to create this story. My favorite scene is the time Becky jets to Miami with a Hail Mary plan to save her faltering art world career. She throws an over-the-top party to impress a gallerist that ends in comic disarray but somehow doesn't daunt her in the slightest. Becky's "go big or go home" spirit is never more apparent than in this scene, and I had a blast making it up. As for hardest to write, I would say: the final chapters. When you spend years with a character, the journey's end is always painful—in this case especially so, given what Becky has coming to her.

Q: What was your experience writing a character who can be seen as an antihero? Was it a challenge to make Becky someone readers can root for and empathize with even as her actions break the law and sometimes hurt others?

A: In fact, I relished the fraught challenge of writing the rise and fall ▶

A Conversation with Emily Gray Tedrowe
(continued)

of a character like Becky. When women are portrayed in fiction as wrongdoers it's most often in the realm of personal or domestic life: the story of a wife cheating on her husband, or a mother abandoning her family. I wanted to write a female character who is so criminally ambitious, so devoted to her own devious goals, that she will stop at almost nothing to get what she wants. I wanted readers to *marvel* at Becky more than I wanted them to empathize with her. That said, Becky does care (sometimes) about (some) people, notably her fellow town residents and Ingrid, her best friend. I hoped that by showing her devotion, even when it is misguided, I could entice readers to deepen their understanding of Becky although they might not be able to excuse her actions.

Q: Why do you think we're so fascinated with con artists like Becky, both in literature and in real life?

A: My sense is that many of us appreciate a big life. And con artists, for whatever their faults, live big lives, full of drama and danger and the thrill of getting away with something. Of course, the big lives—especially the criminal kind—are often best appreciated from a safe distance, which is why we enjoy these people when they are depicted in fiction or journalism . . . less so when they pop up in our own day-to-day reality. One aspect of the con artist life is how isolated it is, by necessity. Becky Farwell has a moment where she craves someone to talk to about it all, just one hour of conversation with another con artist, someone who carries as much of a secret burden as she does. We may be fascinated by these cons, but despite the spectacle, they live lonely lives at heart.

Q: If you could pull a Becky Farwell and illegally buy one piece of art, what would it be?

A: I have to confess that I play this game, mentally, almost every time I walk through a museum. I have a physical response to art I love, whether it's a sudden urge to touch a sculpture or to hold a painting in my hands. Writing the scene where Becky indulges a similar urge was pleasurably cathartic. As for what I'd love to fantasy-buy, I can see myself emulating Becky's go-for-bust attitude by taking home an incredibly beautiful, incredibly large photograph I've loved for many years. It's called *The Flooded Grave* by Jeff Wall, and it's in the Art Institute of Chicago, where I'm lucky to visit it frequently. Wall makes large-scale staged photographs; ▶

A Conversation with Emily Gray Tedrowe
(continued)

The Flooded Grave depicts a watery grave
that is also an actual aquatic habitat,
sea stars included. It sounds macabre,
but I actually find it playful and even
soothing. I can see myself hanging it in
our apartment—if I could find the wall
space, that is. ∽

Behind the Book

Con artists tend to fascinate people, and I'm no exception. When the true story of Rita Crundwell hit national news in 2012—Crundwell being the Illinois small-town government employee who embezzled nearly $54 million over twenty years—I pored over the articles and reports. I was amazed that someone could steal so much, for so long, from the very people she continued to work with and live near. Soon, though, I noticed my mind following a different track. Most people asked, "How did she get away with this?" Meaning, the ins and outs of the financial crime itself. While I wanted to know that, too, what I couldn't stop wondering was "What was it like?" Meaning, how did it feel to accomplish such a crime? What might be the inner experience of a person carrying out years and years of a double life? What mental and emotional arrangements were necessary, was there a place for guilt and shame, and what about the endless fear of getting caught? How do you chat about the weather with the next-door neighbor you're stealing from?

For a novelist, these types of questions are endlessly compelling. And for me, they signaled deep interest in a subject. But the kicker, the moment I knew I wanted to write a fictional version of ▸

Crundwell's story, was when I found out that the FBI and other investigators did not believe, for quite some time, that it could be a woman alone who pulled off such an epic crime. From that point on, I moved away from the actual and into the imaginary: I created Becky Farwell, math prodigy, Daddy's girl, hometown hero, who is blessed and cursed by an overwhelming obsession for owning art.

Once when I was in my early twenties, I was visiting MoMA in New York. Out of the corner of my eye I caught a security guard racing across a gallery toward a person who had reached out to touch one of the paintings. "You're not allowed to hold them?" is what I overheard, in a surprisingly earnest tone. After I left that room, and the security guard's emphatic explanation that no, you are not allowed to hold the paintings, I spent the rest of my visit amusing myself by imagining which of the many priceless works of art I might like to pluck off the wall and hold in my hands. Van Gogh's *The Starry Night*? How about one of the Jacob Lawrences I loved so much? Definitely that gem by Elizabeth Murray.

These sensations—and the forbidden temptation they reveal—were given to my character Becky, who has that same burning physical need for art but also the capability to do what it takes to procure treasures she can hold anytime she wants. But although Becky has a true eye for art, and eventually a lot of money to play with, she struggles to crack the social code of the coastal elite until she learns its rules the hard way. In the art world, money (even vast sums of stolen money) can't always buy connections. An important characteristic I gave Becky is a natural ability for cultivating people, whether that's church supper clubs or dealers who work only with a select group of patrons. She also becomes an expert at switching between two disparately different communities, and those back-and-forths were the most fun for me to write.

Whether she's wearing Rockports or Manolos, Becky Farwell strides easily into any gathering, racking up deal after deal, full of brash confidence that is the signature of a true con (wo)man. To me, living that kind of double life isn't too far removed from the way each of us puts on varying personas for different scenarios. My hope is that readers who may be horrified by Becky's crimes can understand and perhaps even empathize with the desires and fears that lead her to risk so much. ◡

Reading Group Guide

1. What does art mean to Becky? Why do you think she is willing to risk so much for it?

2. What is the significance of Becky's father not being able to see what she does in the first painting that she acquires? Does this mark a turning point in their relationship?

3. Why do you think Becky chose not to leave Pierson and go to college after Hank's death? How might her trajectory have been different if she had? Would she still have created her Activity?

4. How is Becky's friendship with Ingrid different than her friendships within the art world? Why do you think she's able to feel close to Ingrid in a way that she isn't with anyone else? Why is it so important for her to have the constant of Ingrid's friendship throughout the book?

5. Becky wonders what it's like "to have just your one regular life and to be *content*" and feels that this desire sets her apart from others. Do you think she's truly unique to feel this way? Are there any other characters who Becky views as

being content, but are shown to
have their own hidden desires?

6. What role does social class play
   in the book, both in Becky's
   interactions in the art world
   and in her relationships with
   Ingrid and the other Pierson
   citizens?

7. Why do you think the author
   chose to set the book primarily
   in the 1980s and 1990s? Do you
   think Becky could have gotten
   away with the same scam today?

8. What is the meaning of Tracy
   Moncton's statement at the trial?
   Why is it so significant to Becky?

9. What do you think the unopened
   letter from Becky's old math teacher
   said? Why doesn't Becky want to
   read it, in that moment?

10. Were you satisfied with the ending,
    or were you hoping for a different
    outcome? Do you think Becky's
    punishment was just?

Ch:

Becky: Independent
Trying to make it
Quantitative more talent;
self taught
Ethical?

- cheek: didn't do
the right thing - but
author acts like it
was okay. wait for
remorse
Tough situation - private
dad

Setting - not much at all
Plot? - girl growing up
episodes of pursuing
tonight, there would be a
mystery in the cheek,
Plot - girl moving through ~~episodes~~
episodes of life - mystery
yet.